Praise for Maureen Lang

## The Oak Leaves

"A tender account of unconditional love and the deeper joy that results from overcoming the odds, Lang's latest is recommended for all collections."
**Library Journal**

"Lang has written a novel that's close to her heart, in which a mother's love for her child knows no boundaries. This book is heart-wrenching but heartwarming at the same time."
*Romantic Times BOOKreviews*

"Beautifully touching and completely absorbing, this bittersweet novel will entertain. . . ."
**compulsivereader.com**

"Drawing from her own life experience, Maureen Lang invites us to experience the honest disappointments and glorious discoveries that come from mothering a son others may see as 'different,' yet God sees only as His beloved child."
**Liz Curtis Higgs, best-selling author of** *Thorn in My Heart*

"I couldn't put this book down. Vivid, compelling and deeply moving, with issues that touch the soul, *The Oak Leaves* was a story that lingered in my heart. . . . Every moment you spend with this book is worth it."
**Susan May Warren, award-winning author of** *Reclaiming Nick*

## On Sparrow Hill

"Wonderful characters are written with style, grace, and charm. Keep the tissues close by!"
*Romantic Times BOOKreviews*

"*On Sparrow Hill* is a wonderful combination of contemporary and historical romance, offering two equally intriguing plotlines that will capture your imagination from the get-go. . . . Maureen Lang has done it again—created a story that will burrow its way into your heart."
**Christianreviewofbooks.com**

"Two times the story lines equals two times the romance in this book. Lang creates a fine tension between the characters that makes the romance jump off the page."
**novelinspirations.com**

*My Sister Dilly*

# Maureen Lang

Tyndale House Publishers, Inc.
Carol Stream, Illinois

Visit Tyndale's exciting Web site at www.tyndale.com

Check out the latest about Maureen Lang at www.maureenlang.com

TYNDALE and Tyndale's quill logo are registered trademarks of Tyndale House Publishers, Inc.

*My Sister Dilly*

Designed by Beth Sparkman

Published in association with the literary agency of WordServe Literary Group, Ltd., 10152 S. Knoll Circle, Highlands Ranch, CO 80130.

**Library of Congress Cataloging-in-Publication Data**

Lang, Maureen.
    My sister Dilly / Maureen Lang.
      p. cm.
    ISBN-13: 978-1-4143-2224-7 (pbk.)
    ISBN-10: 1-4143-2224-0 (pbk.)
    1. Sisters—Fiction.   2. Mothers of children with disabilities—Fiction.   3. Women ex-convicts—Fiction.   I. Title.

    PS3612.A554M92 2008
    813'.6—dc22                               2008024429

Printed in the United States of America

14    13    12    11    10    09    08
 7     6     5     4     3     2     1

*For Kris*
*This book could not have*
*been imagined without*
*your help and input.*
*My deepest appreciation.*

## ACKNOWLEDGMENTS

Although only one person's name is on this book, it couldn't have been written without the help and input of a variety of people. Many thanks to my sister- and brother-in-law Kris and Jay for their advice. Kris, you inspired this story in more ways than one. Thank you both for never tiring of my endless questions. I wish your experience with hospitalists and intensivists wasn't firsthand, but I'm grateful for your generosity and strength in sharing that with me.

And to my sister- and brother-in-law Marj and Rand, who didn't mind all of my questions about hog farming, and my future son-in-law Connor for being the go-to guy about the financial investment world. Also a thank-you to my niece Linda and her husband, Chris. How wonderful to have an ex-cop and a paramedic in the family so I have two ready resources to pester!

Special thanks to Siri Mitchell, who made it through my rough draft and whose encouragement helped me meet my deadline.

I'm so grateful to Tyndale and in particular Karen Watson, Stephanie Broene, Kathy Olson, and Sarah Mason, whose generosity and encouragement exceed my ability to reciprocate my gratitude in equal measure.

Finally my deepest appreciation to Kellie Waremburg, whose own experiences taught me so much about what my character Dilly might have faced, how she endured and overcame. Many thanks.

Maureen Lang, 2008

## PROLOGUE

RAINDROPS SPATTERED the windshield of my car, leaving see-through polka dots. Then they came down harder, each thwack pummeling any remnant of symmetrical design. Instinctively I reached for the wiper. But my hand stopped midway, almost as if it knew before my brain told me movement would be the wrong thing to do. A parked car, across from a schoolyard, with someone inside . . . lurking . . .

Even I, childless at thirty-five, knew such a scenario would attract the interest of school staff or a parent, if not outright suspicion. So what if I was a woman with no record. It wasn't as if we carried that information on our foreheads. Even a momentary misunderstanding would be embarrassing and, considering what I'd come here to do, probably make a news story or two.

*Hannah Williams was questioned by police today . . .*

So I sat. I would have welcomed the cover of rain if it hadn't sent the kids back inside as they waited for the parade of squat little yellow buses lining up to collect them all. Most of the children, the ones who were mobile anyway, were herded inside, but several of those in wheelchairs were given shelter under a wide red awning attached to the play yard. Umbrellas appeared; hoods went up. Children were wheeled out to the ramps attached to the bus, where they were locked in, chair and all. Then the first little bus zoomed off, making room for another just like it to take its place.

I had no idea there would be so many students in wheelchairs. Rubbing my forehead, feeling the start of an ache, I acknowledged my own ignorance. But what else was I supposed to do? I had to try spotting her because I knew without a doubt that was the first thing my sister Dilly would ask. "Have you seen her?" Followed quickly by, "How did she look?"

But there were dozens of kids who each looked around ten

years old, strapped to a wheelchair with a headrest. From this distance and through the rain, I guessed the ones with pink or yellow raincoats were girls, but who knew if others in green or light blue might be girls too?

I sat there anyway until the last little bus rolled away, never sure of my target. I'd failed Dilly again.

# 1

THE PRISON was in the middle of nowhere; at least that was how it seemed to me. Not many property owners must want a facility like that in their backyard, even one for women. So there were no crops of housing developments taking up farmland around here the way they seemed to everywhere else. Not that I thought much about farmland, even having grown up in the middle of it. The only green cornfields I'd seen since I'd left for college were from an airplane as I jetted from one end of the country to the other.

"Are you here for the Catherine Carlson release?"

I looked up in surprise as not one but a half dozen people seemed to have appeared from nowhere. I'd noticed a couple of vans and cars farther down the parking lot but hadn't seen any people until now. My gaze had been taken up by the prison, a forlorn place if ever I saw one. Even the entire blue sky wasn't enough to offset the building's ugliness. Block construction, painted beige like old oatmeal. If the cinder walls didn't give it away, the lack of windows made it clear it was an institution. The electric barbed wire fencing told what kind.

Two men in my path balanced cameras on their shoulders, and in front of them a pair of pretty blonde journalists shoved microphones in my face while another thrust forth a palm-sized recorder. One on the fringe held an innocuous notepad.

My first impulse was to run back to my car and speed away.

But Dilly was waiting. I clamped my mouth shut, gripped the strap of my Betsey Johnson purse, and walked along the concrete strip leading to the doors of the prison. There was an invisible line at the gate that not a single reporter could penetrate. But I knew they'd wait.

At the front door, a woman greeted me through a glass window. Dilly was being "processed," she told me, then said to have a seat. I turned, noticing the smell of inhospitable antiseptic for the first time. Hard wooden benches were the only place to sit. Evidently they thought the families of those in such a place needed to be punished too. I'd have brought a book if I'd known the wait was going to be so long; there wasn't even a magazine handy to help me pass the time.

Only thoughts. Of how I would make up for my failures. I'd told Mac, my best friend—and somehow it seemed he'd become my only friend—that this was the first step in fixing things. Keeping a broken past in the past. Dilly's . . . and mine.

I remembered the day our parents brought my sister home from the hospital just after she was born. The excitement was as welcome as the warmth of the sun shining through the bare trees that early March afternoon. Everyone smiled, and even though Mom was moving kind of slow up the stairs to our farmhouse, she smiled too. It was the kind of excitement you see when there's a new and hopeful change, like at weddings.

I was five, and even at that age I knew my parents had waited a long time for my sister. I heard Mom say once that she'd envisioned a houseful of kids, but the Lord hadn't seen fit to bless her with a productive womb. I think I wondered what my mother would have done with a bunch more kids when I seemed to be in the way of other things she did: lunches with friends she'd known all her life; making decorative quilts and pillows she sold at fairs; canning fruits, pickles, and jam; or endless work on the farm. In retrospect maybe it was a surprise they'd even had me and Dilly; she must have been so tired at the end of the day.

I wondered later if everybody was happier because things you wait for seem better once you finally get them. But in recent years I thought everybody in town might have been relieved there weren't a whole slew of kids born into our family.

"Go take a seat, Hannah," Dad had said to me after Mom told us I couldn't hold the baby unless I was sitting down.

I skipped over to Aunt Elsie on the couch and hopped up next to her, holding out my arms as my mother made the careful transfer. It wasn't like holding one of my dolls, even though the blanket was made of the same soft material my plastic babies enjoyed. Unlike my dolls, my sister was warm and squirmy. Dad told me not to hold her too tight, so I put her on my legs and pulled back the cover to get a good look at her.

Her eyes were closed, and she wore a pink cotton bonnet. Even then, the straight lines of her brows had been drawn, which later filled in so well. Her cheeks were splotched red and white, and her arms and legs moved in four different directions. When she opened her mouth, I saw her flat gums, no hint of the teeth to come someday. I thought she was the prettiest thing I'd ever seen.

"She's a dilly," I whispered to Aunt Elsie, who'd taught me her favorite word for the things she liked. It came from a song called "Lavender Blue," and while my parents spent so much time at the hospital in those last couple of days, that was what my aunt and I had been doing—going about farm chores singing of things being dilly.

The name on my sister's birth certificate was Catherine Marie Williams, but neither Catherine nor Cathy nor even Marie ever stuck. She was Dilly from that day on.

Nearly thirty years later, here I was, ready to bring Dilly back home to our farmhouse.

Finally I heard something other than the distant sounds of an institution. Closer than the clatter of plates somewhere, something nearer than the echo of a call down a corridor. I heard the click of an automatic door lock, followed by the swish of air accompanying a passage opening.

Dilly. Instead of prison orange, she wore regular street clothes.

Was it possible she was taller? Did people grow in their twenties? She was still short, having taken from the same gene pool I'd inherited, but I was barely an inch taller now. Spotting me right away, she dropped her black leather suitcase on the floor. For a moment the case looked vaguely familiar, but that thought was lost when I noted a shadow of someone standing next to Dilly. My eyes stayed on my sister. She flung herself at me before I had the chance to go to her.

"Thanks for coming," she said, and her voice was so wobbly I knew she was fighting tears. I choked back my own.

"Thanks?" I repeated. *Thanks?* How could I not come?

"It's a long way from California."

I laughed. "Yeah, another galaxy."

The woman beside Dilly stepped closer and I couldn't ignore her any longer. She was tall and thin, dressed in jeans but with a more formal black jacket that somehow didn't look misplaced over the denim.

I pulled myself away from Dilly and accepted the woman's handshake.

"I'm Catherine's social worker, Amanda Mason. We just finished our exit session and she's all set to go."

Dilly held up a folder. "Probation rules, contact names, phone numbers."

"Formalities, Catherine," Amanda said. "Nothing out of the ordinary."

It was always something of a surprise to me that others outside of our hometown knew my sister by any name but Dilly. She certainly looked ready to go home, wearing a spring jacket I hadn't seen before, carrying a suitcase I now recognized as one I'd left behind when I headed to college so long ago.

"I didn't know you'd have luggage," I said when she picked up the black leather case. I didn't know what else to say.

"The women are allowed to purchase certain necessities during their stay. Clothes, mostly."

I knew that, because Mom had told me I could send Dilly

money—no cash, just cashier's checks or money orders, no more than fifty dollars at a time—but somehow I never connected that money with actual purchases. It wasn't like there could be a regular store inside a prison.

"Socks," Dilly said with a grin. "My feet still get cold."

When we were little, we shared a full-size bed, before our parents finally bought a set of twin beds. I still remember her icicle feet in winter. "You have a suitcase full of socks?"

"Just about. They never let me keep them all in one place till today. Guess I didn't know I had so many." Then she turned to the other woman and set the suitcase down again. "Thanks, Amanda. You—" Something caught in her throat, and she stopped herself. "You did so much for me." She put both of her hands on the woman's forearms, and the social worker didn't even flinch.

Amanda shifted her arms to take Dilly's hands in hers. "I haven't done enough," she said. "Not nearly enough."

They hugged and I watched, wondering if the prison movies I'd stopped watching since Dilly's arrest had given me the wrong impression. No hint of inmate animosity toward those in power here.

"Keep praying, though, will you? I won't stop needing that."

"You don't even have to ask."

Then Dilly slipped away and I had to turn and follow her or be left behind.

Prayer. That was what Dilly had asked for. All our life we'd been told to pray. On our knees, right after we got up, right before going to bed, and as often as possible in between. I might have had faith as a child, but by the time I was in high school, I began wondering what I was praying to. Some light in the sky that saw all the suffering in this world and didn't lift a finger—a supposedly all-powerful finger—to do something about it?

I'd given up prayer years ago; spiritually, long before I left home for college. Physically, once I stepped foot outside my parents' home. I eyed Dilly, trying to see if she'd been serious about the request or said it because that was what the other woman wanted to hear. But Dilly was looking ahead, walking out the door.

The reporters were still there when we stepped outside. I meant to warn Dilly, to make some sort of plan about getting to the car as fast as we could, telling her in advance which way to go.

But when Dilly came upon them, instead of hustling past, to my amazement she stopped. For a moment she looked to the ground, then to me, and I thought I saw a hint of uncertainty before she took an audible breath. "I just want to say one thing." Her voice trembled slightly, and she paused long enough to look down at the sidewalk again, then at each one of the reporters.

"When I did what I did so long ago, I didn't have any hope. When I stepped into this place, I didn't have hope. But that's all changed now because of the Lord Jesus."

I stared, aware of the silence that followed as the reporters waited to see if she was finished. But that wasn't why I couldn't find words or even the gumption to pull her along to the car. What was she *talking* about? Between this obviously rehearsed statement and the request for prayer, it was as if she'd "done found Jesus," as Grandpa used to say.

A barrage of questions shot from the reporters.

"Are you going to see your daughter?"

"Are you going to try to regain custody?"

"Has your husband forgiven you for what you did?"

Dilly didn't answer a single question. Instead, she looked at me, then toward the parking lot. It took the briefest moment for me to realize she didn't know where to go, which car was mine, so I led the way. I pressed the keyless remote to unlock her door before she reached it. She struggled a moment to get her bag into the rear seat, then settled herself just as I slid behind the wheel.

One of the reporters, the one I'd mistakenly believed harmless because the only technology he held was a pad of paper, had followed us to the car. He tapped on the window. I saw Dilly reach for the button, but quicker than her, I touched the window lock.

"I was only going to crack it," she said.

"Do you really want to hear what he has to say?"

He was yelling now, his young, impassioned face nearly pressed to the glass. "Did it take prison to teach you you're not the one to take matters into your own hands? that your daughter's life is just as important as anyone else's?"

Dilly and I exchanged glances. I put the car in reverse; there was something militant about the young man that made me want to get away from him, spare Dilly from anything else he had to say. I'd seen judgment in people's eyes before and I was sure Dilly had too. This guy might be a reporter, but he wasn't an unbiased one. If such a kind existed.

Dilly stared at him, the brows everyone noticed on her, so thick, so dramatic, now drawn. A moment ago she'd found the courage to speak about something most people kept to themselves: faith. Now she looked like the Dilly I'd known when we shared the same roof. Timid, malleable. Maybe hoping I would take her away as fast as I could.

I backed out of the spot even as a thousand questions came to my mind too. I wanted to resist asking, though, unlike the guy with the notepad. His emphasis had been all wrong. He'd asked about the effect of prison, unconcerned about what Dilly really believed these days.

I still felt awkward after being away from her so long. But even that wasn't enough to keep me quiet. Once an older, wiser sibling, always so. I figured it gave me the right to be nosy.

"Did you mean what you said back there?" Since I was navigating out of the now-busy parking lot, I had to focus on driving, avoiding the need for eye contact.

"About Jesus?" She looked behind us at the reporters now packing up. "Wouldn't have said it if I didn't."

"What did you mean?"

"Just what I said."

I didn't know how to rephrase the question to get an answer I could understand, so I found the silence I probably should have stayed with. Once we pulled away from the prison grounds, Dilly touched my forearm much as she had the social worker's. I spared a quick glance, keeping both hands on the wheel.

"I've changed, Hannah. God changed me."

I wasn't yet sure I believed her. I wasn't the only one who'd grown up in a house where rules were more important than people, work more important than any kind of play, keeping up an appearance of holiness more important than living a holy life. We'd both vowed never to set foot in a church once we moved out of our parents' house, and I'd kept my end. I thought Dilly had too. I knew she'd stopped going to church after she got married. But lately . . . Did they even *have* church in prison?

"Since when has God done anything for either one of us, Dil?" I asked.

"I wanted to write you, tell you all about it—"

"Right." Even I heard the cynicism. I'd received exactly three letters from her the entire six years she'd been in prison, despite the hundreds I'd written. Well, one hundred, anyway. That first year. After that I just sent money orders as I made my plans. True, I'd made those plans without input from her, but I'd made them to benefit both of us.

Her eyes, brown like two spots of oversteeped tea, shone with sudden, yet-to-be-shed tears. "You know me, Hannah. I'm a talker, not a writer. I tried a thousand times to write, but every time I did, my brain froze. I can't explain it on paper. It's something I wanted to tell you in person."

"What about last Christmas? I visited you then."

She let out something that sounded a little like a *Ha!* but not quite as cynical as me. "In front of Mom and Dad? Are you kidding? I couldn't explain it with them there." She sat back in her seat, and laughter squeezed out one tear, leaving her eyes dry. "Not that everybody wouldn't have liked to see a good argument—from Mom and Dad about what grace and forgiveness really mean and from you about . . . about *everything*. The inmates would've laid bets for a winner, except if nobody drew blood they wouldn't have been able to figure out who won."

I didn't know if she was being sarcastic or not, since our family didn't argue. We hid all our resentment and anger, especially from each other. Even now I held my tongue. For a moment I felt like I was back home, preparing to listen to one of Dad's endless sermons at the family altar he'd set up in the corner of the living room.

I sucked in a breath. "Okay, let's have it, then."

But Dilly didn't reply. She shook her head, her whole body facing me instead of the dashboard. "I will tell you, Hannah. Everything. But not right now. Not yet. I need to know something first."

I glanced at her again, prepared for the questions I knew she'd ask.

"Have you seen Sierra?"

I nodded. "Yesterday."

"They let you? Nick's mother let you—you know, in the same room? You talked to her? How is she?"

I shook my head. "I went to her school. They wouldn't let me into her classroom, but they told me she was there. That she's all right. Then I waited outside until the buses came, and . . ." I was tempted to lie, to tell her I'd seen Sierra close enough to prove what the school receptionist had said, that Dilly's daughter was okay. "I saw all the kids get on their buses, and they looked happy."

Whatever joy, whatever light I'd seen in Dilly's eyes since the moment she mentioned her daughter's name began to fade before I'd even finished talking.

"So she wouldn't let you see her?"

There was no way I'd describe the phone conversation I'd had with Nick's mother; I didn't use that kind of language. Nick had never really taken charge of his own daughter's care, but his mother had taken full responsibility for Sierra. One thing she'd stipulated: no visits from anyone in our family.

"I've got to see her," Dilly said, so low I barely heard her.

I knew seeing her daughter was only the beginning. I knew what she really wanted, but I wasn't sure what *I* wanted. Did I really want a fight to restore everything to the way it used to be or should have been? What if we won?

But I reminded myself that when determination was greater than fear, people could do just about anything, even take charge of someone like Sierra.

All I had to do now was make sure that determination stayed stronger than my fears. All I had to do was convince myself, and then Dilly, that I wouldn't let my fears stand in the way.

Because if I knew Dilly—and I still did, even when she seemed different—my guess was that our future held three of us together. Somehow, in some way.

Me, Dilly, and her daughter, Sierra.

But not God.

# 2

ON THE two-hour trip home, Dilly asked me too many questions, when all I really wanted to know was how she'd survived six and a half years in a women's detention center. Instead of letting me initiate anything, she asked about LA and my job. When I corrected her by labeling it what it was, a *former* job, her jaw dropped and stayed open so long I could have counted molars.

"You quit your job?"

I nodded.

"Why?"

"I'm doing a little freelance investment counseling online, so I'm not totally shut off. But I couldn't do the whole job from here, so I quit."

Dilly's exquisite brows gathered. "What do you mean, you couldn't do it from here?"

"I'm staying, Dil. Here in Illinois. In Sugar Creek."

"What? You? Are you out of your *mind*?"

I laughed. Maybe once, years ago, I'd have thought this decision crazy. But moving back home had been the goal for so many years that I couldn't remember any others.

Before I could speak, Dilly shook her head. "No, no, no, this is all wrong for you, Hannah. I thought you were happy in LA."

If only she knew. "I was. But now I'm home." I checked the rearview mirror, switching lanes. "Did you know the Roland house is empty? The house Tina Roland's grandmother lived in for so long, right around the corner from the deserted depot? When she passed away, none of the family wanted it. It's been on the market for over a year, so I'm getting it for a steal."

"Whoa. You—you're buying a house? In Sugar Creek?"

"I figured you and I could live there. You don't have a job yet, and you can't go back to . . . where you were living." I didn't mention Nick, who was living happily ever after with girlfriend number three in the same farmhouse he'd shared with Dilly, while his mom kept Sierra with her. "I didn't think you'd want to go back to Mom and Dad's. Although . . ." Checking the mirror again, I was annoyed by the tailgater behind me and hoped it wasn't a reporter. "I just got back in town three days ago. If I'd known your parole meeting was going to be moved up by two weeks, I would have had all of this figured out. As it is, I hired Abby and Kyle Anderson to paint. They just got married a few weeks ago, did you know? Mom told me they'd do a good job and could use the money. I guess so! What, aren't they about twelve years old?" I laughed at my own wit. "Okay, they must be at least nineteen or twenty, but not old enough to be married, if you ask me."

I ignored my sudden recollection that Dilly had already been married at that age. No sense bringing up that disaster. "And I have some new furniture on order from Springfield. We can't move in until next week at the earliest, so for the time being we're stuck at Mom and Dad's."

I'm not sure Dilly ever stopped shaking her head, despite my soliloquy on the state of affairs. "You're crazy. Why are you moving back? You couldn't shake Sugar Creek dust off fast enough when you went to college."

I shrugged. "That was a long time ago."

Feeling her stare, I concentrated on my driving by switching lanes again to get away from the car following too close behind. Unfortunately the car made the same change, adding concern to my annoyance. Maybe it *was* a reporter.

"The parole board thinks I'm moving back home with Mom and Dad."

"And so you are. Today. You have a week to let them know you'll be moving." I glanced at her still-stunned face. "It's not as if you're moving very far. Why should a couple of miles make a difference to the parole board? Besides, they'll understand the minute you tell them you'll be moving away from the hogs."

She smiled, but it didn't quite reach her eyes and certainly not her eyebrows. "This is the kind of thing they told me to avoid—changing my plans. I think they liked the idea of me living with my parents." She still stared at me, looking suspicious now, the very emotion I hoped to avoid. "You didn't answer my question. Why are you doing this?"

"I have enough money saved to pay cash for the Roland house, if I wanted to. I saved every bonus I earned over the years and had more than my share of roommates to cut down on expenses. I'll still be doing some consulting, which will pay the taxes and gas and utilities, and I can get a job to pay for groceries and incidentals if necessary. You were planning to work, right? We don't have a thing to worry about, at least financially."

Now she stared straight ahead. "Sounds like you have it all planned."

"Money's my job."

Just then the phone in my pocket jingled. The tune "You've Got a Friend in Me" immediately identified the caller as Mac. Over the years many songs had characterized our relationship, but that one from *Toy Story* was my personal favorite. The classic Simon and Garfunkel "Bridge Over Troubled Water" had defined us after our brief, three-month office romance ended. Such songs aided me in keeping to my determination about our friendship never reverting to what it had been before. It was just a friendship now. I'd convinced myself that was why we'd been close so long. Mac had gone through one girlfriend after another, more than one of them my former roommates. Once it came time to commit or bail, he always chose the latter.

Glancing at the car clock, I noted it was two thirty—twelve thirty LA time. He was having lunch in his office again. I flipped open the phone.

"Well? Did you pick her up?" We rarely exchanged greetings; they went obsolete with the advent of identifying ring tones.

I shot a grin Dilly's way. "She's right here, free and clear. We're on our way to my parents' house."

"I'd say to tell her congratulations, except she wouldn't care about well wishes from a stranger."

"I'll tell her anyway." Holding the receiver over my chin instead of my mouth, I conveyed Mac's message.

"Thanks," she said quietly. Too quietly.

"She says thanks," I told him. "Mac, you really need to go to lunch now. Away from your desk. Your back is going to stiffen up if you don't get up and move around." Turning thirty-five had been rough on him, with the first onslaught of back pain after years of playing too hard at racquetball, volleyball, and baseball. I'd just turned that age myself and half expected the same sign of decline, but so far nothing. Thank God. I caught the thought. *Thank God* was a phrase I used all the time. But not today. Not since picking up Dilly.

"Yeah, that's why I called," he said, and I could tell he was smiling, "for you to tell me what to do. I must miss you or something."

"Ditto that. But we'll get used to it. So get up; pretend your cell phone is me pulling you out the door. And take your jacket. You're going to Ralphie's and it's always ten degrees too cold in there."

"I don't need my jacket. I only take it because I end up giving it to you." But I could hear him shuffling around, so he must have been taking it anyway. "I'm going to look pretty silly putting this thing on a phone."

My voice went with him down the stairs, out the door, and down the block to the best pita restaurant within walking distance. I asked him about his morning and details of the work, familiar with the investments he mentioned. All the while I offered nothing of my day, not with Dilly hearing every word. I couldn't very well tell him about how she seemed different. About the way she'd referred to God as if He'd taken up residence inside her. And about how when I told her I was here to stay, she hadn't gotten all teary-eyed with the joy and gratitude I'd been expecting all these years. So I kept asking questions instead.

As usual, he knew something was wrong.

"I'm not going to ask," he said after he had placed his order, "but later, when you can talk, you're going to tell me what's going on out there. Got that?"

"Got it," I said. "I guess I should go, though. Dilly's been ignored this whole time. Not very nice of me."

"Okay. You'll call me later, then? Or should I call you?"

"You call me. My schedule is a lot easier to predict than yours these days. I'll *always* be available." I wanted to laugh but somehow didn't find the statement as funny as it was meant to be.

Flipping the phone shut, I caught Dilly's gaze again.

"See."

That was an odd word all by itself, with nothing leading up to it. "See what?" I asked as I looked in the rearview mirror again, relieved to see no one behind me. Sometime during my conversation with Mac, the tailgater had disappeared. *Thank . . .*

"What you just said to your friend—what was the name? Mac? It sounded like a guy's voice."

I nodded. "What did I just say?" As if I had to ask. She'd missed the humor in my last statement to Mac too.

"You've never been happy in small town USA, Hannah. I wanted you to come back to welcome me home. I have a lot to tell you that I want to say in person. That's all." She aimed her face right at mine. "You're not moving back because of me, are you?"

"Of course not," I lied. "I can name any number of reasons for leaving LA: the traffic, the smog, the crowds, the materialism, the wildfires, the mudslides, the water shortage. . . ."

"How many reasons can you name for choosing to come back *here*?"

That wasn't so easy, but I was brilliant. "Mom and Dad are getting up there in years. They're going to need our help soon."

She laughed loud and long. So much for my brilliance.

"Plenty of people in town can do that, starting with Aunt Elsie and Uncle Steve. They're ten years younger and they're the first ones Mom and Dad go to if they need something. They don't need you or me."

"That doesn't mean they won't use our help if they can get it."

To that Dilly had to concede. Work, to our parents, was a "blessing." It didn't particularly matter what kind of labor, just that a need was getting filled. If you were there and healthy, you were expected to work.

Unfortunately, that was the only excuse I could come up with, but it didn't matter because we were almost home and Dilly was looking out the window. She was obviously finished talking. Her face possessed an expression of anticipation and excitement that inspired in me both confusion and envy. Had I ever once given the flat, monotonous landscape of central Illinois such a look?

I lifted my gaze from the road ahead, trying to see what she saw. There was only the same endless shade of green. Occasional dark green trees served as windbreaks between young, light green crops. Even the roadside weeds were green. Granted, green was easy on the eye, but it was just so endlessly boring.

The only thing breaking up the landscape around Sugar Creek was Cyd Helferich's ancient wooden grain elevator. It was tall and square, painted black as if it were Chicago's Sears Tower transported to the middle of a cornfield.

Dilly pressed the button to roll down her window, but I'd forgotten to unlock it. She turned to me with a grin. "Roll down my window!"

I pushed the button so she could do it herself, and she did, a moment later sticking both arms out and waving frantically.

"What are you doing?"

"Waving to Mr. Helferich! Can't you see him?"

I looked up and, sure enough, there was Cyd on the roof of his unused elevator, where he'd built a wooden platform, adding lawn furniture and a white picket fence. Even I had to smile, seeing Mr. Helferich wave in return.

Cyd Helferich's father had been the last to use that old grain elevator; once they built the taller, galvanized steel ones in town, he delivered his grain directly there, just like everybody else. But Cyd didn't want to tear the old thing down; it'd been in his family at least four generations. So he converted it to his personal control tower. Through binoculars and a telescope he watched everything that went on in Sugar Creek. He tracked storms, crop dusters, and road conditions, not to mention someone driving too fast or any car parked along the side of a road. For flat tires his interference was fine; for hoping a car might provide a place of privacy, it was not. He was the bane of every teenager around with a penchant for speeding or hope for time alone with a date.

He'd no doubt been told to expect Dilly today.

I didn't slow down even when Dilly slid her arms back inside quick enough to honk my horn as we whizzed by. Cyd leaned over the railing to wave Dilly home, and I couldn't help but worry if he'd made those railings strong enough to hold his considerable girth.

Within the next five minutes we came into town. No one could miss the huge grain bins. The fans seemed to run all year round, and you could hear the whir throughout Sugar Creek. On the other side of the street was the gas station. It hadn't changed since I was in high school, so I knew it looked the same to Dilly. Next to that were the coin laundry and the only dry cleaner to be found within this town or the two neighboring towns. Seeing these first buildings reminded me why I never felt happy to come home. It was just too plain. No flowers, parks, or fountains, not even a sign welcoming visitors to Sugar Creek.

There was a row of small houses between that first intersection and the main part of town. They'd all been kept up well enough, although nothing like the expensively landscaped suburban houses I knew in California or saw in New York. No one was trying to keep up with the neighbors here; they were happy with perennial flowers and the same bushes that had been planted decades ago. Each house was small, neat, clean—and plain.

I couldn't avoid Main Street to get to my parents' farm on the other side of town. Dilly looked around like she was glad to be here. Her gaze lingered on the grocer where she worked when she was in high school but barely skimmed the bank with its flat brick front, then the post office next to that. The sole restaurant in town was the Coffee Spot Café, easily the only building most people might find appealing, with its red and white striped awning and a chalkboard sign out front where Bruno, the owner, posted the day's specials.

On the other side of town, I slowed the car at the lane leading up to my parents' house. Dilly must have seen that nothing, absolutely nothing, had changed. The oak tree, just as huge; the old chicken coop that had been converted to a workshop and occasional bunkhouse; the metal machine shed, as neat as ever; the steel feed bins reflecting a blinding glare in the sunshine. And beyond those, the four confinement sheds for the hogs still stood, canvas rolled out of the way above the screened windows and fans on to circulate the air.

*Shed* was probably too modest a description, but that was what Dad always called them. Each one held four hundred hogs, from a few weeks old to nearly six months. When I was little, Dad used to breed hogs on-site, but he'd joined some kind of co-op and had young ones delivered when they could leave the sow's side.

I stepped out of the car. No breeze today, which meant the air hung heavy with the familiar odor from the buildings. I'd grown up knowing pigs were actually clean, intelligent, curious animals, but even so, there wasn't a thing to be done about the stench wafting from manure pits below each building.

I watched Dilly over the top of my Honda. She sucked in a

lungful, then coughed and laughed. "I guess I didn't miss *everything* as much as I thought."

I'd barely retrieved Dilly's bag out of the backseat before Mom came down the stairs from the kitchen door. She waved a dish towel in her hand as she trotted toward Dilly, all five foot one, 110 pounds of her wiggling like a puppy reunited with its littermate.

"You're home! You're here! Come on over here, young lady."

None of us were especially tall, but Mom was the most petite. Her skin sagged more since she'd turned fifty, revealing bone structure that wasn't nearly as fragile as we'd guessed all these years. She'd once pulled a four-hundred-pound sow off a piglet, which we all thought something of a miracle. All she'd done was quote from the Bible, something about considering the ant. She said they could carry five times their own weight and credited God with giving her nearly that strength to save the squealing piglet.

Dilly seemed to welcome the attention from Mom. I scanned the kitchen porch for Dad, but the door had slammed shut with only Gretchen, the old Lab, following Mom. Gretchen could still wag her tail, but even that effort was slow, arthritic, as she squirmed her way between Mom and Dilly.

Mom held Dilly away, scanning her face as if looking for signs of sickness. "How you doing, honey? Glad to be home?"

"'Course I am, Mom." I saw her gaze roam over Mom's shoulder. "Where's Dad?"

Now Mom pulled away altogether, still clutching the dish towel in one hand and looping her arm through Dilly's with the other. "He'll be back any minute now, for sure by supper. We're having your favorite: pork roast and corn and mashed potatoes and gravy."

"Sounds like Dad's favorite," I said as I passed them by with Dilly's bag.

"Sure, his too," laughed Mom; then she smiled at Dilly. "But I always remember you enjoying our Sunday roasts, so I made it special for you. How you doing now, honey? You still look a little thin. I guess now you're home we can fatten you up. I made a cherry pie for dessert."

"Can I have it with ice cream?"

"Sure can!"

If either one had asked me, or if either one had noticed I was there, I'd have said it was Mom who needed the fattening up. Dilly wasn't as thin as she'd been during the trial or those years leading up to the awful crescendo of that night of her arrest. It wouldn't have taken more than a glance at her then to know something was wrong and had been for quite some time.

I wondered if Mom had ever noticed back then.

The kitchen table, right in the middle of the large oak-laden room, was already set for four. The scent of pork and garlic filled the air, something I hadn't smelled in years. I'd been home for Christmas on a number of occasions, the only other time such a meal might have been expected, but those meals hadn't happened, not with the depressing trek between home and the women's detention center.

"You take Dilly's bag upstairs to your old room, Hannah. It'll be just like old times, having both you girls home again and sharing the same room."

Exactly what I was afraid of.

I went through the kitchen to the hall on the other side, past the bathroom, and up the steep, narrow stairway. How many times had I tripped up or down these stairs on loose carpeting, a shoe-string, or just plain sleepy feet? I topped the last one, following the hallway past our parents' room and to the small bedroom in front under the eaves. It was impossible to stand anywhere but in the center here, with two twin beds shoved under the sloping roof-line. The room was barely more than a cubbyhole compared to anything I'd lived in since, including a dorm.

The same pictures hung on the walls—embroidered bunnies with halos hovering above their floppy ears. A polyurethane wooden cross hung above the threshold behind me, and the Twenty-third Psalm was blazoned into a plaque hanging just below the window. Reminders in every direction of the faith my parents had wanted to brainwash us with.

I put Dilly's suitcase on her bed; mine was stuffed under my own, still half-full. I'd only taken out what I would need for the few days I'd be staying. Once either a couch or bed was delivered to the Roland house, I planned to be out of here and take Dilly along.

I sat on my bed, reluctant to go downstairs. I knew I wanted to be with Dilly, but I was suddenly unsure she wanted the same. The happiness I'd seen in her eyes when we took the cutoff toward town was the expression I'd expected when I told her I'd be staying in Sugar Creek.

Six and a half years I'd planned to come back, to make up for what I didn't do all those years ago. I'd never begrudged the skipped vacations to save money, the roommates I lived with whom I couldn't stand, the bonuses I immediately put into a high-yield account without taking a penny for myself.

Breaking things off with Mac.

But not a tear from her, not a grin, not a spark. Nothing until we drove into Sugar Creek limits.

# Dilly

I look around the familiar old kitchen, a place I dreamed of often enough from behind bars. Funny that I never once dreamed of the farmhouse I'd shared with Nick, even though I'd spent so much time there after Sierra had been born.

"Need help with anything, Mom?" I ask while she's stirring something on the stove.

"Nope. We're all ready for you, honey. Just waiting on your dad now." She sends me a quick smile but her eyes look apologetic. "I'm so glad you're home. Your dad is too, but you know how he is. Not any better with hello than he is with good-bye. I expect he wanted to give me a little time to welcome you home on my own first."

"It's okay, Mom." I can tell she's making an excuse for Dad. I know he has a hard time being around anybody showing a lot of emotion. Maybe he thought I'd be so happy to be home after all this time that I'd make a fool of myself. Get down and kiss the ground or something.

I smile at the image as I reach down and pet Gretchen.

In the living room, I see my old piano. Mom wrote to me some time ago that Nick hired somebody to bring it here. I should say he arranged for someone to bring it, since Mom told me Dad had paid for the move.

I sit on the piano bench. Funny how some things come back when you need them. I haven't seen a piano in over six years, and yet once my fingers touch the keys they know just what to do.

A number of hymns come to mind and I want to play those, but since Dad isn't home yet, the notes of an old Carole King tune come out first. Carole King has been my favorite ever since I heard her when I was a kid. Even then she was considered a classic. So I sing "Home Again," something I've hummed off and on for years now and couldn't wait to play. Here I am, finally living the words.

I close my eyes against tears as the words spill out, knowing there is just one more thing I need to do now.

Be with Sierra.

# 3

WHEN I came downstairs, Dilly was at the piano in the living room with Gretchen at her feet—a sure sign that Mom was lax on the regular rules today, at least about animals in the house.

Mom sat on the couch with the huge picture window just behind her, through which I could see the two-lane road and soybean crop on the other side. I'd heard Dilly at the piano, playing an old Carole King tune. I supposed she was attracted to the artist because Dilly herself sounded a little like Ms. King.

Dilly always played hymns when Dad was home, but one afternoon he had overheard her singing King lyrics and ripped into the house claiming such music didn't edify the soul. Luckily the song had been "You've Got a Friend," and Mom convinced Dad the lyrics had meant Jesus as the friend. That calmed him down. Funny, that was one song I hadn't chosen among the many "friends" songs I'd used on my phone to identify Mac.

The song from Dilly's pure voice now was the one about coming home. She'd had that piano her whole life, a more constant companion than I'd ever been. When she'd married Nick, the piano had gone with her, and now here it was, back with her again.

She finished the song, then stood.

"That's it?" Mom's disappointment saturated the words. Maybe even she was tired of only hymns being played in that room. "You aren't going through the whole album?"

"I will if you want me to. Before Dad gets home. But can I make a call first?"

Mom and I exchanged glances, and I could see her surprise and wariness just as clearly as I felt such things in myself.

"Of course. You can go upstairs if you want some privacy." Mom followed her from the living room to the archway leading to the kitchen.

Dilly stopped. "There's a phone up there now?"

"In our room—your dad's and mine."

But it was only another step to the same old phone in the kitchen. "No thanks. I'll just use this one."

Receiving the words as an invitation to listen in, both my mom and I took seats at the kitchen table. Not that we wouldn't have been able to hear every word from the other location anyway.

"Is Nick there?"

I exchanged another glance with Mom. I knew Dilly would call either Nick or his mother, Sharon, since that was where Sierra could be found. As much as I detested Nick, I was glad she'd chosen to call him.

Dilly identified herself. I wasn't sure who had answered, but I guessed it was Nick's newest girlfriend or the eight-year-old daughter she'd brought with her. Mom had filled me in on all the details of Nick's life since he divorced Dilly: how long each girlfriend had lasted, how many times he'd been arrested for DUI, how Sharon might be as pleasant as a sour prune but at least she'd taken on managing Sierra's care. Like a rock, despite Mom's offer to help. All Sharon had accepted was a check to help cover the expenses of an occasional trained babysitter when the state-supplied respite worker couldn't make it. She'd also accepted the name of someone who would be a responsible caregiver. That particular form of help had paid off; the babysitter Mom had recommended was Esther, whose family attended Mom's church. She effortlessly brought back every inside scoop.

I glanced at the clock. Almost five. Through Mom, I'd learned Nick had kept his job as a mechanic and probably worked early hours. If they had any kind of schedule, they might be sitting down to supper, the same as my parents would be doing when Dad got home.

A hint of annoyance crossed my mind as I waited, along with Dilly and Mom, for Nick to answer Dilly's call. Why wasn't Dad here? For the past six years he'd seen his daughter only in a sterile family visitation room, surrounded by dozens of other inmates receiving their own visitors. How could he treat this like just another workday? He should be here. . . .

"Yeah, Nick?"

A pause as he said something.

"I'm with my parents. You probably know why I'm calling, so I'll get right to it. I want to see Sierra."

If it was supposed to be okay if we listened in anyway, I found myself wishing we had a speakerphone and could hear both sides of the conversation. From Dilly's face, eyes closed as if to stop a sudden flow of tears, I knew his reaction wasn't what she'd hoped for.

"But you could talk to her. DCFS says I can see her if you say it's okay. They don't need your mother's permission, just *yours*."

Another silence as she listened.

"Come on, Nick. She's my daughter."

I closed my own eyes, hearing her tears in that plea. A jab of pain ripped through me, and the same words that had driven me since her arrest played automatically. *If you'd been here for her back then, none of this would've happened.*

*I'm here now.* I gripped the edge of the kitchen table, fighting the urge to stomp over to Dilly and rip the phone from her unsteady grip and lay into Nick. My mother must have guessed my intention, because before my chair could scrape the floor, she laid a restraining hand on one wrist. But it wasn't enough. I started to move anyway.

"You will?" The hope in those two words didn't stop Dilly's tears, but they did stop me. Her tears magically changed to ones of hope. "And you'll call me? When? Tonight? . . . Oh. Okay.

Tomorrow, then. You'll be at work all day—" Her words were cut off again. "Okay. Tomorrow night. I'll wait."

My mother and I nearly tripped each other getting to Dilly once she hung up. Even as I hugged her, wanting to hear the details, guessing at some, I started planning. The pathetic urgency in Dilly's voice during that entire conversation made her tenuous position clear. After years of dealing in the financial world, I knew desperation was the last thing you should reveal in a negotiation. The problem was, I didn't know how Dilly could be anything other than desperate just now. Nick held the power, and we all knew it.

"Let me guess," I said. "Sharon won't let you see Sierra?"

Dilly nodded, brushing away a fresh tear with the back of her hand. Then she shook her head as if to clear it. "But Nick sounds like he's okay with it, and it's only his permission I really need. He'll call me tomorrow."

"It'll work out; you'll see," Mom said. "They'll agree to let you see your own daughter."

I nodded even as I silently called my mother the same name I'd called her most of my life: *ostrich*. She never saw the bad in anyone, even when it was right in front of her. I was not an ostrich; I was a planner. A determined one.

"It *will* work, Dilly. You made a mistake, but you've paid your debt. The parole board said so. It's not Nick's place or his mother's to tell you otherwise."

"DCFS said I could see her—"

"Exactly." I nodded. "They said you could see her so long as Nick agrees. Things are different now. Nick and his mother will be made to see that. You're not dealing with this alone, the way you had to before—which was thanks to Nick, I might add. You have me *and* the system Sharon has set up. We'll make them see it the way it is now, Dil. There's no reason you shouldn't be with Sierra."

Dilly smiled. She must have caught my determination. "You're right, Hannah. The Lord's in control, not Nick."

Nothing I'd said could have inspired that, but at the moment I didn't care that I wasn't the one responsible for the hope growing again in her eyes.

"Praise be!" my mother said. The phrase made me want to cringe. I never could figure out why she was always thanking God for one thing or another, like a harvest we'd all sweat to produce or the successful send-off of another load of hogs that my father fed and fretted over every single day.

Tires on the gravel lane just outside the kitchen door caught my attention. Speaking of not seeing the bad in anyone . . . there was my father in his pickup truck. I watched him get out of the truck, thinking how old he looked. He'd gained a little weight since I'd seen him last Christmas, but only in the middle. His face beneath the seed-advertisement baseball-style cap was still narrow, and his arms and legs, through denim and flannel, were rail thin.

But he didn't head to the house; instead he went straight to the closest hog shed to check on the stock.

I was vaguely surprised by two things: he hadn't come straight in, though he must have seen my car and known I'd brought Dilly home, and he was alone. For some reason I thought his delay might have been in gathering up family members to give Dilly a proper reception. I don't know why I expected such a fanciful thing as a welcome-home party.

"Mom," I said as she went to the stove to check on dinner—a meal that would no doubt be served ten minutes after she heard my father walk through the basement door to shower downstairs. "Maybe we should have a little welcome-home party for Dilly tomorrow. Invite Aunt Elsie over for lunch; Aunt Winnie, too. Maybe some of Dilly's old friends."

Dilly nodded. "I was planning to call Sandee in a while—she's about the only one I've kept in contact with. She'd come."

"That's a fine idea. Elsie already called about coming by anyway." Mom pulled the roast out of the oven, and it sizzled and smelled enticing, but despite that, my stomach rolled over. I hadn't been inside a hog building in over ten years, but I still saw the keen brown eyes of a pale pink pig looking me right in the face, curious about me, about anything that came in and out the door, about whatever was set before them.

"Better let Gretchen out," Mom said over her shoulder.

I did so, because I knew Dad thought all animals were the same, even ones that were supposed to be pets. I'd once chosen a piglet from a prize-winning sow at a neighboring farm, hand-fed it, kept it clean, trained it to walk at my side by guiding it with a stick up and down the lane surrounding the back forty acres. I'd named her Chloe and walked her every day that spring and summer, until she was lean and obedient and eager to please. She'd been six months old when we won grand champion, and I loved that 220-pound pale pink bundle.

But we returned from the fair just in time for the next shipment of hogs. Chloe went with them even though I begged my dad to let her stay. I never ate pork again.

Even poor old Gretchen wasn't any different from the hogs Dad raised, although like Chloe, she had a name.

Dilly set about helping Mom put the finishing touches on the meal, as if she'd been doing so every day forever. I watched until Mom told me to fill the glasses with ice and water.

Somewhere along the way we heard the basement door bang shut, and a moment later the shower spigot turned open downstairs. I can't remember a day my dad's hair wasn't wet at the supper table.

My father wasn't a tall man. His lack of height didn't diminish his strength, however, as he was known for having pulled down a barn all by himself in two days, one beam at a time. When it came to hard work, my father's was the name that came first in the minds of Sugar Creek citizens.

I'd tried, through the years, to tell myself this was something to be proud of. Instead what I saw was the man who'd never once told me he loved me, rarely said *anything* to me, really, unless it was to assign a task or quote a verse from the Bible.

Dad came upstairs just as Mom finished putting dinner on the table.

"So you're home," he said to Dilly, who stood not three feet away.

Dilly didn't wait for Dad to hug her, which was probably a good thing or it would've never occurred. She pitched herself at our father as if fully confident he'd want to hug her back. He raised his arms, those spindly limbs that were as strong as steel, and put them awkwardly around her, patting her shoulder once.

"It's good you're home," he said. "All that business is behind us now."

That was, of course, code for, "Let's never speak of this again, because I won't."

"There is something, though, Dad," she whispered.

He was already shaking his head, as if that could stop her.

"You already know God used everything to work together and bring me closer to Him. I just wanted to say it's still that way. I've never been closer to God than I am right now, and that's not going to change. Not ever."

Dad looked into Dilly's eyes as if trying to read her soul instead of her face. Then he nodded. "God can use us all, girl. Even somebody just out of prison. He didn't come for the righteous; He came for the sinners."

The words cut me for Dilly, the way he made it seem like Jesus hadn't come for people like Dad, just ones like Dilly (and me, no doubt). But it didn't seem to have an effect on her. She just hugged him when she should have been stepping away.

I shook my head without a word, then sat down to eat.

# 4

I LAY in the twin bed opposite Dilly's, wanting to ask her a million questions, wondering why I felt like a stranger to my own sister even though we were back in the same room we'd grown up in.

"So what's it like to be free?" I succeeded in sounding casual.

Our room was dark, unlike the way it had been most of the years we shared this room. We'd both outgrown night lights.

Dilly yawned. "It's great." Then I heard her stretch.

"But what was it like, Dil? being in that prison all those years?"

The silence made me regret asking. Maybe it was too hard to talk about.

"It wasn't all bad," she said at last. "I learned a lot. I know you don't want to hear about it, but there were people who came and taught me things I never knew about the Bible." She rolled over and faced me, but I knew it was too dark because I couldn't see her. "You know what I figured out, Hannah? That Mom and Dad are like cheesecloth when it comes to God. They let some of the truth seep onto us but kept back the best. Like the parts about God loving us even when we make mistakes. I don't think they meant to be that way; they just see mistakes easier than the rest."

She paused, then went on talking when I didn't respond. "I had a chance to do a lot of thinking these past years. I guess I left their church too soon. Sometimes I think if I'd kept going instead of leaving when I married Nick, I never would've ended up doing what I did."

"If you'd stayed in that church, you wouldn't have married Nick; you'd have married somebody who went to church too. Sierra wouldn't have been born."

"No, I mean if everything else were the same, only I still went with Mom and Dad and kept up with people in their church. There are good people there."

I had no reply, neither an attack nor a defense of the parishioners. All I knew was that they hadn't been there for Dilly, but I didn't blame them. She was, after all, *my* sister. Growing up, nobody had known her better than I had. Nobody. And I hadn't been there for her either.

"But I guess it doesn't matter now, to think how things might have been. At least in prison I got to go to school every day," she said. "Right there on the grounds."

"A school . . . about God?" I could hardly believe that; hadn't prisons banned religious material for a while?

"No. A regular school. Some people got their high school diplomas, but I already had that. I got a college diploma. In social work."

I sat up. "What? I didn't know. Do Mom and Dad?"

"Mom does. I don't know if she told Dad."

I lay back down, satisfaction soaking through me. "I'm proud of you, Dil. That's great. I guess you're right about these last years not being all bad." I sighed. "A college degree. It's what I've always wanted for you."

"Not exactly from the fancy university you graduated from, but it's my degree and nobody can take it away from me. God made it happen, Hannah. And once I get back into Sierra's life, once she knows I haven't died or abandoned her or whatever she must be thinking, everything will be okay. God's got a hand in what happens, so I know it'll be all right. And it's going to start tomorrow night, soon as I hear from Nick."

I wanted to caution her, remind her that I was pretty sure Nick Carlson—or Sharon—wasn't apt to take direction from God, no matter what Dilly believed. But I also wanted her to hold on to whatever hope she had. So I lay silent, feeling like a stranger again.

"What about you, Hannah?" she asked after a moment of nothing but darkness. "Why did you come back home—I mean really?"

I didn't know what to say. Until today, I'd been so sure of everything. Driven, Mac used to call me. Getting a call that my sister had poisoned her four-year-old daughter and then slashed her own wrists had a way of changing my course in life. Finding out they'd both survived and Dilly was going to jail had given me a goal. I was never going to let her down again.

But now . . . I wasn't sure she was going to welcome my help, no matter how much she needed me. So I didn't answer. I didn't know how.

"I thought you'd never leave LA," she went on, filling my silence. "Well, maybe for Chicago or New York, but not to come back here. And that guy you talked to earlier—Mac—sounded like you two are pretty close. Is he anybody special?"

"Just a friend."

"No future there?"

"Not as anything more than a friend."

"Is he—you know, gay or something?"

I laughed, although this wasn't the first time I'd been asked such a question. Never by anyone who'd met Mac; only by those who knew my best friend was a man.

"No."

"When you're dating other people, how does it feel to tell them your best friend is a guy? Don't your dates get weirded out?'

"Some; it's a good test, to see how much they trust us." I didn't have to tell her I hadn't been in a serious relationship since Mac, for the very reason I broke things off with him. Telling someone my future was in Nowhere, USA, was undoubtedly a death sentence to any lasting relationship.

Silence returned, but Dilly didn't fall asleep. I could tell she was still awake from her breathing. A few minutes later I heard her start humming another tune from the Carole King album. I didn't recognize it at first, but when I did I whispered the title. "'Natural Woman'?" I shook my head. "It's a good thing I can hear Dad snoring. What do you think he'd do with sensual lyrics like that?"

"I'd just explain the Lord is the lover of my soul."

I laughed outright. "I don't think Dad would consider the word *lover* chaste, no matter who the lover is."

"Yeah, I guess I'll keep this one to myself for a while. Sometimes that song helps me get to sleep."

Dilly rolled over, and soon the humming stopped and her breathing became even. I glanced at the clock. Not even ten.

I lay there, waiting to get tired. I'd been up since six, so sleep should come any minute. What else was there to do once the sun went down around here? I knew I'd be up when the glow came back over the horizon.

Shifting position, I contemplated the first trip to the grocery store I'd make soon. The Roland house had been left with a refrigerator, and it was empty. I planned to stock it with the kind of food I'd grown used to eating in California, the kind Mac and I loved. My guess was Dilly would like it too. Anything would be better than prison food, and I intended to put that memory fast and far behind her.

The first meal I'd make in my new kitchen would be vegetable pizza . . . one of Mac's favorites. . . .

# Dilly

Hannah probably thinks I'm sleeping, but I'm nowhere near ready to doze off. That's one thing I learned in prison: how to make your breathing sound like you're sleeping. It's something you pick up when you're forced to share a room with a total stranger.

Instead I'm lying here thinking about being back in my old bed for the first time in twelve years. I married Nick right out of high school, and Mom and Dad left our room the same as it was when Hannah and I slept in here as kids. It seems like a waste of space to me; Mom should have turned it into a quilting room a long time ago. But I guess she likes to do that downstairs so she can sew even when she has a visitor. Can't do that up here.

It's weird to be here again, almost like the past years never happened. In some ways I wish that were true, but then Sierra wouldn't be here. I know a lot of people think it might have been best if she'd never been born, especially when they remember what I did, but if they only knew she's the most wonderful thing in my life, they wouldn't dare think such a thing.

Being here in this room again with Hannah makes me remember what she said when I phoned to tell her I wasn't coming out to California for college after all, the way she planned. I was marrying Nick Carlson. There was a long pause, like she was trying to think of something to say.

But evidently she couldn't think of anything nice, because she really let me have it. She said I shouldn't limit my choices to Sugar Creek. I shouldn't limit my knowledge to high school. I shouldn't limit my future to marriage. She made it sound like I was already living in some kind of box just by staying in Sugar Creek, and not going to college made the box smaller, and marrying Nick turned that box into the smallest cube somebody could fit inside and still barely breathe.

Sure, I understand *now* that she was right about marrying

Nick. He's two years older than me but three years younger than Hannah, so it's not like they were classmates or would've ever dated. We weren't allowed to date, anyway, so my parents didn't even know Nick and I were seeing each other until we decided to get married. Back in those days I couldn't resist his charm, even knowing my parents wouldn't approve. When Nick decides to be nice, not many women can resist him—whether he's wearing a wedding band or not.

My point is, Hannah didn't really know Nick when she told me not to marry him. I don't think she had anything against him at the time; she just didn't want me to get married so young. I never even told her how he cheated on me before our first anniversary, while I was pregnant with Sierra. Hannah has a way of saying "I told you so" without using the actual words.

I love my sister, but her coming back here isn't right. *So help me, God, if she did this for me . . . Well, what am I supposed to do about this, Lord? You know better than me that she's always been pigheaded.*

I'm tempted to laugh at my prayer, because I'm the one who never minded working with the hogs when we were growing up. Hannah hated it. And it turns out she's the pigheaded one.

But I can't laugh; it'd give away that I'm not really asleep. I guess I have to give it away anyway, though, because I realize I have to use the bathroom. It sure is good to be home, even though my parents are probably still ashamed of me and my sister thinks I'm so pathetic she's here to rescue me. At least I can use the bathroom like everybody else: privately. I get up and find my way to the narrow stairs, praying all the way down to the bathroom.

*Lord, I don't know how I'm gonna do it, but somehow I've got to show them all I'm okay now. Ready to work, ready to take care of Sierra again.*

*All I have to do is prove it. If I can. Somehow.*

*Because I am ready, Lord. Right?*

*Right?*

# 5

THE JINGLE of "You've Got a Friend in Me" pierced through my pillow and into my dreams of a bright California sun reflected like jewels from tips of waves rolling in from the ocean, and Mac . . .

Mac.

He was the only one who called no matter what the time. I pulled my phone from its warm spot and opened it.

"Hey."

"You sound sleepy."

"Yeah, but that's all right. I'm awake. Everything okay?"

"Sure. I told you I'd call. You didn't say much on the phone earlier."

I looked at my sister's bed. With my eyes fully adjusted to the darkness, I could see it was empty. But even with the freedom to talk about things now, I suddenly didn't want to. I wasn't anywhere near ready to admit what I'd worked for these last six years wasn't going according to plan. My plan *was* working; I just couldn't prove it. Yet.

"I didn't want to let the conversation go on too long with Dilly sitting right next to me. That would've been rude."

"So she's happy you're there? She's moving in with you?"

"She has to let her parole officer know about the change, but yeah, I think so."

This was the first time I'd ever held something back from Mac, and I sensed in the long pause that he knew it.

"I'm thinking I'll stop by on my next trip from New York."

"Stop by where?"

"There. Where you are."

I harrumphed—that's the only word to describe the sound I made. "*Stop by* Sugar Creek? Nobody *stops by* here. Even if you found a flight through Springfield instead of Chicago, it's an hour drive one way without a single stoplight once you leave Springfield."

"Okay," he said slowly. "How about if I just make it an official visit? As my little old granny used to say to me own sweet Ma, you'll know I'm coming and can bake me a cake."

Now I laughed outright, more myself since we were no longer talking about the potential debacle I'd made of my six-year goal. He'd never known either of his grandmothers, and he'd never once referred to his mother as sweet. Not since she walked out on him and his dad when Mac was eleven. "Sure, I'll make you a cake with my own two hands and my mother's oven. White or chocolate?" I knew the answer to that and proved it by beating him to it. "Chocolate."

"Okay, then. I'll be there Friday afternoon. You know what kind of frosting I want?"

"Whipped cream."

Whipped cream was the last thing on my mind. Friday meant he had time to stay, at least until Sunday if he didn't have to be in LA or New York until Monday morning. Right here in my parents' makeshift bunkhouse. In corn country. Somehow I just couldn't picture it. Mac with a cornfield behind him? wearing overalls and a plaid shirt? No way.

"You're sure you want to come here? There's not much to see. Or do."

"I'll get to see you and meet your family. I decided I want to be able to picture you there, where you're living, the people you'll be spending time with."

"I've told you about my family, Mac."

"Told me about your family?" He huffed. "Names, what they do, how you celebrated holidays. You didn't like their church. That's about it."

"So if I tell you more details now, I can save you the trip?"

"Nope. I went online before I called and made my reservations already. I'm coming. But tell me more anyway."

I paused again. There was a reason I rarely spoke in detail about my family. I had to sift through plenty of memories I'd rather not share. "Dilly is the one everybody loves. Even Grandpa loved her, and we weren't sure he could love anybody. They're both a little like him, my mom and dad. Let's just say they picked up a lot of habits from him. He could be nice enough, but really he was selfish and cheap and strict and judgmental.

"He was volatile sometimes too. When he was in a bad mood, well . . . he's the one person in the family we were all afraid of. Grandpa lived with us until the day he died. He used to take naps, every single afternoon. Nobody—not even my mother, his own daughter—wanted to wake him when it was time for dinner. Saying he'd wake *startled* just doesn't describe it. His whole frail body would just about jerk out of the chair; he'd either gasp or yell, whichever was on his lips that day, and have this mad-dog look in his eye for a full second or two until he was fully awake. Mom always said it was because he had memories of Korea. Do you know who we sent to wake him, every single time?"

"Dilly."

"That's right. In our family, she was the one voted least threatening. The one whose face would calm him the quickest. She's a lamb; always has been."

He didn't say anything—didn't have to. Dilly was a lamb convicted of attempted murder. Some lamb.

"She's different than she was when she was married to Nick. She found religion."

"Oh no!" He didn't just laugh; he guffawed. "Now she's a religious nut?"

I shouldn't have been surprised by his words, but somehow I was. I knew he was, at best, an agnostic with only the slightest interest in Christianity. It was hard to live in LA and not think the religious right was out of touch. But once, after a Thanksgiving meal the two of us shared without contact from either family—those members of the world we were supposed to be most thankful for—he'd told me he wanted to know what made so many otherwise logical people believe in something they couldn't see. He'd just been dumped by a girl who told him she couldn't commit to him because he didn't share her faith in Jesus Christ. Mac was always telling women *he* couldn't commit because they weren't compatible enough to spend the rest of their lives together, and here was a woman who found him lacking instead. Spiritually, anyway.

"Dilly's not nuts," I said.

He paused, a clear indication that he'd detected my whiny tone. "I'm sorry. I didn't mean anything by it."

"Yeah, I know." I sighed. "Let's not talk about my family anymore, Mac. Tell me what you'll be working on tomorrow."

"You don't want to know. I'm meeting with Crayton in the morning."

I moaned. We both knew how that meeting would go. He complained about everything, from the size of investment returns to the color of the check. We chatted about that awhile, then about the microwave popcorn and Diet Coke he'd eaten for dinner, then about the pain in his back. When I asked him if he'd seen a new movie that had just opened, he was silent.

"Maybe I'll wait and see it with you."

"What, here? We'd have to drive back into Springfield, if it's even playing there."

"That's a problem?"

"You bet."

He paused again. "Guess I just miss you, Hannah. I've got all this time on my hands and nobody to fill it with."

"Sounds like you need to start dating again."

"There's just one problem. Who am I going to date without one of your roommates to hit on?"

"There's always Dilly, when you get here."

He laughed and I laughed with him, but somehow the thought didn't sit well with me anyway.

"I should get some sleep, I guess. Morning comes early in this house, like it or not. And I need to get over to the new house and see if I can hurry things up for us to move in."

"What's the rush?"

It would be dawn before I exhausted the list of reasons to want out of here. The hogs, my dad, the way my mother went from blind to placating, and of course my own guilt automatically associated with having no desire to work with the hogs on a farm where the cycle of animal needs never ended. "You'll see when you get here."

"Good night, then."

I whispered the same, pulling the phone from my ear.

"Hey."

"Yeah, Mac?"

"What happens if . . . What'll you do if this new life . . . if it isn't what you expected? Like if Dilly doesn't get to be with her daughter again?"

"I'm not counting on failing again. It's going to work out."

"Maybe it'll work out differently. What'll you do then?"

"You mean what's plan B?"

I heard him let out a breath. "Will you come back? Here, to LA?"

I wanted to tell him what he wanted to hear, that I'd be back someday. "I don't think so. Sierra's not going anywhere, which means Dilly's not. I'm here to stay."

Nothing for a long moment of dead air, which often wasn't unusual for us. We'd been known to watch the same movie on television from either end of a phone connection, with only the occasional laugh, snort, or yawn traveling the airwaves until the end of the movie.

"Okay," he said at last. "I'll see you Friday. I got directions online. I should be there about five thirty or six at the latest."

"Okay."

Then I hung up. I didn't have a plan B, because plan A was going to work. It had to.

# Dilly

Aunt Elsie is the last remaining guest. Aunt Winnie and Sandee left a half hour ago, Aunt Winnie to this afternoon's stack of bills and Sandee to rescue her husband from their children.

Between us two classmates, Sandee definitely got the better end of life's deal. I didn't think that at eighteen years old, though. I'd been married only a few months when she went ahead and got married too, but instead of being her maid of honor as she'd been for me, I was the matron. Ha, a matron at eighteen. I remember thinking I was the lucky one. I mean, look at Nick and look at Russ. Nick turns heads and Russ is what my mother once called "pleasant." And Russ is . . . well, a *nice* guy. You know what that means: boring. That's what I believed then. But I was wrong. Nick could make a living being a mechanic, making just enough to pay the bills after spending most of his money on beer, cigarettes, and other women. A guy like Russ can be trusted. Respected.

"The Lord has turned all your sadness into joy." Aunt Elsie's words break into my thoughts. "We can praise Him for that and pray it'll work out for you to take care of Sierra again."

"I'll need those prayers, Aunt Elsie," I tell her, and I mean it. "I have a feeling it'll take a miracle to change Nick's mom."

"Sharon is a tough old bird," Aunt Elsie says with a grin that's probably supposed to soften the words, but I know she doesn't like Sharon any more than I do. "If God can change the heart of a pharaoh, how much easier will it be to change the heart of a widow living in the Midwest?"

"I don't know why she's so bent on keeping charge of Sierra," Mom says. "Lord knows it hasn't been any easier on her than it was on you, Dilly. Sierra's bigger now; you'd think Sharon would want to share the burden."

I shoot a gaze my mother's way for calling Sierra a burden. Why is she always so worried about offending everybody except me? She frets over meals she brings to church for the potlucks there, she's been known to pull out rows of stitches if her work isn't up to par with other quilters in her group, and a weed wouldn't dare spring up in her garden, especially when she serves iced tea on the porch that overlooks the yard. Everything has to be perfect for everybody else.

But I don't say anything; I never do. That was one thing I didn't learn in prison: how to really stick up for myself. I just kept to myself and still do.

"I don't know how you can compare Sharon's experience with Dilly's, Mom." I hear Hannah's voice and it comes as no surprise. She's always tried to defend me. "For one thing, Sierra is in school for almost six hours a day now. And didn't you say Sharon has a respite worker and a babysitter you found from your church? Dilly didn't have any of that. All she had was a jerk of a husband and a child who never once slept through the night—"

I hold up a hand because I don't want to be reminded that people might want to feel sorry for how my life used to be. "Thanks, Hannah, but can we not talk about this anymore?"

Aunt Elsie reaches across the cushion between us to pat my hand. "None of us could have known how hard it was for you."

It's a funny thing about compassion. It should make you feel better—I'm pretty sure that's how it's intended most of the time. But for me it's only a reminder that Sierra and I most often just inspire pity. As if we don't have value for other things, like the way she can laugh and move in certain ways so you know what she's trying to say. As if she can't bring joy just by being present.

I get up and leave the room. I have no idea where I'll go, except maybe upstairs. It's not really a sanctuary because it's Hannah's room too, and I have no doubt she'll follow me if she thinks I'm upset. She's such a fixer she doesn't even know when something's not fixable.

But the doorbell sounds and I turn that way, thinking the silly thought that I've been saved by the bell. It's the kitchen bell that rings; no one uses the front door, not even strangers. The lane coming in from the road travels right alongside the house, and the stone-paved walkway leads directly to the closest door in the kitchen. Mom might have decorated the porch with homey, cushioned furniture and sewn a Welcome sign to hang above the front door, but no one ever goes that way.

I open the door. A man in brown is standing there, and I hear the motor running in his delivery truck nearby. He doesn't ask for a signature, just hands me a long, brownish red box and tells me to have a nice day, then trots back to his truck.

As he drives the loop back out to the road, I look at the label. To my surprise it has my name on it, and it looks like a flower box. Somebody sent me flowers? To welcome me home? Other than Sandee, I don't have any friends this generous.

"Expecting a delivery, Mom?" I hear Hannah ask. I glance up, and she's standing only a few feet away. Probably planned to follow me in my escape, just as I expected.

"No, not me." My mother's voice comes from the living room. "Maybe it's for you. You've been ordering all kinds of things since you got home."

"Nothing that a driver could deliver to the porch that fast." She steps closer to me and I turn around with the box. "Flowers?"

"I . . . guess so. They're for me, but I have no idea who could've sent them."

"Only one way to find out." Hannah reaches into a drawer and hands over a razor-edged box cutter.

I have the lid off in no time, but red tissue paper hides whatever is inside. A large card is taped to the top of the tissue, and I take it out of the envelope.

The words are like a match to me, burning my hands, searing into my brain. Not with heat, but with fear and shame and humiliation. I want to crumple it, but it's a thick card and won't easily bend.

"Well?"

"I—I—" My hands are trembling now and I don't want to see whatever's inside the box. I can't let Hannah see it, and I sure don't want my mother and Aunt Elsie to, either. So I stuff the card back in the box and grab the whole thing to my chest, then run out the door.

I stop at the trash bins on the far side of the machine shed.

"Dilly! Wait!" Hannah catches up with me at the garbage cans before I can stuff the box inside. "What is it? What's wrong?"

Tears are rolling down my face, but I don't care. How many times has Hannah seen me cry? It doesn't matter, because I've seen her cry plenty of times too. We didn't have a television in the house, but on the rare occasion we'd sneak off to a movie in Springfield, we both cried at the end, whether it was happy or sad. Maybe it's a product of living in a house where emotions aren't supposed to be revealed. They have to come out somehow.

I try stuffing the box under the lid of the garbage can, but Hannah pulls it away from me. The lid tumbles off and a cluster of stems falls to the ground, topped by withered flowers, long dead.

"What in the world . . . ?" Hannah stoops to retrieve the card. "'These were alive on the day you tried murdering your child. But we put phenobarbital into the water, and when it dried up, we continued to neglect it. Just thought you'd like to see the results of what you meant for your daughter.'" She looks at me after reading those horrible words out loud. "Oh, Dilly, who could do such an awful thing?"

I pick up the box from the ground, gathering the stiff and browned flowers, whose thorns are as sharp as if still protecting a bloom. I stuff them back inside, ignoring a spot of blood on one of my fingertips.

Hannah bends down to help. "I don't know who could be so cruel, but I intend to find out." She looks at the box for a return address; it's marked Dwight, Illinois, about an hour and a half north of us. "We'll take this to the police in Springfield . . . or a lawyer. . . ."

But I'm already shaking my head. "I know who sent it, Hannah. They're part of a group of activists who think people like me get off too easily." My tears are gone, brushed away with a couple of fierce swipes. "They're harmless."

Hannah looks at the box, half-crushed, ugly. "I'm not so sure about that." Then she puts a hand on my shoulder. "I'm so sorry, Dilly. Sorry someone would treat you this way."

"I *agree* with them. Half the newspapers that covered my case talked more about cerebral palsy than what I did. They talked about all the families in this state that don't get enough help, that only get respite workers if they can find somebody on their own. They talked about sympathy for *me*—the one who tried to commit murder—instead of for Sierra."

"But it's only right they should have had sympathy—"

"Don't!" I scrape my fingers over my face, trying to get rid of any evidence of more tears that are escaping. "I've had lots of time to think about this. It's more complicated than just feeling sorry for the tough time I had. What do you think people felt after they read my story? That Sierra drove me to do it? That when you get down to the bottom of it, people like her are worthless anyway, so why punish somebody like me?"

"No. Like you said, it's complicated."

"What's going on, girls?"

Mom and Aunt Elsie are standing on the kitchen porch, Gretchen still huddled in a furry, somewhat matted ball, but wagging her tail at the unexpected company.

I open the lid of the garbage bin and toss in the box.

"You sure you don't want to pursue this?" Hannah asks me quietly. "Sending dead flowers to somebody might not be illegal, but it's cruel. It's harassment."

"What do you want me to do? Somebody like me, just out of prison, file a lawsuit?"

I can see she thinks it's a mistake, but she throws the card in on top of the dead flowers.

# 6

ALL DAY I'd known one thing was just under the surface for Dilly: waiting for Nick's call. When at last the evening came and the phone rang, Dilly rushed to answer it. By the time she hung up, none of us had to ask how it went. Nick had refused, no doubt per his mother's instruction.

Dilly hovered over the phone with the receiver back on its cradle. I saw her shake her head, not at me but at the wall. "I don't get it, Lord. I thought this is what You wanted too."

Her words had been barely more than mumbled, but I heard every one. Before I could try thinking of some way to help, Dilly turned to me. I wasn't far, just at the kitchen table. She stared at me as if trying to decide what she wanted to say. Or building up courage for something clearly on her mind.

"Hannah, will you take me for a drive?"

We all knew her license had expired and she'd have to take a new test to get back on the road. Not that she had a car anyway.

I exchanged a glance with my mother, sensing my dad's attention too. They were both at the kitchen table, my dad with today's paper, Mom with a crossword puzzle. No one said anything. I grabbed my purse from the cabinet next to the door and led Dilly outside.

"Anywhere in particular?" Even as I asked, I had a feeling I knew the answer. My premonition sent a rock to the pit of my stomach.

"Sharon's."

"Are you sure you want to go? I mean, right now, when you're . . . angry?"

She looked at me, at the ground, then at me again. "Who says I'm angry? I'm just . . . just *inspired*, that's all."

Her voice trembled as if she wasn't sure she believed her own words. That was when I knew there wasn't so much anger *or* inspiration as something else. Fear.

Maybe there was a reason for that fear. Confronting Sharon might not help her cause. "Okay, let's just think this through. This is Nick's decision, really. Maybe you should see him first."

She shook her head. "He won't listen to me. He's never listened to me."

I wasn't convinced this was the best way to go, and Dilly's stare wasn't changing my mind.

"You don't think I should go?"

"I just don't want you to get in any more trouble, that's all."

She was shaking as if it were dead winter and here she was dressed in jeans and a short-sleeved shirt. "I can't just sit back and do nothing. God gave Sierra to me. Yes, I screwed up. But I'm better now. God knows I'm better. I know He wants me to be with the child He gave me. I feel it deep inside. So I've got to talk to Sharon. Maybe if she lets me in long enough, I can get a glimpse of Sierra. I need to see her, Han. I've gotta try, anyway."

I heard the desperation in her voice. It would've gone straight to my heart even if I hadn't seen the look in her eyes. She was right. "Okay." I grabbed one of her hands, if only to stop the trembling, and led her to my car. "We can do this, Dilly. I'm with you."

Sharon's house was ranch style, on the very edge of town, surrounded by an acre of grass. I wondered who kept it up, if Nick did or Sharon herself or if she paid someone to do it. The wood trim on the house and shutters was freshly painted, the lawn neat and sculpted at the edge of the long driveway. It was an inviting place, with colorful flowers along the walkway and under the windows. As though somebody who wanted to please others lived here, somebody who liked people. Funny how appearances could be so misleading.

"I can go to the door first," I suggested, unbuckling my seat belt. "Maybe alone, though. If she sees two of us she might get defensive."

"Sharon Carlson is never on the defensive," Dilly whispered, despite the fact that my windows were rolled up and Sharon's doors and windows were closed.

"Sure she is," I said. "She just makes it look offensive."

I moved to open my side of the car, but Dilly's hand stayed me. "I'm the one who needs to do this, Hannah. I'll go."

I wanted to protest but knew she was right. Even so, instead of getting out, she sat there, still. Eventually she put a hand on the door lever, opened it slowly, but didn't move from the seat.

About to ask what was wrong, I leaned forward far enough to catch a glimpse of her profile. Her eyes were closed. Leaning back in my seat, I let her be. Maybe prayer wasn't such a bad idea. Even if God wasn't listening, I believed going through the motion of thinking about what could happen, including consequences, could be effective at changing the person doing the praying.

Then she got out, slamming the door in its place. Almost immediately I heard the dogs from Sharon's backyard. She'd once bred German shepherds, but my mother told me she'd gotten out of the business when she took on Sierra's care. No more puppies in those kennels out back; just the adult dogs left now, those she hadn't sold off.

I watched Dilly walk up to the front door. Before she'd even knocked, I pressed the button to open my window, then shut off the engine.

Luckily for Dilly, there was no window on Sharon's front door. No peephole either. And from the corner where Dilly had chosen to wait, she wouldn't be spotted from the living room window. Sharon might see my unfamiliar car, but in the dark she wouldn't be able to see me. If she wanted to know who was at her door, she'd have to open it first.

Dilly waited so long I wondered if anyone was home. Finally a light clicked on over the porch. It was only twilight, but almost instantly, as if they'd been waiting for the familiar lure, bugs floated beneath the glow. The door opened and light shone through the screen, but only for an instant. Then the wooden inner door slammed shut.

"Please open the door, Sharon," Dilly said. "I only want to talk to you."

"Nick said he'd tell you you're not welcome here."

"He did; don't worry." Dilly's voice was loud enough to go through the closed door, so it easily reached me. "I didn't come to argue with you, Sharon. I only want to be with Sierra."

"And I'm telling you to go away."

"I . . . can't. I've just got to see her. Please? Please let me in."

"I'll call the sheriff if you don't leave right now. Don't think I won't get him over here and have you hauled back to jail. For trespassing. Disturbing the peace. Violating your probation."

"Please, Sharon," Dilly said, so gently I could barely hear her. "I'm not doing any of that. I want you to see me so you'll know I'm different. I know I made horrible mistakes, ones I regret more than I can describe. But I'm okay now. All I want is to see my baby girl. To let her know I'm still here, tell her not a day goes by that I don't think of her and love her."

"If you'd had your way she'd be dead. I'd say that ended your rights to seeing her for as long as she lives."

Dilly opened the screen; it squeaked as she pulled it out of her way. Putting a hand to the doorknob, she leaned close. I guess Dilly must have imagined Sierra herself on the other side, because she caressed that door as if it were alive.

"You're right. I made the worst mistake any mom can make. And I know you're taking good care of my little girl. Nick says so. So does everybody in town. I'm grateful, really grateful. But I've just got to see her, Sharon. I'm begging you. Please, please let me in. I won't stay but a minute. Just let me see her, touch her."

"I'll do no such thing. Now go on home."

"Please, Sharon. I'm her mother."

"You might have given her life, but you tried taking it away."

"I was wrong, so wrong. Please. Let me in."

"You're just a pile of selfishness standing out there begging me like this. You think it would do *her* any good to see you after all this time? She won't know where you've been. She's probably forgotten you by now, and if she has, that's best. For her. Now get out of here before I call Tom or Nick. Or both. Go on."

I saw Dilly sag against the door as if the life had been sucked out of her. She sank to the doorjamb, the screen wobbling behind her as it tilted at the top but made room for her at the bottom.

I left my spot and went to Dilly. The screen door protested again as I opened it wide enough to lean over my sister. She was crying softly, her shoulders shaking.

"Come on, honey," I said gently. "She's not going to change her mind. Not tonight, anyway."

But Dilly shook her head. "She's in there, Hannah. Right on the other side of this door."

She stood quickly in a burst of unexpected power. One small fist formed and she pulled it back, ready to pound on the door she'd caressed only a moment ago. I was too late to grab that fist, but suddenly, as if some unseen hand did what I wanted to do, Dilly was still. The fist opened to a palm reaching upward that landed soundlessly on the wood, slid down, then up once. Her other hand rose to brush away her tears.

Then she turned to me. I pulled her close, ignoring the tears on my own face. I led her to my car, opening her side, and let her in along with a moth who flew beside us.

And we went back home.

# Dilly

All my life I've believed it's best to put the things I don't want to do behind me. Like when I was a kid and Dad assigned chores, I'd do the things I didn't want to do first. I've never minded farmwork, but some jobs are better than others, like checking feed lines is better than spreading manure.

Or homework. Even in grade school I'd get it over with so it wouldn't be hanging there in my mind while I tried having fun in my make-believe world. I'd pretend Dad's chicken-coop-turned-bunkhouse was my own home, complete with loving husband and kids, but it wasn't any fun until after I had my homework done.

Or like when I knew I had to face Nick after the first time I found out he was seeing somebody else. Get the confrontation behind me. I was stupid enough to think guilt would actually make him stop.

Putting the hard stuff behind me is why I once thought I needed to put my life behind me. Face the end once—and *do* it—and you're done with it.

Right now I'm sitting next to my dad in the car, and we're on our way to the Coffee Spot Café. It's the last place I want to go. When I was in prison and I thought about coming home someday, this was the one place I knew I'd have to face sooner or later. Which to me meant sooner, because if I put it off once I might put it off again. And again. How many times would I have to face what I'm facing right now? The quick breathing, the sweaty palms, the sureness I'll say the wrong thing.

Let's face it. Nobody else in this town has been in prison. Yeah, others have made mistakes, but few of their mistakes have been as public as mine. Everybody from one end of Illinois to the other knows. If they didn't hear about it by word of mouth, they read the details in the newspaper. Whatever the reporters initially missed got covered in the trial, most of which was transcribed later in the local paper.

Marcy Simpson could have an affair with the seed salesman and Lucas Burgher could gamble away his wife's inheritance, but that wasn't written on the front page of the news, archived and ready to show anybody in case they missed the gossip the first time around.

I glance over at my dad; he's not saying a word, as usual. He could talk my ear off if I ask him about the hogs or crop prices or church, but not when it comes to what I'm thinking about right now. I should just say, "Hey, Dad, if anybody looks at me when I step inside the Coffee Spot—like they don't know what to say to a jailbird—can you help me out? break the ice?"

But I'm afraid he'll look at me a good long time, then tell me whatever I fear right now is just another consequence of my sin. And he'd be right. Being forgiven doesn't take away the consequences.

At least at this hour there will be mostly men, other farmers like Dad. Somehow they don't scare me as much as the women in town scare me. You know, the mothers who love their kids better. *Ha.* If only they could understand. I *know* how to love Sierra. They don't realize I never, ever stopped loving her, even though I did what I did.

Okay, I have to stop thinking about what I did, or they'll see it all over my face. I can't forget it, and I know they won't either. But if I'm thinking about it, then for sure nobody will talk to me.

I shouldn't have volunteered to come along. What was I thinking? *Father God, You'll have to help me through this one.*

It's too late to change my mind now anyway. Dad pulls to the curb only a few doors down from the café and gets out of the car. I can't just sit here; I have to follow.

My palms are sweatier than ever, my stomach nauseous. The first day I got to prison was like this, even though I was so glad to get away from the jail where they held me through my trial. Nothing could be worse than that.

But this fear is different—it's not completely unknown.

I follow Dad through the door, and the old bells that Bruno put in years ago jingle. Not just one bell. Lydia worked here for thirty-some years, and when she went hard of hearing, the owner, Bruno, kept adding bells until you could hear that door opening from one end of the shop to the other. They were probably still called Lydia's bells even though Mom told me Lydia had finally retired a couple of years ago.

I step inside and look at the sandwich bar first. That's where most of the farmers sit with their breakfast or coffee, because nobody wants to sit at a table alone. The bar is like one long table of them all sitting together.

Everybody has his back to the door, but now I notice one table is taken. I recognize Cyd's wide girth—the stools at the sandwich bar would've made him look like Humpty Dumpty on a very slim stick. I stop clenching my fists. He'll talk to me, because he talks to anybody and everybody. I could sit at his table. *Thank You, Lord.*

Two faces turn around to see who just entered. Harold Pestich farms several thousand acres, and both his boys are in college studying agriculture. The boys, I recall, have long ears just like their dad, which according to Mom means they're smart. I guess you have to be to keep adding acreage the way the Pestich farm is growing.

Mr. Pestich looks at me but doesn't say anything. He turns back to the sandwich bar, and I begin to doubt Mom's guess about long ears being connected to higher intelligence since he can't come up with anything to say to me. Not even hello after how long I've been away.

I swallow hard and wonder if I should just turn around and wait for my dad in the car. Nobody's going to talk to me.

Next to Mr. Pestich somebody else is looking at me, somebody I haven't seen since my arrest. Tom Boyle is four years older than me, so while I was growing up, I knew him by reputation only, since he was the star baseball player. Everybody knew Tom, which is why he probably didn't have any trouble being elected sheriff.

He catches my eye and I'm ready to look quickly away to save him the embarrassment of the awkward moment, but then he smiles and I can't look away after all.

"Welcome home, Dilly."

More faces turn then, but it's like a miracle. Maybe it was the sincerity behind Tom's welcoming face, but other people turn around and say welcome home too.

# 7

BY FRIDAY morning, we were closer to move-in condition with the Roland house. I still called it that, even though it was all mine. Well, mine and the bank's. I'd taken out a mortgage for tax benefits, but the money to pay it off was invested with just enough liquidity to meet the monthly bill.

The living room and two bedrooms were painted beige, clean but neutral, and the kitchen was buttercup yellow. No furniture had been delivered yet, for which the newlywed painters had expressed their gratitude. The carpeting was to be delivered and installed today, so not having to worry about floors or furniture had made their job about as easy as it could be.

Which meant tonight and tomorrow night, if Mac survived the whole weekend as planned, I couldn't offer him a comfortable place to stay. He'd be bunking out in what was once a chicken coop. Try though I did, I still couldn't picture it.

I glanced at my car clock—just past eight in the morning. I was parked on the street, waiting for Dilly at the Coffee Spot Café. I honked the horn to draw Dilly's eye when she came out of the diner, still wondering why she'd volunteered to go with Dad. How could she survive speculative conversations about the price of crop bushels and hogs or about who was planting what on which fields? Who could possibly care? At least she'd had the sense to ask me to pick her up after an hour.

She waved, but in the worst possible way. For me to join her. It didn't take her long to understand I wasn't getting out.

"Come on inside," she said as she approached. "Have a cup of coffee."

I shook my head. "Mom offered me some at home. I'm fine. Hop in. We'll head over to the house and get some work done so we can move in that much faster."

She didn't move, just stuck her hands in the pockets of her jeans, looking from the diner back to me. "I need your help, Hannah."

My interest perked. "With what?"

"There are seven people in there right now I need to impress. Not including Cora, who's waitressing, and Stan, the morning cook."

"What are you talking about?"

She came closer to the car, leaning in the window on her forearms. "I was sitting in there and had this idea. The only way I'm going to get Sharon to change her mind is to convince this entire town that I'm capable of taking care of Sierra again. I figure the more people I get on my side, the more likely I'll get to see Sierra."

I had to admit this wasn't a bad idea. People had a way of taking sides, and in a small town such lines were drawn pretty clear and pretty quick.

"The Bible says being nice to your enemies is like pouring hot coals over their heads," Dilly continued. "That's what I'm going to do to Sharon. Only I'm starting with Tom Boyle and Mr. Helferich. They're inside."

I looked at the café door. "Okay, I can see why you want to impress Tom Boyle. If he doesn't think you're a threat to Sierra, he won't be convinced by Sharon that you are. But what about Cyd Helferich?"

"He's been sweet on Sharon for years. Mom told me."

I couldn't remember ever having my own jaw drop wide open just like that. "Mr. *Helferich*? The town spy? Doesn't he weigh like three hundred pounds?"

"What difference does that make? His heart's just like yours and mine. And Sharon doesn't have many real friends, so he's about all she has. If I can make a good impression on him . . . Will you come inside, Hannah? help me?"

This was exactly what I'd been dreaming of—Dilly asking for my help, and my being here to say, *Yes, I'll help. Whatever you need, anything at all to make up for not being here years ago.* I pulled on the handle to my car door and followed Dilly inside.

Although the daily meeting of area farmers had the potential to last all morning, based on weather conditions or who popped in and out, I could tell things were already winding down when I came in.

But since I saw the value in Dilly's plan, I determined to stretch out the visit as long as I could. From their welcome, I could tell the task would be easy. I'd just returned after having abandoned this little town for fifteen years and rarely visiting. Evidently now that I'd come back, they were ready to see me as the prodigal who finally found the wisdom of small-town living.

After assuring everyone I was glad to be home, confirming that I'd bought the Roland house in town and that the newlyweds were indeed painting it for me, I felt as though I'd done my best. A half hour not at all wasted, if it helped in Dilly's cause.

Tom Boyle didn't seem difficult to impress, if I was reading him right. I'd forgotten he was just a year younger than me. I heard he'd married Misty Shoemacher, who'd left him for someone she'd met on the Internet. No one heard from her for a couple of years, spurring all kinds of rumors (according to my mother) about how she might have been murdered by some online predator, but then Misty had called an old friend and told her she was happy as ever, with two kids and another on the way. My mother assured me everyone was glad she was still alive, even Tom in a sad sort of way.

He was built solidly, with hair that was abandoning him and a belly that was growing a little soft. But from the way he smiled at Dilly, I thought she wouldn't have to do much to convince him not to listen to any of Sharon's complaints.

"Your dad here tells me you've got a fella coming to town this week," Cyd said to me.

I'd just glanced at my watch, wondering how much longer we'd have to stay, but now I looked at my dad, thinking how easy he'd made it, and for Cyd of all people. Everyone would know once Mac got here. Why tell Cyd ahead of time?

"You bring him round the tower, you hear?" Cyd said. "I've got quite the view from up there. He might enjoy it."

I nodded, even as the reminder of Cyd's grain-elevator-turned-traffic-tower made my heart sink. When Mac drove into town, he'd be subject to Cyd's intelligence test, the one Cyd issued for every visitor to Sugar Creek.

The most direct entrance to town was from a narrow road off the interstate—Route 84. It was a straight shot to town—up to the last two miles. At that point the main road took a curve. And not just any curve.

In a land where the only bumps in the road were man-made bridges over culverts draining the flat farmland, most of the roads were laid out in even patchwork squares, like fringe on the farmland itself. Maybe that was why the curve was so well marked—*because* all the roads but this one were so predictable. Maybe it was because when the wind blew snow or crop dust over the lines, it was harder to see the warnings. So along with the curve being painted in bright yellow stripes, a row of arrow signs pointed it out. Just in case the driver couldn't believe the road was actually going to curl.

Anyone with eyesight good enough to drive would be inclined to follow that curve. In fact, the road was on a slight embankment making even the wheels want to go that way. A person would have to intentionally force a car to go straight along that stretch of road.

But if they did, they wouldn't drop off the pavement. Almost at the last minute before following that bend, if the driver was observant and not swayed by all the arrow signs and bright yellow lines, he'd see a nondescript, curbless, rather humble road that offered a way to go straight and altogether miss the only curve in the county. And that was the road to Sugar Creek.

Nearly every visitor's first time to town included following the curve, only to go about five miles out of the way before seeing a sign at the only stoplight in the next town over pointing to Sugar Creek in the direction you'd just left. A county officer's joke, I guess. Letting drivers go ten miles out of their way made anyone grateful to finally arrive in Sugar Creek.

Cyd's land was the first farm you'd pass once you turned around. I pictured Cyd up there on his homemade deck—quite an engineering feat, I had to admit—watching the cars go by. He always said if they knew how to follow directions they would have ignored the bend and gone straight; thus, his intelligence test. Resisting the curve despite the signs coaxing you against going straight earned you an A. Follow the curve: F minus (an F by itself not being sufficiently humiliating). There was no grade in between, he explained, because there were only two options.

I found myself imagining what grade Mac might earn, because sure as I knew Mac and Mr. Helferich, one would certainly be assigned.

I continued to listen to the conversation around me, certain only the aftermath of a California earthquake or wildfire could create intimacy there that friends and neighbors shared here every day. Everyone who happened to be in the Coffee Spot Café just now was in on this conversation in one way or another, either participating or listening.

Then I marveled at my own thoughts. It was impossible not to know your neighbor's business with this kind of networking going on, and that was bad, right? But I'd forgotten it came with something not easily found in Southern California: community.

I savored the word, realizing it was the first really welcome thought I'd had about Sugar Creek since returning.

I'd planned for Dilly and me to spend the day at the house scrubbing empty cabinets, washing windows, and watching the carpet installation, then cutting the lawn and trying to locate where the Rolands kept perennials so we wouldn't mistake any for weeds.

All I really needed now was furniture, which was promised next week. Besides living room furniture, I'd ordered a new bedroom set for Dilly's room and a daybed for my own. Each piece was reasonably priced, in a traditional style to match the house. I'd sold my furniture from LA and didn't miss a stick of it except the Dania couch. But it was far too modern for any house in Sugar Creek.

The only furniture I considered taking was my bedroom set, which Mac said he would keep in the once-empty second bedroom at his condo until I decided if I wanted to sell or have him ship it to me. I'd bought that set on credit when I first started my job and paid it off during my first year of work. It wasn't that I loved the Martha Washington mirrors and smooth cherry finish; I'd bought it without realizing it reminded me of home, with its country style. By the time I realized the meaning behind the purchase a year later, I was able to afford all new furniture but only had time to purchase the sleek couch I'd left behind. That was right around the time I'd received news of what Dilly had done, followed by her trial. All that had changed my life and my spending habits for the years I remained in California, saving money to come back.

Mac promised he'd never use the country-style bedroom set. To be honest, I don't think he liked it. He assured me it would be there for me when I visited, and he'd let dust protect the finish.

Mac. Didn't he know if I ever came back to LA I might not want to leave? Which was precisely why I didn't plan on returning. We might have joked about the four seasons in southern California—dry, fire, rain, and mudslide—but there were plenty of other amenities to make up for those minor drawbacks. The ocean I loved, the mountains, the best restaurants and shopping in the world, not to mention winters that didn't require mittens, snow boots, or scraping ice off windshields.

Besides, LA wasn't here.

I sighed. Mac had been on my mind all through that visit at the Coffee Spot, knowing he was due to arrive today. Before leaving my parents' house, I'd swept and dusted Dad's bunkhouse, changed the sheets on the cotlike bed, and made sure the mousetraps were empty. Mom had promised to roast a chicken, something I knew Mac would eat. Unlike me, he'd eat pork, but I knew he'd want to see the entire farm, and somehow offering pork after looking a live pig in the eye just didn't sit well with me.

After I gave Dilly the grand tour of the house, we decided to start our work in the kitchen. Most of the cleaning supplies we'd need were already there anyway.

"Do you think you could take me into Springfield on Sunday, to church?"

Although I fully expected Dilly would want to go to church, the request still surprised me.

"You're not going with Mom and Dad to their church?"

"It *would* probably help my campaign to sway people to my side of things, once they know there are two sides, but I can't go back there, where everybody knows me. Not yet, anyway. I have a friend in Springfield and she invited me to her church. It sounds like the kind of place I need." She looked at me. "You might like it too. Besides, I'd like you to meet my friend."

If I was going all the way to Springfield I wasn't likely to just drop off Dilly and wait in the parking lot. "Okay, but we might have Mac with us. If he's still here on Sunday." That would be interesting. Besides trying to envision Mac with a corncob pipe, I also couldn't imagine him inside a church. "Who's your friend?"

"Someone I met in prison. Her name is Lana and she was released about a month ago. We went to classes together, only she was released too soon to get a degree. But she's smart. I'm pretty sure she'll follow through and finish now that she's out. Her dad's a teacher and always wanted her to follow his profession."

"What was she in for?"

"Drug charges." Dilly held up a hand to stop another question. "She only got involved because of her boyfriend, and he's out of the picture." She looked out the window, adding, "At least for the next three to five."

"I'm going to have to trust your judgment on this kind of thing, Dilly," I said, back to my big-sister, know-it-all voice. "But if you have any suspicion—any at all—that she's involved with drugs again, you'd be better off ending that friendship."

She looked at me with her thick brows drawn. "Do you think I don't know that? I'm not letting anything take me back to jail, Han. Nothing, not even if you drive me completely crazy."

Her last words surprised me. "What do you mean, if I drive you crazy?"

She shrugged and picked up a bucket I'd left near the sink. I stared at her back, wondering if I should let the comment pass, as she obviously wanted me to, or pursue it.

I came up behind her. "No, really, Dil, what did you mean?"

I noticed she was using cold water to fill the bucket, so I reached over to change the faucet to hot so the bubbles would mix better and it wouldn't be so uncomfortable to the hand when rinsing out the rags.

She stepped back. "*That's* what I mean."

I shut off the water altogether and turned to her. "What are you talking about?"

She pointed at the sink, then dropped that hand to lift the other and sweep in the rest of the room or the whole house. I wasn't sure which.

"You bought this house for *both* of us to live in, Hannah. Without telling me. Even if I could get excited about the idea, you never gave me a chance. You picked all the carpeting, all the wall colors—you even ordered furniture for me! Who do you think you are, my new warden?"

I stepped closer, putting my hands on her arms because I could see she was shaking all over, and I hoped my touch would steady her. "Of course not, Dilly. I just wanted to make things easier for you, that's all."

She shook off my touch, taking a step back. "Easier? As in, take care of *everything*?"

I folded my arms on my chest because they were just dangling there after she'd shaken me away. "I thought you'd appreciate my help."

She folded her own arms, rubbing her palms against them as if she'd been shaking from being cold. She didn't speak for a long, silent moment, but I could see whatever anger she'd had was fading away. I still didn't know what had caused it to begin with. She even smiled, although it was a little one. "I do, Hannah. But can I tell you something? I hate the color of this kitchen."

I laughed. That I could deal with. "Well it doesn't really matter, does it? You're not the one who likes to cook, so I guess I'll be spending the most time in here."

Her smile grew wider. "Then I guess I'll just have to get used to it."

Hours later, after Dilly and I left the house and were headed back to our parents' farm, my gaze fell on Cyd's grain bin in the distance. For a moment I was half tempted to go to the curve just outside of town and wait until I could flag Mac down. But I wouldn't have known what kind of car to look for—it could be anything from a Ford GT to a Ferrari Spider. He didn't mind spending money on such expensive rentals, but he often settled for common cars, too. All he really wanted was variety. It reminded me of the way he dated.

Precisely why I was glad to be his friend, I reminded myself, and not his date. Still, I didn't deny I couldn't wait to see him again.

# 8

COOKING WAS the one thing I had in common with my mother, although I preferred to do it while my guests were already with me so I could be busy stir-frying or mixing something while chatting over appetizers.

Not so my mother. Mac hadn't even arrived and she was already fussing over the final preparations for dinner. I was reminded how she always wanted everything to appear easy, which was why she did the challenging parts of a dinner presentation in advance. Somehow she kept her gravy free of lumps, the meat from cooling to room temperature, and her steamed vegetables crisp. No guest ever saw her fret over a single item on the menu.

Those of us in the family did, though. As I came out of the bathroom after my shower, she was transferring au gratin potatoes from the pan they'd baked in, which was a bit too browned at the edges, into a covered casserole dish with nary a tinged edge to be seen. She slipped it into the microwave before turning around to greet me.

"I'll be out of your way in a minute," she said.

"Out of my way?"

"For you to frost that cake you made this morning."

I glanced at the corner of the counter next to the bread box, where I'd left the chocolate Bundt cake under my mother's glass cake dome. "I wasn't going to frost it. Just serve it with a bucket of whipped cream and put a plop on each piece."

"Oh, now, honey, you're not going to land a husband serving dessert like that."

My first reaction was to tell my mother *no thanks* on any cooking advice. I'd learned more than enough on my own, and no doubt healthier than she was used to. Instead, I questioned the more obvious topic. "Land a husband? Who said I was trying?"

"Why else would a man come all this way if he isn't looking for a wife?"

I shook my head. I knew this would happen. "I told you, this is just a visit from a friend, Mom. Nothing special."

"Uh-huh."

Not even a word, but she'd convinced me she wasn't buying my claims about the friendship status between Mac and me. When I'd told my parents about Mac, my father asked only the typical questions: Did I meet him in church? Was he a man of faith? To which I said no, we met at work. My mother wanted to know all that too and more. I'd assured her we'd worked well together, respected each other's opinions, and even consulted one another on more than a few projects, but never once had I said we'd dated.

Dilly came into the kitchen just then. "What's nothing special?"

"Your sister is trying to convince me this Mac person is just a friend."

"That's what she keeps saying." Dilly grabbed an olive from the table and popped it into her mouth. "I guess we'll have to wait until we see them together to find out the truth."

"I've told you the truth."

Dilly shook her head. "Mom and I are both holding back judgment, mainly because of something Mom noticed. Because of something you *haven't* said about this guy."

"What haven't I said?"

"Go ahead, Mom," Dilly said with a grin. "Tell her your theory."

Mom pulled oven mitts off her hands. "You've never said he's like a brother to you. For somebody who's just a friend, we think leaving that out means something."

I ignored an oddly formed lump in my throat. "Has it occurred to you that since I don't have a brother I just didn't think of the comparison?"

"So, he *is* like a brother?" Dilly asked.

My mother had taken up a whisk to whip what looked like hollandaise but stopped, looking at me too.

"Okay, he's like a brother to me. Satisfied?"

Truth was, every once in a while I had some thoughts (not to mention dreams) about Mac that were in no way brotherly. I'd learned to ignore them.

Hearing wheels on the gravel outside made me head to the door, grateful to be out from under their scrutiny but, more than that, excited about Mac's arrival. The blue balloon I'd attached to the mailbox had no doubt helped him know which farm was ours, and since it wasn't even six o'clock I assumed he couldn't have had much trouble with finding the cutoff from the interstate. Maybe Cyd would give him an A.

Gretchen gave a halfhearted bark at the unfamiliar car, but her wagging tail and slow, careful steps off the porch were a dead giveaway that she wasn't much of a watchdog. I knew my mother would be looking out the kitchen window, and maybe my father from the living room too, if he put aside the newspaper long enough. And Dilly had followed me to the door, so I knew she was watching.

Though he'd only driven from Springfield, the modest black Toyota was streaked with mud just above the wheel wells. Not that I cared, because my eyes went to Mac just as he stepped out of the car. He left his door open, the chime sounding because he'd left his keys in the ignition. I couldn't resist the hug he offered, no matter what my nosy family thought. I'd hugged him plenty of times and never once had I come away thinking we were one step closer to an altar. I wasn't sure what my mother would think, but I was pretty sure my father believed folks who went about acting like family ought to get related.

I had to admit after not seeing Mac for more than a week, and now seeing him here in these surroundings, he looked awfully good. He was going to be hard to explain as just a friend. There was absolutely nothing objectionable about him. Not movie-star handsome (as seemed more obvious in LA) but attractive nonetheless. Brown hair and eyes, tall enough for most women to comfortably date at just under six feet, a smile that made you want to smile with him, and a scar on the bottom of his chin that offered an instant icebreaker.

I knew he switched tales about that scar as often as he switched girlfriends, depending on the audience. One tale was that he'd been thrown from a horse as a child and hit a rock. To a male audience he might say he'd gotten into a fight in high school and the other guy had pulled a knife. To another group he'd been in a car accident and the air bag had smashed his cell phone into his face. I told him that story was particularly suspect, since the scar looked older than most modern, compact cell phones. And it wasn't that big a scar.

To his credit, he always grinned after his made-up stories, letting his audience know they were just that, especially after a particularly embellished one.

But I knew the truth behind that scar. In college he'd jumped off a diving board too close to the edge of a pool, hitting the bars on the nearby stepladder. Jumped? No, he'd been pushed by a girl he'd just broken up with and didn't want to admit his failure—either to save himself from injury or from dating someone with maniacal tendencies to begin with.

"I can't believe you came all this way," I said.

"Hey—" Mac held me away from him, hands still on my shoulders—"you crying? We're not even at the movies."

I touched my cheek, aware of the tears for the first time. "Yeah, that's why I'm crying. There's no theater here, not even television, no good restaurants. . . . But you're here anyway. Don't say I didn't warn you."

He pulled me to him again, but only for a moment. He closed the car door behind him and looked around. The late afternoon sun hadn't reached the horizon, and as I looked around the farm to see it through his eyes, I had to admit what he saw no doubt matched his imagination of the picture-perfect farm. Not a weed in sight, flowers beginning to bloom along the side of the house, the surrounding crops just inches high but promising greater things to come under the endlessly cloudless blue sky.

And not a whiff from the hog buildings. The wind was headed out to the field. I almost felt like calling up a "praise be" from Mom.

"I'll show you around later, or maybe in the morning if that's okay. Come on in. Might as well meet the family." I started walking, but just as we reached the porch, I turned abruptly. "Promise me one thing?"

He nodded.

"You'll forget all the things I've said about my family," I whispered, "at least while you're here?"

He put his hands back on my shoulders. "Hannah. How bad can they be? They produced you."

I wanted to say something about how I'd come to be myself in spite of my background, that the me he knew had actually been born in LA, or at least reborn, but none of that came out.

Gretchen was the first of the family to greet Mac. He patted her shaggy hair, then held open the door for both of us. I gently nudged Gretchen aside and led Mac in.

My dad was in the kitchen when I opened the door, a sure sign he'd seen the hug outside. If he hadn't, he'd have stayed oblivious in the living room, waiting for me to bring the visitor to him.

Or maybe he was in the kitchen because it was almost six and dinner was about to be served.

"Everybody," I said, unable to prevent the slight breathlessness to my voice. I sounded like a sixteen-year-old. "This is Gideon MacIntyre. Mac."

One by one, I introduced my family, starting with Mom, who was the closest, and finishing with Dilly. I knew he was most curious about her.

"Hope you're hungry," Mom said, pouring water from a pitcher into the glasses. He'd get used to the taste of well water, if he got past the cloudy look or waited until the sediment sank to the bottom.

"Starving," Mac said. "That little bag of pretzels on the plane didn't last long."

Still watching the water in the glasses, seeing it cloudier than I expected, I headed to the laundry room, where my mother kept soda. "Diet Coke okay?"

"Only Pepsi in there," Dad called. "Ever since your aunt Winnie bought stock, that's all we buy around here anymore."

"Sit down," my mother invited. "Sure, we like to support the family. It's how things are around here, you know."

I came back from the laundry room, wondering what Dilly had thought of that statement. What kind of support had she received when she needed it most?

"So you've come from LA," my dad said.

"Actually New York, on my way back to LA. Hannah's abandoned me. She used to make the miles shorter, but now I'm on my own in between."

"I thought they were going to give you a new partner?" I asked.

Mac nodded, accepting the Pepsi. "They promoted Brian, but he didn't come with me this time."

"Brian! He just started."

"Premature, I agree. But I'm hoping he'll be okay." He turned to my parents, who stood beside the table. "No one, of course, can live up to your daughter. She's a natural in the investment world."

I felt my parents' bewildered gazes travel my way, as if they'd never considered what I'd been doing for the past ten years since I graduated from UCLA or, if they had, never considered that my work made much of an impact. Or that I might be good at it.

"Mom roasted a chicken and made au gratin potatoes," I said, drawing attention to the waiting table. Thanks to me, there wasn't a single fried item on the menu, although my mother's potatoes did have more butter and cheese on them than I ever would have seen—or served—in California.

"Great. But hey—did you . . . ?"

He let his question taper off, but I knew what he was looking for. I cocked my head to the countertop. "It's over there."

"Are you talking about that cake?" my mother inquired, her gaze following Mac's. "Such as it is. I told her to frost it."

"Nah," Mac said, pulling out the chair my mother had motioned for him to take. "She used to frost cakes until I talked her out of it. If she lets everyone take a scoop from the whipped cream carton— or the bowl if she made it herself—you can get twice as much on your slice as if she'd frosted just the top and sides. Trust me, it's a better deal."

Everyone laughed, and my gaze fell to Dilly. She looked shy and uncomfortable, and at first I attributed it to six and a half years of having only women's company. The friendly, hopeful Dilly who'd just been here with my mother and me seemed gone. But what about this morning at the Coffee Spot among male farmers whose ages ranged from twenty-two to seventy-five?

Before me was the Dilly of high school: cautious, uncertain. The one I'd promised would blossom once she followed me out to LA for college. But she'd married Nick instead.

We made it through dinner. My father talked about farming and how many generations his family had been working the same fields, my mother about the town's history, linking a local Civil War hero to his descendant who had been killed in Iraq. As I listened, I silently marveled that my parents seemed so friendly and normal. Maybe if everyone in the world only knew each other over limited time periods we wouldn't have so many opportunities for bad memories. Even my dad was friendly and talkative, the way he was to everyone but Dilly and me. He didn't quote a single Bible verse. By the time the meal ended, I was convinced Mac must have thought I was crazy for having left this companionable seat of familial bliss.

"That was the best meal I've had in months, Mrs. Williams," Mac said to my mother.

"You left room for Hannah's cake, I hope?"

"I always have room for cake."

"I'll have the coffee up in no time."

"Did Hannah tell you about our GPS system here?" my dad asked Mac while Dilly and I cleared away the dishes.

He shook his head, looking between my father and me. Wisely, he said nothing specific; I was pretty sure he'd wonder why a farmer would need directions anywhere, if he imagined this GPS to be anything like the one in his car. Dad explained how a satellite tracked yield conditions at harvest time, making the whole job of planting, fertilizing, and harvesting for the following year a more exact science as to the needs of the soil.

"I was going to show Hannah how it all works, first on the tractor and then through our computer," my father went on. Use of my name had me listening closer. Since I'd never once shown an interest in the farm, I wondered at his statement. "I figured she's got that fancy education; we might as well use it around here, now that she's home."

I smiled, but I was pretty sure everyone except my father knew it wasn't a sincere one. Converting crop yield to sales wasn't my line of investment.

"And we'll have Dilly here back up in the John Deere starting tomorrow," Mom said.

My gaze flew to Dilly, next to me, but she wasn't looking my way. I should have known we'd been too lucky for the past few days, with not a single word spoken about Dilly and me getting back into our old farmhand roles.

"Are you sure you'll have time for helping out around here, Dil?" I asked. "I thought you were going to start interviewing."

"I've looked online and submitted résumés to a couple of places. I figured I could put in some hours around here until I start getting some interest."

That made sense, except it didn't explain why she wasn't making eye contact with me.

"Dilly has a degree in social work, Mac. She put these past years to good use."

"Congratulations, Dilly. That's great."

"My options will be limited because of my record—"

"Maybe you want to see how that GPS works," Dad cut in. "We've still got some light left in the day. Come on outside, Mac."

If Mac noticed my father's rudeness, he was gracious enough not to mention it, except to send a glance Dilly's way to convey that he'd have been interested in what she had to say if she'd had an opportunity to say it. Then he set aside his napkin and followed my father out the door.

"I'll come along," I said, "if I'm the one who's going to take on this job. You'll keep the coffee hot, Mom?"

Much later, after my father had shown Mac every aspect of the equipment taking up space in the machine shed (each piece explained in detail: the planter, combine, tractor, field cultivator, drill for planting wheat), after we returned inside for cake and coffee, after my mother had cleared away the last of the dishes, I asked Mac if he wanted to see where he'd be sleeping.

My parents were not ones to condone unmarried men and women spending time alone together, and somewhere in the back of my mind I considered this. But it was ridiculous for them to think I hadn't been following my own rules for the past fifteen years, and so I refused to feel guilty about going outside with Mac and taking him alone to the bunkhouse. I even closed the door.

"Well?" I asked, flipping on the electricity. A tent of light shone down from above, illuminating my scrubbing efforts earlier.

"They're great. First impressions, anyway."

I knew he meant my family, so I shook my head. "No, I mean about this place. It's kind of like camping out, with canvas covering the screens instead of real windows. If you get cold, there's a heater in the corner you can turn on."

Mac was looking at me, not at the heater or at our surroundings. "Do you think I'm suddenly not believing all the tales you told about your parents?"

Why did he never let an ignored topic rest? "No. But it did

occur to me they were a lot more charming to you than they've ever been to me and Dilly."

"They were charming. And yes, I noticed your parents were less than charming to you, but isn't that how families are?"

"So you *do* think I've exaggerated my tales about how judgmental they've always been to me and Dilly? You think we're just a normal, healthy, happy family?"

He shrugged. Perhaps seeing my dissatisfaction, he came closer and put his hands on my shoulders. "I'm not saying how you feel isn't valid. You're the one who grew up here."

I let out what was supposed to be a short laugh, but it sounded more like a sigh. "I grew up here, but I still feel like an outsider. And my parents don't do much to change that."

Keeping an arm around my shoulders, he led me to the cot and we sat down. "Your dad does seem less aware of you and Dilly than other dads I've been around. Even my own."

I rested my head on his shoulder, relieved he understood, amazed I'd doubted for a moment that he would. "It's as if he doesn't even like us."

"He's just one of those old-fashioned man's man types. More comfortable around guys, only not gay."

I laughed. "If my dad knew he had to be explained that way, he'd for sure think everybody from California is crazy. You included."

"I'm glad I came," Mac said. Now he did look around, then out the window at the last rays of the sun setting over the soybean field across the road. But his expression changed in those moments from the peaceful placatory role he often played with me to something else. His brows lowered slightly; the corners of his mouth went straight. Not exactly a frown, but definitely solemn. "Much as I hate to admit it, Hannah, I think you'll be okay here."

"Yeah, I'll be okay."

I didn't know what else to say about that, especially since his tone of voice hadn't been much happier than mine.

"So, how come you played the quiet one tonight?" I asked Dilly after she turned off the light in our room.

"Your friend and Dad didn't leave much room for anybody else's words."

I accepted that. "Why didn't you tell me about agreeing to work for Dad?" No sense not airing things right away.

I heard her fluff her pillow, pull back the covers, and get into bed before answering. "Mainly because I just don't feel the way you do about farming, Hannah. I don't mind working with Dad. He likes it too. You'll see when you start working with that GPS system."

"Dilly . . . I don't know if I'll do that, at least for any length of time. I really am planning to do some investment consulting, and that'll take up a lot of my time."

"I guess you'd rather do that than work on the farm."

"Just like you'd rather do something related to your degree. Wouldn't you?"

"I hope so. If I *can* get a job in my field. I knew I'd have a tough time getting into social work with my background, but that's what appealed to me when I chose what to study. I had a call earlier—my first interview is next week. Tuesday. I'll need to renew my license before then, though."

"No problem. I can take you to the DMV on Monday. Great news about the interview, Dil. At the risk of sounding like Mom, I'm going to tell you it'll all work out. It has to. You've worked too hard and I won't let you give up."

"Because my only alternative is working with Dad the rest of my life?"

"Because you should be able to use your talents."

"From God," she added. Not exactly what I would have said, but I didn't argue.

"Did you ask Mac about church on Sunday? Will he still be here?"

"Yeah, he'll follow us in his car and go on to the airport after the service."

"He's a nice guy, Hannah. I don't know why you say you're just friends."

"Because that's what we are."

"Sure."

I didn't want to argue the point, especially with Dilly. After all, if it hadn't been for her I probably would have continued dating Mac—at least longer than the few months we lasted all those years ago.

And then where would Mac and I be?

Probably with one more memory of another broken relationship.

# 9

IN THE morning, I reminded my father about the time difference between LA and our central time zone, making it clear I wouldn't wake Mac by seven if my father expected to share breakfast. My goal was to avoid one of my dad's usual morning Bible quotes around Mac. The one about God's compassion being new every morning was the first that came to mind. My father's interpretation of it was anyone who slept past dawn was bound to miss such a blessing.

My father went about his morning chores, showered, dressed, then went into town on his own.

I kept an eye on the bunkhouse door, surprised to see it open shortly after Dad left. When I went outside on the porch to greet Mac, I knew what must have awakened him. The gentle breeze we enjoyed yesterday had faded, leaving the pungent scent of hog manure wafting gently—and thoroughly—around the house.

He'd pulled on jeans and a T-shirt, but his hair was still tousled as if he'd just gotten out of bed.

"Come on in for a shower and breakfast," I called.

"So you think that smell is me and a shower will wash it away?"

"What smell?"

"Funny."

He joined me on the porch, where I handed him a cup of coffee. He didn't take a sip. "I think I'll have to go inside before I can swallow anything."

"Welcome to the farm."

He followed me inside. "How come I didn't smell this yesterday?"

"Depends on the wind. It usually blows out to the field, but when there's no air movement or it shifts, voilà! You're reminded of what's in all those buildings over there."

He raised his T-shirt to his nose. "Maybe I better store my clothes in here."

"You can sleep on the couch down here tonight if the air doesn't start moving again."

"Deal," he said over his shoulder as he made his way into the bathroom.

Before long we'd eaten the breakfast my mother put before us: eggs, bacon, toast, and juice. Soon Dilly joined us.

"We ate the last of the eggs," I said to Dilly, looking at Mom's empty pan.

"She already ate, while you were in the shower earlier," Mom said.

Dilly nodded. "I was going to ask Mom to take me into town."

"I can do that," I said. "I was going to show Mac around, take him by the house." I looked at Mac again. "Maybe you'd like another cup of coffee at the café in town. You might be able to help Dilly's plan."

He eyed her, but she didn't speak. I filled him in.

"The more the merrier," I finished. "Care to join in?"

"As long as having a Californian in on it won't hurt the cause in the long run."

"All you have to do is pretend you're interested in farming, and everybody will love you."

"Now, Hannah," Mom said from the sink, "pretending is lying."

"Then just listen to all the farm talk and try not to fall over dead from boredom."

We'd been at the Coffee Spot for less than a half hour and I knew Mac was thinking my perceptions were totally off-kilter again.

Had I feared he'd be bored? He looked far from it. Everyone in town must have taken some kind of charm drug. They welcomed Mac and laughed over Cora the waitress's ten-year-old grandson mistaking him for a movie star. Mac certainly received star treatment, the way they asked questions about California and, once they learned he was in investments, about how to diversify their money.

I'd lived in California for almost fifteen years including college, held the same degree Mac did, received the same licensing training, worked the same job, but no one asked me a single question. Like the loyal friend he was, Mac did try including me in the conversation, but it was clear everyone thought someone who'd grown up in town must not be bringing much new knowledge to the community table.

When Cyd Helferich arrived, everyone shouted his name, and it reminded me of the way characters on *Cheers* used to shout, "Norm!" Not that the Coffee Spot and a bar had anything in common, except maybe a feeling of fellowship, each in their kind.

"Well, Cyd?" my dad prompted while Cora poured Cyd some coffee. "You probably already knew what kind of car Hannah's visitor was driving before he made it into town. What'd he get?"

Mac looked at me, perplexed.

"I should have explained your arrival was under surveillance, Mac. You probably don't remember seeing a tower on the road—"

His brows shot up. "The one with the fence on the top? Who could miss it? I was going to ask you about that, if you knew who built it. I was hoping to see it up close."

I smiled, guessing he'd probably upped his grade at least one level by showing such interest. "Cyd's the architect. Well, he didn't build the actual grain elevator; that's been around forever. But he converted the top to a flat patio. He'll take you up there if you'd like."

"I was wondering how you get up there," Mac said. "I didn't see stairs."

"There's a ladder inside," Cyd chimed in. "Good and sturdy, too.

Have to be to carry me up there. Tell Hannah to bring you around later this morning."

Most eyes remained on Cyd, obviously waiting for the grade he'd assigned this popular visitor, while once again Mac looked my way to finish my explanation. "Cyd watches the roads around here," I said. "If he *happens* to be up there when someone new comes to town—" someone snickered at my choice of words; I thought it was Tom Boyle—"he checks to see if they miss the cutoff. Did you?"

"Almost. But you told me it was a straight shot from the expressway."

That was true; I'd emphasized no matter what, don't turn the wheel.

"Well, Cyd?" my father prompted again.

"This here fella's getting the first A minus ever issued," Cyd announced.

A hoot of laughter followed. "What's the minus for?" I asked, knowing Cyd's penchant for F minuses, but never with an A.

"That was for a little veer over the line at the last minute," Cyd said. "Ran right through some soft ground just off the road. But I didn't mark him to a B, since it's an act of faith to keep going straight when you think the road's about to end right below your tires."

Mac nodded. "I did almost follow that curve. I only saw the straight road at the last minute."

"Congratulations," I said. "An A minus from Cyd means you're as good as born here."

We stayed a while longer, finishing another cup of coffee, hearing stories about other visitors who'd gotten lost, even beyond the stoplight a couple of miles down the road. I stopped listening after a while, convinced of Mac's acceptance. Instead I eyed Tom Boyle, wondering if I should tell him about Dilly's flower delivery. Dilly hadn't mentioned it again, but who knew what someone was capable of if they thought sending such a heartless thing was okay? Tom had always been reasonable; he might think he should know, just to be aware of it in case anything else happened in the future.

"He a friend of yours?" Mac whispered over his coffee cup.

"Who?"

"The tall one you've been studying the last few minutes."

"According to small town rules, *everyone* is a friend around here."

"Town sheriff is a good one to keep close. Has he been here long?"

I could tell Dilly was ignoring our hushed voices on purpose, although she could probably hear every word since we were seated at the same booth.

"Born and raised. He graduated a year behind me in school."

"Married?"

"Divorced."

"Interested?"

"Me? In Tom?"

His silence confirmed the question. "I'm not here to find a husband, Mac."

"You've been putting off starting a search for six and a half years, Hannah. Now you're where you wanted to be. No excuse not to start looking, is there?"

I shrugged, sitting forward in my seat, bending over my coffee. His words might contain a hint of truth, but finding a husband here was the last thing on my mind. That would mean staying in Sugar Creek forever. I couldn't entertain that thought just yet, even if staying was the main part of plan A.

The rest of the day went quickly. We went to the house and Mac approved of all my choices, from the carpeting to the color of the walls. Afterward we went to see Cyd, who gave us the grand tour of his traffic tower grain elevator. Mac was especially impressed with that, which made Cyd extend the tour to the most minute detail, citing the date it was first built, how much grain it had once held, how many miles he could see from the top, how many accidents he'd reported to send help all the quicker.

When we returned to my parents' house, I knew something was up. We'd planned to go to Springfield for a movie and invite Dilly along. But Mom and Dilly were in the kitchen up to their elbows in hot dog buns and potato salad.

"Good news!" Mom greeted us. "I was talking to Aunt Elsie and mentioned we have a visitor." She shot a smile Mac's way. "She said she wanted to meet you, Mac, so I thought why not have them over for a wienie roast? And why just Aunt Elsie and Uncle Steve? Why not the Johannsons? And the Hertzbergs? Aunt Winnie, too."

I exchanged looks with Dilly, wondering if she'd had any part in it. But I could tell the idea didn't appeal to her any more than it did to me.

I hid my thoughts, even from Mac, although from my lack of eye contact he'd probably guessed I was less than thrilled with the evening ahead. But Mom was clueless as usual, especially when both Mac and I volunteered to help. Willing participation had always equaled excitement in Mom's book of life.

# Dilly

When I was little I used to look forward to a neighborhood wienie roast like no other event. But here I am, lingering alone upstairs in my room while everyone's gathering on the lawn outside. Everything is perfect this evening, with a gentle breeze carrying away the odor from the hog buildings. It's still just cool enough to make everybody welcome a fire.

Even Hannah is downstairs already, but that's because she's hovering over Mac the way she's been hovering over me since I got back. Hovering as if to protect him from something, like she's afraid all of us will make her look bad for having grown up here, as if she had a choice and chose badly.

I have to admit it's nice having her worrying about somebody else for a while.

I'm trying to figure out what's going on between them. Maybe it's just my general lack of experience around guys (not to mention lack of confidence, thank you, Nick) that makes me think it's impossible to be "just friends" with one of them. Mac's a nice guy, kind of cute if you like the city type, so how is it she can be with him without wondering if he's ever thought of her as more than a friend? That's what I would do.

I shake my head at my reflection in the mirror above the dresser. Hannah's a lot more confident than I am. Why do *I* have to wonder what value I am to others? I'm supposed to be a Christian and get my value from God.

I remember a time when Hannah and I were younger that makes me recall she wasn't always confident. She was about seventeen at the time, so I must have been twelve. Mom and Dad weren't home, and she was in our one and only bathroom. I needed to use it, but she was just shaving her legs, so she let me in. I don't think Mom or Dad knew she was secretly using Dad's razor on herself.

When she told me other kids would point and stare if we had hairy legs, she convinced me shaving was a vital practice every girl needed to follow. After she showed me how to do it, she made me agree to a pact: if either one of us is ever in a car accident and put in a coma, we'll come in and shave the other's legs—or worse, if we ever grow a hair on our chin the way Aunt Winnie grows one, we'll make sure we have tweezers in our purse so we can take care of it before anyone else sees us on our deathbed. We laughed about that for quite some time.

I glance at the clock. I have to go downstairs sooner or later. Mom's probably wondering what's taking me so long. She thinks I actually want to do this thing tonight. She suggested I bring out my guitar to lead the singing around the bonfire. Just what I don't want to do—have everybody staring at me, probably wondering what it was like to be in prison. Remembering what I did that sent me there to begin with.

But I can't put it off. I go downstairs, where it's so quiet in the house I know everybody's already outside. This isn't the normal time of year for this kind of gathering. We don't have the straw bales to sit on like we do in the fall, and we've already moved the clocks forward an hour, so it's not nearly dark enough. But the sun will probably have set by the time we're finished eating, and the fire right now has only one important purpose anyway: cooking hot dogs.

I go outside, but my feet feel heavy.

Aunt Elsie is uncovering a basket of chitlins and holding them over the food-laden picnic table toward Mac, who stands on the opposite side. As I'd expect, Hannah has a horrified look on her face even as Aunt Elsie is practically daring Mac to try one.

"What is it?" he asks.

"Chitlins." Aunt Elsie and Hannah say it at the same time, although with very different tones.

"And that is . . . ?"

"You don't want to know, believe me," says Hannah.

Despite the warning in her tone, he picks one up. "Hey, if we can eat hot dogs without knowing exactly what's in them, I think I can try one of these."

I smile. Mac's a friendly guy; I have to give him that.

"Round here, chitlins are the hide of a pig," my dad says from behind a full plate of food, to which he adds his own helping. "We cut it into the size of the small squares you see here, fry it up and press the fat out to use for oil. What you have left is chitlins."

I'm just glad the food is getting all the attention, until Joanna Zoll comes up behind me and gives me a hug. She's been friends with my mother since before I was born.

"Nice to have you home after your ordeal, honey," she says, too loud. Everybody filling up their plate at the food table looks at me.

I reach for a paper plate. "It's nice to be home." I murmur the words, hoping if she says anything more she'll match my lower volume.

"Well, of course it is, after everything you've been through. I'll just guess you have some stories to tell, don't you, dear? About what it was like, you know, where you've been?"

My hope that she'd speak more quietly was for nothing. I want to run back up to my room, but that would only call more attention to myself. So I stand still and shake my head. I reach for the spoon in my mother's famous potato salad, but the thought of eating anything makes my stomach roil. I'll stuff my mouth anyway, though, because nobody expects you to talk with your mouth full around here. After putting too much potato salad on my plate, I grab a chitlin.

I don't know how I'm going to make it through the rest of the evening.

# 10

THE MORNING after the wienie roast, Mac said good-bye to my parents as they went off to church dressed in traditional Sunday best. Mac, Dilly, and I took two cars and headed to church in Springfield; I, at least, was grateful to follow Dilly's lead and wear blue jeans.

I led the way to the church with Dilly reading directions, Mac following in his rental. While we drove, I couldn't help wondering what he'd thought of last night. It must have appeared easy to present a perfect facade, with plenty of homemade food and lots of close-knit neighbors and relatives. After roasting marshmallows for s'mores and eating Norma's homemade peach pie, Dilly had finally relaxed enough to sing and play her guitar. The patriotic songs we sang in between the hymns everyone knew must have made us all seem like actors out of an old-fashioned movie. Mac sang along to "This Land is Your Land," "America," and a few folk songs my aunt Elsie had taught us when we were kids. By the end of the evening I'd been convinced that Mac thought Midwestern life might be as corny as the folk music we sang, but it *was* full of face-to-face community instead of the virtual kind found in most big cities.

Which made me wonder what he thought of this morning, too. I think he's only gone to church once since I've known him, with that girl he dated for a while. What was her name? I couldn't remember. I wondered if this church would offer some of the same tight-knit community feeling our parents' church offered.

The church turned out not to look like a church at all, at least from the outside, but rather more like a college campus. People dressed in orange-striped vests with matching orange wands waved us into the rapidly filling parking lot, as if directing airplanes into assigned gates instead of cars into efficiently planned spots.

There were so many vehicles filing in I thought they must be giving something away or at least be very good at brainwashing.

"They must be doing something right here," Mac said as he joined Dilly and me to follow a walkway toward the biggest building.

"Just what I was thinking," I said, only I didn't say more because I didn't want to hurt Dilly's feelings. She was clearly excited to be here.

"How are we ever going to find your friend?" I asked Dilly.

"She said to meet her by the bookstore, which is supposed to be easy to find on the main level."

"They have a bookstore?" Mac said. His interest irritated me, if only because it no doubt added to Dilly's enthusiasm. "I've been looking for something to read on planes now that Hannah has deserted me."

I glanced at him, not thrilled with his choice of words because you can't be deserted by someone who's been telling you for over six years that she was leaving. But I knew he only meant it as an indication of his missing me.

Lana was nothing like my image of a drug dealer—or user. She looked like a Sunday school teacher, with neat blonde hair just long enough to be pulled off of her forehead behind a pale blue ribbon. She was dressed in a modest sweater set and jeans that looked like they'd been ironed, with a crease at the bell bottom. Beside her was a man who could only be her father, dark haired but with a gray beard, sturdy rather than slim. Robust, I would say, after he greeted all of us with hearty handshakes.

"And which of you is this Dilly I've heard so much about?"

Dilly raised her hand.

"God blessed my Lana through you, young lady. I'm grateful for that."

"It was the other way around, really. I knew the Bible, but Lana knew God. We stuck together and others left us alone." She smiled. "I'm not sure either one of us could have made it through science class without your letters, though."

"I was just glad the letters made it through the censors!"

They laughed, explaining about some of the scientific terms being called into question until their teacher at the detention center verified that the terms weren't some new code for getting drug information back and forth—merely chemistry calculations.

Looking at Dilly and Lana, and even her father, I had to respect their cheerful attitude about the whole thing. The two had a past in prison—and such a recent one too—but they could already laugh over it?

We filed into what turned out to be a large auditorium with deeply cushioned, theater-style seating. Just avoiding the hard wooden benches at my parents' church was enough to sign me up for this denomination. If I was looking for such a thing. Plus, the lighting was inviting. Dim, with a stage gently illumined, blues and greens reflected off of full band equipment.

The music was as out of sync with my vision of church as Lana was with my image of a drug dealer. The band started playing almost as soon as we sat down. They played tunes I didn't recognize but that were lively and upbeat, like something I'd hear on the radio. When a woman came forward, the music slowed. She started singing about somebody loving her, and I nearly forgot where I was.

"Wow," Mac said right into my ear after that was over.

I might have agreed, except by now I was growing suspicious. This was a performance, all of it, and a darn good one too. But did it really have anything to do with God, or was it just part of a very effective marketing plan? I looked around. There must have been over a thousand people here. Something had to be pulling them back every week. It wasn't the guilt my parents had used on me growing up. What was it?

By the end of the service—which included a sermon filled with as much Scripture as anything I'd heard as a kid, only less fire and brimstone and more everyday life—I had to admit I was glad I'd come. We went back to the bookstore, where Lana's father took Mac under his wing. He ended up leaving with a stack of books that would last him a month's worth of LA-to-NY trips.

I wondered if he'd still want to read them once we left this place. Maybe the brainwashing would end when we were far from the fancy lights, the professional-quality singers, the smiles that lit the faces of every person we saw.

Since we had a couple of hours before Mac had to be at the airport, we accepted Lana's invitation to go out to brunch. Mac insisted on paying for all of us. He'd never been as good at hoarding money as I was, but never once had I seen him struggle with generosity.

Evidently the buoyancy from the service lasted through a tasty meal and good company. Lana's father, Walter, tended to dominate the conversation, but because he was humorous and intelligent even I didn't mind.

Somewhere around the middle of the meal, though, I remembered that all too soon Mac would be getting on a plane again. He'd go back to LA, to the life I'd known and loved for the past fifteen years, where everything was convenient and the variety of entertainment endless, where there was beauty from man-made architecture to natural mountains and a huge ocean that changed from hour to hour, where I could work at a job I loved and was good at. And where, though people might let you put them at arm's length, it was impossible to feel really alone. Most of the time.

I knew I'd miss him, but I envied him too. He got to leave.

We'd left Mac's rental car in the church parking lot, having met Lana and her dad at the restaurant. From there they went home. I drove back to Mac's car, the crunch of gravel of the outer church drive considerably quieter than it had been going in among so many others. There were still a few cars left, placed here and there in the huge parking lot, but for the most part the building looked deserted. The church was on the outskirts of Springfield, with a

housing development going up on one side, crops on the other
for as far as the eye could see. Typical central Illinois topography
outside this small city. Flat.

I pulled my car next to Mac's, turning the engine off despite
knowing we'd be here only long enough to say good-bye. He was
all set to go.

"Good-bye, Mac." Dilly was sitting in the backseat and put her
hand out to shake his. "It was nice meeting you. I'm glad you're my
sister's friend. She's happy when you're around."

Mac looked from Dilly to me. "Isn't she always?"

"You probably think so," Dilly said.

I wondered what she meant but wasn't at all sure I wanted it
explained in front of Mac. He already had a healthy ego; he didn't
need to know he had such a powerful impact on me, one that Dilly
had noticed in so short a time.

Mac climbed out of the car and came around to my side, as
I'd expected. He'd want me to get out of the car with him for a
whole-deal hug, and I was only too willing to comply.

I opened my car door and he reached in to take my hand,
helping me alight as if I were eighty and he eighty-one and he'd
been helping me out of a car for the last sixty-five years. He didn't
let go when we were both standing. Whenever he was between
girlfriends, he often held my hand, hugged me, put his arm around
me when he sat close on a couch. But that had always been
the extent of it—chaste and friendly, his need for human touch
outweighing the fear that others might think such contact should
be reserved for those on an intimate basis. I'd long since accepted it
for what it was: a knee-jerk reaction to having someone he trusted
nearby.

I didn't mind. I enjoyed the touch too. And we both knew it
didn't mean anything.

He broke contact only to reach in and retrieve the book bag
he'd left beside me on the front seat.

"Do you know how much reading I'm getting done now that I
don't have you talking my ear off on those long flights?" Even as he

spoke, he rested the books on the roof of my car, taking me back for another embrace.

I rested my head on his chest, on the soft knit of his pullover shirt. It was a safe, familiar place to be. A couple of days on a hog farm hadn't altered his scent. I recognized the brand of anti-perspirant he used, the hint of his shaving cream, the Downy he'd been using in the rinse cycle ever since I told him why my clothes always smelled so fresh.

"See, I told you this move would be good for both of us."

He squeezed me tight and didn't reply. For a few seconds I thought nothing of it. I didn't want him to leave, but I knew he had to. He didn't belong here; he was LA and New York, Rodeo Drive and Wall Street. Money and yachts belonging to our best investors, and parties and nightlife. The only nightlife here was had by the crickets.

But he was still standing there, wordless, motionless. Holding me. I could have fallen asleep, I was so comfortable. Still, the length of the embrace might have been viewed as odd, and I was vaguely aware of what Dilly could be thinking.

"What are you doing?" I asked after what must have been nearly a full minute.

"What else?" He sighed, looking out at the gravel parking lot and beyond, to the crop nearby that was roughly the same three- or four-inch height as the ones we'd left behind in Sugar Creek. "Watching the crops grow. That's what people do around here, isn't it? Even just outside a big city like Springfield?"

I laughed, pulling away. "Big city? Well. There's not much to see this early in the season."

He pulled away too, his brown eyes boring straight into mine. "You have a good home here, Hannah. I came here half wishing your worst stories were true. That way I'd have a chance of your coming back to LA. But I'm glad I came. Now I know better."

I didn't tell him it wasn't as nice as he thought. That this weekend had, for the most part, been like the breeze that wafted away the stench from the hog sheds. It had been a misrepresentation, a perfect image of something that was anything but. Everyone had been so friendly they'd made it seem like the Midwest was as trouble free as a Norman Rockwell painting. I knew it wasn't, but trying to convince Mac of that right now wouldn't do him any good. "I told you I was here to stay."

His smile was lopsided, more so than ever. "I didn't believe you."

"But now you do?"

He nodded, even as his brows drew closer together. He pulled me close again, and for a moment he held me too tight, but I clung to him, too.

"I'm gonna miss you," he said.

"You'll wake up tomorrow in LA and be as busy as ever. You'll barely know I'm gone."

He grabbed his books and led me to his car, his free arm still around me. "Not a chance."

After pressing a button on his keychain, the trunk popped open. He threw the books in on top of his luggage, then pulled me gently toward him by the lapels of my jacket.

"There's just one thing, Hannah. You said before that our friendship was bound to change, that we both knew it, have known it all along. That was another thing I didn't believe, but after this visit I guess I'll have to. So . . . maybe I shouldn't be calling as much as I have been.

If he thought I might argue—and maybe he did, because I *did* want to—I knew I couldn't. Two thousand miles between even the best of friends was bound to come between us. I'd known that years ago.

"I guess so."

"Okay, then. This is it. Really good-bye this time."

I wanted to shout something. *You mean really, really, I'm never going to see you again?* But I kept silent. It amazed me how much emotion, how many tears and sighs a person can hide, just by standing still and keeping a forward gaze.

"You'll send me a Christmas card anyway, won't you?" he teased.

I was impressed by his light tone. I tried to match it. "And a birthday card." I failed; there was a crack right in the middle of the *birthday*, when the lump in my throat clogged my voice.

He looked like he might hug me again; he leaned closer, his hands reached out, but he held back, straightened. Cleared his throat. "Guess I'll get going."

"You won't have any trouble finding the airport?"

"Not with the GPS." He grinned. "It's not as impressive as the system you'll be working with, but it'll get me there."

I wanted to shout again, tell him I never wanted to work on soil assessments or crop predictions no matter how fancy John Deere equipment became. But I held back; I was stronger than I thought.

He got into his car just as Dilly emerged from mine so she could move from the backseat to the front. From my side view I saw Dilly wave with me as Mac drove off, but I couldn't look at her. I was afraid I'd see sympathy, and I knew that it would crumble whatever strength I had.

# Dilly

I've never had what I consider a real job. All the years I lived at home, I worked with my dad on the farm. When he wasn't keeping me busy, Uncle Steve sometimes hired me to help him out with his hogs.

During high school I took a job at the grocery store and worked there while I dated, then married Nick. I worked until the day Sierra was born. After that I stayed home. I'd planned to go back to work part-time, leaving Sierra with my mom on the days I was gone, but we figured out pretty quick that Sierra was going to need more attention than other babies. So I stayed home to take care of her, which was the best job I've ever had. She needed me.

In prison it was either work or go to school, and I never minded school, so I decided to get a degree if I could. I knew Hannah always wanted me to go to college. The truth is I chose to go to school because the jobs they offered, like working in the laundry or in the kitchen, didn't appeal to me. I don't mind hard work, but if I'm going to work, I'd prefer to be outside or with kids.

I was one of the few who went to the prison school because I wanted to be there. I wasn't eligible to have my time cut for taking classes. For some people, every day they went to school cut their time by a day. All they had to do was show up; they didn't have to learn anything.

But I wanted to learn. I couldn't take books back to my cell, so I had to do all my work during the school day in the room they assigned as a classroom. And they didn't make allowances for the times I had to see the psychologist, had visitors from home, or went to my Bible study.

I found out I can work and learn, even under pressure.

Right now I'm standing in front of an office building in Springfield. I drove here in Hannah's car, the longest trip I've made on my own so far. I'm dressed in a skirt, the first time I've had one on in years. It feels good, but I miss my tennis shoes. Instead I'm wearing flat beige shoes that I bought ten years ago. I never wore them much, so they look almost new, and nowadays you can wear just about anything and call it style if it looks good. At least that's what Hannah says. But I'm not so sure. Ten-year-old shoes aren't old enough to be vintage or new enough to be fashionable. They're just old.

I'm not going to worry about how I look. I told myself this already on the drive here, but I tell it to myself again.

I go inside and ride the elevator to the third floor, the way the lady who called me said to do. I sent them my résumé from prison on my last day there. This is the first place I chose because they work with kids who have one or both parents incarcerated. I thought it would be a good fit for me. At least they won't think my past is so odd if they work with other people who've been in prison.

I find the right suite number and open the door. The office is beige, like my shoes. The walls, the carpeting, the furniture. There is a metal desk to the left, but no one is there, so I take a seat on one of the plastic-covered metal chairs and wait. I realize the office is anything but plush. The desk must be as old as I am, and the plastic covering on the chair next to me is torn. Behind the desk is a row of beige file cabinets and a copy machine, and sitting on the desk is a computer style I recognize from the prison system. I didn't know how old it looked until I saw the one Hannah brought with her from California.

There is an open door behind the desk, and I can hear women's voices. I look around for some kind of bell—you know, like they have at a dry cleaner or in the butcher department at the grocery store, so people who come by can get the attention of whoever's working in back. But there's no bell. So I wait.

There is a clock on the wall above the copy machine, and I try not to watch as five minutes pass by. I'd been exactly on time for my appointment, but now, since no one knows I'm here, I'm technically late.

I decide I should try to get the attention of the voices in the office.

"Excuse me? Hello?"

No response. I try again.

The voices stop, then resume again in lower tones. I couldn't hear what they were saying before, only a loud word now and then mixed with intermittent laughs, but now I can hear hushed tones.

Finally someone comes out. It's a woman probably five or six years younger than me, dressed in cotton pants and a short-sleeved casual blouse. She sends me a smile but it's not a welcoming one. She looks away, as if nervous or shy. I understand what that feels like, so I don't hold it against her.

But she doesn't say anything. She goes to the seat behind the desk, and before I can introduce myself or ask about the Mrs. Marshall I'm supposed to see, another woman emerges from the office. She's wearing a suit; it's brown and probably cheap because it doesn't fit her all that well and it's made from the same material as the skirt I'm wearing.

She holds out her hand to shake mine and smiles warmly. I try to relax, but so far I'm still nervous. I've never been on a job interview in my whole life. I only got the job at the grocer because Sandee told the manager about me; I never even filled out an application.

"Are you Catherine Carlson?"

I nod. I need to take a deep breath so I can talk, but I don't get a chance because as quickly as the smile on her face appeared, it disappears.

"I'm afraid there's been a mistake and we've wasted your time. I'm so sorry."

"Excuse me?" I don't know what else to say.

"We reviewed your application and, based on the grades you earned at Midvale, we were so eager to hire you we failed to scrutinize a few important facts." She glances at the girl behind the desk, and I wonder if the woman in the suit is trying to lay the blame on the girl.

But knowing I went to school in the women's detention center means they hadn't missed the important part about my past. What *had* they missed? I'd told them everything on the application.

I don't move; I need more of an explanation than this.

"Yes," she continues, answering my unvoiced question about details. She reaches over to accept what I instantly recognize as my application from the girl behind the desk. "Your grades and behavior reports are wonderful, and the classes you took are just right for the jobs we have here. The problem is your original conviction: child endangerment. We can't have someone with such a conviction working with children, even if we are more flexible about hiring from Midvale. I'm sure you understand."

I don't, but I nod because that's what she expects me to do.

"I'm very sorry. I wish there was something we could do. You really ought to apply for office jobs or working with adults, you know. This just isn't the right place for you."

I nod again, murmur the only thing that comes to mind, which is, "Thank you for your time," and walk out the door.

I'm shaking by the time I reach the elevator, and all I want to do is sit down and cry. I can't even see my own daughter; what made me think anybody would want me around somebody else's kids? But it's what I want to do, and God knows I'm not going to hurt anybody.

*God knows. . . .*

I punch the button for the elevator to stop at this floor. I never thought getting closer to God would solve all my problems, but I did think life would start to make sense. Will I ever be able to get past my mistakes and use the passion for kids that God Himself must have put in me?

I suck back my anger and tears as the elevator door opens. Another woman is standing in there, so I clutch the strap of my purse to hide my trembling hands. Thankfully she has already pushed the lobby button.

I barely make it to my car before the tears gush out.

# 11

BY THE Thursday following Mac's visit, Dilly and I were ready to move into the house in town. Despite being more than sixty years old, the place smelled brand-new, between the paint on the walls, the carpet on the floors, and the fresh varnish on the new furniture. I finally spent the money I'd saved all those years, and it smelled good.

The only old item in the house was the piano, which we'd hired Dad's occasional workhand, Beacon, and another friend of his to move. Cyd came to tune it after that, in exchange for Dilly playing a dozen hymns that even I enjoyed. There was something about live music that brought beauty to a moment, however otherwise mundane.

Although Dilly had been given permission by her parole officer to move in with me, she had no luck in getting a job despite filling out more than a dozen applications. She never did tell me what happened with her interview on Tuesday; she wouldn't say a word when I asked. I wondered if transportation would have been a problem, even though I assured her we could share my car until she could afford one of her own.

In the meantime our parents were doing their best to keep us busy (idle hands being the devil's tools, or so we'd been told from toddlerhood). Although she hadn't shown much interest in driving my car, Dilly was soon driving a John Deere tractor almost every day, mowing ditches and waterways. I wouldn't have dared do the same. I could just imagine what my father would say if I'd gotten too close to the field and crushed a few rows of corn. He'd have crop prices already calculated and be able to tell me just how much my inability to gauge a mow line had cost him.

He'd also tried to get me to join him in daily chores, grinding grain, keeping it cooled and stirred to prevent rotting, making sure the water and feed lines to the hogs were clear and clean. I remembered how much time walking the pens could take. The same hogs stayed together from the first time they were sorted to the day they left, the bosses having established themselves in each pen. Sick ones were transferred to an intensive care pen before any of the stronger hogs had a chance to pick on the weaker ones. But when I continued to be absent for morning chore time, I assumed he knew his open invitation had been declined.

I could not, however, escape the guilt that came with not working a consistent job. My online consulting took up less time than I'd hoped, mainly because people wanted to meet with me face-to-face instead of through a computer screen. At Dilly's suggestion I called her newly adopted church and asked about volunteer work. I was connected to a food ministry drive that helped coordinate donations of everything from homemade jams and jellies to corporate donations of nonperishables. Not a member, not even a believer as they would define it, and I was working for the poor of Springfield through Central Community Church.

But nothing I did helped me stop missing Mac.

He was as good as his word. He didn't call or e-mail as often as we'd been used to. And when we did talk, he seemed distracted, his mind elsewhere. Was he already pulling away, not missing me? If so, it would explain the growing distance between us in these last few weeks, a distance that had nothing to do with miles. He'd mentioned reading the books he'd bought at church and that he'd been in contact with Walter, Lana's father, via e-mail. That surprised me. He was striking up a friendship with someone in the Midwest while allowing that same distance to come between us?

Each time a call ended, I was left so lonesome for the old Mac I wondered if we should have contact at all. Maybe no contact would be less traumatic.

Since I wouldn't talk about Mac and rarely talked to him, it should have been easy to stop thinking of him too. If only that were true. Time let me down. It hadn't faded my feelings for him at all. What those feelings were, exactly, I refused to dwell on. All these years I'd resisted defining them, and now, missing him as much as I was, they seemed all too clear. Mac was far more than a friend to me. He'd always been more than that, but that was the only relationship that could work for us. It was the only kind of relationship I thought I could trust with him.

It didn't help when Dilly sang her favorite Carole King tunes. On occasion she'd sing "So Far Away" and I had to leave the room if I didn't want her to see my tears gather.

I had tried getting Dilly to go to church alone on Sundays, but my work with the food ministry convinced me to accompany her. The woman on staff to whom I was accountable had a way of expecting me there on Sunday morning. And so I went.

It made Dilly so happy that I couldn't complain. For six years I'd considered how to make up for letting her down so long ago, and I was good at following my plan. Going to church to please her was just part of what I'd been doing. So far I'd shielded her from seeing her name ravaged on several online blogs run by advocates for persons with disabilities. I'd protected her from one overeager newspaper reporter's phone call (and once I'd investigated her previous bylines, I knew she would have no sympathy for Dilly) and another call from an irate man who'd received her application and wondered how someone with her record had the audacity to apply for a job with proximity to kids.

Despite my efforts, Dilly's day for almost a month finished the same way, an ending I couldn't prevent or change. It started with a phone call to Nick and ended with his refusal. He couldn't do a thing to change Sharon's mind about Dilly seeing Sierra. Couldn't or wouldn't.

But one evening around the time Dilly would have picked up the phone, someone knocked at our door. I saw through the kitchen window that it was Tom Boyle.

I showed him inside, and he took off his sheriff's hat, looking around at my redecorating efforts. The house was typical of the postwar boom. The kitchen was next to the living room, where the front door was located. No family room or great room, no study, no master bath. None of the luxuries most homes in California offered.

"The place looks nice, Hannah. You've given this old house a real face-lift and then some."

"Thanks, Tom." But I was curious as to why he'd come, decked out in his uniform and in the squad car no less. "Did you stop by looking for decorating tips?"

He smiled, shifting the brim of his hat in his hands. I could tell he was uncomfortable. Dilly had followed me to the door, and for some reason I had an image of another time Dilly had seen Tom outside the Coffee Spot. Hadn't he been the one who arrested her?

"I was looking for Dilly," he admitted, nodding his head her way.

# Dilly

I hear what Tom says about looking for me, and I'm curious.

"Couldn't it wait until morning, Tom?" Hannah asks. "Won't you see each other at the Coffee Spot?"

I glance at her; she sounds nervous.

"No, I'm afraid I had to come by tonight. Right about this time, to be exact."

"Why, Tom?" I ask. I'm actually glad to see him. Whenever I see him, which is almost every morning at the café, he always asks how I'm doing, what my dad has me working on, if I've seen Sierra yet. He's one of the few people in town who treats me just like everybody else.

"It's Nick, Dilly. Or I should say his mom. She's tried calling him a few times round about this hour of the evening and can't get through. She says you call every night to see about Sierra."

"That's right." I say it like it's the most natural thing in the world, and it is, because I'm a mom calling about my own daughter. I'll do it every day for as long as it takes until I can see her and check on her in person.

"You've got to stop doing that. Sharon's going around town telling everybody you're harassing her son, trying to convince him to let you see Sierra."

"That's the truth." I sink into one of Hannah's chairs. They're ridiculous chairs, with huge armrests that make me feel like I'm a kid again, I feel so small in them. But I have to sit because of those first few words Tom had used. So I clarify. "The part about me trying to convince him to let me see Sierra is true, but not the part about harassing him."

Tom looks between the two of us, first at me, then at Hannah, as if words are beyond him and any help from her would be welcome.

Hannah comes to my side, sitting on one of the cushioned armrests. But she doesn't even look at me; she's looking at Tom.

"What else is she supposed to do? All Nick has to do is say yes, and she can see Sierra. It's his decision, not Sharon's."

Tom twirls his hat one more round, then comes to sit on the matching chair just opposite. The chair doesn't look so silly beneath him. I realize I don't want to hear what he has to say; I don't want to be talking about this at all. I want to go back into the kitchen and use the phone to call Nick again.

But Tom is talking and my ears register his words anyway. "Do you think he's going to go against Sharon in this? If he did, you know what would happen, don't you? *He'd* have to take care of Sierra, and everybody in town knows he can't do that. He just can't, Dilly. He's got to do as his mother wants this time."

"If he took on her care, I'd help; he knows that."

Tom clamps his lips shut, and in that moment I figure out that even if I've convinced more than half the town I'm fit enough to visit Sierra, allowing me to have full care of her is another thing altogether.

"So you're here because of a complaint against Dilly," Hannah says. She sounds calm again, competent as usual. I don't think I can speak. "Whose? Sharon's or Nick's?"

I stare hard at Tom, wanting to hear his answer. For some reason it matters to me. If it had been Sharon, well, who wouldn't expect she'd try something like this? But if she's convinced Nick to formally complain against me . . .

"Nick called me this afternoon, asked me to come by tonight around now. To get you to stop calling. It's not helping your fight, Dilly. You've got to find another way."

I lean forward, elbows on my knees, head in my hands, face down. I shake my head. "I don't know any other way, Tom. Nick is the only legal way to Sierra."

And that's the truth. We even tried something legal but not quite ethical—calling Esther, the babysitter-spy who reported to Mom whatever went on in Nick's or Sharon's house. We wanted to see if she might take Sierra to the grade school playground when Sharon was out. But evidently that jig is up. Esther hasn't been asked to babysit since I returned to town.

"What if we sued for visitation rights?" Hannah asks.

She's mentioned this to me before, but we haven't really discussed it because I think she's every bit as sure as I've been that eventually Nick will give in and somehow convince his mother. But the longer time goes on, the less likely that seems.

"You'd have a jury with an opinion just like this town," Tom says. "They'd see Sharon taking good care of her for more years than Dilly did. They'd see her record. It'd be a waste of money if you ask me."

I look at Tom. "What do *you* think? That I'm unfit to ever care for her again?"

"What I think doesn't matter."

But it does, probably more than Tom suspects. Tom not only represents a healthy percentage of the town's opinion, but he's been the one person who makes people comfortable around me. If *he* doesn't think I should have custody . . .

"It does matter, Tom," I say.

"I don't know," he says slowly. "You come from a good family, Dilly, and everybody's getting to know you again. But people might have forgotten how things used to be when you took care of Sierra all by yourself. Nobody ever saw you in town back then, the way you stayed home with her all the time. They never saw it was hard on you or that your marriage wasn't working, that Nick used to cheat on you, because he's settled down these past few years. He's held his job, paid his bills. He's not what I'd call a good dad to Sierra, since I don't think he visits her, but he's been a good dad to Adrienne's little girl. That's all anybody sees these days. Or remembers."

"But they'll never forget what I did? Is that what you mean?"

Silence says everything.

As usual, Hannah can't let it go on for long. "They've forgotten that she had total, complete care of Sierra? Maybe it was her choice to stay home all those years because that was the only choice she had." I hear her take a deep breath, as if she's afraid to lose control. "Nick wasn't the only one not helping. Where was Sharon when

Dilly and Sierra needed her? Do you know Dilly didn't sleep through the night *once* from the time Sierra was born to the night she was taken to the hospital? That's four and a half years of sleep deprivation, mixed with worry and hard, unending work. Have they forgotten that Nick, the husband she still loved back then, flaunted his girlfriends and never lifted a finger to feed Sierra, change her clothes, bathe her, monitor her medication, take her to the doctor, comb her hair, talk to her . . . ?"

I hear my sister's breath coming faster again, and her tone has grown harsh in spite of that first deep breath. Her eyebrows are drawn, her mouth tight with anger. "I was in the courtroom when all those facts came out, Tom, and I'm not going to forget them the way everybody else in this town has. No one was there for her. Not me, our parents—nobody. Day after day of isolation. All any one of us had to do was . . . show up."

I stand now because the anger she has is aimed just as much at herself as at anyone else—I can see it on her face. Reminding herself of whatever failures she thinks she has on my behalf isn't going to do either one of us any good.

"That's enough, Hannah. He knows about the trial. He was there too."

Tom rubs a hand on the back of his neck, and I bet he wishes he were anywhere else than sitting in Hannah's living room. "People have a way of forgetting circumstances behind crimes. I'm sorry, but that's the way it is."

Hannah puts a hand on my shoulder, but I shrug it away. "I just want to *see* her, Tom. I don't care if Sharon stays in the same room the whole time. Sierra was my whole life—"

I stop myself. I'm not sure why, except that I don't know what Tom believes. If Sierra was my whole life, why did I do what I did? Wasn't what I did selfish, because I couldn't handle my life back then?

I go to the windows, three cottage-style openings that were the only thing I liked about this house when I moved in with Hannah. Like something out of a magazine. They offer a view of the matching maples that bend over the street in the front yard. At this moment I want to be like my mother and let wishful thinking take over. *Everything's going to be all right,* I want to say to myself. But I can't make myself believe it.

"I never meant to hurt her, you know." I say the words over my shoulder, still looking out the windows, my arms hugged close in front. "I just . . . didn't want to *be* anymore. And I couldn't leave her behind." I pat my palms on my upper arms. "Guess I didn't know Sharon would've stepped up like this. To be honest, I didn't know she had it in her. I didn't think she liked anybody, her son or me or Sierra either."

"Yeah," Tom says gently, "Sharon's a funny one. She likes those dogs she keeps out on her place better than she likes most people. Ever notice that? How some can like animals but not people?"

I hear his voice, that same one he uses at the Coffee Spot when he talks to me. Warm and friendly, which makes everybody around me comfortable too. I guess he never gets to use such a tone when he pulls someone over for a speeding ticket or takes in somebody who's drunk and disorderly.

Now he steps closer and puts a hand on my shoulder. For one wild moment I want to bend my head so my cheek touches him, but thankfully I catch myself. Tom's just one of those nice guys. . . . He's nice to everybody.

"I don't know if it'll help any," he tells me, "but I'll stop by Sharon's on my way home tonight. I'll tell her you'll stop calling Nick, and I'll see if she'd be open to giving you some supervised visits. I'd be willing to be there too."

I face him fully, my heart filling with hope and gratitude, so much that I grab the hand that fell away from me when I turned around. "You'd do that for me, Tom? Really?"

"Sure, why not? Like I said, it might not do any good, but it's worth a try."

"Will you call me? Tonight, I mean, after you leave? To tell me what she says?"

As I'm speaking, I'm leading him to the door to send him on his mission all the quicker. He nods, then opens the screen door and lets himself out. From the door I watch him get in his squad car with the first bit of hope I've felt in a long time.

That hope lasts exactly one hour, until Tom calls to let me know Sharon refused. He assures me he'll try talking to her again, but right now it's hard to believe it'll do any good.

# 12

THE FOLLOWING afternoon while I was working online, Dilly came in earlier than I expected. She'd been up and out just after dawn, probably doing hog chores with our father. She usually stayed on the farm until after lunch, which bothered me because it meant I had to eat alone, but I didn't complain. Aloud. Then she ran errands or stayed with our parents until midafternoon or dinnertime at the latest.

Today, though, it was just past one and the front door was already banging shut.

"Mail call!" Her voice was more cheerful than I expected given last night's disappointment. Maybe Tom's offer to keep at the effort was helping.

I left the little room at the back of the house that used to be called a sunroom but was now my office. Although it was squared with windows overlooking the yard, it was shaded by trees and heated and cooled just like the rest of the house. It was a perfect spot to work. I met Dilly at the archway to the kitchen, seeing immediately that she was laden not just with the normal advertisements and bills but with a bulky padded envelope.

"Expecting a delivery?" I asked her. I knew I wasn't.

"Nope. It's for you." She thrust it my way. "From California."

I glanced at the return address curiously. My old boss had sent me some paperwork not long ago, a personal file of investment research material I'd inadvertently left behind. But this was marked with Mac's address.

Considering I hadn't talked to him in several days and he hadn't mentioned sending something, I was as confused as I was excited. In fact, our whole conversation had lasted less than ten minutes—record short in our history.

It was a book, and I could tell immediately that it wasn't even a new one. From the title I saw it was an argument for Christianity, against atheism. I flipped through the pages and they were rife with highlights, underscores, pencil marks, and notes in the margin.

"Hey! That's one of the books he bought at church," Dilly said.

"Looks like he read it," I replied.

"Read it! From those pages all bent and marked up I'd say he could write a thesis on it."

"There's a note." I unfolded it. "He says he would have sprung for a new copy for me but wanted me to see all the places he liked in particular."

That was like him; he was always telling me when a good part of a movie he'd seen was coming up. But the note was unsatisfying. Friendly but impersonal.

"Wow!" Dilly's eyes were fairly starlit. "Maybe he's found faith. A new creation, just like the Bible says."

I wanted to smile, simply because it was impossible not to feel some of the joy oozing out of Dilly. But I just looked at the book. Mac . . . a new creation?

I'd liked the old one. The original.

"I hope you read it, Hannah. You should call him and thank him for it. But can I borrow you for something else first?"

Anything to put off talking to Mac about this book. "What is it?"

"Better sit down." She pulled me with her free hand to the kitchen table, where she tossed the rest of the mail. "Adrienne Robinson is working at Farm and Fleet. You know, Nick's girl-friend? I want to go there and ask her about talking to Nick. Will you come with me? drive me up to the store?"

I was no longer sure this was a worthy postponement to doing something else I didn't want to do. "Farm and Fleet's only ten miles up the road, Dil. You don't need me to drive you that far."

"But I do need you for moral support. Actually, I was thinking you'd be the best one to approach Adrienne first. I don't know how she'd feel about me, as I'm Nick's first wife and all. Will you do it? If she can get Nick to think about bringing Sierra to his house once in a while, I might get to see Sierra there."

"I don't know Adrienne Robinson at all. She didn't grow up around here, did she?"

"No, her family's from Springfield, I think. Mom told me Nick met her through some cousin or something. But I talked to my friend Sandee, and she said she's met Adrienne and she's not half bad. I don't know what she's doing with Nick if she's got anything going for her—Oops. Forgive me, Lord; I shouldn't have said that. But anyway, if she's got an ounce of compassion, maybe she'll help. What do you think?"

I took a deep breath, setting Mac's book on the table with the rest of the mail. "I'm not very diplomatic, you know."

"Yes, you are," Dilly insisted. "You get people to trust you with their money. How much more appealing can you get?"

"I'll try," I said. But even as I agreed, I wasn't at all sure she had the right person for the job.

The Farm and Fleet parking lot was never empty, and today was no exception. But the paint department, where I was told we could find Adrienne, was deserted. We roamed the aisles, and I wondered if I'd ever been served by Adrienne without knowing it while I was choosing colors for my walls.

"Can I help you?"

There stood a young woman wearing a red T-shirt over pale blue jeans. Above the pocket was a tag identifying her as Adrienne. She was certainly pretty, and in some ways similar to Dilly in the shape of her face and her light brown hair. But her wide eyes were greenish gray instead of brown, and she didn't have the same striking brows. She might have passed for Dilly's sister sooner than I would have, though. If Nick had been trying to forget Dilly, he'd chosen the wrong woman.

She stopped approaching us halfway down the aisle, so far away I could see that she'd abandoned her idea to be of service. "Oh . . . you're . . ." She didn't finish, but I could see as easily as Dilly that she'd recognized one or the other of us. She turned away. "I'll see if I can find someone else to help you."

"No! I mean . . ." Dilly quickly quieted her tone. "It's actually you we came to see, Adrienne. Not to buy anything. I'm sorry. I hope you don't mind."

She turned back to us, crossed her arms, and stayed still while Dilly and I moved closer. "Why would you want to see me?"

"Just to talk to you," Dilly said. She looked at me, and I knew I was supposed to take up the next line, but I still hadn't figured out the details of my part. All I could do was present the facts in a less emotional way than Dilly.

"Dilly's between brick walls," I said, keeping my voice low, adding a smile. "In the form of Sharon and Nick."

"What does that have to do with me?"

"Well, for one thing we wondered if you've ever been in such a spot with them—between the two of them, that is—and maybe figured out how to change either one's mind on a matter. Any advice?"

She shook her head. "I can tell you right now Sharon is not going to be the one to change. I know you want to be with your kid again. Everybody in town knows it. But I think Sharon has a point. If Sierra's forgotten you, isn't that best? I mean, for her? Since you can't turn back time and make things the way they were when you took care of her all the time anyway?"

"Nobody wants to go back to the way things were," I said. "The past is past. But if Sierra can have Dilly in her life, even for a little bit of time every day, wouldn't *that* be best for Sierra?"

Adrienne turned her gaze back to Dilly. "Sharon says Sierra must think you're dead. Why don't you just let her keep thinking that? It's kinder than having her wonder where you've been all these years, maybe remember that you tried to . . ."

Adrienne was considerate enough not to finish her statement. Dilly nodded and lowered her eyes toward the floor. Adrienne started to turn away.

"You have a daughter of your own, Adrienne." My voice was still low, but I was getting desperate for her to understand, and a touch of that came out in my tone. So much for me presenting the facts with less emotion. "You know how you'd feel if somebody wouldn't let you see her."

Her arms unfolded, hands falling to her sides. "Okay, so I feel sorry for your sister here. But what do either one of you think I can do? Convince Nick to take care of Sierra so he can decide who gets to see her and who doesn't? How would that be possible? We both have full-time jobs; my own daughter is at day care. Sierra's school day is only six hours long, and me and Nick work eight- and ten-hour days. Sharon's retired. She's got nothing else to fill her time except those dogs, and they don't need much from her anymore. She's the only one who *can* take care of Sierra."

"We don't expect Nick to take on Sierra full-time. Just take her home with him for a few hours, maybe on a Sunday afternoon or sometime when he's not working, and let Dilly see her?"

Adrienne was already shaking her head. "And you think Sharon won't see through that? All these years, he's never once taken Sierra home for a visit. Now you come back and he suddenly shows an interest in being a father to her?" She turned away. "I can't help you."

Dilly followed Adrienne's retreat, grabbing one of her arms but quickly letting go. "I don't want him to do anything without Sharon's knowledge. I just want him to take a stand. I don't have any other options. Please, please help me? If you can think of any way, any way at all, to get Sharon to change her mind, or to get Nick to help me somehow . . . I just don't know what else to do."

"Sharon's taking good care of Sierra. The school is taking good care of her too. She's as healthy as can be, considering her condition. You don't need to worry about her."

"It's not worry," Dilly said. Her brows lifted, imploring the other woman to listen and believe. "I just want to . . . to love her. She used to smile when I talked to her or sang to her or massaged her arms and legs or washed her hair. She couldn't tell me she loved me, but she did, just like I loved her. I want her to know that love is still there."

Adrienne tilted her head to one side, as if considering the weight of Dilly's words. If there was a disconnect between the love Dilly showed and the history of what she'd done, it was all muddled now. No one could doubt Dilly's love for Sierra.

"Is Sharon doing that for her?" Dilly whispered. "Making sure there's love in Sierra's life, not just . . . good, clean care?"

I looked at Adrienne's face. Dilly's words had clinched it.

But Adrienne turned away again, and for the barest moment I thought I'd misread her. Maybe she wasn't sympathetic after all.

Two steps off, she paused and gave Dilly her profile. "I'll talk to him. But I don't think it'll do any good."

Then she walked away.

# 13

IT WAS only nine o'clock, but Dilly was already in bed. She liked to get up before the sun did and went to bed early because of that.

I'd seen her reading before turning her lights out, something I used to do more of when I lived in LA. Since coming back to the Midwest I didn't do a lot of the things I'd enjoyed there. Contacts through my job had supplied a good portion of entertainment in the form of dinner parties and social events (no big business here, apart from farming), Mac used to supply me with Starbucks every morning (no Starbucks to be found in Sugar Creek), even in my most frugal times I'd go to movies (no movie theater here, either), and I'd loved to go bicycling on endless paths through high country and low (risk biking along the narrow, high-speed roads around here?). I also used to try new recipes with strange ingredients I could only find at specialty stores (no such store in sight). I knew I could still read a book—I could order any volume I wanted online—but somehow I'd lost the desire.

These days, when I didn't go to bed early like Dilly, I filled my head with satellite television. News shows abounded. True, it was mainly *bad* news, but I liked to tell myself I was at least keeping up on current events.

My phone jingled the familiar friend tune, and I eagerly opened it.

"So . . . did you get my book in the mail?"

Despite the question, Mac's voice buoyed my spirit. He'd not only saved me from watching a news story worthy of yet another

nightmare, his call assured me that even if we were drifting apart—
which often felt more like Mac rowing away—he wasn't out of my
life altogether.

His book was on the kitchen table, where it had stayed since I
received it the day before. "Yes. Thank you."

"Aren't you going to call me a cheapskate for sending you a
used book?"

"Nope. Of the two of us, we both know I'm the miser."

"Have you looked at it? read any of it?"

"I saw all your notes and highlights."

"But you haven't read any of it."

I didn't answer. I was still glad he'd called, but my insides were
sinking fast.

"I wish you would."

I yawned. "I suppose I could look at it a little now. Maybe it'll
put me to sleep."

"Go ahead, make fun of something that really matters."

His hurt tone was obvious. In all our years of friendship, good-
humored sarcasm had always been a part of it. Was that what
Christianity did—killed a person's sense of humor? Maybe that was
why my dad didn't have one.

"I've never been interested in reading books that tell me how I
have to live my life. You know that, Mac. You didn't used to like
that sort of thing either."

"It didn't tell me how to live, Hannah. It made me think about
things I never really thought about before, about how incredible it
is that any of us are here to begin with. How incredible this planet
is. The moon is a miracle; do you know that? Can you see it yet
tonight? It's not dark enough here, but I can't look at it anymore
and not think everything around us has to be more than just
chance. And if it isn't by chance, which revelation about how we
got here—and why—makes the most sense?"

I bristled. "Look, if you want me to get Dilly, I'm sure the two
of you can have a nice little worship service together."

"Whoa!" He laughed. "You sound peeved."

I was, irrationally so. He was only trying to share something with me. But I knew this message already. Everything else in the world had been bulldozed out of my childhood to make room for what he was trying to tell me now. Maybe he thought it was a different message, a new one because to him it was good, but I knew underneath it all, it was the same. Rules. A God who judged. A vengeful one.

"I'm just not particularly interested in things like this. It boils down to the same thing my parents have told me all these years: don't do this; don't do that. Watch what you say; somebody's always around to point out your sins. And now you . . ." I let my words drift off, not wanting to accuse him of something he wasn't yet guilty of.

"You think I'm going to be one more person telling you what not to do?"

"No, not really." My thoughts went from bad to worse, and I couldn't seem to control my mouth. I lunged ahead. "For as often and as long as we've talked lately, I don't think you'll be telling me much about anything anymore."

"I thought that's what you wanted. For us to adjust. You there. Me here."

I nodded even though I knew he couldn't see such an action. I didn't trust my voice.

"And you go to sleep earlier than you used to. The time difference doesn't give me much time to call. But you know," he added, more gently, "the phone rings at both ends."

"I just thought you might be busy these days. Are you dating again?" I was proud of my light tone. "Without me there for convenience, you're bound to want to find somebody to pass the time with."

"I've been busy reading. I know that sounds weird, but it's true. I'm learning for the first time in a long time, Hannah. And I wanted to talk to you about all of it, especially that book, but I guessed you might react this way so I just sent it."

I noticed he skirted my question. Was he dating or wasn't he?

I hid my desperation to know; pride was a wonderfully protective agent. "My reactions have never stopped you before. Remember when you went skydiving? I didn't want to go, I didn't want *you* to go, but that didn't stop you."

"This is different. This is . . . life changing."

"So's skydiving if your chute doesn't open."

"I really called to tell you I'm coming to see you this weekend."

My heart did a flip with the surprising announcement. I didn't think he'd ever come back to Sugar Creek; at least that was what I'd tried to prepare myself for.

"Any particular reason?"

"Actually there is a reason, but I wanted to talk to you about it in person."

"Sounds serious."

"It is."

"What's it about?"

"I'd rather talk to you face-to-face."

"Come on, Mac, you know I'm just going to pester you to give me a hint." My mind raced, combining past experiences with present fears. He *must* be dating. "I thought you'd only use the word *serious* if you were getting married or something."

"I'd like to get married," he said.

My heart seemed to stop altogether. Never, in the seven years I'd known him, had I heard Mac admit such a thing. This really was serious.

"I've been thinking about a bunch of different things lately. Marriage is one of them. So are honesty and truth."

"Bad things to wish for in an election year," I quipped. "No truth to be found then." I had to make a joke of things, otherwise I'd cave in to the panic that could be held only so far away and only for so long.

"You can push me away all you want with your humor or your bitterness about God, but I'm still coming. Friday. Tell Cyd to be on the lookout for me around six or so. I'll see you then, but I probably won't call."

He hung up, and I had no choice except to fold my phone away. My pulse was erratic; blood jumped through my veins, tapped at my temples. He was coming all the way to central Illinois, to talk to me in person. About truth . . . and no doubt about this newfound faith of his.

# Dilly

I'm sitting at the table in my parents' kitchen, my mom filling out all the paperwork for me to be added to their health insurance as an employee. Growing up I guessed I'd spend at least some of my life doing farmwork of one kind or another, but I didn't think it would be for my dad.

My mom's asking me about certain things she doesn't know automatically, like my social security number. She's already filled in my full name (Catherine, not Dilly), address, and birth date. Then she asks my dad about job title and number of hours I'll be working.

I don't know why it's my mother who does all the paperwork in the house, but she does. She opens every piece of mail, pays every bill, and fills out everything from tax forms to rebate requests. My dad's the one who likes to tell everybody what to do, but in this area it seems to be my mother who has the real control.

The windows of the house are closed, but even so I hear a car on the graveled lane just outside the door. Dad is closest to the window and he pulls back the rooster-flecked curtains my mother hung years ago.

"Too early for the mail," Mom says. Her gaze goes to the coffeepot on the counter. "I'll have to make more coffee if we have a visitor."

"Nope, not yet," my dad says as he stands. "Don't know who it is. Might not be staying."

This interests me as well as Mom, I can tell when we exchange glances. My dad knows every single car and its owner in town, and then some.

Dad opens the door before anyone has a chance to knock.

"Hello." It's a woman's voice, friendly and just a little breathless. I stand and so does my mother. Visitors are common but not strangers.

"I'm looking for—oh, there you are. Catherine Carlson?"

I nod, but I remain behind my dad. He isn't much bigger than me but I realize all of a sudden that I don't like strangers anymore. When I was a kid, I wasn't afraid of them, and when I was married to Nick but home all of the time taking care of Sierra, I never came across any. The ones I encountered during my trial and while I was in prison must have changed me without me knowing it, because here I am, not wanting to step out from behind my father.

"I'm Alice Matthews from the *Sentinel*, and I was wondering if I could talk to you? I'm interested in doing a closure piece on your story."

"There's no story here," my father says gruffly. He's like a Chihuahua with the bark of a German shepherd. "You're wasting your time."

The woman's smile fades and she looks from my dad to me. "Oh, really? Perhaps you should decide that for yourself, Ms. Carlson."

"No story." I choke out the words because my throat is dry and I can feel my hands shaking. This total stranger is trying to take something from me, right in front of my parents. She wants *me* in that story of hers, so everybody can read about my mistakes all over again.

"I really don't know why either of you would be hesitant to speak to me. I think the public has an interest in cases like this, and—"

"We're putting all that behind us," my mother tells her over my head. They're like buttresses, one in front of me, one behind me. I'm glad they're here, both of them.

"Maybe I can help do just that by putting closure on this case. Don't you think Catherine would like to tell her side of the story? tell how she's dealing with the memories of what she did? According to the law, she's paid her debt. People might be interested in knowing how that plays out in real life, the debt paid, life after prison."

"Nobody wants all that to be out in public again," Dad says, and I don't even mind that I feel like a kid again, with my parents chasing away the bogeyman.

"It's a memory that shouldn't be forgotten. Not by anyone, so we can learn how to avoid something like this in the future. Or . . ." She pauses and is just outside the screen door, so I can see her face clearly. One brow lifts, and she looks straight at me. "If you think you were justified in what you did, you can say so in my article."

Adrenaline fires through my limbs, stopping hot at my fingertips. I saw plenty of confrontations in prison, but I always avoided them by keeping to myself. That's all I want to do now. "Please leave, and don't come back."

Then my dad shuts the door. He does it with a thud, and I've never been so grateful.

I go back to my seat, because now my legs are shaking along with my hands. It's good to sit down. Both of my parents remain at the door, peering through the curtain that hangs on the window portion. I wait to hear something from outside: first her steps down the wooden stairs, then the car door slamming, and finally the gravel again as she follows the loop around and back out to the county road.

I still feel the remnants of adrenaline, the tingles here and there. I don't want to make eye contact with either of my parents. I know their goal was the same as mine—get rid of her—because they're just as ashamed of what I did as I am.

My dad takes his seat first, and then my mom.

"What's left to fill out?" Dad asks.

I look up, my gaze going to him, then to my mother, who puts her reading glasses back on. For the first time in my life I celebrate the way my parents can sweep anything under the rug, even an elephant this big, as if it never entered the room.

# 14

CYD CALLED to announce Mac's arrival into town, five minutes before Mac pulled into my driveway. I asked him how he knew it was Mac, since he'd no doubt rented a new style car, and Cyd told me Mac beeped his horn and waved out of a shiny blue convertible Thunderbird just like he was coming home.

Mac hugged me as if nothing at all had changed, as if no time had passed since the last time we'd spoken or seen each other. No long days without phone calls, no subtle stiffness in the calls we did share.

When Dilly came up behind me, he hugged her, too.

"Hey, thanks for taking me to church that day, Dilly. And for introducing me to Lana's dad. Between him and those books, I'm learning all kinds of things I never knew before."

Dilly was blushing, looking between Mac and me. "I still have a lot to learn myself."

"I guess we all do."

She nodded. When they turned to me, no doubt my face wasn't quite as welcoming as it had been a moment ago. They exchanged a glance like they had some kind of conspiracy going.

"You'd better watch out, Hannah," Mac said. "God's after you, too, and He's got you surrounded."

I ignored the comment. "Are you hungry?"

"Are you kidding?"

We went into the kitchen, where I'd prepared Thai shrimp,

sesame seasoned green beans, and a strawberry salad. For dessert I'd made a low-fat cheesecake and decided to serve it with blueberries. I'd had to drive all the way to Springfield for half the ingredients.

My mother had also delivered potato salad in honor of Mac's visit. I would have appreciated the gesture except she made sure I was aware the bunkhouse was available for Mac's use. The salad was a bribe against my wrath, since she must have guessed she was the only one worried about everyone in town seeing Mac's car in my driveway all night long.

Mac and Dilly were polite during the meal, not entirely dominating the conversation with all things spiritual. But I could tell they were eager to talk about such things, especially since it was Lana's father who had answered so many of Mac's initial questions and Dilly wanted to hear more about him. I was gracious, though, which wasn't as hard as I might have imagined. The God they seemed to be talking about—loving, wanting what was best for them, a knowable Creator—wasn't the kind of God I remembered hearing about as a child.

"When I was in prison," Dilly said as we lingered over the table after dessert, "I felt God's protection. It was like I was invisible to people I knew could hurt me, and that was a miracle. But now that I'm out . . ."

She hesitated and I watched her closely. She never spoke of her time in prison, and I never pressed the subject. But I did want to hear how her life now compared to her life before.

"Yes?" I prodded.

"It's just that I thought God's plan would be easy to figure out. I know what I did was wrong, not only for Sierra and me but from God's point of view too. He was the one who gave us life. I had no right to try ending either one. But I know He forgives me for what I did."

She played with the last bit of cheesecake left on her plate, twirling a lone blueberry. "After I realized God did love me after all and that I wanted Him in my life as much as He seemed to want to be with me, I thought things would be easy. I decided I'd never do anything so selfish again. I thought I had the same goals God had." She smiled sadly. "With God on my side, how could things not work right? I thought He'd want me to take care of Sierra again." She looked at me. "I know I won't get custody of her, but I thought I'd be able to visit, you know? I thought He'd make that much easy."

"You know what Mom used to say about God." I hadn't intended to sound bitter, but I knew I had to finish anyway. "He's not a genie, there to grant our wishes."

Dilly nodded. "I actually think she's right on that one."

"You don't have visitation rights now, Dilly," Mac said. "But that doesn't mean it won't happen or that it's not what God wants too."

I saw Dilly give him a grateful nod. Now why hadn't I said something like that instead of what I'd said? I smiled Mac's way. No wonder I didn't want to lose him as my best friend. He always said the right thing.

It was after seven already, and Dilly refused a third cup of coffee. She stood. "I'm off to my room."

"You don't have to go," I called after her.

"I'm going to take the phone in there and call Sandee. I haven't talked to her in over a week." She grabbed the handset from the wall and left the room, nodding a good night Mac's way.

And we were alone.

"So."

"Yep."

Awkwardness had never been part of us, Mac and me. At least not until recently, and not in person until this moment. I needed something to do, some way to spend the uneasy energy inside me. But between dinner and dessert Dilly had cleared the table while I loaded the dishwasher, so there were only the dessert dishes left. I stood to fidget with them but finished far too soon, especially since Mac helped. I was free before I knew what to do with my nervousness.

"Mac—"

"How about we take a walk?" he asked. "Your cooking made me eat too much."

"Sure, blame the cook for your gluttony." I was glad to have something to tease about. "How about a walk around the yard? It's a big yard, and I can show you the flowers I haven't killed yet."

We went outside through the sunroom. The sun was low in the west, promising a colorful setting. That moon Mac had talked about would be out soon, the one that was a miracle according to him.

"You said you wanted to talk to me about something, Mac," I began. "Something serious."

"Yep."

We were near the side of the yard, where a row of daylilies and daisies were thriving and shardlike green leaves remained from the irises that had bloomed and faded.

"Care to expand on that?"

He stopped our stroll, facing me. "Now that I'm here, I'm finding this harder to talk about than I expected." He put his hands in his pockets, withdrew them. Looked over my shoulder, then back at me. "It's part of the reason I haven't called very often lately. Everything I've been learning points to truth. Truth is important, Han. More important than I realized."

He took a step closer to me, closer than usual. I took a step back, but he put a gently restraining hand on my shoulder and closed the gap again. There was only one reason for his hesitation. He must believe whatever he had to say would hurt me. If he was seriously dating someone and had come here for one last good-bye, he was right. I tried to prepare myself for the hurt to come, feeling it already.

I managed to turn around, giving him the back of my shoulder. I could speed along the conversation by telling him that even if the truth hurt, if it was important enough for him to make this special trip to see me, he ought to just let it out. But I didn't, because if he was getting married or something, I knew that really would be the end of our friendship. And that was one thing I didn't want to hurry.

"I came here to tell you something I've wanted to tell you for years."

That wasn't exactly the opening I expected. I turned back to him. He started to say something else but held back again. He looked around, first at the flowers beneath us, then at the sky, which was just taking on a pinkish hue. "I guess this is as appropriate a setting as any. In a garden, under a painted sky."

I wondered what the setting could have to do with honesty but said nothing. I aimed my face downward so he couldn't see me close my eyes and wish I were somewhere else.

"I love you, Hannah."

I didn't look up. I waited. But the silence didn't explain what I'd just heard, or if I'd heard what I thought I'd heard. He loved me? Well . . . of course he loved me. We'd said that before, and it meant we were the best friends of all. Was this some sort of gentle prelude?

I looked up slowly. "I love you too, Mac." I wanted to do something silly, like jab his arm like I would a brother if I had one, but I didn't.

"No, I mean I *love* you, Hannah." He ran a hand through his dark hair. "This isn't exactly the way I thought this would happen. I guess I pictured it being like *When Harry Met Sally* . . . well, without jumping into bed like they did. I think I'd like to marry you before we sleep together." He stopped himself, looking like he'd swallowed something sour. "That didn't come out right at all. Look, let's start over. Forget everything I just said. Except the part about me loving you, because it's hard to screw up three little words, at least those three little words."

I was stunned, like I'd been Tasered but with no pain. He'd just used the "three little words"—along with a reference to marriage—and he was talking to *me*. Mac. To me.

Suddenly he started laughing again and I knew it was all a joke. I had no idea why he wanted to joke about such things, but that's what it must have been. He slipped his hand back around mine and led me toward the house, where my dad had delivered a set of outdoor chairs as a housewarming gift. I'd found out he bought them at an estate sale, but they were in such good condition I didn't mind. I was reminded where I'd gotten my own ability to be cheap.

Mac led me to one of the chairs and I sat. He pulled up another chair and placed it right in front of mine so that our knees were touching. I was wearing shorts and he had on khaki pants because he'd worked that morning before getting on a plane. Casual Friday, travel attire.

Whatever.

I was too confused to think coherently.

The thing was, he never let go of my hand. In fact, once we were seated, he leaned forward and took my other hand, holding both of mine in his.

"I'm thirty-six years old and have been on more dates than I could count. I've had women ask me out and tell me they thought I was their Prince Charming. But I couldn't have bungled this any better than I have. Some prince."

"Mac," I said, looking at him closely, "what are you doing? Is this some kind of joke?"

"Only the performance, not the truth behind it." He squeezed my hands and put his face so close to mine I thought that for one instant he was going to kiss me. "I've loved you for years, Hannah, and the funny thing is, you never guessed it. You've been so focused on coming back here, you didn't see anything else."

His words did nothing to dispel my confusion. "I was supposed to see you loving me when you were going out on all those dates?"

"I had to pass my time somehow," he said with a grin. "And before a few weeks ago, I didn't think there was anything wrong with men treating women like I did: as a tool to pass time. Hey, I was honest to a certain extent. I never let anyone think our dates were anything other than casual. I lived for convenience, ease, and comfort, with my version of honesty."

"And now?"

"I want to live with truth, and that has to start with you."

"So you came here, to Sugar Creek, to tell me you love me."
I shook my head. "I'm here, Mac. Here. And you live in LA. Why
are you telling me this now? Just for the sake of the truth you
mentioned?"

He nodded. "Yes. That, and I've been thinking about Dilly."

I tilted my head. "What does Dilly have to do with this?"

"You came back to take care of her. You've scrimped and saved
and put your life on hold for her, and you followed through. But
ever since I came here, saw the kind of life people live around
here, how Dilly is . . . I don't think she needs you as much as you
expected. And in spite of how nice it is, I don't think you really
want to stay here with her anyway. You can come back to LA."

I breathed in deeply, so deeply that it made me cough. I pulled
one of my hands from his, even though I didn't want to, to cover
my mouth. I wasn't sure what to feel. I wasn't exactly numb—my
heart was beating in a frenzy, but a good frenzy, because having
Mac love me wasn't like having just *someone* love me. This was Mac.
Worthy, wonderful Mac.

But my confusion was just as real as the giddiness growing
inside of me. Had he just said he expected me to move back to
LA? While we sat in my own backyard, on chairs that belonged to
me, here in the Midwest? He knew why I was here. And Dilly did
need me, no matter what he mistakenly thought.

"Mac—"

"Okay, that's the wrong tone of voice," he cautioned softly. "Like
you're going to follow it with something I don't want to hear."

"Remember after we broke up, when we said the attraction part
was off-limits from then on? that our friendship was more important than anything? What happened to that rule?"

He shrugged. "I broke it. So sue me."

I stared at him. I knew his face so well, with deep brown eyes,
the scar on his square chin. His nose was somehow perfect, even
with a minor slant where it jutted out beneath his eyes. I'd heard
him tell someone once it had been broken in a car accident, the
same one that caused the scar. But it wasn't true; he'd been born

with a slightly crooked nose. Maybe that was part of the reason truth was so important to him now, because he'd violated it so many times over such mundane things.

"I'm here, Mac. Here to stay."

He shook his head. "That's why I've never said anything, because you were so convinced living here is the right thing to do. And in the last few weeks I tried distancing myself, accepting that you made the right decision. I tried convincing myself you'd be happy here. Here's the thing, though: I don't think you are happy here. Maybe if Dilly didn't have your parents, or if she had full-time care of her daughter again, she might need you. But she doesn't."

He was wrong. Totally, completely wrong. "How do you figure that? I bought this house for Dilly—"

"She'd be just as happy under your parents' roof."

"No, she wouldn't. And besides, she's bound to be able to see Sierra sooner or later. Once that happens, she'll be there every minute she can. I'm not sure she'll be able to hold a regular job, other than working for our parents. And what if she gets depressed again? Taking care of a child so fragile, it might happen. I need to be here, to watch for the signs, to bolster her. It's what I've been working for all these years. I can't just abandon that plan now."

Mac shook his head. "I'm not asking you to get on a plane tomorrow and come back with me. We'll figure all that out later. All I'm asking right now is if you love me. Could love me, not just as a friend."

"I . . . could," I said. But even as I admitted to this, I couldn't help but feel the pull of another truth, one he didn't seem to believe. "I can't leave Dilly. I can't. She spent over six years in jail; her life is ruined for any real job she's ever wanted; she can't even *see* her daughter anymore. And it's all my fault. I should have been here for her."

He was quiet a moment, and so was I. How was it possible to feel elated and hollow at the same time?

"You've dated countless other women, Mac," I reminded him. "And you *did* care for a few of them; I saw it. You could have married before this and lived happily ever after if you really wanted to be married."

"Maybe," he said slowly. He leaned closer again. "But anyone other than you would have been second choice. You were always first."

I pulled away, folding my arms, my back as stiff as the chair behind me. "I can't come back to LA."

"Well . . ." He studied me a moment. "I did consider moving here. If absolutely necessary."

Now I felt like laughing. "You're kidding, right? You'd be miserable here, and trust me, work isn't as easy online as I thought it would be. Accounts aren't exactly rolling in."

"Does it matter where we live, Hannah? If we love each other?"

I wanted to jump from my chair, pull him into an embrace, kiss him for the first time in seven years. But I couldn't. I knew it *did* matter where we lived, in the long run. I was willing to be miserable in Sugar Creek, but I wasn't going to drag him into that recipe for doom.

"You can't live here, Mac, and I can't leave," I whispered. "Dilly will never leave Sierra; she's never going to get custody of her, and so she's here to stay. And I'm not going to leave Dilly. I'll never, ever leave her."

His brows drew together. "But Dilly isn't the same person who did what she did all those years ago, Hannah. She's—"

"Yeah, yeah, a new creation."

"That's not actually what I was going to say. She's not alone, even without you here."

"The only people here now are the ones who were here before," I reminded him. "And what good were they then?"

"You've changed; maybe they have too. Dilly must have. She says she has."

"No, she hasn't. Not really. Not underneath. She still needs someone to look after her, to help her."

Mac lifted a hand to stroke my cheek, and I let him. This was a whole new feeling, being aware that his touch did mean something to him and now I could let myself believe what I'd thought all along, what it meant to me.

"You're the fixer, aren't you? Isn't there any room in your life to think about someone other than Dilly? How about thinking of yourself once in a while? or me?"

Giving in to my restlessness, I stood. "You and I don't have the same past as Dilly."

I had to move, to do something with this sudden animation inside of me. Being pulled in two different directions made me want to gather it all back together, and to do that I had to be moving. I had to switch locations, despite the thought that out here I wouldn't give in to the growing realization that if I wanted to kiss Mac, he'd let me. Welcome me.

I'd get us more coffee. Decaf.

But there, at the sunroom door, stood Dilly. And she didn't look like she was going to let anyone pass by.

# Dilly

"I can't believe you." The words come out of my lips, but just barely because my jaw is so tight my teeth don't even separate to let them out.

I don't think I've ever felt rage before, at least not like this. Sure, I've been angry with Nick for cheating on me all those times, but deep down I thought it was my fault. First, because I got pregnant so soon. I didn't blame him for looking somewhere else when my body was so swollen and I was sharing it with a baby. Then, after Sierra was born and she needed me the way she did, I grabbed whatever sleep I could, whenever I could. I didn't have the energy to be a wife to him.

But this. This *isn't* my fault. I never asked her for her help.

"What's wrong, Dilly?"

I look at my sister and I hate her for what she's done, how little she thinks of me.

"You!" I turn away, clasping my hands together to keep them from shaking.

Hannah comes to me, her face full of concern, and puts a hand on my arm, but I jerk away from the contact.

"What is it, Dilly?"

We're in the sunroom and there's barely enough room for the three of us with all the furniture she's piled in this room, furniture that's way too large, between the couch and the desk with the computer on it, a file cabinet, and a lamp table. But there's a narrow path that leads from the outside door to the one into the kitchen, and I dart back and forth like a pacer on steroids, needing to use up this energy inside of me somehow or I'll pull out her hair. I've seen it done in prison; I could probably take her, even though she's a little taller than me.

"I *asked* you if you came back here because of me." I never make eye contact with her but she knows I'm talking to her. Then

I stop and come up to her nose to nose. "You said you *wanted* to leave LA. You said you and Mac are just friends. You said you came back for Mom and Dad. I knew all that was a lie, but I let it go. I told myself not to read into things, because you're capable of making your own decisions. But now! How could you, Hannah? Think that of me? Do this to me?"

"What have I done? I didn't do anything—"

I turn away, pace again, and start mumbling. I know no one can understand me, but that's my goal. I babble about ruining one more life, that I'm not going to accept the blame for this one, no matter what. And I bring God into it too, because I'm so mad it even reaches heaven. He didn't do a thing to prevent another life from being ruined. Even as part of me knows I'm sinning, I can't stop my thoughts or my muttered words.

I stop only when my pacing circuit passes Hannah again and she steps in my limited path.

"Whose lives do you think you've ruined, Dilly? You're free now and forever, and we're not done fighting for Sierra. She's okay; you know that."

"I'm talking about yours, Hannah!" I cock my head Mac's way; he stands by the doorway, probably thinking the last thing he wants to do is join this family. "And his!"

"Am I missing something?" Mac asks quietly.

"You and me both," Hannah says.

Oh, come on. They're not stupid! Neither one of them gets it that Hannah's treating me like I'm some kind of head case? I heard what she said, and she said it, all right.

I heave in a deep breath. "Okay. I came in here to check on the status of an application I filled out online. I was sitting right there, at the computer." I point to Hannah's desk, which sits off to the side as far as the room limits allow. Under a row of open windows. "I heard everything you said, from the time you sat on the patio." I glare at Hannah with so much anger she leans back a little farther from me. "You've put your life on hold all this time so you can take care of me?"

"You make it sound like a bad thing, an unreasonable thing. I wasn't here when I could've made a difference, Dilly. I had to do something to make up for—"

But I raise a hand to stop her. "So now I find out I'm responsible for ruining your lives too? How am I going to pay for that? How many ways has my mistake ruined things? And how long are you going to let it keep going?"

Hannah puts her hands on my shoulders so I can't move away, even though I want to. "Dilly, it's not that at all. I'm the one who wasn't here for you."

"Because I was such a failure at being a mother—a wife, too—that I couldn't handle my life."

"I never said—"

"No, you didn't have to say any of that. I've said it to myself enough. I'm a waste of creation, can't take care of myself let alone someone else."

My sister shakes her head. "No, Dilly. I didn't know how hard it was for you, not until the trial. I wanted to pay for *my* mistake, because I'm to blame too, for yours."

"No, Hannah. You're not. I'm the one who did what I did. Me. Alone." Without another word, I try turning away.

But Hannah grabs at my hand, and it takes all I have left to wrench it back. "Leave me alone, Hannah!"

Then I run from the room.

# 15

I TURNED to Mac, more sure than ever where I was needed most. I didn't need to speak. When our eyes met, I could see he heard my thought. Surely he believed me now.

We waited for Dilly to return, a long, silent, awkward wait. Mac no longer spoke of loving me, and I could barely look at him. I was torn inside, ashamed at how I wanted to throw myself at him, forget all I'd worked for. But the rational me prevailed. I was to blame for Dilly running out. I should have told her the truth, somehow found a way to let her know I was here because of her— because I *wanted* to be here for her.

So, silently, I looked out the cottage windows in the front of the house, waiting for Dilly to get back. She couldn't stay away forever, and she couldn't have even gone far; she hadn't taken my car, not with Mac's rental in the way of mine tucked inside the single garage.

Finally I called my parents' house, to see if she was there. It would have been a long walk, but we'd walked to town plenty of times when we were kids. I was pretty sure I'd made my inquiry sound like an incidental reason for the call, as if I'd only wanted to let them know Mac might be late but that he'd be using the bunkhouse. Mom was glad, offering to cook breakfast for all of us as no doubt her way of conveying gratitude and approval of Mac's respectable intentions.

Dilly, however, wasn't there.

I considered calling her friend Sandee and refrained. No sense having the whole town know we'd had a fight.

It was late, after eleven. I knew one thing—Mac was getting tired, even if he was worried about the situation. He'd no doubt been up early in the NY time zone. He needed to go to my parents' bunkhouse.

Just as I was about to say so, I saw a car pull up in front of the house. A squad car. My heart pounded and I rushed outside, hearing Mac close behind.

No sooner had I stepped onto the front porch than my erratic heartbeat eased. There she was, safe and sound. With Tom Boyle behind her.

The moment she saw me I knew what she was thinking: I'd overreacted. I was hovering. I was worse than our parents. But she didn't say anything, just walked past me into the house.

I smiled awkwardly at Tom.

"I found Dilly at the café," he said. "Thought it might rain, so I offered to drop her off."

"Thanks," I said.

Dilly was already in the house, but Mac stood at my side. The two men exchanged nods.

Tom started to turn away, then stopped. "I probably shouldn't say anything, but I know how close you are, so I will. Not being able to see Sierra isn't getting any easier on her. I told her I'd talk to Sharon again, but I'm not sure it'll do any good. I didn't want to give Dilly any false hopes, so I guess I didn't help much." His gaze went to the door where Dilly had gone inside. "I wish there was somethin' I could do, that's all."

"We all do, Tom," I said.

"Well. We'll leave it in God's hands," he said, replacing the hat on his head. "Good night, then." He nodded again toward Mac, going back to his squad car.

I watched him drive off, the noise of his engine fading, leaving only the sound of crickets around us.

"I guess I'll head over to your parents' house," Mac said. "Unless

. . . Do you need anything? Do you want me to stay? to talk to Dilly?"

I shook my head. "She probably won't talk to me tonight anyway." Not that I wasn't going to try. But what could Mac do except remind Dilly of what she thought I'd given up?

I followed him to the side of his car. "Mac," I said as he put his hand on the door, "I'm sorry."

He smiled, though his face was tired and he didn't look all that happy. "For what?"

"For not giving you the reaction you wanted tonight."

"And what was that?"

"Oh . . . maybe not what Harry and Sally did, but for not booking the next flight back to LA with you."

He pulled me close and my heart leaped. "I'm a patient man, Hannah Williams."

Before I knew what he was doing, his mouth came down on mine. Not long, not passionately. Barely more than a graze, really. But never once had he kissed me there, at least not in the last seven years.

"Good night, Hannah," he said.

I went inside, but Dilly was nowhere to be found. The kitchen was unlit, and the bathroom between our bedrooms was open and dark. Neither was there light coming from the crack beneath her bedroom door, but since it was closed, that's where I knew she was. The door was open when she wasn't in the room.

"Dilly." I tapped lightly as I called her name.

"I'm tired."

But I couldn't just go away. "Are you still angry with me?"

Nothing.

That said it all.

# 16

BREAKFAST WAS to be at eight, which I told Dilly about through the bathroom door once I heard her up and around the next morning. She didn't say anything, but by the time she finished and I was done with my own shower, she was already gone.

She couldn't avoid me forever; we shared the same roof. Still, I couldn't deny a certain amount of anger. How could she be angry with me for wanting to *help* her? It made no sense.

I drove to my parents' house and, to my surprise, found Mac already at the kitchen table.

"The wind was coming from the direction of the house today," he said as he greeted me with a raised cup of coffee. "I smelled your mother's cooking and it drew me right inside."

I nodded and poured myself a cup, hoping the caffeine would help me think. Not that I hadn't been doing that instead of sleeping. All night.

My father passed me the cream, while my mother smiled and chatted about a bird nesting on the unused front porch. I wondered how long my parents would be oblivious to the argument going on between Dilly and me. Didn't they wonder where she was? why she hadn't come with me?

Once Mom stopped talking, Dad leaned forward, refusing another cup of coffee. I thought he might leave, either for the hog sheds or for town. But he looked at me, then at Mac. He was probably going to invite him out on a tractor. Mac might actually like that sort of thing. Once.

"Your mother was just about to ask your friend Mac here what his intentions are toward you, Hannah. It's a good thing you're here, so you can hear his answer."

I looked up, whatever brainpower I'd hoped to attain from the coffee now far out of reach. Mere caffeine wouldn't bridge the gap. "What?"

My mother laughed as if it were a lighthearted joke. "He's come a long way to see you a couple of times now, Hannah. But we're happy you have such a nice fella in your life. As a friend, or whatever he is."

Mac put a hand over one of mine, which to him might have been only friendly but to my parents was probably equivalent to a marriage proposal—or at least the intention of one. I tried pulling away, but he increased the pressure and grinned my way.

"Hannah and I have known each other a long time, but she's been concentrating on coming back here for so long I don't think she's thought much about anything beyond that. For now we're just friends . . . really good friends."

"Sounds like you're hoping that might change," Mom said.

I didn't want to look at him. I wanted to sink into my mother's polished wood floor, but my eyes went to Mac anyway. Just in time to see him nod.

"Okay," she said, pushing a stack of pancakes his way. "Eat up. You've answered our questions just the way we hoped. You know, we were wondering why Hannah decided to move back home after all these years, but this answer from you doesn't really explain that. In fact, it makes it harder to understand. Hannah? Do you have anything to say?"

Since the floor was no closer to changing to the quicksand I'd desired it to be a moment ago, I knew I had to answer. I glanced at my father, blaming him for this whole conversation. What happened to my family never talking about personal things? My dad's favorite way of talking to me was through Bible verses, usually ones that conflicted with whatever behavior he saw in me at the moment. And he never encouraged my mother to speak her mind, least of all about Dilly or me. He chose *today* to change his policy?

"I wanted to be with Dilly," I said. "She . . ." I'd been about to say *she needs me*, but I caught my tongue. She didn't want to need me. "I thought she might want some help, until she's settled."

"No need to drink your sister's cup," my father said.

I glanced at Mac, glad that he'd only recently taken up reading the Bible and probably wouldn't recognize half of the verses my father twisted around to suit his purposes.

"Dilly's already settling in nicely," Mom said.

My father nodded. "She's working for me and your mom. She could live here if she wanted."

"But she wants to get a real job," I said.

"What she does now is a real job. She's my first full-time employee. What's not real about that?"

"I mean in the area she studied. She has a degree."

"Yeah." My father's tone revealed his opinion of that. "Your mother told me about that. In social work or some such nonsense. Seems to me social workers work with kids. No school in this county—or state, or country—is going to hire her to be around kids with her record. I'm just glad I didn't have to pay for that wasted education. Foolish children are a grief to their father."

"Where is Dilly this morning, anyway?" Mom asked. "I thought she'd come out for breakfast with you."

"At the Coffee Spot," I said, adding silently, *I guess. . . .*

My father stood, having finished the portion of pancakes he'd been served before I even walked through the door. "I'll swing by and get her then. I was headed over to Springfield for a part I need for the tractor and told her I wanted her to come along."

He grabbed the hat he always wore, which hung by the kitchen door, and left. I watched him leave, only the residue of his words left behind. *Foolish children . . .*

"What's on your agenda today?" my mother asked as she filled my glass with juice.

I hadn't the faintest idea. Mac's trip had been a surprise from the start, and everything that had happened since his arrival hadn't left me time to figure out entertainment in this land of perpetual boredom.

"Your dad mentioned a pitch, hit, and throw contest going on somewhere around here this morning," Mac said. "Maybe we could go to that."

A bunch of local kids playing baseball. Now wouldn't that just compare to the last Dodgers game he'd been to?

While my mother took up with what fun that would be, naming names as to which child she thought would win, my mind went to the mess I suddenly found myself in. Mac, the man I'd strictly defined as my friend for the last seven years, now revealed he was in love with me. If I was honest with myself, something I hadn't allowed myself to be regarding Mac for a long time, I had to acknowledge the idea of him loving me was about the most wondrous news I could imagine. Stunning, really. I think I was still soaked in shock.

But I couldn't think of it without remembering Dilly's reaction. Her anger was so real, so deep, I didn't think anything could bridge that. And how was I supposed to try bridging it if she wouldn't even talk to me?

My life was suddenly far more complicated, when all I'd done was carefully plan. Why weren't things going according to plan?

I wasn't in the mood for baseball of any kind, least of all with a bunch of kids, but since there was nothing else to do, I said nothing as Mac drove us to the field in his rented Thunderbird.

"I'm surprised your parents didn't come along," Mac said as we walked toward the nearly full bleachers overlooking the pristine diamond.

"My parents?" I almost laughed. "They love sports, but that's not something they let themselves talk about outside the family. Competition can't be good for the soul, you know."

He caught my exaggeration; I could tell by his smile.

"You've always said your parents are the kind of Christians that give Christianity a bad name. Do you still think they're that way, now that you're back?"

"You mean now that I can look at them with the eyes of an adult?" I shrugged. Were they relaxing some of the rules I resented growing up because my dad had a radio in the shed these days and my mother wore slacks sometimes instead of only dresses? I still had the feeling they judged everything I said and did. I couldn't imagine why Dilly spent so much time over there, when I'd seen firsthand that my father remained ashamed of what she'd done. Although he did cover up those feelings when they were at the Coffee Spot.

"I don't know if they're different or not," I said. "I hope they are, for Dilly's sake, since she's there so often."

Once we were seated, we picked out the kids that my mother had told us about from names on jerseys. How she knew which kids were the best without having attended a single game, I wasn't sure. I supposed the stars were written up in the local paper, which she read as routinely as she read her Bible.

But my mind wasn't long on the sport, even though Mac seemed to enjoy it. He was particularly impressed by a boy who was smaller than the others. Those in the outfield moved in when he came to the plate, but with his first swing the boy smacked the ball far beyond every one of them.

My eyes wandered. I considered getting popcorn from the concessions stand, but I knew the bees were always attracted to the soda and candy, so I stayed put.

Until I saw a familiar person standing in line.

Adrienne.

"Mac," I whispered, even though there was no possible way she would have heard me from so far away. "Nick's girlfriend, Adrienne, is at the concessions stand. She said she'd talk to Nick about bringing Sierra to his house so Dilly could visit her. But that was a couple of weeks ago and we haven't heard a thing. I'm going over there. Want something?"

He shook his head. "Do you want me to come along?"

"Only if you want to."

"I'm not sure it'll do any good. Is she alone?"

I looked back, seeing a child next to her dressed in a baseball uniform. A girl.

"I think she might have her daughter." I scanned the area. "But I don't see Nick."

"I'll wait."

I nodded, then left his side.

Adrienne was second in line by the time I got there, with three customers between us. I stood there until Adrienne was served. As she started walking away, I left the line.

"Hi." I greeted her with a smile. "Remember me?"

Adrienne stopped and with some difficulty shifted a box of Skittles to the same hand holding a cup of soda, freeing her other hand to land protectively on her daughter's shoulder. Surely she wasn't afraid of me?

"You must be Adrienne's daughter," I said, smiling at the child. She looked like Adrienne, only her hair was lighter, what I could see of it from the ponytail sticking out the back of the baseball cap. "Are you competing today?"

She shook her head, at the same time slipping behind her mother. Maybe she read caution in Adrienne's demeanor.

"But you're on a team," I said.

She nodded this time.

"Do you have a regular position, or does the coach switch you around every game?"

"Look," Adrienne interjected before her daughter could speak, "I know why you want to talk to me, and I don't have anything to say. I mentioned to Nick about taking Sierra for an afternoon, but he didn't go for it. I'm sorry. I can't help your sister." She started to walk away.

"Wait," I said, my voice still friendly. "I just wonder if Nick really knows how important this is to Dilly. And you. Do you know? Your daughter is about Sierra's age, I think." I glanced again at her daughter. "Are you nine or ten?"

"Eight," she answered.

Adrienne continued walking again, and her daughter followed.

It occurred to me I was as persistent as those bees I'd tried to avoid at the concessions stand, but I couldn't stop now. "Dilly really needs some help, Adrienne. We're at a dead end with Sharon. Isn't there any way Nick might be convinced to help?"

"Sure, if . . . never mind." She picked up her pace, pulling her daughter along. "Would you leave us alone now? We came to watch the players."

I didn't give up. "You were going to say something," I coaxed. "What was it? An idea?"

She turned to me, and the candy in her precarious hold fell to the grass. Her daughter was quick to pick it up.

"Go back to our seats, peach," she said to the girl, handing her the drink and letting her keep the candy. "I'll be right there." She turned to me. "I can't believe you want me to help Nick's wife. I'm already living in her shadow, and you want me to bring her back under his roof in living color?"

"What? What do you mean?" I was confused but could think of only one way to interpret her words. "Nick was a terrible husband to Dilly. I can't believe he still has any feelings for her, if that's what you think. He cheated on her for years."

"She was his wife though, wasn't she?"

"Dilly isn't any competition," I assured her. "He's never once called, and if he had any hope whatsoever in that regard, he'd know the quickest way to get to Dilly is to get her to Sierra. I don't see that happening, do you?"

Adrienne didn't look my way. Her shoulders, once stiff, fell lower. "Nick doesn't care one little bit about Dilly. Or Sierra, for that matter. I'm not really sure what he cares about." She lifted her eyes to me. "But he married her, at least."

"And cheated every chance he got," I reminded her. "I don't hear about that happening these days, and you know that wouldn't be a secret for long in this town. You could talk to him, Adrienne. If anyone could change his mind, it's a woman he's been faithful to."

Her gaze fell on me again, but she didn't move. "I did ask him," she said, then gave a half smile. "I just didn't make it sound like something he needs to agree with."

"Could you talk to him again?"

She hesitated, but eventually she nodded without a word.

# 17

ONCE THE competition ended, neither Mac nor I was interested in eating after my mother's big, calorie-laden breakfast. So we skipped lunch and went to the only grocery store in town, planning our dinner as we walked the narrow aisles. Then we went home and seasoned burgers made of vegetables that we spent the afternoon slicing. I made a spinach salad while Mac crushed ice for a lemon squeeze appetizer. We sliced and pureed fresh peaches to be mixed with yogurt and gelatin for a frozen dessert. When it was time, we set the table with new dishes I'd purchased. All with Andrea Bocelli singing in the background from my iPod's speakers.

It was like it had always been. Mac and I worked well together no matter what we did: travel from one end of the country to the other, advise clients on how best to invest their money, plan and prepare a meal. Evidently neither of us wanted to jeopardize the team for the sake of an admission of love we weren't yet sure how to handle.

Dilly came in just as I folded the last napkin in the shape of a tent. She stood at the kitchen table, no doubt seeing it was set for three. I hadn't exactly expected her, but I'd hoped she'd be here.

"I don't want to be a third wheel," she said, staring at the table. "I'm not all that hungry anyway."

"You'll be hungry once we start grilling these burgers." Cheerful and tempting. Who could resist that? "How about a lemon squeeze while we wait?" I went to the counter and held up the pitcher.

She didn't move for a full second. Instead of letting her decide, I poured a drink and handed it to her.

"We have to talk," she said. "I don't want to, but we have to."

I agreed.

"Do you two want some privacy?" Mac asked. "From what I hear about sisters, they usually have all kinds of secrets."

He'd tried making a joke of it, but I wasn't feeling any more lighthearted than how Dilly looked at the moment. I wanted him to remain, though if Dilly felt otherwise, I would go with that.

"Dilly?"

"It's okay with me if he stays, since you two don't have any secrets from one another—" She cut herself off and put a finger to her chin, looking more irked than amused. "Oh yeah, except one: the fact that you've loved each other for years but didn't admit it because I was standing in the way—the needy sister who had to be taken care of first."

I moved closer. "That's not it, Dilly. Tell her, Mac."

But he was silent.

"Mac?"

"It's true, Hannah."

"Well, at least he's honest *now*." Dilly put the icy drink on the table, as if by drinking it she'd be accepting a gift from the enemy.

Mac shook his head. "It's true that Hannah planned to come back here all along. She thought anyone who might be interested in her should know her future was here, not in LA. So she kept everybody at a distance, as if she were only alive for a certain amount of time and that would be it. Death. Cut off. Don't form any lasting bonds." Then he looked at me instead of Dilly. "Except one bond she never let go. The one we had."

"You're not helping, Mac," I said.

"And you're not being honest if you don't admit everything I'm saying is true. But I don't blame Dilly. I'm okay with the way it's been, because all along I knew there was a reason you were putting me off. But you still cared too much to let me go. You didn't want me to be a memory in your life any more than I want you to be one in mine. So what if we waited all these years? Who knows what would have happened if we didn't?"

"You might be married, for one thing. Have kids," Dilly added.

Mac shook his head. "I doubt it. We've both been too busy building careers. So what, exactly, are you feeling guilty about, Dilly? How you ruined Hannah's life? mine? Well, get this. We're not ruined. We're both doing just fine. No guilt required."

"Okay, fine," she said, although I knew she wasn't convinced. "Then go back to LA. Both of you, where you belong. Leave me on my own two feet."

Mac and I looked at each other again. There it was, the real source of her guilt. And once again, I was to blame. I didn't think she could manage on her own, and there was no way I was leaving. And that *was* the truth.

I didn't have to say so, though.

Dilly took a step backward. "Do you both think I'm so incompetent that I'm a complete bust?"

"No, Dilly, that's not it at all. I'm just saying life is hard right now. I want to help you get to see Sierra. And once that happens, I want to help you take care of her because I let you down before."

"*You* let me down? And how were you supposed to know, Hannah? I never once asked for your help. You didn't even know how it was with Nick; I made sure of that. Nobody told you he was a lousy husband, never home to help with Sierra, always sleeping around. Do you know what he did on that night, the night that I . . . ?"

I shook my head, although I knew a little of it from the trial. He'd been out all night, even he admitted that. With another woman.

"He *told* me he was going to Jan's house. That was the girl of the week. He said he'd be at his girlfriend's house and not to wait up." She laughed, but there was no delight in that sound. "I sat beside Sierra and I knew it wasn't in me to go on anymore. I'd thought about it before, but I wasn't sure I could go through with it. Until that night." She turned away, reenacting the same pace she'd done the night before out in the sunroom, only here she had more room.

"The main thing was for Sierra not to feel anything. No pain. I just . . . I just wanted her to go to sleep and not wake up, because I wouldn't be here to take care of her if she did."

She stopped, looking at me. "But I was wrong. I'm to blame, Hannah, because every time I had those thoughts I should've asked for help. I didn't want anybody to know I didn't have it all under control. I wanted to go to bed every night at least with my pride." She laughed that same humorless laugh. "Nick wasn't there to sleep with, but I had that pride, because I had it *all together*."

Anger glinted through her tears. "Now I've got no reason to ask for help. And you're here anyway. Don't waste another minute of your life, because there's nothing here to help. I don't have Sierra. I know I won't get custody of her, so I won't need the kind of help I needed and never asked for before. I thought that's what God wanted for me, but I guess I was wrong. So you can leave. Go."

In that moment I saw I shared some of her anger. With God.

"Don't you see, Dilly?" I said. "You're making the same mistake now that you made then. Don't you want my help in trying to see Sierra?"

"All I've done since I was released is ask for help. I've asked you, Tom Boyle, Nick, Adrienne. I learned my lesson about trying to do everything myself."

I just shook my head. I glanced at Mac again instead of keeping Dilly's eye contact. Asking for help might be part of it, but I still didn't trust her, and now she knew it for certain. If Dilly never got to see her daughter, what would that do to her? Send her on another spiral downward, so she didn't want to be anymore?

I wasn't going to let that happen. Not on my watch.

"Nothing is going to be decided right now, Dilly," Mac said. His voice was soothing, the same one he used on me after I occasionally let a heartbreaking movie bring out all the emotions I'd been busy stuffing away. "The important thing is that Hannah is here for you. What's so bad about having a sister love you enough to want to see you get settled into a new life on your own?"

"Nothing, if she thought I was capable. No. She comes back to

town and *buys* a house, for pity's sake! She's planning to live out the
rest of her life in a town she doesn't even like because she thinks
I'm going to try killing myself again someday."

I couldn't have said it better, but I turned my back to her. I went
to the sink, busying myself with rinsing the cutting board, the
knife, dishes we'd used to prepare the meal.

"Okay," Mac said, his tone still soft, reasonable. "It seems to
me you both have jobs ahead of you. Dilly, you have to convince
Hannah you are capable of taking care of yourself. What about the
faith you've been living out since you were released? You didn't
have that before, but you've got it now. Doesn't that play into how
you plan to take care of yourself?"

"Yeah, it does."

"Then, Hannah," Mac said, coming up behind me, putting his
hands on my arms, standing close, "you have to be willing to look
at Dilly differently. Not right now, not this minute. But consider
letting her do some of the things you're always doing for her now.
You can't expect her to fly if you keep carrying her everywhere
yourself. You have to get out of the way."

"I'm not—"

Dilly stepped closer. "You're always doing stuff for me, Hannah,
and not even complaining about it. I know I probably take advantage of you, but you're just so easy to impose on. Mac's right. We
both have to change, starting right now."

I turned to her. This conversation had gone on long enough,
as far as I was concerned. Mac was right about nothing being
resolved tonight, though. I needed Dilly not to be mad at me
anymore. I needed to lighten the mood, get beyond the anger, the
disappointment. I smiled. "Does that mean she can't eat the meal I
just cooked?"

"*You* cooked?" Mac teased.

I welcomed his grin. He was always so quick to read my line of
thinking.

"How about I serve?" Dilly asked. "And do the dishes?"

"Now that," Mac said, "is a deal we can't refuse."

# 18

WE PLANNED to go to church on Sunday in the same way we'd done a few weeks ago, Dilly and I in my car, Mac following in his rented convertible. On the way to our parents' house to pick up Mac, Dilly and I didn't talk about everything we'd discussed the night before, but I sensed Dilly's hopefulness returning and her anger toward me lessening. She volunteered to drive my car and let me go with Mac to Springfield, so I let her. I hopped into Mac's convertible and we drove off without a thought to how my hair would look by the time we arrived.

When we were on the highway, he reached across the seat to take my hand. This was definitely something new.

"Do me a favor?" he asked over the wind.

I nodded.

"When we're sitting in church today, pretend you don't already have a bunch of head knowledge about everything. Forget how you were raised."

"I know how this church operates," I said. "I've been going every week for a while now."

"And . . . ?"

"And . . . what?"

"Is it making sense to you?"

"Some of it." I looked out my side of the car, pointing out to Mac the crop duster in the distance as it dropped a cloud over cornfields that stretched to the horizon. Before coming home,

I hadn't known anyone still used that technique. The sight was well timed, since I didn't want to carry on the conversation he had initiated anyway.

I knew Mac didn't welcome abandoning his topic. He pulled his hand away, putting both on the steering wheel. This faith business had become important to him, but what could I say that wouldn't end up hurting his feelings or making me say something I didn't believe?

"Speaking of head knowledge," I said, "it seems to be a pretty standard rule not to marry outside the faith. How do you feel about that?"

"Talking about marriage already, Hannah?" he asked with a glance. "We haven't been on an official date in seven years. You're ahead of me."

"You marry who you date, as one pastor said to me somewhere along the way."

"So don't date the wrong person."

"And for you, that could be me. About the faith thing, that is."

"I've been doing some thinking about that, Hannah. Here's what I came up with. You do have faith; you've had it all along. Why else are you so mad about the way your parents raised you? They didn't match up with what you thought was faithful. They followed the rules but didn't love you, at least the way you needed to be loved. They followed the rules and weren't there for Dilly, so it seemed like they didn't love her either. Maybe that's what you're so angry at . . . not at God, just at the people He put in your life to show Him to you."

I didn't want to listen, although a few of his words stood out as stark truth. "I don't want to talk about this anymore, Mac."

"Oh, sure, okay." His dramatic tone reeked of sarcasm. "What was I thinking? I shouldn't be talking about spiritual things on the way to church. I get it now."

Thankfully his glance was affectionate, so I knew he wasn't taking offense and didn't want me to either. The whole topic made one thing obvious to me: we might have been loving each other from a distance, but maybe there was a reason God hadn't let it go any further than it had. I wasn't the right one for Mac, and God knew it.

"What was the name of the girl who dumped you a few years back? the one who said she couldn't date you seriously because you weren't a devoted Christian? You should look her up."

"That was Kim, and no thanks. I heard she found some Bible thumper and got married."

"Too bad she didn't know you'd turn into one. She should have waited."

"My heart was already taken, even back then. That was the real reason she broke up with me. She saw me with you and the light went on."

"Oh. Sorry."

"Don't be. And she wasn't the only one, by the way."

I stared at his profile as he kept his gaze on the road. Others had broken up with him because they thought he was interested in me? This was news.

During the service, I tried doing what Mac had suggested—listening to everything with new ears. I did have to admit coming to church wasn't the chore it had been growing up, but until today I'd attributed it to the improved music and the relaxed atmosphere in everyone from the jean-clad pastor to those bold enough to wear shorts to church.

Somewhere during the course of the service, I began to wonder if Mac was right. *Did* I have faith inside of me, only I just didn't want to link it up to the kind my parents had tried to teach me?

Afterward, we lingered in the church parking lot, not exactly the most scenic place to hang around, but somehow this good-bye was even harder than the last, with nothing resolved. The three of us talked about mundane things, keeping to safe topics like the music from the service, Mac's upcoming travel schedule, my own consulting work. Eventually Dilly said her good-byes to Mac and ducked into my car, but when he invited me to sit for a moment in his car, I nodded and slipped into the convertible next to him in the front seat. It was wide open with the top still out of the way, and even though the parking lot was emptying out, I felt open, exposed. Shy.

Mac took one of my hands again. "I've been thinking all weekend about how to say good-bye to you," he said softly, both of his hands around mine now. "Should I kiss you, or should I not."

"Definitely not," I whispered.

He stared at me, as if he could see behind my halfhearted protest to the truth. He moved closer.

"Positively not," I added for emphasis. "Don't kiss me, Mac. If you do, it'll mean we really are something more than friends. Until I know where I'm going to spend the rest of my life, I don't want anything to end that friendship."

He smiled and stroked my cheek. "I think it's too late for that, Hannah. We're more than just friends already. And besides, I told you I haven't ruled out moving here." He grinned. "If enough of my clients don't want to follow me as an independent, maybe your dad needs a partner. He's getting up there in years, isn't he?"

I laughed. "You, a hog farmer? Right." I could not laugh long, though, because just as I realized I'd relaxed, Mac pulled me closer and kissed me after all. Gently at first, then gradually more firm, as if he didn't want it to end. Neither did I. His kiss hadn't changed in all these years, with its power to move and melt everything inside of me. I knew I should pull away, but for a moment longer I didn't. I enjoyed this renewed part of us, this one part I hadn't let myself think of for so long.

He remained close, resting his forehead on mine. "Sorry?"

"Do you want me to tell you the truth, or what I should say?"

"Why? Are they different?"

"I should say you shouldn't have done that, and then I should say yes, I'm sorry you did. But the truth is I'm not."

And then he kissed me again.

# 19

SUNDAY AFTERNOONS were for rest and enjoyment, but that was the day I pretended to be a farmer. True, I had no aspiration to become one, but I was determined to sustain the perennial garden that I had acquired with the house. How hard could it be to grow what were essentially weeds that sprung up wild along the road? Trouble was, I only wanted the kind that provided flowers.

As I dug in the soft, black dirt, my mind flitted between Dilly and Mac. Of course I did what all women in love did: I wondered what Mac was doing. If he was thinking of me. If he missed me. When he would call next.

I was positively girlish.

But then my thoughts would return to Dilly and I would know I was doing the right thing by not pushing anything forward with Mac.

"Hannah! Hannah!"

Turning, I saw Dilly running from the back door of our house, tears streaming down her face. All thoughts vanished except of my sister. I scrambled to my feet, dropping the tool I'd been using to dig out weeds and pulling the gloves from my hands, hindered by fingers that suddenly turned shaky, hot and cold all at once.

I stumbled toward her. "What is it?"

She stopped before me, and now that my hands were free, I threw the gloves aside and grabbed her by her arms. Her tears were unstoppable.

"It's . . . Sierra! I just got off the phone with Nick. Oh, Hannah!" She pulled me close, hugging me tight. "I'm going to see her! Right now, this minute, before he changes his mind. Will you take me? I can't drive; I'm too excited. And scared."

"Scared?"

She stood clear of me, wiping her palms on her jeans. "He told me to go to his mother's house."

"Sharon's? Does she know you're coming?"

She nodded. "She must! Nick said he called her right before he called me."

I couldn't believe it. "Sharon changed her mind? Just like that?"

Dilly's slight shoulders bobbed up, then down. "I don't know and I don't care about details, Hannah. Let's just get over there before she changes her mind."

It took only five minutes to get to Sharon's house on the edge of town. I saw the van Sharon used in the open garage, but no sign of Nick's car. The dogs must have heard us pull up; they were already barking from the backyard.

I looked at Dilly, thinking she would rush out of the car. But she was sitting still now, eyes closed. Praying again, as she had the last time we'd come to this house. Or maybe she was waiting for Nick to drive up. She'd need his support, I was pretty sure of that.

Finally Dilly moved, opening her side of the car.

"Do you want to wait for Nick?" I asked.

Dilly shook her head. "If Sharon agreed to this, why wait?"

The front door opened just as we approached, but it wasn't Sharon who stood there. It was Adrienne, Nick's girlfriend. She held open the door. "Nick took Sharon over to Cyd's. They're having dinner."

Dilly stopped short. "You mean . . . Sharon's not here? Nick, either?"

"Nope." She smiled broadly. "It's just me and Sierra. And my daughter is here too. Come on in."

Still Dilly didn't move. "Did Sharon know I was coming? Nick said he called her."

"Yeah, before he picked her up to take her to Cyd's."

Dilly grabbed my hand, as if I were an anchor making her stay where she was. "So Sharon doesn't know?"

"Are you kidding? She wouldn't have left if she'd known. Come on in."

Dilly took a step forward, then another. The third one led her to the step at the porch, but only one foot made it up. She stopped. She turned to me, still clutching my hand. "Should I?"

There have been few times I've been dumbfounded in life, but this was one of them. We'd talked about cutting Sharon out of the decision by having Nick take Sierra to his house, if only for an afternoon. Maybe he would have provided for Dilly to be there without Sharon's permission the first time. Such a circumstance had called for Nick taking charge, putting his foot down. And once Sierra knew Dilly was back in her life, Sharon would change her mind. She was bound to. That was something no DCFS agent would object to.

But this was something else altogether. Morally *and* legally.

"I . . . don't know, Dilly. Let's just think about consequences first, okay?"

She lowered her face. Her shoulders went round. Her hand fell from mine. "I was so sure this was it, my answer to prayer." When she looked up, she stiffened, but I could see the struggle on her face, the urgency to go in stopped by confusion.

"You and Nick set this up?" I asked Adrienne. I could see Dilly didn't want to violate rules any more than I did, even as much as it tormented her to have rules keeping her from Sierra.

"Yeah, we decided this was the best way to do it."

Dilly shook her head. "I don't want just one visit with her, though! I need Nick to be here so I can come back regularly."

Adrienne frowned. "Look, Dilly, Nick and I went to a lot of trouble to figure this out. We thought you'd be grateful."

She nodded, extending one hand, palm up, toward Adrienne. "I am! I am. I just . . . I'm not sure what to do."

"You wanted to see Sierra. She's right inside." Adrienne held the screen door wider.

Dilly leaned forward again, but it was as if her feet were stuck in wet cement.

"Adrienne," I said, "Dilly's on probation. Sharon could make things hard for her if she really wants to, and coming here without her permission might just make her mad enough to cause trouble."

"I thought you only needed Nick's permission. That's what he said. You have that."

"Verbally—to you and not to Dilly. Sharon could make it seem any way she wants if she finds out about this. Whose side do you think Nick would be on?"

Dilly latched on to my hand again. "I know you're right, Hannah. But she's just inside—I've got to see her." She moved both feet onto the stair.

I didn't let go. "Your first instinct was the right one, Dil. Let's go back before this whole thing turns around and blows up."

She ran a hand across her forehead. "You're right, I know you are. But . . . I've just got to look in on her. For a minute? Just a moment?"

"The amount of time doesn't matter, Dilly. It won't matter how long to Sharon."

Dilly nodded, and now she leaned my way but made no progress forward.

She shook her head, as if bugs were flying an orbit around her and she wanted to be rid of them. "This is hard, Hannah. I don't know if I can do the right thing."

"You—you're not going through with it?" Adrienne asked. Her face was incredulous. "Do you know how hard it was for us to convince Sharon to leave? I had to tell her I'd babysit whenever she couldn't find somebody, as if I want to do that! I barely have enough time with my own daughter without dragging her over here to watch somebody who might die on me any minute."

The words infused Dilly with movement. She wrenched her hand from mine. "She's not going to die!"

I snatched her hand back, which must have been enough for

Dilly to remember why she'd hesitated in the first place. She stood a step below Adrienne, and I heard her take a deep breath.

"I'm sorry, Adrienne," she said softly. "There's nothing I want more than to take you up on this offer. I want to see her more than anything."

Adrienne shook her head. "All I know is that sometimes you have to bend rules. Sharon's rules, anyway. And that's all you're doing. Is Sharon worth not seeing your daughter after all this time?"

"No, she isn't. But I can't risk what she'd do. This moment, going in and seeing Sierra once, might cost me getting to see her regularly in the end."

She turned away before Adrienne could speak, as if allowing Adrienne any more words would add too much temptation.

I turned to catch up.

I wanted to say something, to be the cheerleader I should have been years ago. To bolster her even though I could see each step that took her from Sierra was like a step into hell . . . or at least away from heaven.

"You're doing the right thing—"

A car from the street caught my attention and I stopped. I didn't recognize the car, but I did recognize its driver. And the frantic passenger opening the side door before the vehicle had even come to a stop. Her graying hair was in its usual bun at the back of her head, but a few thin, errant strands rippled in the air as she jumped out of the car.

"You stop right there, young lady! I'm going to call Tom Boyle this minute and have you arrested. Coming here under this sort of trickery! Do you think I wouldn't have found out? I knew something was going on. And I was right."

Sharon's words were barely clear, the way she ranted and waved her finger Dilly's way. I stepped between them because Dilly was in no shape to defend herself, with new tears streaming down her face, her entire body shivering.

"You don't understand, Sharon." I held a hand out like a referee at an unfair boxing match. Each faced the other, but Dilly hardly appeared ready for a fight. She looked ready to curl up into a fetal position. "Dilly and I were just leaving. As soon as she found out you weren't here, she wanted to leave. She thought you knew; she thought you were here."

Sharon's face pinched, revealing wrinkles not yet permanent. "I don't believe a word."

Adrienne came off the porch, and from the other side of the car I saw Nick's shadow. He was dark and short, not much taller than Dilly. I never knew what women saw in him, except Dilly said he once made her feel like she was the only woman in the world. Before he started seeing other women, of course.

"It's true, Sharon," Adrienne said. "I couldn't believe it, because me and Nick went to so much trouble to let her come here. But she wouldn't come in once she found out you didn't know anything about it."

Sharon was clearly skeptical, but Nick's brows rose. "You see, Ma?" he said. "I told you she was different now. You know they're telling the truth—you haven't been gone long enough for Dilly to have any kind of visit."

She looked at her son, her lips tight in exasperation. "I keep telling you, Sierra doesn't know where she's been all this time. Do you think if she could understand, she'd want to see her mother after what she did to her?"

"Sharon." Dilly stepped closer and I stood back, knowing no mediator was necessary anymore. Not with Dilly's pleading tone and Sharon's anger now scattered toward Nick and Adrienne too. "I'm not dead, and she deserves to know. All the years in the past don't matter anymore. I'm here, and I need to see her. Every day. I want to be in her life again. I want to take care of her."

Sharon's mouth twisted on one corner. "No jury in the country would give you custody of her again."

"I just want to be with her. As often as you'll let me, with you right in the room, or Nick, or anybody else. Tom Boyle, my parole officer, a social worker, whoever we can get until you trust that I'm never going to do anything to harm her again. I never wanted to harm her in the first place. I just . . . I couldn't . . . I didn't know how to take care of her on my own as well as you can, I guess."

Sharon crossed her arms, which seemed to soften her rather than adding a barrier. At least she wasn't stiff as stone.

"Ma," Nick said, "why don't we all go inside right now? I don't see any harm in Dilly seeing her own daughter. I don't know why you wouldn't want Dilly's help. Like she said, she doesn't need to take on full care or even be alone with Sierra. She just wants to see her. Where's the harm in that?"

"What if Sierra doesn't want to see her? None of us here know what really went on that night or leading up to that night."

"I can tell you what led up to it," Nick said. "Dilly did everything for Sierra, everything you're doing now, only around the clock and by herself. And if I hadn't been a jerk, maybe I'd have been able to get her some help, like you have now."

I saw Dilly and Nick exchange glances, as if Dilly wanted to say thank you.

"I should have asked for help," Dilly whispered.

In that moment it didn't matter that Nick still wasn't living up to his responsibilities, that he continued to allow others to do everything for Sierra. He'd come to Dilly's defense, and that counted for something.

Dilly looked at her former mother-in-law. "I should have asked for your help back then, Sharon. I'm sorry I didn't."

Sharon's arms unfolded, and she sighed. "You all feel this way? that she should see Sierra?" She looked around at the faces nearby, even skimming mine.

"We do, Ma. So does Cyd. I told him what I was doing today."

Sharon's brows lifted. "You told Cyd you were bringing me to his house as part of a scheme? And he was in on it?"

"He said he'd come back here with you if you made a fuss."

She let out a breath, and it was one of defeat. I'd heard that kind of sound before—from myself. "I have one thing to say, and I'll say it to both of you. I don't know what God was thinking to let either one of you have a child. But if she's going to be in Sierra's life, it'll have to be for good. Consistently, you understand? You just can't come by when you feel like it; you have to be part of a routine. That's all she knows. Routine."

A leftover tear in the corner of Dilly's eye winked a sparkle, tumbling down her cheek. "I can be here every day! Well, in the evening, when she's here. I'm working out on my dad's farm during the day, and she's at school then anyway. Just say when, Sharon. I'll be here."

Sharon glanced at her watch. "It's dinnertime now, and neither Nick nor I have eaten. You haven't, have you?" she asked Nick, suddenly skeptical of that, too. "Did Cyd really have dinner waiting for us?"

Nick nodded. "He was going to tell you everything during dessert." He grinned. "Guess I should go call him. He's probably out on his tower, expecting we had some kind of accident on the way there."

"Why'd you come back, anyway?" Adrienne asked.

"Ma said she forgot her purse, but I told her she didn't need it. Said she had some kind of medication to take with a meal."

"Shows you how much you know. I didn't trust this whole thing from the start." She eyed Dilly again. "And you knew nothing about it? Nothing?"

Dilly shook her head.

"Okay then. Come inside." But when Dilly moved to immediately obey, Sharon caught her arm. She must have squeezed tight, because even though Dilly's arms were as thin as mine, flesh oozed out above Sharon's grip. "I don't forgive you for what you did to her, Dilly. I think you were weak and foolish and stupid, and I haven't decided yet if you aren't still that same weak and foolish girl. I'll be watching you. And you will never, ever, be alone with Sierra again. Do you hear me?"

Dilly said nothing, only nodded, eyes wide. Then Sharon let go, and Dilly was the one to lead the way inside.

# Dilly

There she is, my beautiful little baby. Instantly I see she's still the same, just as I imagined. Bigger, maybe, and her hair a little longer than I used to keep it. Bigger tennis shoes on her feet. But she's my baby, my little baby girl. Right here, so close I can touch her.

I move closer, one slow step at a time, even though what I want to do is run and scoop her up and twirl her around. All this time I've been praying to see her, thinking about being with her, but suddenly I realize at least some of what Sharon's been saying is true. Who knows what Sierra has been thinking since I've been gone?

"Hi, Sierra. It's Mommy."

I'm standing beside her now, and she looks up at me, past me, back at me, the same way her gaze used to float before. Sometimes it hit the target, sometimes not.

Her arms move, both of them at the same time, as if she's trying to tell them to do something. I tell myself she's trying to hold them out to me, so I kneel closer. I take her flailing arms gently in my grasp, land them steadily on my shoulders.

"Hi, honey. Oh, boy, have I missed you."

I don't even realize I'm crying until the tears are coming down my face, but I scrub them quickly away. I don't want her to think I'm unhappy because I'm anything but. I haven't felt this happy since . . . since I can't even remember when. Since the day she was born. I knew this was someone I could love and who would love me, wouldn't judge me, control me, or cheat on me.

"I'm so happy to see you. I've thought about this day for a long, long time. I'm sorry I've been away all this time. But now I'm back, and I'm going to spend as much time with you as I can. A little while every day, if you're not too busy." I smile because she's groaning, but it's a happy groan. Her arms are moving again, along with her legs.

"Do you remember one of our favorite songs? 'Hush, little baby; don't say a word. Mama's gonna buy you a mockingbird. . . .'"

As I sing the rest of the song, I know she's trying to sing along, the same way she did when she was littler. Her gaze hits me often, and her brows are happily raised. Joy washes through me, greater than ever, because now I know what really matters, why I was born, and what my future holds.

# 20

IN THE days that followed, Dilly met the routine Sharon demanded for visits with Sierra. My sister never missed a day, was never late, and stayed as long as she was allowed. She brought her voice, her guitar, and joy behind every song she sang.

On the days I came along, I watched Dilly become someone I'd never known before. She was sure of the care she provided for someone so fragile, never shying from what needed to be done. She tended to the feeding tube that sustained her daughter and got rid of soiled diapers whenever necessary. She changed her daughter from school clothes to pajamas, never uncertain as to the most comfortable angles for arms and legs going through armholes or pant legs. She wiped drool from Sierra's chin, used a motorized suction machine to draw secretions from Sierra's mouth, held her through seizures, massaged lotion on her arms and legs. Eventually Sharon even let Dilly bathe Sierra and wash her hair, braiding it into pathetically thin strands that she prettied with ribbons.

And all the while Dilly's eyes shone, as if she were the one being served instead of Sierra. As if she were the one being showered with love.

As I watched, I wondered if I would have learned all of this if I'd been here for Dilly years ago. Could I hold Sierra through a seizure without stiffening myself or panicking? Could I speak to her gently, soothingly, without revealing my own fears? I watched, intent on learning, because even if it was true that Dilly might never share custody of her daughter again, I knew if I was going to be any help at all I would have to get beyond my own discomfort and learn to care for someone I wasn't sure could withstand my awkwardness.

I might, in time, achieve Sharon's way, I supposed. Competent. But I preferred Dilly's way, as though each act of service was a privilege. For the time being I could only watch. I wasn't yet bold enough to act on my desire to help.

Dilly kept so busy with her days at the farm and her evenings at Sharon's that I rarely saw her. I was tempted to spend some time at the Coffee Spot, I was so desperate for company. But I didn't. Instead, I found my own busyness. I continued to do my online consulting, and I spent more time with the food ministry at church. But even there I was alone, tallying and sorting canned goods and other nonperishables.

Mac called almost daily. We'd slipped back into our friendship. With so much distance in between, there seemed little choice. We never spoke of the future, but I could tell that every time I gave a positive report about Dilly and her new, fulfilling routine, he believed more strongly than ever that I would be back in LA soon. It was only a matter of time.

Part of me wanted to believe it too. But I wouldn't let myself. I'd prepared myself to stay by Dilly's side, and I wasn't ready to give up that job just yet.

My evenings became routine too. On the days I didn't accompany Dilly or go out to my parents' house for dinner, I'd clean up my kitchen, go to my sunroom office to check e-mail one last time for the day, then settle in to watch the news shows. It wasn't a particularly thrilling routine, but this wasn't and never would be LA.

One such night I clicked through my favorite channels, stopping at the local news, wondering if the rest of my life would be spent this way. I'd been afraid of Dilly falling back into a depression; maybe I ought to worry about that for myself.

The picture of a woman flashed on the screen. She was thin, her long hair bedraggled as if she'd just gotten out of bed. But what caught my attention wasn't her unkempt appearance or the prison-garb shirt she wore in what was obviously an arrest photo. It was the look in her eye. Desolate.

I turned up the volume, connecting to the loneliness on the woman's face.

"Carla Morelo of Springfield was taken into custody today after allegedly killing her seven-year-old severely handicapped daughter. Authorities say Morelo, thirty-five years old, took her daughter's life 'in order to end her suffering.' The child, Molly Morelo, suffered from a severe case of cerebral palsy. Mrs. Morelo is being held on a two-million-dollar bond and will be evaluated to see if she is fit for a trial. For a report on the incidence and variety of cerebral palsy we'll go to Dr. Jeffrey Pitman. . . ."

I stared at the screen, abhorring the thought of connecting to any part of this woman. Immediately a jolt of guilt and pain seared into my chest. The face they'd shown was of a woman as lost and despairing as Dilly had once been. The only difference was that she'd succeeded in half of what Dilly tried to do, and this woman's wrists hadn't been taped.

I shut off the television, irritated with the news and my own routine for having seen it to begin with. All of the reports were the same, showing a state of affairs that let the world come to a place where mothers could do such a thing to their children.

It's sin, they would have said at church. Not of the child, the victim, but was it a sin of the mother? Could I see Dilly in that light? She was a victim, too.

Sudden restlessness filled me, fueled by frustration and something else I couldn't identify. Fear? A refusal to revisit that part of Dilly's life, that nightmare?

I fairly stomped into my bedroom, pulled off my cotton shirt and thrust my arms through a T-shirt, then put on a pair of shorts and my running shoes. I hadn't jogged since leaving LA. There wasn't a jogging path to be found in this corn county, and there weren't enough residential streets in Sugar Creek to go any distance. The roads surrounding town were narrow and used by the kind of drivers Cyd was famous for calling Tom about. But I ran anyway, around the block, then again, then down the other four blocks of town and started over. I ran and ran and tried to make my mind a blank.

# Dilly

I hang up the phone and stare at it for what feels like a long time. I know Sandee called because she thought she'd be the best messenger for this, but I wonder if that's true. I wish I didn't know what she just told me. I wish I'd taken five more minutes to get home and had missed the call altogether. I wish I could be ignorant a little longer.

I go to the living room and click on the television. It's already set to a news channel, but they're talking about a hurricane in the Bahamas and I click it off. The Internet. I can control that and find out all I need to know right now.

I didn't have free access to a computer in prison and didn't own one before that, so I don't know much about them. Learning to use a computer was the one thing I really welcomed my sister teaching me after we moved in here.

I do a search for the name of the woman Sandee called me about. Carla Morelo. A picture of her pops up with a story next to it. I stare without reading. She's got that same not-really-there look I saw in the mirror just before my own arrest.

I want to cry, but something else is going on in my head that I don't welcome. *What do you call it when you're glad somebody else falls into the same pit you've fallen into?*

I stuff away everything I'm feeling right now, the good and the bad, because if I think about it, maybe I am—just a little—relieved that it's somebody else people are talking about in connection to this kind of crime. But then I realize it's only going to bring up comparisons, and my name is bound to come up again.

My insides shrivel.

I think of this woman's child, her precious but handicapped child, that she's dead now. Forever dead.

I thank God He didn't let me succeed. I thank God for Sierra's life, for her smile, for every breath she takes.

I pray this girl, whose mother succeeded where I failed, didn't suffer.

I pray the woman, this Carla Morelo, somehow gets through these next few days, because they will be tough, even though once she comes out of the shock it'll get tougher.

I just sit there, staring at the picture where mine had once been.

# 21

THE MINUTE I stopped running, pure exhaustion getting the best of my intentions, her face came back. Her eyes turned to Dilly's; her guilt turned to mine.

By the time I admitted my own depletion, I could no longer jog. I glanced at my watch, which I'd forgotten to remove. I'd been jogging only forty-five minutes, but I walked home anyway. Being wrung out in under an hour was a sad testament to how far behind I'd left my LA lifestyle.

The sun was almost gone for the day as I trudged up my front porch. Dilly was back from Sharon's. She'd taken the car and it was back, safely tucked into the garage. Instead of going right in, I sat on the cool cement step, knowing I'd better shake the memory of the news story if I was to present a pleasant facade to Dilly.

Thirst sent me into the house at last, and I went straight to the kitchen for ice water. The room was empty, and from there I could see no light from Dilly's bedroom down the hall. Taking my water with me, I went in search of her. There were few choices: the yard, the basement, or the sunroom.

I checked the sunroom first, where I saw a dim light from the monitor on my desk. Dilly was bent over it studying something.

"How was Sierra tonight?" I asked. Goodness, I was a better actress than I gave myself credit for. Dilly would never guess I'd just tried exhausting the life out of myself.

"Fine, just fine."

So much for worrying about an attentive audience for my performance. Dilly hardly let herself be distracted by my question or my presence. She was still intent on whatever it was she was reading. I looked at the screen, and the glass nearly slipped from my hand.

There was the face again. The Springfield woman's face.

"Dilly! What are you doing?"

At last she looked up, perhaps perplexed by my condemning tone. "Sandee called and told me about a woman in Springfield who was just arrested. I wanted to find out more about the case, so I'm seeing what's online. She's right there; her name is—"

"Yes, I heard." I was tempted to reach behind the chair and yank out the plug. If it would have removed from Dilly's brain whatever she already knew about the case, I would have done it in an instant.

"So you know why she was arrested?" Dilly asked quietly.

I nodded.

"I need to contact her."

My heart rate sped. "Why?"

"Because I know what she's going through. I know what's ahead for her." She pushed away from the desk and leaned back in the chair, hands in her lap. She was quiet and still, but my eye was caught by her fingertips. They were trembling. "She has to know she can get through it."

"She can find that out the same way you did."

Dilly shook her head, clasping her hands together. "Shouldn't I try to help her? let her know that if I made it, so can she?"

"But you didn't kill your child. They might ask for the death penalty in her case."

Dilly shook her head again. "They won't, not with the moratorium on death penalties still in effect. They wouldn't have anyway."

"Just because executions are on hold in this state doesn't mean death sentences are illegal. If that advocate group that's hounded you has any influence, that's what they'd want."

Dilly turned back to the face on the screen. "She might welcome it if they do want to put her to death. At least at first, the idea of it."

I set what was left of my ice water on my desk, then bent over Dilly with one of my arms around her shoulders. "Forget this, Dilly. We were bound to hear about something like this happening again sooner or later, but you don't have to do anything. . . . You don't have to relive everything you already went through."

Dilly wheeled backward on the office chair, freeing herself from my touch long enough to stand and move to the other side of the desk.

"I know what she's going through, right this minute. It says online that she's being put on a suicide watch." Dilly put her palms to the sides of her face, rubbing backward so her skin pulled momentarily tight. "Sounds like they're doing her a favor, doesn't it? Wanting to protect her from herself?" She sank onto the couch behind her, covering the top of her head, skinny, sharp elbows pointing up. She started to rock, back and forth, back and forth, finally lifting her eyes to stare straight ahead. "They'll put her into a room all by herself, a room with a camera in it, placed so there's nowhere to hide. And they'll put her in a suicide suit." Now she rubbed her neck, as if she could still feel the material. "Thick, scratchy. Like a dress but no sleeves, and with Velcro in the back. No shoes, no socks, no bra, no underwear, no sheets on the bed. Nothing to use against yourself. If she refuses to eat, they'll threaten her and say they'll take her to the hospital and feed her with an IV. And when she does eat, if she does, everything will be given to her on Styrofoam, no utensils. She'll have to break off a piece of a cup to scoop up what's on the plate. Or use her fingers."

Dilly took a deep breath and I wished she would stop, but I could see she had more to say. "She'll be in that room twenty-three hours a day, without anything—no paper or pencil or books or anything except the noises outside the room. They'll let her out for an hour, to shower and maybe make a phone call but nothing else. Other inmates that see her will stare and whisper, and word will get around right away that she's the one on the camera. The monitor they have is in the hall, where everyone can see it—guards, inmates as they pass from their cells, everybody. Men, women—it doesn't matter. Oh yes, they'll see her sleep and she'll hope the gown doesn't twist or roll up over her hips when she doesn't know it. They'll see her eat with the Styrofoam or with fingers like a baby. They'll see her go to the toilet, too—it's right there in the room. They'll hear the guards curse at her and tell her not to complain that she's cold without a blanket, not to ask for anything, not to speak because she shouldn't have done what she did. And she'll know . . ." Dilly was crying now, and I neared her slowly, cautiously, until I was right there in front of her, pulling her into my arms. "She'll know she deserves it all because of what she did."

"No, Dilly, no. Shhh . . . It's all right now."

I stroked her hair, letting her cry, wishing such memories could be wiped out. I wished for a place like heaven, where I'd heard there weren't any more tears. Just then, I wanted to believe such a place existed and that God wanted us there so that Dilly could hope to go someday and never cry again.

"You—you believe in heaven, Han?"

I looked at her, not knowing I'd uttered any of my thoughts until Dilly's overrunning eyes bored into me, asking that question. I had to nod, because if I didn't, it would disappoint her. And so I did.

She hugged me close. "In there . . . all I had was God, and then He sent me Lana and others who knew about how He really is. That He . . . He forgave me. And I made it through." She wiped away her tears. "So I've got to be there for this woman now. You see it, right? How could I just shrug it off and not do *something*?"

I wanted to argue, to say it was too late to do the kind of good that would have made the most difference, when it counted. Before her child was dead.

Dilly grabbed my hands and I felt the tears that had been wiped onto her palms. "How could I not be there for someone else that I'm capable of helping?"

"But what about you, Dilly? What will it do to you to think about somebody else going through what you've been through? It won't help you forget."

Dilly reached up and stroked my hair, as if suddenly the roles were reversed and she knew more than I did. "I won't ever forget anyway, Han."

Maybe comforting someone else might help. I nodded. "Then write to her, Dil. If that's what you think is best."

# 22

I AWOKE the next morning hoping Dilly's plan to write to Carla Morelo had changed, but it hadn't. As she was leaving for the farm, she mentioned that she wanted to call her parole officer to verify the correct address for the jail in Springfield. I volunteered to do that, and once Dilly was gone, I told the officer about Dilly's intentions and asked if she thought it was an appropriate thing to do.

Instead of the caution I hoped for, she said it was a good idea. So much for trying to gain a tool for changing Dilly's mind.

When the call ended, I went to the sunroom, intent on working. Instead, I stared at the telephone.

It was already past noon here, which meant Mac was halfway through his morning at work. Perhaps he thought I'd fallen asleep earlier than usual last night, and that was why I hadn't called as I'd said I would. Perhaps he didn't even notice that I'd intentionally skipped contacting him.

During the night I wasn't sure why I'd done it, but after spending hours mulling possible reasons, I knew my instinct had been correct. Listening to just some of the indignities and hardships Dilly had been through, I knew I could never really make up for allowing her life to get to such a point. Those wounds that had been created weren't yet toughened into scars; they weren't even healed over and might never be. She would, no doubt, struggle with such memories the rest of her life. She'd said as much last night.

So I couldn't leave her. I knew now I'd been right all along. And if I couldn't leave, the only option for Mac and me was for him to live here, too. In the Midwest. Something I knew, without a single doubt, could not happen.

How would I tell him? I hadn't nearly the experience Mac had at dating, but he'd always said he'd never break up with a woman on the telephone or, worse, in an e-mail. But what other option did I have? I couldn't go to LA and talk to him in person. Going back, being there with him again, being so far from Dilly, I might be talked into a selfish decision. I was determined to stay with my sister, but I knew my weakness for Mac could outweigh my determination to do what was best.

I'd have to call him, sooner or later. If not, certainly he would be calling me.

I tried working but accomplished little. Realizing it was useless, for the rest of the day I killed time as best I could—watering the flowers, walking to the grocery store. After I ate dinner and cleaned up the kitchen, I resorted to my mother's way of passing time, doing the crossword puzzle in the local paper. I wasn't ready to go back to the news shows just yet.

The phone rang and I leaped to answer it, then held back. As I glanced at the clock and saw it was eight o'clock, six o'clock LA time, I knew it would be Mac. He could have just got home from work, an early end to the workday.

I hovered over the desk, seeing his number pop up with caller ID. It rang again and again, all through my silent battle. If I didn't answer it, I could put off ending things.

But I couldn't stop myself. I picked up the receiver.

"Hi."

"Hey. I was starting to think you weren't there. Everything okay?"

"Yeah, fine."

"I got home around eleven last night," he said, his tone so normal I wanted to record it, have it permanently etched in my brain for those days in the future when I couldn't hear it anymore. But what a silly thought. Of course I would never forget. "Not as late as I thought it could go. Did you forget to call?"

"No. I didn't forget."

"Fall asleep?"

"No. I didn't fall asleep."

"Okay, what's up? You okay?"

"I'm okay."

"No, you're not. Why didn't you call?"

I should have rehearsed what I wanted to say. Instead, I'd thought about the consequences of telling him what I knew I had to tell him. Consequences like missing him, the conversations we shared, the memories we had. Like the loneliness that would come with not having him in my life. I thought about how it wouldn't change his life all that much, because he hadn't gotten out of the practice of dating. Knowing he'd genuinely cared about some of the other women he dated in the past would show him love could come again, and in all likelihood would, once he let go of me.

But none of those thoughts had brought me any comfort, then or now, and none helped me decide how to begin.

"Hannah?"

His gentle prompt made tears spring to my eyes, hot and stinging. I sucked in a breath of air, hoping it would steady me, clear my brain. But it didn't. "I . . . can't really talk right now, Mac. I'm right in the middle of . . . an investment return timeline. Can I call you back?"

"No." More firmly now, any trace of the lighthearted tone he usually spoke with gone. "What's wrong?"

"Nothing," I assured him emptily.

"That's not true. I know it isn't; you know it isn't. I've been reading your voice for years."

It was true; he was right. He was always right. But I still couldn't speak.

"Something's up," Mac was saying through my thoughts. "Tell me what."

He'd begun the conversation for me, simple as that. All I needed was to be honest. The very trait he'd come to desire lately.

"Something happened yesterday, Mac. Something that made me

rethink this whole idea of us. I know that lately . . . lately it seemed like things were going really well for Dilly. It seemed like she's going to be okay, that her life is going into a good routine, one she could handle and still be part of Sierra's life."

"Yeah, that's true. It is. Isn't it?"

"Yesterday there was a news report about a woman right over in Springfield who killed her handicapped daughter."

I let that sink in, hearing him give a little groan.

"Dilly didn't take the news well. It brought up a lot of memories. Oh, Mac. I can't even tell you what she's been through, it's so awful. And now this whole thing seems like it's taken away the happiness I thought she was just getting back, since being with Sierra again."

"You can't control her happiness, Hannah, any more than you can control anything else in her life."

"I know."

A pause—long, awkward.

"So what does this have to do with us?"

I knew he'd ask that, but I hadn't been brave enough to prove I knew what he was thinking by saying it first. "I can't leave, Mac. I know it seems like she's a lot stronger, not afraid to ask for help. That she has my parents' support now and Sandee's and not even full care of Sierra. But she's not strong. I need to stay with her, to make sure these past few years in prison really are behind her, in her mind, too."

"She's not as needy as you seem to think."

"You didn't see her last night. Telling me things she'd gone through, how humiliating it was, how guilty she still feels, even with all that faith she says she has."

"Her faith is real, Hannah. Even when it looks shaky, it's there. I already know how that goes."

"You do? And how's that?"

"Whoa. Is this Hannah Williams? Asking me about faith this time?"

"If it relates to doubts, if you have them."

He sighed. "I don't have doubts. I just thought when I figured out there really is a God, if He really does love me, He'd fix my life the way I want it. I thought the same thing Dilly told us she believed, that her will and God's will would automatically be in sync. Naive, I know. But I'm learning. It's not my plan anymore; it's His."

"Maybe us together isn't part of the plan, Mac. Not with you there and me here."

"And you don't see that changing?"

I hesitated. What I wanted was to go back there; what I needed to do was stay here. "No."

"Then I'm coming there. This weekend."

"I don't—"

"No protests. I'm coming there, and you can't stop me. I have a Monday presentation I can't miss, but I can fly from Springfield to LaGuardia Sunday night."

"Mac—"

"No arguments, Hannah. If I'm going to be moving there, I'll need to assess things a little differently this visit. I knew it would be a possibility, but I'm not sure I was taking it seriously enough on my other visits."

"Mac—"

"Look, you've been there most of the summer. I think by now you'd know if there was any hope of your leaving anytime soon. You're telling me there isn't. We'll make plans this weekend, about how we're going to earn livings." His voice held none of the horror and uncertainty it should have held. He sounded eager, convinced. Back to being sure of himself. "We'll be partners again. We can do this."

"You're not thinking clearly," I said. "You've never lived in the Midwest, and what little time you've spent here has been quaint and appealing but not real. It only gets real when you've lived here month after month, seen the same crops grow, heard the same people talking about the same people, nothing to do, nothing to see, nowhere to go. I won't even talk about how long the winters are. It's not for you."

"It's kind of you to be concerned, but try not to make my decision for me before I've even had enough time to really consider it. I might fit in better than you think."

"You'll *never* fit in. You don't get to be a local just because you marry one. Do you want to know the official definition of a local? Your *grandmother* has to have been born here. You'll be miserable, and I won't take the responsibility for that. I won't."

Instead of listening, I could hear him laughing. "So now you're trying to control my happiness, too? Give it up, Hannah. I know I can't make a decision this big without serious consideration and time, so it makes sense to move up my trip. I'll see you Friday."

He hung up before I could say anything more.

# 23

FRIDAY APPROACHED slower than I expected. I should have been dreading his visit, knowing there had to be a way to show Mac he didn't belong here, couldn't possibly consider living here. He could wave at Cyd, spend time at the Coffee Spot, and chat with my parents, but none of that would disprove what I knew to be ultimately true: Mac was a city boy. The slow pace of country living would drive him crazy. How many folksy hot dog roasts could satisfy a man who preferred sushi? I could also mention to him what the hog farms around here did, and with nary a redwood to be found—or any forest, really—to balance the atmosphere. The landscape might be monotonously green, but lifestyles here were anything but.

I would demand he think of his career, and that would undoubtedly make him see reason. Unless he wanted to be traveling every single week instead of just a couple of times a month, this was not the place for him. And if he were traveling day in and day out, we might as well stay where we were, him in LA and me here.

My argument would work. It would work because it was valid.

But even as I came to such a conclusion, fully convinced I could prove him wrong and myself right, another part of me wanted something else. Part of me *did* want him to throw every caution aside, give up everything in proof of his love.

I knew such thoughts were foolish. In the long run, having Mac give up everything for me was not only illogical, it was no doubt the first step toward a greater heartache. How much worse would it be to face a divorce in the future than a good-bye now?

Dilly wasn't home when Mac arrived on Friday evening. She was at Sharon's. Mac and I could have gone to my parents' house for dinner, since my mother had issued the invitation when she found out he would be using the bunkhouse again this weekend. But I'd declined.

Providing Mac pleasant company to pass the time wasn't on my weekend agenda. I would feed him, but that was it. I intended to show him firsthand just how limited the options were around here.

He came in the front door, his smile so comfortable and familiar I had a hard time not reciprocating. When he set his briefcase aside, which I was mildly surprised he'd brought in from the car, he leaned closer for an obvious kiss. But I turned my face so that his lips landed on my cheek.

"The cold shoulder?" he asked with a grin.

"No, not cold. Realistic."

He laughed. "So if we were to get married, you wouldn't kiss me?"

I turned away without answering, and he followed me to the kitchen. I'd decided to make the typical meal served at the Coffee Spot or one that my mother might have made. There was no health craze around here. Fried chicken, thickly coated in breading, dripping with the grease in which it had been cooked. Potatoes fried in oil and butter. Coleslaw, heavy with mayonnaise instead of the light dressing I knew Mac preferred. Bread and butter, and the best beverage for my purpose: buttermilk. (I hated the stuff.) For dessert, fried apple fritters awaited, to be served with cream. Whipped with sugar, of course.

I predicted it would take no less than a week to rid my stove of all the grease and batter speckles this meal left behind.

I wondered if he noticed the artery-clogging oil sheen that came with his plate after I piled it with food.

"This looks . . . filling," he said.

"Better get used to it if you want to eat around here. People do lots of manual labor. That means lots of carbs."

Instead of replying, he covered one of my hands with his. "Is that what you plan to do this weekend, Hannah? Convince me I'd hate living here?"

I nodded. No sense denying it.

"What if I said I've been thinking about things since our phone conversation the other day? that I've decided to really consider *all* the ramifications of moving here?"

"I'd say that was a good idea." Such a statement was the beginning of reason over emotion.

He set aside his napkin. "You know what I've been doing all week? Preparing the strategy for the Liddington account. I'm presenting in New York on Monday. It's good, Hannah." He leaned forward, and I saw something in his eyes I'd seen a million times before when we were working together. "I'm ready for it, and all I have to do is set it out in front of them. They'll go for it; I know they will."

I believed him. I'd seen it happen before.

"My work this week reminded me how hard it would be to go independent, with limited access to more of the kind of accounts I have right now."

I stared at him. None of his words matched the assurance and hope for the future all over his face.

He watched me through a pause, then leaned forward again. "But here's the thing: I'm still willing to consider moving here." When I started shaking my head, he put up a palm to stop me. "Listen. If we want to be together the rest of our lives, we have to work this out. One of us is going to have to see the other's way through this. So—" he patted my hand once—"you know what my agenda is this weekend? To convince you to come home, to California. We *both* have to consider moving, Hannah."

I sat back in my chair, pulling my hand from his and folding my arms. But he didn't sit in front of me long enough to read whatever body language I was sending his way. He pushed back his chair and left the table, telling me over his shoulder to wait for him. In a moment he was back, his briefcase in hand. He placed it on the other end of the table, opening it and pulling out something wrapped in stiff, colorful paper. He handed it to me.

The paper wasn't sealed, so it came away easily. I held a small glass globe, filled with sand and tiny seashells.

"I thought you might be missing the ocean by now. I was going to wait and give it to you for Christmas, when you're knee-high in ice and snow around here. Something told me not to wait."

I tumbled the globe in my palm, watching the sand alternately bury, then reveal the little shells inside. It was an authentic piece of the ocean I'd left behind, the ocean I loved to walk beside. The ocean that was like me—sometimes the waves danced with happiness, but most often it was calm, a calmness some might mistake for monotony. I knew, though, there were all sorts of moods waiting to roll in, never the same for long, sometimes rippling just beneath the surface.

Even as I gripped the cool glass, instantly loving it, I looked up at him. "But I told you, Mac. I can't come back."

He pulled me from my chair at the table, taking the globe from my hand and setting it on the paper beside my plate. Then he put his arms around me. "I'm not asking for a decision right now, Hannah. Just don't count out anything. Not even coming back."

But I already had.

The telephone rang and instinctively I reached for my cell next to the bed. I opened it, knowing it could only be Mac at such an unusual hour. But when I answered, the telephone rang again. A real ring, not the tune I associated with Mac. I had the wrong phone.

Why would he be calling me now, and on the landline? Even in my groggy state I realized we were in the same time zone, at least for today and most of tomorrow.

I fumbled past my clock radio, in the process pushing my cell phone to the floor.

"Hello?"

"Hannah, it's Mom. Dad needs Dilly here right away, and you better come too. We can't get hold of Beacon or Ed. I called your uncle Steve, and he's on his way."

I sat up, pulse pounding before my eyes were even wide-open. "What's happened? Is Dad okay?"

"Something's wrong out in one of the sheds. Your dad heard the hogs making some kind of ruckus as soon as he came down this morning. He went to check and came back only long enough to tell me to call for help, but I haven't got much to give him yet. Could you wake Dilly?"

"I'll get her, Mom. We'll be out there as soon as we can."

"Better hurry."

I threw off the covers, knowing I didn't have time for a shower even though I'd no doubt be seeing Mac, too. He wouldn't sleep through car arrivals and any kind of commotion in the sheds, merely yards from the bunkhouse screens.

I went to Dilly's room. She was already stirring. It was almost the time she'd be getting up anyway.

"Did I hear the phone?" she asked just as I opened the door.

"Yeah, it was Mom. Something's going on out in the sheds, and they want both of us out there. Better get dressed."

I followed my own advice, choosing old jeans and a T-shirt—a must if I was going to be of any help inside the hog sheds.

We were out on the farm in less than fifteen minutes, which I thought impressive. The sun was already casting a pink glow on the horizon, but all the lights in the kitchen, porch, and lane were still on. I eyed the bunkhouse, but there was no light coming from there. Perhaps Mac was still asleep.

I headed toward the kitchen in search of Mom while Dilly scrambled from the car straight to the sheds. I found my mother on the telephone.

"No, Nora, tell him to stay home. He won't be any help with a broken arm." A pause. "Yes, you tell him thanks anyway and to stop out later after Dieter figures out how it happened. Yes. Okay. Bye, then."

Nora was Beacon's wife, the man who took care of the hogs if Mom and Dad ever needed help. He'd once told Cyd to install a beacon on his tower to warn drivers when he was on the lookout for speeders (having been caught doing that very thing himself), but Cyd had refused, saying such a warning would defeat the purpose. Cyd had called him Beacon ever since, and the name had spread.

"Beacon has a broken arm?"

"Happened yesterday afternoon, Nora said. Fell off the roof at home repairing some shingles." Mom was at the kitchen door then, and I would have followed her out, but I heard the water running in the bathroom. I assumed it was my father.

"Dilly went out to the shed. She thought Dad was out there."

"He is."

"Then who—"

Mac stepped into the kitchen, fully dressed in jeans and a blue cotton shirt. He sent all of his shirts to the cleaners, both work and casual if they were cotton, so they sported similar crisp fold creases. I immediately made up my mind to keep him away from the sheds, no matter what the trouble was out there.

"Good morning," he said, coming to my side. He refrained from much contact, except for a brief caress of my arm. "I heard the noise from the sheds about a half hour ago, but I'm sorry to say I thought it was normal. Your mom says there's trouble; I'm ready to help."

I would have laughed and said, *No, you're most definitely not,* except it would have hurt his feelings. I didn't think *I* could be much help, and I'd grown up with the sheds out back. What did he think he could do, especially dressed that way?

"That would be great," my mother said. I'd been too slow while squelching my first reaction. She hurried out the door and we followed.

"What's the trouble?" I asked as Mom led us toward the second shed. I already heard the squealing, definitely louder than usual.

"A couple of slats broke and some of the hogs fell in. We don't know how many are down there."

I nearly stopped dead, but I didn't want to alarm Mac any more than necessary.

My mother stepped up her pace. "I'll see if I can find coveralls for both of you. You can wear Beacon's, Mac, but he's not much taller than Dieter, I'm afraid."

I stopped and pulled Mac to my side, letting my mother continue without us. "Mac, maybe you ought to stay out here."

He tilted his head to one side, brows drawn. "You think I can't handle this?"

"I can pretty much guarantee you've never smelled anything like it."

He grinned. "You've never been inside a guys' locker room. Now come on."

The stench was already present, with no wind on this early morning, but I knew this was nothing compared to the pit. I could still recall helping out as a kid when my dad pumped the contents out to the "honey wagon" twice a year to fertilize crops. The smell lingered on our skin for days, and all the town kids at school would call Dilly or me names, depending on who helped, because it was impossible to wash away.

My mother produced only one jumpsuit and a pair of rubber boots, all of which she offered to Mac. The coveralls were made of heavy, dark canvas and weren't exactly pristine on the outside but were clean enough on the inside. Mac's forearms were left exposed; so were the bottoms of his jeans and his white leather jogging shoes. I found myself praying Beacon had big feet before I even realized what I was doing.

He didn't. Mac couldn't get one boot on.

"You can use them, then," Mom said, handing me the boot she still held. "At least you'll have something."

"That's okay. I don't care about these clothes." I handed the boot back to Mac. "If you take off your shoes, it'll probably fit. Believe me, it's worth a try." I had access to my full wardrobe for replacement; Mac didn't.

He nodded and slipped his shoeless feet into the boots. Soon we were climbing the three stairs at the back of the building. Despite the furled-back screen covers and the fans on full blast, this was the source of the stench. It wasn't any worse in here than it was outside, at least on this end. Hogs nearby looked up at us, eyes wide, squealing nervously at the uncommonly close quarters and no doubt at all of the unexpected company. Despite not liking confinement hog farming, I'd learned to begrudgingly respect my father for never overcrowding the pens, using the least amount of drugs to keep them healthy, and receiving piglets who were allowed six weeks instead of the minimum three before taking them from the sow. Pigs that lived less stressfully produced tastier meat, so he always said.

Mom opened the nearest gate and I let Mac go in before me so I could clasp it behind us. To his credit he didn't hesitate, despite being immediately surrounded by two-hundred-pound hogs who came to see who we were.

I slipped around Mac, gently kneeing snouts away. My father and Dilly weren't at first visible, but I heard the commotion in the far corner. The area had been cleared of pigs, revealing two missing cement slats. And there, sprawled out on the remaining slats, were my father and Dilly, hands and arms out of sight beneath them. The squeal of at least one hog was deafening, and suddenly I saw why. My father had one frantic pig by the ears, and Dilly had a back hoof.

Mac plopped between them and I watched as something must have overtaken him, something that certainly hadn't been born or bred on the California coast, except perhaps as a need to save something alive. He grabbed the nearest hoof and between the three of them they yanked the animal up over the edge, nearly landing on Mac's lap. The pig lay there heaving, barely squealing now, and my father came behind me, hose in hand, and tossed the nozzle to me. He went back to the hole in the floor, and I opened the nozzle to a gentle spray. In the process of rinsing the filth off the animal, I spattered some of it on myself.

"How many are down there?" Mac asked. His breathing was

tense, as if he didn't want to inhale but had no choice. Whatever had possessed him to get that hog to safety appeared gone, and for a moment I thought he might heave. But he didn't.

"We don't know yet." My father was leaning over again. His reach couldn't be nearly as long as Mac's, who joined him. "Get that light on 'em again, Sooz," he yelled to my mother. "Hannah, go out to the machine shed and get the other beam from under my bench. Make sure it's working first, then come back."

I went to follow orders, with a last glance at Mac. He, like my father and sister, was bent over the six-foot-long, three-foot-wide opening, peering down into a pit of hog manure.

# 24

THE FLASHLIGHT had dead batteries, so it took twice as long as it should have to return after finding replacements. I rejoined them in time to see another hog pulled from below, my father on one end, Mac on the other.

"It would make more sense to get down there and push them up from below," I heard Mac say just as he swung his legs over the side.

"No!"

The word came from all of us at the same time, but from me the loudest. I ran forward, the heavy flashlight falling from my hands.

"I'm the only one tall enough—"

"The fumes'll kill you, boy," my father said. "Stay right where you are."

Mac looked at the pit, then at my father and finally at me. I'm not sure he believed my father's words until he saw my face, which I was sure held stark horror. And it had nothing to do with the image of him swimming in manure. It had everything to do with the memory of the Pepperwells. They'd lost their father when he'd gone into a pit too soon after pumping it out to hose it clean.

"Why isn't it killing the hogs down there?" Mac asked, shifting once again with his legs straight out behind him.

"You don't want to take any chances," Dilly said. "See that one? Mom, shine the light over there."

My mother's flash went in the direction of Dilly's finger, and I moved close enough to add my own light to it. There, floating in the wake of a hog thrashing by, was the carcass of another. It could have drowned from fatigue, but it might have been the deadly methane from decaying fecal matter.

I held my light steady as the three of them—my father, Dilly, and Mac—waited until a pig flailed by. Most often it would be Mac who would grab an ear to stop the frantic hog. A new panic overcame the animal at the slightest touch, setting off a deafening squeal, but I knew it was the only way to save them. The drenched hog would wrench and fight, and slippery hands would lose him, only to have another grab what could be grabbed.

There was no more time for talk, no time for fatigue. They hauled another up, then another. Dilly and I took turns with the light and with rinsing; my mother held her light steady. It was only Mac and Dad who could manage to lift the animals over the edge, while Dilly or I would latch on to what we could to settle the agitated pig and keep it from falling back in once they neared the upper edge.

Uncle Steve came, and he and I and Dilly worked on the other side of the hole. When someone had a chance at grabbing any portion of a hog, the others rushed forth to assist. I stopped counting after ten hogs were pulled out.

We could save only those that came under us. My light more than once flickered on a few hogs at the other end, too far away for us to reach. At last my father turned off all the lights, even though by now the sun had risen. Despite the circulation it offered, he ordered the curtain siding closed, so the only lights were ours, the strong beams from the flashlights. Pigs began swimming toward the light.

Tired hogs were easier to pull up than frenzied ones, but getting them close enough to grab remained a problem for many. Dilly and I went to the other end with lights and sticks, shoving them through the slats in the hope of scaring them toward our end. It worked with a couple, but soon the light revealed no hogs moving of their own accord.

I had no idea what time it was, only that the sun had been up a long time. I imagined exhaustion was taking hold of Mac, too, and his back had to be hurting from all that lifting. He was even filthier than I; manure seemed to cover him from hair to boot. I knew once any remnant of adrenaline was gone the details of what he'd been doing these past several hours would sink in. Once he got over the loss of life, he'd be disgusted at least, sickened at worst. He wasn't used to this kind of environment. I made up my mind to take him over to Sandee's brother-in-law, who was a doctor.

"There's no more we can do from up here," my father was saying.

"But there might be some left alive down there," Dilly said. "How can we hear with the racket the rest of the hogs are making? I think—"

My father was already shaking his head. "We can't do more today. Bring the honey wagon around, Dil. We'll pump out what's down there and count the losses."

I went to Mac's side. "We might as well get cleaned up. My dad and Dilly don't need our help with the pump. Do you, Dad?"

"No."

I led Mac away, wishing my father would send a thank-you out with us but knowing he wouldn't. I walked toward the gate and the door beyond, seeing the rest of the hogs, sensing their stress was lessened but still present. As I looked down at the slats, I wondered how many hogs were still down there.

I closed my eyes, refusing to dwell on it.

"Mind if I get in that shower first, Susie?" my uncle asked my mother once we were outside.

She looked at me and I nodded. I guessed Mac and I would survive another twenty minutes. We could use the machine shed hose to remove the worst beforehand anyway.

My mother went inside the house to find Uncle Steve some clean clothes to wear on his way home. Uncle Steve wasn't nearly as tall as Mac, but he was definitely stockier than my father. I was curious to see what she came up with that could possibly fit.

"There's another hose over here," I said, leading the way to the far side of the machine shed. I found the hose and attached a nozzle so I could control the force of the spray.

Mac and I went to a grassy spot in the sun. I knew the water would be cold, but there was nothing to be done about that. At least the day was warm.

I was grateful for the task because no matter how hard I tried, I found it impossible to make eye contact with Mac. It wasn't that I was distressed about the loss of life we'd just experienced, although I was. But to my shame, my inability to look Mac in the eye was because of embarrassment. Not over my filth; his was worse than mine. But over the fact that the filth was part of my family's business, and if it weren't for me, Mac would never have had to go through these past few hours.

He offered to hose me down first, and I let him, wishing I could laugh at the joke he made about writing to the guy on cable who investigated all of the dirtiest jobs in the world. Instead, I welcomed the water he held over my head as it ran through my hair, down my face, over my shoulders. Mac wouldn't be able to tell my warm tears apart from the cold water pouring down my cheeks.

He handed me the hose and pulled off the rubber boots. I could tell he was intent on the job of getting clean; he barely even looked at me. I made a quick rinse of him in the coveralls, but he took those off too. I couldn't reach to put the hose over his head, so he bent over and I sprayed his hair much as he'd done for me.

At last I twisted the nozzle and the water stopped. I turned away, dropping the hose, shivering once. Mac had his back to me, the heavy cotton and thick denim molded to his body. The worst of the muck was gone, but I knew the smell would linger. His jeans were probably a total loss. Such heavily soiled fabric would never be the same.

"We can go in the basement and use the shower spigot down there; that's where my dad showers every day."

Mac was making himself busy by brushing water from his thighs, but he still hadn't turned around. I was proud of myself. Despite knowing today had no doubt proven to Mac what I'd known all along—that he couldn't and shouldn't consider living around here—my tears had shut off much the same as I'd turned off the hose. This day had served my purpose as no other activity could.

But not having Mac able to look at me threatened to demand I face the coming loss right away.

"Mac—"

He turned his head so I could see his profile, and when I moved to walk around him, he reached out an arm and caught me around the middle.

"Don't move, Hannah. Just stay behind me, will you?"

"You can't even look at me after this? I know you must absolutely hate the idea of living anywhere near a hog farm right now—"

"Shut up." He laughed lightly. I'd always hated those words. My mother had taught us they were the equivalent of swear words, which I'd told Mac before, and so he usually refrained from using them. But that they came with a laugh confused me.

"Excuse me?"

"I can't look at you right now. I *want* to, believe me. But your shirt's all wet and I know that's not your bathing suit you've got on and—just trust me, I'm trying to do the right thing for once in my life. I'll go in the bunkhouse for some clean clothes while you shower. Then, after you're done, I'm going inside for my own real shower. Am I supposed to go in through the kitchen? I saw your uncle go around the house."

My mind was still trying to sort through what had just happened. He wasn't angry over how he'd had to spend this Saturday? Disgusted? Instead he was struggling with . . . lust?

"You should go in the basement door. It's just around the corner where my uncle went in, you'll see it. I'm not sure Uncle Steve is finished yet, though."

I followed Mac around the machine shed and he moved closer to the bunkhouse. Uncle Steve and Aunt Elsie were just coming down the kitchen door stairway. He was dressed in his own clean clothes and she was carrying a sack, no doubt his soiled clothes to be laundered. They each went to their own cars as Mac and I approached.

"I'll use the shower first," I said. "Give me ten minutes, okay?"

He nodded, and I stopped short, remaining behind him and out of his line of vision.

"And . . . Mac?" There was one more thing I needed to warn him about, if he was already struggling to keep his mind as pure as a baby's. "The shower in the basement. It's completely open—not a bathroom. It's just a spigot from a pipe in the rafter and a drain on the cement floor. No doors."

He moaned. "Great. Now I have to fight with myself not to go in nine minutes after you instead of ten."

I knew I shouldn't have laughed. Making light of this awful day was the last thing either one of us should be doing. Wasn't he seeing that if the other things he'd witnessed lately were miracles— the moon, his own transformed interests, his new quest for truth— then today's event couldn't be discounted as a miracle, either? Something God had timed to teach Mac just how horrible farm life could be?

But here I was, suddenly lighthearted because Mac was struggling to keep his mind pure—about me. Talk about miracles . . .

He went inside the bunkhouse and I hurried to the basement. The cellar was on the other side of the house and this was a section set off exclusively for my father. In summer or winter, he came in here to clean up before stepping into the rest of my mother's clean house. There was a shelf of strong soap, cheap shampoo, and plenty of towels along with my father's clean clothes. Thankfully for me, Dilly now had a shelf full of her own, and I chose a pair of her old jeans and a clean T-shirt.

When I went upstairs, my mother was cooking and I wished I could smell something other than the lingering scent of manure. It seemed to be in my nostrils, in my hair follicles, in my pores, all so deep no soap, no matter how potent, could reach.

"I still stink," I said to my mother as I took a seat at the kitchen table.

· She nodded, and part of me wished she wouldn't have agreed so easily. "You know how it is, Hannah. Every time your father cleans the pit and fertilizes, it takes a few days for him to air out. And this is worse than that."

"Wonderful. Just wonderful."

Mac had a nasty surprise in store. *Mac!* I popped from my chair and it nearly toppled behind me. Thoughts exploded, and a new rush of adrenaline shot through my veins. He was due back in New York on Monday morning. *The Liddington account proposal!*

I needed to share my horror with Mac. I ran from the kitchen, ignoring my mother's call following me. But the bunkhouse was already empty, and by the time I returned to the kitchen, I heard the downstairs spigot open and water rush through the pipes.

"What's wrong?" my mother asked as I came in. She'd followed me to the door, probably to see where I'd been headed, but now she went back to the stove, where she was frying toasted cheese sandwiches for a late lunch. None of us had eaten all day.

"I—I need to talk to Mac about something. He has a really important meeting on Monday, Mom. How's he supposed to meet with a bunch of people who've never left the city if he stinks like a manure pit?" I found myself at the threshold to the laundry room door, on the other side of which was the basement door. But I backed away, turning around and walking to the kitchen table, then toward the door and back again, needing to use this sudden burst of energy or I would surely explode.

Mom turned from the oven, wiping her hands on her apron. "Now, Hannah, don't be worrying about something you can't control. How bad can it be? It's not as if he's going to be sidling up close to these people, is it? And there is such a thing as cologne, you know. It'll be just fine."

I didn't stop moving. "Cologne? You mean cover up one over-powering scent with another? What a mix that'll be!"

"Don't go worrying about tomorrow. You know what the Bible says about not borrowing trouble."

I wanted to shake the Pollyannaish naiveté right out of her. I started pacing again. This was all my fault. If Mac didn't get to present this account, Stan, his boss—my former boss—would demand that Mac send his presentation to the new junior partner, Brian. And worse, if Brian did a halfway decent job, the Liddington decision maker might decide Brian could do the job without Mac.

I rubbed my forehead, wishing I'd insisted Mac not come to the Midwest. I'd tried to tell him, but I could have been more persuasive. I could have suggested he come *after* this trip to New York. Why hadn't I?

The door to the basement squeaked, and I heard it open, then close. A moment later Mac entered through the laundry room door. There he stopped, holding up his wet jeans. "Is there any possibility of getting this washed before I leave tomorrow?"

"Leave them on the floor with the rest of the clothes, Mac," my mother said. "I'll see to it right after we eat. You must be starving!"

I glared at my mother and her normal tone of voice.

Mac disappeared back behind the basement door, and when he returned, I met him at the doorway to the kitchen. "Mac," I whispered, staring at him so intently he eyed me curiously, "what about your proposal on Monday?"

He was dressed in a pair of light cotton shorts and another immaculately pressed shirt, this one green. Despite his squeaky-clean appearance, I knew he still stunk just like me. "What about it?" His gaze was on the stove. "You're right about being starving, Mrs. Williams."

"Good, then sit right down. We have sandwiches and pickles and macaroni salad. And chips, too, with some iced tea to wash it all down. Have a seat."

"I didn't think I'd ever be hungry again after the filling meal Hannah served last night," he said with a wink my way. "But here I am, on empty again."

My mother laughed. "You can't expect to work hard all morning and not get hungry. Here you go." She handed him a full plate, the bread perfectly toasted.

I sat next to him, but as I was about to share my gloom and

doom, my mother pushed the iced tea pitcher closer to me. Automatically, I filled his glass and then my own. "Mac, there's something you need to think about. I know you've had a shower, and you're wearing clean clothes. But can't you still smell it?"

He frowned my way. "We're just about to eat, Hannah. Maybe we can relive this morning another time."

"No, listen to me. You still stink. And you'll probably stink all week. You're going to be in an enclosed boardroom on Monday with a bunch of people who won't know what a hog farm smells like until they get near you. Good grief, Mac, you might not even make it to New York if they don't let you on the plane!" I stood, unable to sit still. Tears heated my eyes.

Instead of joining me in my fears, Mac leaned over his plate and started eating. "I'm not going to push the panic button yet, Hannah. I'm too hungry." Halfway into another bite, his brows lifted. He put down the sandwich, sat back in his seat, and looked at me with a grin. "How about we do what you do every time you cut onions?"

I sat beside him, catching on. I hated the way my hands smelled after slicing onions, but I had yet to find an automatic slicer that I liked. Hope stirred in my heart. "Lemons?"

Mac nodded, then looked at my mother. "Hannah rubs lemons into her hands after she slices onions and it gets rid of that smell. Think it'll work?"

"It won't hurt to try. And what about tomatoes?" My mother was clearly eager to believe the best, but then she always did that. I just didn't know Mac could be the same way about something this important. "Don't they say tomatoes get rid of skunk odors? You can try that."

"We'll try both," Mac said. Obviously he wasn't bowing easily to my dire predictions.

As much as it went against my nature to join them in their wishful thinking, I needed to believe it would work too. For Mac's sake. "We can look online to see if we can find any more advice there."

With that little bit of hope I decided I could eat after all. And then I'd not only take him to Sandee's brother-in-law for whatever kind of shot he thought a city person should have after such exposure, we'd go into town and buy every lemon and tomato we could find.

# 25

BY SATURDAY night Mac had soaked in a bathtub full of water and lemon juice, another of crushed tomatoes, and a third of apple cider vinegar. Finally we wrapped him in wet newspapers that were supposed to absorb whatever smell remained. While he sat in the tub of dripping newspapers, I'd called Sandee's brother in law, who assured me Mac should be fine if all of his immunizations were up-to-date.

His hair was dried out from all the concoctions we'd used, but the last bit of my favorite conditioner took care of that. Between the vinegar and the tomatoes, he smelled faintly of a salad, but that was far preferable to the way he'd smelled earlier. The way I still smelled.

After one last shower, Mac's skin was so raw from his scrubbing that he looked as if he'd spent the day at the beach instead of hovering over a manure pit. Which was why we were spending the evening in the bathroom with my most expensive lotion and a container of baby powder in hand. This mix was the last in our arsenal.

This day had been the perfect cap to my side of our argument— an argument I needed to stir up just now for more reasons than one. Because Mac had set the tone earlier, I'd been able to laugh with him while we'd filled the bath with various concoctions. But now we were quiet, sharing the tube of lotion. The skin on his back was smooth and taut, slippery beneath my touch. Since I knew there was absolutely no way Mac could live here, there was also no way I should allow myself to enjoy this task as much as I was. His skin would never be mine to tend.

"It's not as if I'd be taking up hog farming," he reminded me for the tenth time. "I'd still do what I do, just from here instead of New York or LA."

"I told you, Mac, you'd still have to meet face-to-face with clients the way you do now. You'd be traveling so much it wouldn't matter where you lived, except for the airfare costs. It doesn't make sense."

"I'll tell you what doesn't make sense," he said, handing me the tube of lotion again. "Me living two thousand miles away from you. We have to work this out, Hannah. If we can't—"

He stopped himself, and I wanted to ask him what he would have said. But there was only one area of his body left to cover in lotion. He'd slathered his own arms and legs, but now his chest remained. In such tight and intimate quarters it was impossible not to want to keep going, to minister to spots we both knew he could reach. I knew he was contemplating the image just as I was.

Gently he took the tube away from me. "I think I can take care of the rest."

His voice was soft, tempting me to resist, but I knew he was right. He wanted to do the right thing because of his newfound faith, and I certainly understood that. But I knew we also had to do the right thing because it made the most sense.

"I'll wait in the living room," I whispered, then slipped out of the room.

It was late, well past eleven, and Dilly was already in bed. We'd been trying one remedy after another for the better part of four hours, most of the time Mac saying he could still smell the manure. I kept assuring him it must be me he smelled, and he'd started believing me after spraying a saline solution up his nostrils. That seemed to clear his sense of smell, at least for a while.

I stood in the living room, thinking Mac was probably hesitant to go back to the farm, even if only to sleep in the relatively clean bunkhouse. I wouldn't blame him if he was; it was so close to the sheds and there was no wind tonight to carry away the scent. But I doubted he would stay at my house, even if I ignored my own better judgment and asked.

"Guess I'll head out to your parents' house," he said as he came up behind me.

I was staring out at the darkness through my front windows, seeing nothing, trying not to dwell on all my gloomy thoughts. Even ones I wanted to dwell on seemed gloomy, like Mac loving me. It wasn't so wonderful when I was convinced of what was ahead.

He took my hand, leading me to the door. "You don't smell half-bad yourself anymore," he said with a grin.

"Half-bad?"

He took me in his arms, kissing me soundly.

"Thank you for worrying enough about me to do everything you did to help me," he said. "It's been an interesting day."

"Interesting as in the old Chinese curse?"

Mac laughed. "I love you, Hannah."

# 26

AFTER MAC left, I drew my own bath. I didn't bother with the tomatoes or the newspaper method. But I did soak in cider vinegar and followed that with a lathering shower of Lava soap, ending my treatment with lotion and baby powder. By the time I slipped into my bed, I was hopeful I wouldn't stink up the sheets.

In the morning, Dilly told me she would be borrowing Mom's car to drive herself to church rather than tagging along in my car. It meant taking three cars all the way to Springfield, but Dilly needed to return right after the service to spend time with Sierra. She knew Mac would have part of the afternoon free before going to the airport and didn't want me to cut that short to bring her home.

I should have argued. I should have told her it would be just as well if Mac and I did limit our time together. But I couldn't.

At church, we sat in the uppermost balcony, in a corner fewer people chose when it wasn't too crowded. As I sat on the cushioned seat, I knew whatever smell lingered on us wouldn't have been viewed as odd or unusual by many of those attending. Farms of all kinds surrounded Springfield. I wanted to say I belonged here, but even as I contemplated the notion of belonging anywhere, I did find myself glad to be here. Not in Springfield, but here, in this church. Here I could admit it wasn't that I'd doubted God's existence. I'd never done that. I'd just doubted His goodness. His love for me. I still did. I even doubted His love for Dilly and especially for Sierra, even though Dilly didn't seem to. How could she not doubt it, knowing how hard life was for her daughter?

Eyeing Mac, knowing it would be all wrong for us to be together, I couldn't help wondering again why a good God would have allowed us to want something that so obviously couldn't work. *Why, Lord? Are You having some kind of joke on us? Or do You just not care at all?*

The music shifted and a vocalist came under a spotlight. My mind drifted back to the God I'd known growing up, the one who judged everything I did, made sure I had no fun. The one who gave me to parents who I didn't think loved me, at least not as much as they loved rules, work, and others outside our family. I wondered if everyone remembered the disappointments in their childhood more readily than good things or if it was just my own pessimistic nature. I wondered if I should let God define Himself for me instead of letting my childhood memories define Him.

Then I heard Dilly on one side of me and Mac on the other. They snickered. Curiosity piqued, I tried to figure out what they found so amusing. When the vocalist sang the chorus for a second time, I understood. He was singing about the filth on the prodigal child, and I knew they'd found the connection funny. The song was about the son who'd turned his back on his father only to end up wallowing with the pigs.

I didn't laugh, though. I felt too much like that prodigal.

We found Lana and her father in the lobby, and Mac was comfortable enough with Walter to ask him outright if he could smell anything on him. At first Walter joked about cigarette smoke or some illegal substance, but when he assured Mac he had only the faintest odor of earth and vinegar and apples, we knew our efforts hadn't been in vain. There was little fear he'd be banished from the airplane, and no more worries about offending anyone in the boardroom.

Mac put his arm around me even as he looked at Walter. "I'd ask you and Lana to brunch but I have a date with Hannah," he said. "It's part of my ulterior motive to woo her back to California."

"Might as well make a reservation back to LA right now," Walter said to me. "I don't know how you're going to resist the charm from this fella."

I didn't know how to respond, taking a quick glance Dilly's way. Apparently she didn't find the topic funny either.

We chatted a little more, eventually leaving the church. Mac's "ulterior motive" to woo me was soon clear. In the car, he held my hand and told me how pretty I looked in the color of my blouse. He told me with a grin how good I smelled. He said he'd been looking forward to being alone with me all morning.

When we reached the restaurant, we were directed to a booth and Mac slipped in next to me. We ordered our meals, and he soon had me laughing and teasing and enjoying the intimacy of our shared history. It was, by far, the most wondrous date I'd ever been on.

Somehow I managed to ignore what I knew was best, simply because the moment, the here and now, was too good to give up. But when we were silent long enough for such cautions to invade my thoughts, I couldn't help but contemplate what troubled me. Maybe I really had been angry at a God of my own definition, not the One that actually existed.

While we waited for the check, I said as much to Mac.

He nodded. "I know I have a lot of learning to do as far as the Bible goes, but it seems to me you have some forgetting to do. Forget the rules that drove you away from God. Start over."

"I'd love to," I admitted. "I'm just not sure how. Not around here, anyway."

He took a last sip of his coffee. "I don't get it, Hannah. Ever since I've known you, you've talked about your family as if they're judgmental peasants, and now I find out they're good people. Hardworking, smart, honest. They don't seem so bad to me."

"They've always put rules ahead of us, me and Dilly."

"Maybe they thought that's what kids need: direction, instruction."

"They put the rules in front of themselves, too."

"Okay, I agree they might be a little hung up on the way things *should* be. But they love you. They want what's best for you and Dilly."

I shrugged, unconvinced. The bill was delivered, Mac stuck his credit card into the padded folder, and the waiter took it with him.

I wanted to talk about something else, return to the lightness we'd enjoyed during the meal. But even as I longed for that, I had a sudden image of my mother. How many times had I silently accused her of being an ostrich? sticking her head in the sand and enjoying life, enjoying my stern, unloving father as if nothing in the world were wrong?

For me to sit here and pretend this was a date, one more step toward something permanent, was just as ostrichlike as anything my mother had done.

Mac's credit card was returned, and we left the booth and went to Mac's rental. The serious mood between us lingered. I guessed he wanted to say more and I wished he wouldn't, but I knew him too well to think he'd ignore something just because it was comfortable to do so. *He* wasn't an ostrich.

He didn't even put the key in the ignition. He turned to me instead. "Maybe your perception of God isn't the only thing you should look at, Hannah. Maybe your perception of things around here isn't really the way things are."

"My perception?" I shook my head. "If anyone's perception of things around here is off, it's yours, Mac—if you're still thinking you might live here."

He leaned back on the cushioned headrest, a puff of air escaping his lips. "You don't want to live here any more than I do. Knowing that is driving me crazy. These last few years of your life haven't been all that easy. You were worried about Dilly—"

"With good reason."

"Yes. You've been working so hard to make it all right for her, but now I'm not sure you're seeing the whole picture."

I felt my back stiffen despite the soft seat, and I shifted to face him fully. "What do you think I'm missing?"

He paused and I could tell he carefully considered his words. "I've been doing a lot of thinking, trying to figure out what's really keeping you here. You keep saying it's Dilly. She needs you. Okay, I can see you're convinced of that. Somehow you want to make up for letting things get so bad in the past. But don't you see, Hannah? We can't go back; we can't really make up for something that's finished. After something is already done wrong, all we can do is forgive."

I was tired of church talk. I didn't respond, and I didn't look at him.

"I have one question for you, Hannah. Is it really just Dilly keeping you here?"

Now I had to look at him, I was so perplexed. "Why else do you think I need to stay here?" I lifted one brow. "For the hogs?"

He didn't even smile, although my attempted humor was admittedly bad. "Maybe what I should have asked was why you really left California."

"You don't think the answer would be the same for that question as it would be for the other?"

"You tell me."

I pretended to study one of my fingernails instead of looking at him. He'd always been too good at reading me, sometimes better than I could read myself. I might not be ready for the same soul-baring honesty he seemed to be demanding, but somehow I found words forming without taking the time to filter them. "What would you do if you'd had to watch me do all the dating you've done over the years? You were pretty imaginative in your reasons not to get serious. No one has ever measured up. Maybe I won't either."

Reaching over, he took one of my hands in his. When our eyes met again, I saw something I hadn't seen before. He was more than serious.

"Nobody ever measured up to *you*, Hannah. You were the standard. There was never any reason for you to leave California if you were afraid of becoming involved with me again. You've already measured up."

I shook my head, wanting to believe the words, but somehow it wasn't so easy.

"So maybe the other question should still be asked. What's keeping you here?"

"My sister needs—"

Now it was his turn to shake his head at me. "Maybe for now. A little while. Not forever. There's no reason to want me out of your life—unless you're choosing Dilly over me."

I shook my head. "It's not that. I don't know how long she'll need me. How can I keep you waiting indefinitely? And how could I leave her when she's been through so much?"

"She survived. She'll continue to survive without you."

I was still shaking my head. "She almost didn't, once. How can I take a chance again? No one around here helped before. Not my parents or her friends or our so-called wonderful little town." I heard the bitterness, and its intensity surprised me.

"Hmm. And here I thought you were the only one who let her down."

I pulled my hand from his, shifting forward. He put one hand on the steering wheel and one on the ignition but didn't turn the key.

"Think about this, Hannah. Maybe you don't like your little hometown because you're mad at it and everyone in it, including your parents. You're mad at everyone except Dilly, because she was the one who was let down. By everybody around her."

I didn't want to think anymore. Analyzing the situation wasn't going to change it.

The church parking lot was only a few minutes away. My car looked abandoned in the near-empty lot. I wanted to sit still, not leave Mac's side, or go back into the restaurant, relive the last hour of pretending. Laugh and tease and remember LA. I wanted to be on that date again.

Maybe I shouldn't have worked so hard to alleviate the stench on him. At least then I might have been allowed to hope he wouldn't leave.

Mac pulled me closer for a kiss, then smiled as if our last conversation hadn't taken place.

I stroked his cheek, studying his face. "I do love you, Mac. That's what makes this so hard. And this morning just makes it harder."

His smile dimmed.

"I'm sorry, Mac. I don't know what to say that I haven't already said."

"You could say you'll come back." He held my hand and rubbed his thumb across my skin. "I've loved you for seven years. Ever hear of the guy in the Old Testament named Jacob? He waited seven years for the girl he loved, then was tricked into marrying the wrong woman. He had to wait another seven—and he did."

I wanted to cling to such words, an indication that he loved me so much he'd be willing to wait so much longer. But I knew better. "You won't wait, and I can't expect you to. The only reason you've waited this long is because I was right there, either conveniently waiting or finagling my way back into your life every time you became bored with a date. If I hadn't been there you'd probably be happily married right now."

He shifted away, resting both his hands on the top of the steering wheel. "Maybe you're right, Hannah," he whispered.

But those were the last words I wanted to hear.

# Dilly

There's a blank sheet of paper in front of me.

Carla's letter *should* be the easiest one to write. It's certainly the first one I thought of doing, because she's in my spot. But here I am, suddenly wondering whether I'm crazy for thinking I can do somebody else any good.

I write a few words, but they're not good enough. I throw away that sheet, starting a new one on the lined pad on Hannah's desk, where I'm sitting.

Dear Carla,

You don't know me, but you might have heard about me from years ago. I was in the same place you are right now, facing a trial, not knowing the future.

I reread the words and decide to keep going. That's what I wanted back then—for somebody to tell me I'd survive. It couldn't be my mother or my sister; they didn't know any more than I did. It had to be somebody who'd been in my place. That's who I want to be to Carla.

It's hard, though, to give her support without supporting what she did. She succeeded where I failed, but my failure was the best thing I've ever done in my life. God gave me another chance to know Him, to figure out that He loves Sierra and loves me, too, and that He wants both of us to live this life in a better way. The best way we can, same as anybody else, with some happiness in between the struggles.

So a lot of my letter is practical advice about being in prison, about getting involved in a Bible study and keeping to that group so she can avoid trouble from other groups.

At the end of the page I'm not so happy with the letter but I know God wants me to send it. If it helps get Carla into the right group, maybe she'll have a chance to find peace after all.

# 27

DILLY DIDN'T hear from Carla Morelo after writing to her, but she didn't expect to, at least not while the woman was being held under suicide watch. That didn't, however, stop Dilly from writing to her again. And again.

She didn't stop there. She wrote to the defense team and to the prosecuting team, to the judge overseeing the case and to Carla Morelo's family. For someone who'd once told me she had a hard time communicating via letters, Dilly had turned into a letter-writing devotee.

I watched Dilly closer than ever, looking for signs that the campaign to help Mrs. Morelo demanded too high a toll. Every time I cautioned Dilly, I received the same shake of her head. "I'm fine," she'd tell me. "Just doing what I wish someone would have done for me. When you're understood, you're not alone."

I wasn't invited to read all of the letters Dilly wrote, but she did share the one she sent to the judge presiding over the case. In it, she admitted she didn't know Carla Morelo personally but did know the kind of challenges she faced. That life she knew intimately.

. . . I do not know how to briefly describe to you the difficulty of parenting a disabled child. It is like walking around every day with a broken heart. The worries are never ending—there is no escaping from the pain of knowing that your child suffers and that she always will. There is no "getting better"; there is only trying different medications, dealing with the side effects, doing more procedures and tests, using more equipment—always guessing at what is best because no one, not even the doctors, can tell you for sure.

It is also a cruel joke that children like mine and Carla Morelo's do not need very much sleep. When they do sleep, they cannot be left alone in their beds when they wake up. They have to be tended to be sure they are not having seizures. They cannot move like normal children, so you have to make sure they are safe and as comfortable as possible. They cannot reposition themselves like everyone does many times every night. They cannot call out for help if they need it. If you could imagine getting up literally every single night, month after month, year after year, you would see how this would wear on any person.

Add to Carla's life the sad wish of most parents of disabled children (even the parents that are not depressed): the hope that you will live only one day longer than your child so that you can make sure she is taken care of for her whole life. Because no one else will care for your child the way that she deserves.

There is pain in every direction, because you see your child suffer in life but that pain would be worse if she died, if you had to live without her.

Your Honor, I have been in the dark place that Carla was the night she killed her daughter. I wanted to crawl into a hole and just not be anymore. I heard on the news that Carla said she only wanted her child not to suffer and not to wake up. At one time I knew exactly what she meant.

Please forgive me for the length of this letter, and please forgive me for writing about myself. I know that Carla and I are two different people, but we have felt some of the same feelings. I know, too, that she must be punished for what she's done. But it's my hope and my prayer that you will take all of her circumstances into consideration. It's my understanding that Carla received little, if any, help in the care of her daughter. Perhaps if someone had reached out and seen her need, her child would still be alive.

When I read Dilly's letter, my guilt reared up again, but my pain was softened by one thing: the difference in these two cases. Sierra was still alive.

The day of the trial drew near and I knew Carla Morelo's defense team had invited Dilly to attend. As much as I didn't want to go, I knew I would accompany Dilly to the trial.

Despite my lack of sincere support, I smiled when she emerged from the bathroom on the morning we were to go. We'd gone shopping the day before, and she'd chosen a plain gray suit with an A-line skirt. I was so used to seeing her in shorts or blue jeans that she looked like someone else altogether. Someone much older, someone competent and responsible. Someone able to take care of herself.

"Now if I could just wear tennis shoes or work boots instead of these heels," she said.

I looked down at her feet. The heels couldn't have been more than an inch high, but to someone who hadn't worn dress shoes in years, I suppose they might take some getting used to. "You'll be fine."

"I just hope I don't walk right out of them," she said. "I thought the extra half size would work, but now I'm not so sure."

"Want cotton for the toe?" Both of us had grown up lamenting the difficulty of finding shoes to fit small feet. The children's department had plenty, but it was a desert of fashion.

She shook her head at my offer, eyeing me instead. "You look great."

I was dressed in something I'd worn at least three times a month back in California. Mac used to call it my no-nonsense suit, because between the shoes and the straight skirt style, I looked at least three inches taller. Tall was good when trying to instill trust about money—a completely faulty assumption but believed nonetheless.

It felt good to have a reason to be dressed like this again. I just wished I were going to a financial meeting instead of to a courtroom.

I refrained from a caustic comment about neither one of us being *really* ready for this trial. I was going only out of obligation to Dilly. She was going out of sympathy for another human being. Someone to whom she owed nothing.

I knew exactly how to get to the courthouse on Ninth Street and where to park in the pay lot directly across the street. The courthouse itself was huge, redbrick, and fairly new based on the young trees lining the walk. It was an imposing place—just the way it appeared to me nearly seven years ago when I'd come here for Dilly's trial. I ignored the weight at the pit of my stomach as I relived those days when I came here with my parents. Dilly had never used this entrance before; she'd been escorted back and forth from jail under armed guard through another door—an employee entrance? I couldn't recall, didn't want to probe the memory, and certainly wouldn't ask Dilly. For a moment it was yesterday anyway, and I wanted to take Dilly's hand, assure myself it was all in the past, over.

If this was hard for me, I couldn't imagine how hard it must be for Dilly. How could she put all of her own awful memories behind her if she kept reliving them through others? I glanced at her, but she was composed. No one but me could guess what thoughts she might have going through her mind.

To take my mind off the past, I eyed the area as we crossed the street in our approach. Predictably, many people filed up and down the wide concrete staircase leading into the building. My gaze didn't linger there long. There was a cluster of people down the sidewalk. A protest group just gathering?

I hurried Dilly through the revolving doors, not bothering to find out what cause they'd come to support or fight. Inside, we went through security, passing under the metal detectors, allowing our purses to be screened. Dilly had been told the case would be tried on the seventh floor, and we took the elevators up.

We found the correct courtroom and waited, neither one of us saying much, neither one of us making an attempt to talk to anyone in the room. I kept my eye out for any faces I knew, friendly or otherwise.

When Carla Morelo was at last led into the room, I saw she was older than Dilly, even now, so many years after Dilly had tried committing a similar crime. Mrs. Morelo looked worried and gaunt, though she was dressed neatly in a suit surprisingly similar to Dilly's: plain, without adornment. Navy blue instead of gray. Her hair was pulled back and she wore no makeup. I thought she searched the attendees but her gaze stopped on a man seated behind the prosecutor's desk. Her husband? He stared straight ahead, never looking her way.

I knew from Dilly, who'd been following the case more closely than I, that he'd filed for divorce and frozen their assets so she wouldn't have access to their money for bond. He'd claimed in one news report that he didn't want her to be free to either kill herself or have access to their other, healthy child.

Soon the trial began. I didn't want to listen. I didn't want to learn about Mrs. Morelo or how she took her daughter's life. I watched people instead. I studied the jury, comparing them to the one I remembered sitting Dilly's case. There were more women on this jury. Most seemed young. Was that a good thing or bad? And what did that mean? I wasn't sure which side I was on, because there was misery on both.

Now and then the words falling on my ears registered, despite my intention not to listen. As the prosecutor set about explaining the case he would build, he spoke of little Molly, whose world had ended so tragically, contrasting her innocence to Mrs. Morelo's selfish desire to rid herself of an inconvenience.

It all sounded familiar to me—the need for the accuser to concentrate on the victim and not the circumstances around the crime. To portray the defendant as seeking only what was best for herself, turning her back on the concept of right and wrong. I'd have thought the prosecution team entirely without sympathy except I knew the sentence they were after—twenty to sixty years—had shown a certain amount of compassion. If Molly had been a healthy child they would have asked for life.

The court adjourned after one o'clock, late for lunch, but would not resume until the following morning. I would have left immediately, but Dilly went the wrong way when we left our seats. She headed to the defense lawyers, who were packing up their papers.

"I'm Catherine Carlson," she said.

The lawyer nearest us, a tall, thin man with dark hair and thick glasses, turned to her, hand extended. "Nice to meet you in person. Carla would have liked to meet you too."

"Yes, I hope to be allowed to visit her soon."

A woman came up behind the other lawyer, one I hadn't noticed before. She was older, not thin but not really plump, either. Her hair was void of much gray, but I guessed that was because of a hairdresser and not because nature hadn't already taken its toll. A few gray roots showed at her temples.

"Your letters have been a great comfort to my daughter, Ms. Carlson. I want to thank you for writing to her. And for the card you sent to me."

Dilly nodded and the two of them let the glance linger, as if an understanding passed between them that didn't need words.

"I'm sorry for all you're going through," I said when the older woman at last looked my way. "I'm Catherine's sister."

"Ah," she said. "Then you know it's hard on the family."

I nodded.

There was a moment of awkward silence. From my memory of our own awful days, I knew this woman would want to consult with her daughter's lawyers about how the morning had gone, what to expect next. I touched Dilly's elbow.

She started to turn away with me but stopped. "I just want to say I'm praying for you." Her gaze grazed each of the others. "For all of you, really. I know this isn't an easy thing to defend, and I know none of this is easy for Carla, either. But she'll get through it. You will too." She aimed those last words at Carla's mother.

Then Dilly walked beside me down the aisle and we headed to the courtroom door. A slight man, shoulders stooped, sidestepped the officer who stood nearby, jumping hastily in our path to hold open the door. I slipped my arm through Dilly's, urging her with my touch to walk a little faster. I just wanted to be away from everyone, home.

I couldn't help but notice that the man who was so courteous at the door followed us toward the elevator. Something about the way he followed—too closely—made me uncomfortable, but to my relief there were several people already inside when the elevator opened to let us in.

"Let's go straight to the car," I whispered. Dilly was probably as hungry as I was, but I didn't want to linger, even long enough to stop for a sandwich at a nearby café.

The elevator's first-floor button was already pushed, and we floated down without another stop. Everyone, including us, got off at the lobby level.

I looped my arm through Dilly's again and led the way to the revolving door at the front of the courthouse.

"What's the hurry? You're rushing—"

"You're Catherine Carlson, aren't you?"

There it was, the voice that went with the shadow still too close behind us.

Dilly slowed; it was only my grasp that seemed to propel her forward.

"Just ignore him," I said as she looked about to either protest my behavior or answer him.

"Can I take just a minute of your time?" The man didn't let the gap between us widen despite our hurried stride. The door was only a few paces away.

"No," I said over my shoulder.

But Dilly stopped altogether. "What do you want?" I heard only curiosity, not a trace of the suspicion that flooded me.

He stuck out his hand, and to my dismay, Dilly took it. He held it a moment too long.

"I just wanted to know what it felt like to shake the hand of a murderer."

Dilly's hand fell away.

"She's not a murderer," I said, pulling on her arm once again.

"Just because she failed doesn't mean she isn't guilty, same as that murderer you saw in there today. Did you come to support somebody who did the same thing you tried to do?"

I tugged Dilly harder, picking up my pace and forcing her to do the same. I pushed her through the open segment of the revolving door, squeezing in behind her. We were out in the crisp fall air, the parking lot in sight.

The man still hovered, like a helicopter over a news story. The sun was bright after the inside dimness, and the white cement at our feet reflected the light almost blindingly.

"Hey!"

I looked over my shoulder, but the man wasn't shouting to us. He was waving toward someone at the sidewalk. It was at least part of the group we'd spotted earlier, although I saw no banners or posters. They might have been walking harmlessly along the sidewalk, but at the moment they looked like a mob to me.

"This is Catherine Carlson!" the man called out.

Even from this distance, I saw interest followed quickly by recognition ignite several faces. Two broke away from the half dozen or so in the group and headed our way. I yanked on Dilly again and she seemed as eager as I to be away. But we'd taken no more than a couple of steps downward before something hit the back of my ankle.

It was Dilly's shoe, and after it sailed toward me, I inadvertently kicked it farther down the cement stairs.

I let go of Dilly long enough to rush forward and save the shoe from somersaulting any farther away. No sooner had I retrieved it than I turned back to see the man who'd hounded us grab hold of Dilly's arm, keeping her in place while the pair who'd left the group below passed me and took places to surround my sister.

Shoe in hand, I tried getting back to Dilly's side, but two more women pushed by on the cement staircase. Their backs were to me, as if I were invisible. Because I was a step below and they were taller than me to begin with, I felt like a child trying to break in on a football huddle. I couldn't see Dilly, but I heard the man who'd clutched her arm. He was yelling now, and one of the women who'd joined us raised her voice too.

Frantic, I tried pushing my way between the two women. They stepped aside only long enough for me to glimpse Dilly's face. Fear robbed any color from her cheeks, and I thought I saw pain in her eyes. The man still gripped her arm, and I could see from the odd angle and disarray of her suit jacket that he didn't care if he hurt her or not.

"Let her go!"

I'd shouted the words, I was sure I had, but they seemed to echo as if someone else had cried the same thing. I lurched forward, suddenly on the same step as the man imprisoning Dilly, but before I could catch her, the man thrust Dilly away.

Like her shoe had a moment ago, Dilly tumbled down the hard concrete steps.

# 28

I RUSHED to Dilly's side, nearly tripping myself. All I saw was my sister at the base of the stairway, blood on her forehead. Still.

"Dilly!"

She was moving by the time I reached her, to my immediate relief. But my relief reverted back to fear as voices came in too close. I bent over her, shielding her body with my own. The sun was so bright that when I tried looking up I could see nothing, only hear the voices close at our side.

And a scuffle.

People gathered from all directions, soon blotting out the glare and allowing me to see what had happened. Two men restrained the one who'd pushed Dilly down the stairs. The shouting had subsided, but now inquiries came one after another. *"Is she okay?" "Does she need an ambulance?" "Should somebody call the police?"*

I had no answers. I only looked at Dilly, who was trying to sit up but her face tightened and I knew something was wrong.

"Sit still, honey," I told her. "What hurts the most?"

"I—I don't know. . . ." She tried to lift a hand to her forehead but winced at the movement, and her other hand lurched just below her breast.

From the look of it, her forehead was just grazed, like a skinned knee after a fall. I was more worried about her unwillingness to sit up, and she looked positively woozy. I told her to be still, that I'd

239

get help, that everything was going to be all right. Empty words, because I could only sit there, nearly as traumatized as her.

My hands were trembling so fiercely I could barely unclip the latch on my purse. It had been designed for a woman in power, not for what I felt like just then.

"I'm calling help, Dilly. Just lie still."

I still fumbled even after my hand was inside, talking all the while, telling Dilly it would be all right. Someone bent over me and said something and I shook my head, more a refusal to respond than a real reaction to words I didn't hear.

"Someone's already called for help," the voice said, and this time the words made sense. I stopped searching for my cell and clutched the purse, along with Dilly's, close to my chest, still kneeling at my sister's side.

"Did you hear that, honey? Help's already on the way. Everything's going to be just fine."

New sounds and voices added to our surroundings. A siren from the distance closed the gap faster than I expected. The horde of people around us opened up toward the street and I saw two men jump from the front of the vehicle, already slipping white plastic gloves on their hands. Doors slammed; metal clanked; a stretcher bounced out the back door. A man in a dark blue jacket asked everyone to step aside and was soon bent over Dilly, opposite me. Another man went to Dilly's head, holding her steady.

"I'm okay," I heard Dilly say, which was a ridiculous statement considering she still didn't move.

The paramedic opposite me was already examining her—a touch to her forehead, a steadying hand to her shoulder when she unsuccessfully tried again to sit up. He had a satchel on the stair next to us.

"I just had the breath knocked out of me," she said.

I had the horrific memory of a neighboring farmer who'd been hit in the gut by a piece of machinery gone haywire, only to assure his wife he just "had the breath knocked out of him." Then he'd sat down and died, right in front of her.

"I need you to sit still, all right?" As he spoke, the paramedic pulled something padded and circular from his bag. "I'm going to put this around your neck to keep you from hurting yourself, okay? Where does it hurt?"

"Yes—it does hurt, right here, when I try to move." She pointed to her upper side. "But I think I just need to sit still a minute."

The man, whose jacket was embroidered with *Thomas* over the breast, applied the brace around Dilly's neck. Briefly I wondered if Thomas was his first name or last, then berated myself for even having such a worthless thought.

Myriad thoughts, visions, and fears permeated my brain, leaving me nearly motionless while Thomas disappeared for a moment, returning with a stiff board that wasn't much longer than half of Dilly.

"This is a backboard, miss, and before we move you onto it, we're going to tape your ribs in place so nothing is jarred when we lift you. Okay?"

Right over her brand-new suit jacket, Thomas wrapped stiff white bandaging firmly around her chest, barely moving her from side to side to get it around her. Efficiently and in perfect time with one another, two paramedics lifted Dilly onto the board, then transferred her to the stretcher and carried her to the ambulance. I moved automatically to sit next to my sister until Thomas stopped me.

"You'll have to follow in your own vehicle, miss," he said.

"But I'm parked so far away. How will I follow you?"

"We're taking her to Saint Teresa's. Do you know where that is?"

I nodded. I'd been born there. Dilly had been born there. Sierra had been born there, too, and hospitalized there more than once.

Just as Thomas closed the doors and I hurried back onto the curb, a police officer stood in my path.

"I understand you're a witness to what just happened."

"Yes, but I need to get to the hospital and be with my sister." I started to walk past him.

"If you could just look this way a moment, miss. To corroborate that we have the correct suspect in custody? We'll need names and addresses, too, but we can get that at the hospital. We'll be following you there."

He directed my attention to a squad car, before which stood two more officers on either side of a handcuffed man. The man who'd shoved Dilly down the stairs.

"Yes, that's him."

Then I ran off to my car.

# Dilly

If I breathe too deeply it feels like someone's sticking a knife in my side. I feel like I was hit by a truck; every part of me aches. I suppose they'll give me something for the pain now that I'm here at the hospital. People are moving all around me, and I've been transferred from the gurney I was brought in on to a narrow bed in a small room in the ER. I'm a little surprised they brought me to a room with real walls instead of one of the curtained sections, but I'm glad. All I can think of is that this is the same hospital I've been at during the weakest moments in my life: first when Sierra was born, then several times when she was sick and I panicked for help, and then the last time—on the night I tried to kill us. But I've never been in this room, and I'm glad about that.

The ambulance guys are gone, but two police officers are still here. I wish they'd leave; anyone in a uniform and carrying a gun draws attention, and I don't want people looking my way. I feel helpless just lying here, but at least the room limits how many people I can see—or who can see me.

A doctor comes in and removes the oxygen mask from over my mouth. I had liked not having to talk, but now he's asking me questions about what happened and I'm answering him, telling him about my pain. The white coat he's wearing looks too tight, and his breath smells like a mixture of garlic and mint, so I wish he'd give me the oxygen tank back.

I can't sort my thoughts. That guy at the courthouse called me a murderer. I've never been called that before, not even when I was on trial. Not to my face, anyway. It's all I can think about right now. I just want to be left alone, and I start praying for that.

It occurs to me that God knew this was going to happen, and I wonder why I was so blindsided. All I wanted to do was help. I know what Carla did was wrong. I hate what she did. But the punishment has already begun, even before she's sentenced. And she's still human; I know she feels all the hatred people like that guy have. I just wanted her to know not everybody has forgotten she's still a person with feelings.

I guess that guy thought I deserved this for trying to help her. But most likely he would've done what he did anyway, once he found out who I was.

He called me a murderer.

Maybe I do deserve it.

# 29

SAINT TERESA'S was a large hospital by central Illinois standards but nothing compared to hospitals I'd driven by in LA and New York. However, it still managed to provide a maze of corridors and halls in which to get lost, especially for someone as distraught as I.

A police officer found me wandering and told me he would take me to Dilly. He led me back toward the same emergency room entrance I'd run through earlier, only off to the side and into a small room.

"This is actually a personal assault room," he whispered as he led me to the door. "They put her in here since we came along to ask some questions."

His tone suggested they'd done Dilly a favor by providing the private room. But wasn't "personal assault" what had happened?

The place was nearly full with a nurse, a doctor, and a female police officer all standing around the padded examination table upon which Dilly lay. My gaze went straight to her face, where I saw that her forehead was bandaged but they had removed the neck brace and taping from her chest. Although she was still on her back, she didn't look quite so out of sorts anymore.

"I'm okay, Hannah. Really." She looked from me to the doctor. "This is my sister."

I went to Dilly's side, taking her hand. I wanted to believe her, but I'd seen the pain on her face back on the stairs and it didn't appear to have left her yet, even if the grogginess had. "Maybe I'll let the doctor tell me that."

The doctor shot me a smile. "We'll be taking her down for some X-rays in a minute, and we'll want to keep her overnight to make sure that head injury is nothing to worry about. She's right, though. She'll be just fine."

"Why couldn't you sit up before?" I asked Dilly. "Can you sit up now?"

She might have tried except for the doctor's gently restraining hand to her shoulder. "My guess is she has a couple of cracked ribs, so moving around is probably going to hurt for a while. Until we see what's going on in there, we don't want her moving just in case."

"Cracked ribs?" The two words came out as if they'd just offered me ice cream.

"Isn't that bad enough?" Dilly asked.

"If you knew all the possibilities I worried about on the way over here, you'd feel like dancing along with me. Crushed arteries, spinal cord injury, broken neck, brain damage . . ."

"Sounds like you've got a worrier in the family," the doctor said. He turned away before I could reply, although I had no defense. He gave orders to the nurse and told Dilly he would see her again after he received the X-ray films, then left the room.

For the next couple of hours I lost track of time. The police had questions and forms, telling me Dilly would have to sign papers if she wanted to press charges against her attacker. I assured them she would do whatever was necessary and I would do what I could to help, just as soon as Dilly was able.

While Dilly was being x-rayed, I made a couple of phone calls, first to my parents, then to Tom Boyle. Most of all, I wanted to call Mac, if only to shake off the effect of the residual adrenaline in my system. He always had a calming effect on me. But we hadn't spoken in over a week, by my design. I couldn't call him now; I didn't have the time I needed to tell him the whole story.

I spotted the nurse who'd taken Dilly away. She told me Dilly was finished in the X-ray department and with the doctor and had been taken to a room.

"She's being admitted, then?" I asked the nurse, who nodded and gave me the room number.

When I got to Dilly, I found a nurse with her, folding the crumpled suit Dilly had been wearing. My sister now wore what looked to be far more comfortable attire: a hospital gown and light blue cotton socks. She was in the bed with the covers folded back and the head raised so that she was nearly sitting up.

"How are you doing?"

"Okay."

"She'll be just fine and dandy before you know it," the nurse said with a cheerful smile. "I'm going to put you on the dinner list before it's too late. I'll be back in a bit, okay? Is there anything you need before I go?"

"Actually, there is," Dilly said. "Do you know how I can get a copy of a Bible?"

"Well, we don't have our own supply of Gideons, but I'm pretty sure I can dig one up." The nurse winked and left the room.

I neared the bedside, wishing I'd thought to ask Mom or Dad to bring a Bible from home. Heaven knew they had one for every room of the house.

But even as the thought crossed my mind, I questioned the bitterness behind it. Was it habit that had me automatically rail against this faith Dilly clung to? After today I was more eager than ever to believe there was sin in the world. I wasn't perfect either.

There was no way I wanted to talk to Dilly about such a thing. I glanced at the empty bed on the other half of the room. "At least you have some privacy."

Dilly didn't respond. She stared ahead. "I just feel really . . . stupid."

"Stupid! Why?"

"Because I stopped and talked to that guy to begin with, and because if I hadn't lost that shoe I'm not sure I would've fallen. I was off balance."

"Dilly, the guy was twice your size and had a grip on you that probably left a bruise. And you didn't fall. You were pushed. Have you checked your arm?"

She nodded and tried to lift the sleeve of the gown but winced. It was supposed to have been short-sleeved and would have been on anyone with shoulders wider than Dilly's. On her the sleeves hung past the elbow.

I rolled it up myself. There it was, a ring around her upper arm that might have passed for a snake tattoo at first glance. "Ouch," I said for her. "Goodness, Dil, the man was a lunatic. I can't believe a stranger would do this to you."

Her eyes watered. "He called me a murderer."

I sat beside her on the edge of the bed, the bars folded out of the way on this side. "He was crazy, Dil. He was totally wrong." I would have tried gathering her up for a hug but I was afraid the contact would hurt. "Tell me what they're doing for your broken ribs."

"Nothing."

"What?"

"Painkillers if I wanted them. Ribs have to heal on their own, they said. Nothing was punctured, and X-rays showed the ribs are settled into place. I just have to take it easy. No lifting."

I tried to smile. "No moving hogs from one pen to another . . . or hoisting them out of a pit?"

My humor made no impact; maybe it was just as well. I doubted laughing or crying was a good thing for her to do.

"Do you have your cell phone, Hannah? I need to call Sharon. I'm supposed to be there to see Sierra, and Sharon might think I'm shirking and cut me off."

"I already called Tom to let Sharon know what happened. Mom and Dad, too. They said they'd be here as soon as they could."

"I shouldn't have agreed to stay overnight," she said.

"I think it's best. One of the nurses told me they get people in all the time who've fallen down stairs. It's best to make sure everything's okay."

"I just want to go home."

The way she said it made it sound as if she'd cut herself off too soon, before adding, *". . . and never stray outside of town again."*

"I'll take you home in the morning."

"I haven't been in this hospital since I brought Sierra here." Her voice was low, and she looked at the wall behind me, not at me. "She had pneumonia. I almost lost her then, and she was only two years old."

Tears tumbled down her cheeks, and I knew the day had been too much for her. I took her hand, the only thing I knew wouldn't hurt. "It'll be all right, Dil. You'll see."

I looked around and found a box of Kleenex in a drawer on the table beside the bed. Handing her one, I tried to smile but I didn't feel much happier than Dilly looked. I was exhausted.

"Dilly?"

Our mother's voice came from around the corner of the room, at the door that was impossible to see beyond the private bathroom.

I stood. "Yes, Mom, she's here."

Our parents came into the room, both faces aged with worry. My mother's gaze passed easily over me, going to Dilly. They went to the other side of the bed, my father right behind my mother.

"Are you all right?"

I would have expanded on Dilly's nod, told them what both the nurse and the doctor had said, but I noticed another shadow lurked in the doorway. Tom Boyle stood there, looking unsure if he should enter.

I glanced at Dilly, seeing her wiping the last of the tears away. "Look who brought Mom and Dad—you did bring them, right?" I asked. "Or did you all just arrive at the same time?"

Tom stepped into the room. "No, we came together." He kept his face in my direction a moment, as if to give Dilly more privacy or the chance to protest his presence before looking her way.

I saw her try reaching for the blanket at the foot of the bed, but she barely moved before wincing. Between my mother and me, we had her covered in no time, although all Tom would have seen were the pale blue socks. The gown was plenty long.

"Hi, Tom," Dilly said. At least now she had some color back in her cheeks. "You brought my parents . . . in your squad car?"

"Had to get them here as fast as I could, so that seemed the best option."

"Won't you get into trouble for using the car for something that's not official business?"

He grinned. "With who? The town voters? As I saw it, I'd probably have lost a few votes if I didn't get them here as quick as I could."

Dilly gave a thank-you nod.

"You called Sharon?" I asked.

He nodded. "She was surprised you were hurt. Even said she hoped it wasn't bad."

I lifted one brow. Sharon, concerned about Dilly?

"I just said to Hannah that I should go home," Dilly told them. "I don't need to stay, really."

"Don't you worry about it," our mother said, patting her hand.

"Good thing I put you on my insurance." It was the first thing I'd heard all day that almost made me smile. Good ol' Dad.

"So what does the doctor say?" Tom asked. "And what exactly happened? Hannah said you fell down the stairs at the courthouse."

"*Pushed* down the stairs," I amended. "They have a man in custody and Dilly's going to file charges."

Dilly didn't nod in agreement, but my parents' shock-induced questions allowed no chance to talk to her about it. Dilly and I filled them in on what had happened, from the moment the man followed us from the courtroom to when he grabbed her.

"I can't believe it," my mother said. "How could someone do this to you? You're hardly bigger than a minute, and so sweet. No one has a right—"

"I'm not really sure he pushed me," Dilly said. "He just sort of . . . let go, and I went tumbling."

"Same thing," I said, "the way he had a grip on you. You should see her arm. She's all bruised up."

Tom, grim-faced, hadn't said a word through the description. He just stared at Dilly.

"You'll help Dilly with the paperwork and the trial if it comes to that, won't you, Tom?" I asked.

But instead of Tom's voice, I heard Dilly's. "There's not going to be a trial. I'm not pressing charges."

"If you let him off he won't learn not to do it again, Dilly," Tom said quietly.

She lowered her eyes. "I can't do another trial, that's all."

"It'd be different this time," I said. "No one has the right to do what he did. He has to be punished."

Dilly shook her head, and I looked to Tom for help.

"It doesn't have to go to a trial," Tom said. "We need to talk to a lawyer, maybe set up a plea bargain. No trial then."

I looked from him to Dilly, wondering if she'd noticed the *we* in Tom's statement. He was clearly here to help.

# 30

I DIDN'T sleep more than a few minutes at a time that night, and not only because of the trauma of the day. I'd given in and called Mac, which had helped to alleviate some of the stress, but that very same conversation had opened a new vein of anxiety.

For several hours that night, I wrote, rewrote, then rewrote again a letter to Mac.

> . . . so you see, don't you, how hard we're making this on ourselves? Every time I hear your voice, every time I know what you're doing in a day, every time I imagine you calling or coming here, I remember how much I want you in my life. But it just won't work. You can't live here, and I can't leave.
>
> We need to end this, Mac. Once and for all. I ran to you the minute I needed you tonight, and that was unfair to both of us. I won't do it again. I won't call you, and I'm asking— begging, really—that you don't call me anymore.
>
> We both need to accept this as just the way it is. I'm sorry.

The note lacked the kind of grace Mac deserved, especially since I was doing something he wouldn't do, breaking up with him in a letter instead of in person. I could have e-mailed him, but somehow that seemed even more impersonal than a handwritten note, on paper I'd bought when I'd dragged him into a stationery

boutique some time ago. I could have sealed the lined envelope
with tears, because I'd cried most of the night. By the time I went
to the post office in the morning, on my way to the hospital to
pick up Dilly, I thought I was out of tears. But more came as I slid
the letter irretrievably into the mail slot.

I drove away from the post office with the blue box in my
rearview mirror, as if I could see Mac ready to accept the letter on
the other end. There was no taking it back now, and I shouldn't
want so desperately to do that very thing. So I gripped the steering
wheel, ignoring more tears. *All of it had to be said, and the sooner the
better.* I repeated the words like a mantra, wishing I believed them.
For both our sakes.

Dilly moved carefully off the bed, but I could see she was more
than ready to go home. I'd brought the same small suitcase she'd
used when she left prison, this time full of comfortable clothes, a
casual jacket, and her favorite tennis shoes. While she changed in
the bathroom, assuring me she didn't need my help, I packed up
the clothes she'd worn yesterday.

"Excuse me," said a voice at the door, "is this Catherine Carlson's room?"

I was in the mood to be both bold and rude and demand who
wanted to know, but the woman had such a friendly look on her
face that I held back. Still, I refused to let down my guard. "Can I
help you?"

"My name is Karen Stedman. I was there yesterday, at the courthouse. I wondered if I could talk to Ms. Carlson?"

"Are you a reporter?"

She shook her head. "No, but I should tell you I've been
involved with the Advocates for Kids with Disabilities."

"Then I don't think—"

"I came to apologize." She took a step forward, either not

reading or ignoring the tone of my protest and my rigid demeanor. "And to let Ms. Carlson know that our group had nothing to do with the man who attacked her yesterday. We were there because we didn't want the public to forget the real victim in the Morelo case: Molly. Sometimes, when people are so sympathetic to the mother's plight, they want to forget kids like Molly. Or write them off as expendable."

"I'm familiar with the complications. I was there yesterday too. The man called to other protestors, and they came to support him. Against my sister."

"No, no, that wasn't it." Her words remained calm, soft, but she was already taking another step forward, fully inside the room now, as if she'd been welcomed. "That's why I knew I needed to come today, me and my two friends in the hallway. We honestly just came to talk to Ms. Carlson and to tell her how sorry we are that things went the way they did."

"I'll tell her." But she might have doubted that, since the words barely made it through my clenched teeth. I wasn't sure what so offended me; one person from a nationwide group didn't seem enough of an apology, but three seemed like a gang. I didn't want Dilly to have to face any one of them.

"We'd really like to talk to her," the woman said gently.

This time it was I who took a step closer. The woman was older, taller, and heavier, but I felt far bolder. "You'll forgive me if I find it difficult to trust your words."

The bathroom door opened behind me and I was sure my sister heard my cold tone of voice. She was fully dressed, except for needing her shoes tied, and she looked in need of the protection I was eager to provide. Her eyes beneath her concerned, heavy brows held a hint of the fear I'd seen there yesterday.

"It's all right, Dilly," I said. "This lady was just leaving."

The woman did not move for a full second, and I wondered if she would make the retreat I demanded. When she did move, it was toward Dilly. "I understand—and appreciate—that you need to be protected after what happened yesterday. But I hope to just take a moment of your time, to tell you how profoundly sorry I am for what happened."

I came up behind the woman, with her between Dilly and me. She was probably only here because she didn't want her organization implicated in the assault, leaving them open to a lawsuit. "I don't suppose you'll back up that regret by being a corroborating witness against the man who pushed her yesterday?"

"As a matter of fact we went straight to the police station after the incident. We told them we saw it all and left them with contact information saying we'd be happy to testify if necessary. The man was completely at fault for what happened, Ms. Carlson. His name is Johnson, Vic Johnson, and he did attend a couple of the meetings our advocate group held. But none of us invited him to return. He's a belligerent man, and after yesterday he proved whatever methods he'd like to use to help our cause aren't the kind of things we'd like to see." She turned so she could look at both of us. "That's why I've come today. To apologize and to assure you we do not support what happened."

"There won't be any need to testify," Dilly said, and if she didn't have broken ribs I'd have jabbed her to keep her quiet. "I know what your group's goals are. Even that man . . . As awful as he was, I think he probably has one thing in common with me—a desire to see people with disabilities valued in this life."

The woman nodded. "That is what we want." She said the words slowly, carefully. "I've been part of this group for eight years, Ms. Carlson. I remember your case. We did write editorials to local newspapers and to the judges and lawyers involved. It must seem as though we have no sympathy for the circumstances of families, but that's not true. We only want society to value everyone equally."

"Me too. That's just it. I'm your ally and your enemy at the same time because of what I did. But I want the same thing you want. For my daughter to be treated with value."

"Ms. Carlson, what happened in your life was a long time ago. It's been settled in court; you've served the time. We don't go around dredging up old cases, believe me. Unfortunately, there are new ones to call attention to. We fight what we fear most, and what we fear most is that people with disabilities will be discounted. But we don't fight it the way Vic Johnson tried yesterday."

Dilly nodded. "Thank you for taking the time to come here and tell me that."

The woman held out her hand, and Dilly barely hesitated before accepting it. "I'm sorry for all the heartache you must have known already in your young life, Ms. Carlson."

To my surprise, Dilly smiled. It was the first one I'd seen on her in days. "The Bible has something to say about heartaches. They purify us, like gold."

I wondered if she believed it. They sounded like pretty words to me but just words after all. Weren't they?

# Dilly

She just doesn't get it. When we were kids, I didn't mind Hannah telling me what to do. It was easy never having to wonder what was next. Besides, I liked her attention. Okay, so maybe it was because our mom didn't give either one of us the time with her we thought we needed. But I'm grown up now and the feeling that I'm under Hannah's eye all the time is really getting to me.

Not being able to lift anything is getting to me too. This is the best and busiest time of the year. Harvest. What's better than seeing everything that grew out of little seeds ready to feed the entire world? I can see why my parents have kept faith all their lives; it's hard not to when you see a miracle year after year.

I move to pick up the book I'm reading, but it's farther than I think and when I stretch to grab it, there's another knifelike pain in my upper side. But I don't groan, because if I do, Hannah-who-hears-all will be in here quicker than I can blink.

My mind automatically goes back to what I've been thinking about since the courthouse: how much that man—a total stranger—hates me. It's a hard thing to forget. I shake my head at the image of his face, closing my eyes against it.

So instead I start thinking about Hannah. We're sisters, but we just don't understand each other. She doesn't get that I don't want her running my life, and I don't get why she left California to begin with. Oh, I know she thinks it's because she feels guilty about not being here for me, as if having her here years ago might have kept Sierra and me safe. Truth about that is, she wouldn't have been any help at all. I was determined to keep my problems to myself, and living an isolated life taking care of Sierra was what I chose. Hannah has always hated living in a small town, so chances are she'd have just added to my general depression. Leaving behind all the unpleasantness of life would've included leaving behind an unhappy sister.

She doesn't see it that way, of course. She'd see a remake of those years as her being here to somehow fix everything.

But what's done is done, and the more I think about it, the more I'm convinced there's something else to her being here now than doing good deeds to make up for her self-imposed guilt trip. There has to be a pretty strong reason she wanted to leave California—and Mac—even though from what I see he's great for her. If I can just figure out why she really left, maybe I can get her to go back.

Despite my efforts to be so quiet that Hannah will continue to stay out of my room, she shows up anyway. With lunch on a tray.

"Here you go. Whole-wheat pasta and tomatoes with garlic and basil. Some cottage cheese with peaches, a glass of iced tea, and sorbet for dessert. How's that?"

I nod as if grateful, although her healthy food is driving me just as crazy as her attentiveness. I have a taste for boxed macaroni and cheese, but she won't serve that kind of pasta. Or white rice, which is another thing I miss. Or doughnuts, drowning in sugar.

"You don't have to serve me in here, you know." I told her this a few days ago when I first came home, but evidently it didn't sink in. It's not even noon; I'd have gone into the kitchen myself but hadn't been ready to give up my privacy just yet.

"Enjoy the service while it lasts," she tells me with a grin.

Instead of leaving me to eat alone, she sits on the edge of the bed.

"Aren't you eating?" I ask.

"I ate while I was cooking."

So she just sits there, watching me eat. She asks if I'm enjoying my book and I tell her I can hardly put it down, even though that's not exactly true. But she gave it to me and I'm not ready to battle her over little things, too.

I can tell there's something on her mind, but I'm not about to ask. Instead I think I'll tell her what's on mine.

"Have you talked to Mac lately?"

She shrugs, shakes her head, then nods. I have no idea what kind of an answer that is.

"You'd be happy with him, Hannah. What I don't understand is why you're not with him already."

She stands, which was my intention all along—to get her to talk about California (Mac *is* California in my opinion) or leave. But instead of heading to the doorway, she just stands there, folds her arms, and looks down at me.

"Have you thought any more about signing the papers to charge Vic Johnson?"

So here it is, the price of lunch served in bed. One more attempt to change my mind. It's probably killing her that I won't do what she's telling me to do, the way I always have in the past. That's probably why she's having such a hard time giving up on the idea.

"I already told you I won't do it. I don't want to talk about it anymore."

"But—"

I try to sit up straighter, even lean toward her to help make my point, but that knife in my side comes back and I go limp against the pillow again. "Leave it be, Hannah. In fact, leave *me* be."

Her face gets that offended look and she hesitates as if she's not going anywhere, but then she turns away. At the door she stops.

"I'll come back for the tray."

Then she leaves.

I tell myself I shouldn't feel bad, because it's my ribs that got cracked, not hers. The decision is mine. If I thought Vic Johnson had followed me out of that courtroom to purposely hurt me, I'd agree to press charges. But the truth is even though he's probably glad I got hurt, it really was an accident. Maybe he doesn't believe in accidents. Maybe he thinks it's all part of my punishment for feeling sorry for a woman who let her life get so messed up she killed her own daughter.

I don't feel sorry for Carla, though. I just understand her. There's a difference.

# 31

FOR THE next few days, Dilly and I were back to being children again. Bickering ones. There was only one brief season in my life when I recall Dilly aggravating me, and that was when I was in junior high. I was so very grown up, of course, and Dilly so very young. I didn't take well to what my mother called the "compliment" of Dilly's imitation.

There was, however, no imitation going on during this season of our lives.

The tension started when the police followed up on the case against Vic Johnson. I was certain Dilly should follow through, demand justice from the man responsible for her pain. She'd already convinced me she wouldn't pursue a trial, but that didn't mean charges shouldn't be brought against him for a possible plea bargain, as Tom had suggested. Dilly refused. She did not press charges and that was that. I'd even called Tom, but he only told me he would support whatever decision Dilly made. So I finally gave up.

The magnanimity Dilly showed toward the man who'd broken three of her ribs did not extend to me. Even after my surrender about the charges, she appeared to be annoyed by everything, from my healthy cooking habits to my penchant for folding hospital corners on the sheets of her bed. While she was recuperating, her open bedroom door invited me to straighten things up. But I could do nothing right.

I tried convincing myself she was just bored. I certainly knew how that felt. Since she was unable to help while the crops were still being brought in, all she did was stare out the window or call my mother to see how the work was coming along.

She'd also called Carla Morelo's lead defense lawyer. He had heard about the assault, and although I heard her say she was still willing to come to court in support of Carla, he recommended she stay home. Carla had been grateful she'd been there, but the reality of how some people viewed those who shared this crime wasn't helping her morale. He didn't want his client put back on suicide watch, and neither did Dilly.

The only time Dilly spoke in her old tone of voice, warm and soft, was at dinnertime when she prayed aloud for a blessing on the meal. And the only time she wasn't scowling at me was when I drove her back and forth to see Sierra. Although she was unable to help lift Sierra for dressing or bathing, she still sat with her, prayed over her, read to her, sang to her gently. It was only then I saw peace on Dilly's face.

For the first couple of days, while Dilly was still too uncomfortable to drive, I stayed while she visited with Sierra. I'd been with them before, always aware of Sierra's frailty, often moved by Dilly's obvious love for her. But somehow I'd always thought distantly of Sierra. It was hard to know someone I was afraid of, someone I didn't think I could get to know. And yet during those days I saw she was knowable. She loved her mother; I could tell that by the softening of her eyes the moment Dilly walked into the room. I could see she loved music, too, perhaps as much as Dilly did, because her mouth would break open into a smile—crooked though it was, a smile just the same. What I'd once thought were groans were really an attempt to sing, or so Dilly said when she complimented her daughter's efforts.

This was my niece; we shared the same genes. Yet in all my endeavors to take care of Dilly, I'd never once thought to embrace Sierra. I'd told myself that Sharon and the teachers, therapists, and caregivers had everything under control. And with

Dilly in Sierra's life, she had the most loving and attentive care-giver of all. I'd tried assuring myself Sierra didn't know me, had never known me, didn't need to know me. She might not want my attention.

By the second week I vowed I would get over my fears and become an aunt for the first time in my life. Dilly had started driving herself back and forth again, but I offered to come along after one long day of Dilly ignoring me. I supposed being ignored was preferable to arguing, but the result was the same: a heavy heart.

We arrived at Sharon's, who let both of us in. The respiratory therapist was just leaving, a young woman I'd met before who came three times a week. The first time I'd seen her perform her therapy, I winced at the pounding she gave Sierra's frail little chest with small, round rubber mallets. Dilly had explained that since Sierra couldn't move on her own, liquids might settle in her lungs, causing pneumonia. Between this and the nebulizer treatments she received multiple times a day, pneumonia hadn't been an issue since Sierra was a baby.

When Dilly took her seat on one side of Sierra's wheelchair, I sat in the chair just opposite. I took one of Sierra's hands, much the same way I'd seen Dilly do, and I caressed her arm. Her skin was cool and soft, her fingers in mine limp.

"I know you know me," I said gently. "I'm your aunt Hannah. Do you mind if I sit with you and listen to your mom sing?"

I refused to look at Dilly or Sharon, who lurked, as usual, in the corner of the room on a recliner in front of the television. But I could see Dilly out of the corner of my eye, and even from that vantage I saw her brows lift in surprise. I'd spoken to Sierra before but always from a distance.

"I wonder what song she'll sing today," I said. "She knows the ones I like, and the ones I don't like, too. She was a little grumpy toward me earlier. Why, you ask? I guess we all get that way some-times. But she's always happy when she's around you. Did you know that? Of course you did."

Dilly's stare was planted on me, but I kept myself from looking at her and waited until she started singing. When Sierra groaned along, I started singing too. My voice wasn't nearly as pleasing as Dilly's, but I lost all inhibition next to Sierra. I laughed when my voice cracked and apologized to Sierra for having to listen to me, and I thought I saw a lift to the corner of her mouth. She'd smiled!

Dilly's visits weren't as long as they'd been before her fall, since she couldn't help with her daughter's bath or changing her clothes. I volunteered to help, which sent another lift to her brows, but Sharon said she would handle it herself. I was secretly relieved, despite my determination to know Sierra better and to help with her care.

On the way home that evening, I waited for Dilly to say something. I wanted her to acknowledge my efforts, to say it made a difference. To break this glass wall between us. But she didn't say a word.

She didn't even say anything when I listened to the messages on our phone service. The Morelo trial was over; sentencing was scheduled for the following week.

All Dilly did was go to the piano and sing Carole King's "So Far Away." I simply came up behind her and shut the keyboard. She moved her fingers just in time not to get caught.

If she was trying to tell me something, she'd have to use real words and to my face, not some cryptic music message. She knew Mac hadn't called in days and that I hadn't called him, either. If she thought hearing a song about someone longing to see the one they loved was going to make me break down and call him, she had something to learn about my fortitude.

Not that I didn't want to call. Every day when I woke, it was Mac I thought of first. And at night, when I passed by Dilly's room for my own, while I saw her on her knees praying, I would go to my own bed and sometimes be tempted to pray for Mac. But how could I leave him to the care of a God who let everyone's life get to be such a mess?

So instead I would fall asleep just thinking of Mac.

"It's too soon."

I followed Dilly through the kitchen to the garage door, where she paused only long enough to slip her feet into the work boots she wore out to the farm. They were a child's size five and fit perfectly.

"What if you dislodge one of your ribs?"

Dilly straightened to her full height and we were nearly eye to eye. "I thought you wanted me out of here."

"I want you happy, Dilly. And if being out of here for the day will do that, fine. We can go shopping. Drive to Springfield for lunch. Go to a movie."

She tilted her head. "Me getting out of *here*—" she swept the kitchen with the palm of her hand—"isn't the real goal. It's me getting away from you."

"That's what I don't get, Dilly. What did I ever do except try to help?"

With one hand on the screen door that separated the house from the garage, Dilly paused. "When we were growing up, I used to wish Mom would play more games with us. Play dress up and pretend we were fairies or princesses like other kids could do. Take us to the city and buy us those fancy dolls we saw other girls with. I might have welcomed her if she'd ever tried hovering over us then, Hannah. But you could take some lessons from her. On how to step back."

She walked out, letting the screen slam. "I'm walking to the Coffee Spot." She didn't look back, but the words reached me anyway. "Dad'll drive me out to the farm. Don't make any lunch for me."

I watched her go, wondering if I'd ever be able to do something right in her eyes again.

I worked that morning, by habit scanning my e-mail in-box for a note from Mac, wishing the instant messaging would kick in with his ID. Without Dilly here, even though she'd taken the rancor between us with her, my mind went back to the pain I carried without Mac in my life.

Midafternoon, the telephone rang.

"Is Dilly there?"

I recognized the voice, the lack of a cordial greeting. "No, Sharon," I said. "She's out on the farm. Is everything all right with Sierra?"

"She's fine." Her words, as usual, were clipped. But since this was the first time Sharon had called here without an immediate complaint, I wanted to use the opportunity.

"I think Sierra enjoys having Dilly back in her life. Don't you?"

"If you want me to say Dilly is a good mother, you can hang up right now. Yes, she's good with Sierra so long as she doesn't have round-the-clock care of her. Do I trust her? No."

I wasn't in the mood for more tension. "Why did you call, Sharon?"

"I have a meeting with Sierra's support team at school tomorrow."

"Dilly would love to go."

"I can't take Sierra with me, so I'm having Cyd come by for about a half hour until the respite worker gets here. Cyd thought Dilly might want to be here with him and Sierra, and I said it would be all right so long as Dilly isn't alone with Sierra."

"Sharon," I said softly, "do you think you'll ever trust Dilly to be alone with her? What happened was one rash mistake a long time ago. Dilly's changed."

"If she wants to be with Sierra while Cyd is here, tell her to come at two o'clock. Otherwise Sierra will be fine without her."

Then she hung up, my words unacknowledged.

# 32

I DROVE with Dilly to Sharon's the following afternoon. I knew I wasn't needed, but I'd begun to enjoy visits with Sierra. It was Dilly who could make her smile most often, but I'd coaxed a smile or two myself, and they always brought a ripple of joy to me.

Sharon barely acknowledged our arrival. Cyd was already there, reading *Rumpelstiltskin* to Sierra. His voice was rather high-pitched for a man of his size, and he did the best elf impressions this side of the North Pole. Even so, Sierra was fussing despite his best entertainment efforts.

"How are the ribs today?" Cyd asked Dilly once the miller's daughter sent the elf into a green dervish, having figured out his name.

"Much better," she said. "Did you hear that, Sierra?" She took her daughter's hand. "I think I can probably start helping you out more around here. I can wash your hair again, how about that?"

If I'd come to see Sierra smile, I should have stayed home. Cyd's best elfin voice hadn't produced one, nor did Dilly's arrival. Instead, she was fidgety and loud, coughing now and then, quieting only when she went into what Dilly had once called an "absence seizure." She stared off into space and left for a few seconds, but when she returned to herself, she went back to being unhappy.

When Dilly went through Sierra's favorite songs, she didn't produce a single syllable to sing along.

I watched Dilly suction Sierra's mouth, as competent as any nurse.

She asked Cyd if Sierra had received her nebulizer treatment, and he said Sharon had been finishing up with that when he'd arrived.

"Did Sharon say if Sierra slept much last night?" Dilly asked.

"She mentioned Sierra wasn't quite herself today, that's all."

"Her skin feels so damp. Cool, though."

Cyd nodded. I'd noticed that too, but I wasn't sure what was normal and what wasn't. The room was plenty warm, despite the outdoor chill, and if someone was always on their back in the kind of soft and warm clothes Sharon dressed Sierra in, wouldn't they be more prone to sweating anyway?

"It's time for her next med," Dilly said.

"Do you want to give it to her?" Cyd asked. So casually, and yet my eyes flew to Dilly's as quick as hers flew to mine.

"Sharon's orders are that I never do that, Cyd. You know that."

"And I'm saying Sharon's orders are overcautious. She premixed it as usual, labeled with the time. You know how to do it."

A plastic tray with various bottles and syringes sat on the counter. Next to that was a spiral notebook with a tracking list that named various medications, dosage, and administration times for each day. I knew the log was similar to the one Dilly herself had started on Sierra years ago. Sierra had been to so many doctors, been through so many medication changes, it was impossible to keep up without help.

Dilly went to the counter, picked up one of the syringes, and checked the list. Sierra took nothing through the mouth, having been born with such low muscle tone she could hardly swallow, combined with a reflux problem so severe that she needed to take her nutrition through a feeding tube directly into the stomach. Dilly had told me once that if Sierra took anything by mouth, it might find its way into the lungs instead of her stomach, and that could cause real problems in their battle to keep her lungs functioning.

"So when are we gonna see your fella again, Hannah?" Cyd asked me while Dilly kept busy.

It was the question I dreaded but knew was bound to come sooner or later, especially from Cyd. He and Mac always chatted the longest if we happened to see him in town when Mac was around. I felt Dilly's eyes on me, waiting for me to answer.

"I'm not sure. He's pretty busy these days."

"And here I thought we'd be gathering on your wedding day soon. Don't want to wait too long, you know." When his gaze went to Dilly, I felt a hint of relief. "You either, young lady. I heard Tom Boyle talking about you the other day."

I saw Dilly blush as she neared Sierra, though she kept her eyes on the oral syringe as she hooked it to Sierra's gastronomy tube.

"She's too shy to ask, but I'm not," I said. "What was Tom saying?"

"He was telling your father he was blessed to have Dilly as a daughter, the way she's turned out. Got to agree with him there. We're all sorry about what happened in the past, Dilly, but that's all behind you now. You're a fine girl these days, one I think Tom would be proud to have on his arm, if you know what I mean."

"He's never said anything to me about that," Dilly said quietly.

I rolled my eyes, a gesture Cyd caught. He winked my way.

"Sometimes a man don't have a lot of words. Not all of them are like me, you know. Sometimes, especially when he's had a bad time in the past, the girl is the one who has to make sure a fella knows that when the question is asked, the answer will be yes."

My immediate thought was they were doomed, the way Dilly was so focused on Sierra.

Visions of a romantic meal crossed my mind—one I could create for the two of them. Maybe if Dilly were happy in her own love life, she'd stop being angry with me about mine.

Ignoring the pang of regret that I couldn't plan my own romantic meal, I began to consider menu options.

At least one of us could be happy.

"I just think it would be a nice way to pass an evening, that's all."

Dilly wasn't buying my idea, I could tell that before one of her brows so suspiciously lifted. I thought she would be pleased, especially since Carla Morelo had finally received her sentence. Mrs. Morelo had been given thirty years, although no one believed she would serve the full sentence. It sounded harsh to me, but considering the prosecution had argued for the maximum sentence of sixty, perhaps thirty was something to be thankful for.

At the very least, Dilly could put closure on this. She'd no doubt have to face a news story like this again some awful day, but at least she'd know she could survive the memories it evoked, the way she had this time.

Sharing dinner with Tom Boyle was a perfect step in a new direction for Dilly, which was why I didn't give up on my attempted persuasion, no matter how skeptical my sister appeared.

"Inviting him to dinner is a natural thing to do," I persisted. "How would you like to go home to an empty house every day? That's probably why he's always at the Coffee Spot. He'll be eager to agree to a home-cooked meal and some company."

Now she added a tilt of her head to the raised brow. "Even if he's not in the least bit interested in me, you mean?"

"Yes . . . you'd just be sharing dinner like two friends."

"Friends? Like you and Mac?"

Movement in our driveway caught my attention through the kitchen window, sparing me from having to conjure up a fitting reply. "Were you expecting Nick to stop by?" I'd barely finished the question when I heard him at the service door from the garage, rather than the front door. He knocked but came inside at the same time.

"Nick?" Dilly went to meet him.

I saw immediately something was wrong, and Dilly must have sensed it before seeing his face. She was stiff, as if preparing for an assault.

"It's Sierra, Dilly. Mom took her to the ER. She was having trouble breathing. You can come with me if you want."

Dilly didn't waste time answering with words. She grabbed her jacket from the hook by the door and fairly pushed him out first, close on his heels. I took my own jacket and followed.

Much as I wanted to get into Nick's car and hear details of the emergency, I wanted to be cautious. "I'll follow in my car," I called after them. "Just in case we need it."

I had a hard time keeping up with Nick, and with hands gripped to the wheel, I tried to lighten my own mood by comparing his driving to any number of drivers on California highways. But thoughts of California didn't help, since the first thing I wanted to do was call Mac and tell him to start praying.

And then, glancing at the empty passenger seat, I realized I couldn't have called even if I'd found the guts to take one hand from the wheel. I'd forgotten my purse; my phone was back home.

# Dilly

Nick's driving like a crazy man, but I don't care. I don't want to get pulled over for a speeding ticket, so even as I'm asking him questions (most of which he can't answer) I'm looking out the window in all directions for squad cars. I see Hannah in her car behind us trying to keep up.

Nick tells me he doesn't know much, only that his mother called from the hospital. He repeats what he already told me, that Sharon brought Sierra in because she was having trouble breathing. I ask him a couple more times if Sharon said anything else—anything—but he just shakes his head. So I sit, pivoting in my seat, chafing at the shoulder strap of the seat belt because I'm not sitting straight.

The hospital is normally almost an hour away, but we get there in under forty-five minutes. I tell Nick to drop me off at the door, and he does, then pulls away to park.

As soon as the double doors to the ER open, I feel like I'm in a tunnel. I see everything around me, but once I spot the half-open curtain where Sharon is standing beside Sierra's empty wheelchair, I zoom toward her without letting anything else distract me.

Sierra is on the hospital bed, safety bars raised on both sides. She's agitated, coughing and thrashing, but no one is even near her. Sharon is just standing there at the foot of the bed.

I rush to my daughter's side, where I put a hand to her forehead. I barely register that it's cool before Sharon comes at me, pulling my arm away from Sierra.

"What do you think you're doing? What are you doing here, anyway?"

I jerk my wrist out of her hold and turn back to Sierra. "Nick brought me," I tell her over my shoulder.

I notice from the corner of my eye that Sharon is looking around, probably for Nick so she can lay into him. I take advantage of her distraction.

"Hi, honey," I say to my daughter. I put my hand back on her forehead, just to make sure it's as cool as I thought it was before Sharon grabbed my hand away. It is. She coughs, a deep, racking cough that scares me, especially when it seems like she can't breathe in between more coughs.

Then the coughing stops, but even though that's over, she twists around like she's trying to escape pain. I put my hands under her back to lift her slightly and adjust the pillow to see if shifting her position helps. It doesn't. She looks weak and tired, but something is clearly bothering her. Something I can't see is giving her trouble. I wish I knew how to help her.

*Oh, God, if ever I need You it's right now. Please help my baby. Let the doctor be able to figure out what's going on and in record time. Don't let her be in pain—*

My silent prayer is cut short by Sharon. She can't find Nick, who's probably having a hard time finding a parking spot. So she turns back to me.

"You lost your legal right to be here, Dilly, and Nick shouldn't have brought you. I hope you can find a way home, because I want you out of here—now."

"I'm not going anywhere." I say the words quietly because I don't want to make a scene, and I don't want to risk Sharon hating me even more than she already does. But I can't leave. I won't. Not until I know Sierra's going to be all right.

"I might not be able to keep you out of this building, but I can certainly keep you away from Sierra." She presses herself between the bedside and me, but I press back. Instead of Sharon moving me away, the bed behind us rolls in the opposite direction. I grab at the side bar and the bed stops.

"We can't fight about this." I'm still intent on keeping my voice down, so I fairly hiss at her. "You've got to let me stay. She's my daughter."

Sharon doesn't move. She turns her back on me to bend over Sierra like an eagle over an egg.

I go to the other side of the bed.

Sharon looks at me, her brown eyes narrowing. "All I have to do is tell the staff what you did to this child and where you spent the last six years of her life and they'll agree with me."

"Sharon, please—"

I stop because a nurse comes in and Nick's at her side. "Ma, what's going on? With Sierra, I mean?"

He must not have heard what Sharon just said, and I'm not surprised he doesn't pick up on the obvious tension between us. He's never been good at that.

The nurse comes to the foot of Sierra's bed and asks everybody to step away from the sides. She adjusts the bed back to dead center of the station. Sierra is still flailing, and I reach for her again.

"Doctor will be in shortly," the nurse says, then leaves the area.

I look at Sharon, wondering if she'll answer Nick's question or resume her rant against me. When she looks at me, I know the answer.

# 33

AS I walked through the automatic doors into the emergency room, I recognized Sharon's tone.

"For all we know this could be her fault! You shouldn't have brought her, Nick."

"Lower your voice, Ma," Nick said. "Do we have to tell all of Springfield about our family problems?"

Dilly was beside Sierra, who was on a gurney, thrashing her arms, yelling in pain, coughing intermittently, and gagging almost to the point of retching. And although part of Sharon's tone was a necessity over Sierra's noise, Nick was right. Dilly needed to be here.

When Sharon caught sight of me, I saw her moan. *Her, too?* She didn't say those words aloud, but her face said it for her.

"Where's the doctor?" I asked.

"He just left," Sharon said. "The nurse is coming back to take blood samples."

I came up behind Dilly. "Have you ever seen her like this? so uncomfortable?"

Dilly nodded. "Twice. Once with the pneumonia. Another time we brought her here but she was okay after a while." She looked at Sharon, her face hard, as if preparing for a battle. "When I was with her yesterday, Sierra seemed uncomfortable then, too. How long has she been this way?"

"I don't have to answer any of your questions. You lost custody a long time ago."

"She's trying to help, Ma. Just answer the question, will you?"

"I'll do no such thing. I wouldn't have told you I was bringing Sierra in if I thought you were going to bring her. Cyd told me he let Dilly give Sierra her meds yesterday. Of all things! For all we know she could have messed with the dosage and tried killing her again."

Dilly's fists clenched, and I stood close to her in hopes of buffering the attack. Dilly must have thought the accusation didn't deserve a defense, and I should have gone along with that wisdom. But I didn't.

"Sharon, you have no right to say anything like that. I was right there, and so was Cyd. She'd never do anything to hurt Sierra. You premixed the dosage."

"She could have tampered with it. The meds were all together on that tray."

"That's ridiculous," I said. "She didn't do anything to Sierra. I was there!"

"How do you know? Were you watching what she did? Did you see the dosage?" Sharon turned back to Dilly. "I'll see you back in jail yet, young lady."

The hooks holding the curtain jingled as a nurse came into the makeshift room, wheeling a white cart with various colored caps on vials and tubes in the tray. "I'm here to take samples, so if anyone doesn't like that idea, they're free to go on the other side of the curtain."

I stayed beside Dilly, who I could tell wasn't about to move. She still held one of Sierra's arms, singing to her in a futile attempt at soothing. For someone who couldn't move of her own accord, Sierra was suddenly all arms and legs in quick, jerky movements, her back arched. Sharon held Sierra's feet down while the nurse prepared her arm.

I found myself praying before I knew it. Sierra's arms were so thin, her veins were no doubt hard to find. But the red tube filled after the first prick.

The pain from the needle must have distracted her, but soon

Sierra starting moaning again, until it crescendoed into another
string of howls. The nurse stayed at Sierra's side, speaking calm
words to ask her to be quiet, as if Sierra could understand.

At last she gave up, looking at no one in particular. "The doctor
wants chest X-rays and to consult a hospitalist. I'll see about having
you moved as soon as possible." She passed briskly toward the
curtain, but Dilly was quick to prevent her exit.

"Chest X-rays? You mean he thinks she might have pneumonia?"

"Well, of course. Isn't that why she was brought in?"

Dilly shook her head, a quick, spasmodic movement. "Maybe
she has an ear infection? the flu?"

The nurse whispered, "No," freed her arm, then left the
curtained area.

Sharon was only a foot away, her eyes narrowed at Dilly. "Go
ahead; try and make it sound as if you don't know what's causing
this." Although Sharon's voice was softer, her words weren't. I
wondered why she was still so full of hate, so long after Dilly's
mistake.

Dilly turned to Nick. "Do you remember when Sierra was
three? We took her in and it was hard but she was fine after a few
days. Remember?"

Nick looked lost, obviously not recalling the incident.

Dilly returned to Sierra's side, leaning over her. She was still
moaning, but softer now. "They'll check, honey. Don't you worry
now; we'll find out what's going on and make you better. Okay?"

Then Dilly started singing again, but there was something
different about my sister's inability to meet anyone eye to eye.
Maybe she didn't want anyone to see the terror there. But I saw it.

It was more than a half hour before the nurse came back.

"The doctor recommends we take Sierra to X-ray, then up

to the pediatric ward, where they'll be able to make her more comfortable. I'm sure you'll all be more comfortable there too."

I couldn't help but think she was really referring to everyone left behind here in the emergency department.

"They want to admit her?" Sharon asked. "I need to speak to the doctor about that."

"He'll see you upstairs."

The nurse left, and Sharon turned her bleary gaze on Dilly. "I want you to wait somewhere else."

"Ma—"

"I didn't have her barred with those medical privacy laws for nothing, Nick," Sharon said. "I expressly forbade her to be included on Sierra's medical information."

"That was only while she was in prison," Nick said. "But she's home now. She should know what's going on. Come on, Ma."

If Sharon had further arguments, she didn't have time to state them before Sierra was taken to X-ray. We all waited in the hallway while Sharon went inside to assist. Then we waited some more before being taken upstairs to the fifth floor, the pediatric ward. The room was private, offering a bed that looked something like an oversize crib, with high bars that lowered to let the nurses move Sierra onto the neat white sheets. Despite the warm tan color of the walls, with teddy bears appliquéd here and there, it was cooler than the emergency wing had been, so they covered her with a soft white blanket.

Sierra was noticeably quieter, her breathing labored. She rarely coughed despite Dilly encouraging her to do so. Sierra didn't seem to have the strength. The room was large enough for all of us to stand nearby, but the nurses asked us to leave while they settled her. Sharon didn't leave, and I could see Dilly wanted to stay too, but she followed Nick and me out anyway. One scene avoided, at least for the moment.

# Dilly

Today is another real-life nightmare, and I've known my share of nightmares. She's sick; she's really, really sick. I can see it by looking at her. I can hear it in her cough. I can feel it so deep inside of me that I can barely breathe, just like her. *Oh, God . . . Oh, God, please . . .* But that's as far as my prayers go. I can't even form the words around my fears; all I know is I'm begging God to heal my little girl.

I want to pace but I just stand there, outside her room, wishing I were like every other mother and knew each moment of my child's health history without any breaks. I hear someone move toward the door. It's Sharon.

"I'd like to talk to you—alone."

I watch as Sharon walks away and Nick follows like an obedient son. He's never been what I'd call a mama's boy because he's just too wild, but when it comes to Sierra, he doesn't know how to say no.

They slip into a waiting room down the hall.

Hannah moves to follow. "I think we should all have a say in what Sharon decides, don't you?"

I want to caution her not to make things worse, but I can't help myself. I follow. But then, when it would take only one more step to walk to the waiting room, I grab Hannah's arm and hold her back. I can hear Sharon's voice from here.

"It's a mistake to have her here, Nick. Just like it was a mistake for me to let her come back into Sierra's life to begin with. For all I know it's Dilly's fault Sierra is here right now."

"You keep saying that, Ma, but I don't know why."

Silence; shifting around like she must have taken a seat. I wonder if anyone else is in the waiting room, but from this angle I can't see anyone through the open archway.

"I shouldn't have left her with Dilly yesterday. I knew Sierra wasn't feeling well; I should have just stayed home with her."

"You had to go to the school meeting. And Cyd was there. And Hannah."

"Well, it's only Cyd I trust, and he can be so . . . gullible. I'm sure he wasn't the least bit concerned about what Dilly did. When he told me he let her give Sierra her meds, I couldn't believe it."

I exchange glances with Hannah; she looks as if she wants to go in there and defend me—again—but I still have her arm. I look over my shoulder, wondering if the nurses at the nearest station can see that we're obviously eavesdropping. But there's no one around.

"She didn't do anything."

I breathe a little easier because Nick sounds so sure. I've hated this man for cheating on me so many times, but at the moment all I feel is gratitude.

Another silence, then something strange. I know Sharon well enough to think she'd never, ever give in to crying. But that's what it sounds like. Her crying.

"What's wrong? What's going on, Ma?"

Nick has never been good at handling tears; he sounds just as uncomfortable around his mother's tears as he was around mine so long ago.

"I—I've been so tired lately, that's all. She hasn't slept in three nights. All she does is yell and seize. Yell and seize, all night long. And now this." I hear her suck in a gulp of air. "The respite worker stopped coming two months ago; I haven't slept through the night since then. It's just—I don't know how to make it through the day anymore."

She's still crying, and I hear Nick shuffling around. "Don't cry. Just don't cry. Somebody might come in."

I grimace. Nick is as compassionate as ever.

"You don't understand, Nick. What if *I'm* the reason Sierra is here? I'm the one who mixed her meds. This morning I was so tired I didn't realize I poured juice in my coffee instead of cream. What if I gave Sierra the wrong dose?"

Hannah's looking at me now as if we've just scored a coup. But

I know how tired a person can get. I didn't think I could feel sorry for Sharon, but I suddenly realize I've heard enough. I walk back to wait outside Sierra's room.

# 34

WHEN WE returned, Sierra was hooked up to an IV, while one of the nurses was attaching a mask similar to the one Sierra had at home for her nebulizer treatments. Another nurse came and performed respiratory therapy, the pounding on her chest.

I watched, trying to stay out of the way, wincing at the treat ment. Sierra was so weak and thin, the raps on her chest so firm, I couldn't imagine she welcomed the attention. But at least she was used to it; this was the same therapy she received at home often enough.

As all of that was going on, a physician came into the room and extended his hand. "I'm Dr. Faulding." He was too young to bring vast experience, but I latched on to the notion that at least his training was fresh. He looked at Dilly, who stood closest to Sierra. "The X-rays show her lungs are clear—well, no sign of acute pneumonia. I'd like to see the last X-ray that was done on her, so I can compare the two. We'll keep the IV in place just in case anything changes, but for the moment that worry is behind us."

"No pneumonia?" Dilly repeated. Evidently she wanted it stated clearly.

The doctor shook his head.

Dilly bowed her head in what I knew to be a prayer of thanks-giving. I was tempted to raise a thank-you to Sierra's Creator too. It occurred to me as I'd witnessed so much today that God really must have a place in all of this, if life was to matter at all.

"Excuse me, but I'm Sierra's custodian," Sharon said, bustling into the room with Nick on her heels. "And there are some serious questions about this mother's stability. You'll need to address the medical issues to me."

Dilly's head shot up and the doctor looked between the two women, as if surprised one of us would broach any other topic outside the realm of Sierra's care.

"I need to know if Sierra's lab report showed anything unusual."

"Such as?"

"Is there any indication that her meds were administered incorrectly? that she has too much of something in her system, and that's what's causing her discomfort?"

"We've received only a partial report; they'll do a more thorough screening off-site. But no, nothing to suspect that sort of thing so far. Why? Is there some reason you think there might have been a problem with Sierra's dosages?"

Sharon eyed Dilly, and I waited to hear her accusations, however unfounded. I was prepared to admit we'd eavesdropped and tell them the truth, but it occurred to me that it would be our word, Dilly's and mine, against Sharon's.

But Sharon turned away and I shook off my thoughts.

"You know," the doctor said quietly to Sharon's back, "one of the nurses made me aware of your family's history. If you think there is any chance of someone attempting to hurt this child again, you are legally bound to tell me."

Sharon's shoulders sagged and she shook her head. "No, Doctor. I just wanted to be sure no one was confused when the dosages were measured. Nothing more than that."

The doctor held the clipboard to his chest, turning his attention to Dilly. Was he trying to read her mind, her emotion? trying to decide if there was anything else to worry about, other than the obvious health challenges Sierra faced? Or was this nothing more than a typically dysfunctional family? He even looked briefly at Nick and me, perhaps hoping we might add some insight. But neither one of us spoke.

"The first thing we're going to address is her sodium level," Dr. Faulding said at last. He looked at neither woman, as if deciding they had equal rights and he wouldn't show favoritism toward one or the other. "It's off-the-chart low, so we need to get that addressed first. We'll do a bolus feeding of sodium bicarbonate and fluids. The low sodium might account for some of her discomfort."

"And you're sure about the pneumonia? I didn't think she had a fever." Dilly stroked Sierra's arm. "But she's sweating, so maybe she's broken a fever if she did have one."

"No, she's cold and clammy," Dr. Faulding said. "That's different from sweating, and it's from the low sodium." He slid the clipboard under his arm. "Your daughter is very frail, Mrs. Carlson. We'll take one thing at a time, but I must warn you she's anything but healthy right now, with or without pneumonia."

He went to the door. "I'll be back to check on her this afternoon. In the meantime, she's in good care. The nurse will be back to administer the bolus, and we'll see how she responds to this first treatment."

Then he left the room. Not what I would call an excellent bedside manner, but with all of the dynamics in the room, perhaps he just wanted to spare himself more drama than he was used to in a profession that only dealt with life and death.

I stood beside my sister, who looked closer than ever to tears.

"Nothing's changed," Dilly whispered. She turned away from Sierra, as if she didn't want her daughter to see her hopelessness. "They still don't know what to do for her. One doctor says pneumonia; this one says no. Not enough sodium? He didn't even know if that's all that could be wrong."

"They're treating the sodium problem," Nick said. "He seemed sure about that."

Dilly nodded.

Sharon went to the foot of the criblike bed, staring down at Sierra. But she didn't speak.

"Ma," Nick said, "you're tired. Why don't you let me take you home?"

Sharon shook her head but did find the only comfortable chair in the room. There was another, little more than a padded folding chair, but none of the rest of us took it. We all lingered near Sierra's bed, watching her behind the oxygen mask.

"She'll need to be suctioned again," Dilly said.

Sharon seemed incapable of moving. The machine was at her feet. Maybe she hadn't heard Dilly speak.

Nick picked it up, handing it to Dilly. I doubt he knew how to use the thing, even though I couldn't remember a time Sierra hadn't needed it.

Dilly pressed the button for the nurse and, when she came, asked if it was okay to remove the oxygen mask long enough to suction Sierra's secretions. From that point on, nurses came and went, but it was obvious Dilly was more familiar with her daughter's particular care than any of them. They let her do what she could to make Sierra comfortable, including adjusting and readjusting the oxygen mask, suctioning her mouth, holding Sierra when she intermittently coughed, encouraging her all along. The nurses did take charge of the feedings, along with administering medication through the G-tube. Dilly watched even though she'd handled Sierra's feedings so many times.

Sharon was strangely quiet. She stared straight ahead, her gaze vacant, shoulders still so slumped I didn't think she'd have the strength to move even if a nurse had asked her to help.

All the while Nick lingered by the door, looking out of place, extra, like he didn't belong.

When the last of the nurses finally left and Sierra was sleeping, I noticed Nick's gaze rarely settling on Sierra anymore. Instead, it volleyed between the clock and the door.

"Sharon," I said as gently as I could. I wasn't sure any tone would be welcome, no matter how placatory. But I went on anyway. "There's nothing more we can do. Why don't you let Nick take you home?"

I wasn't sure she'd heard me, until at last she looked my way. I tried to prepare myself for some cutting response. But none came. She just stared at me, looking somewhat bewildered.

Nick neared his mother. "Ma?"

Nothing.

"Ma, how about I take you home?"

When Sharon still didn't answer, Nick looked toward Dilly, obviously baffled by his mother's behavior. Dilly did nothing, just stared at Sharon along with the rest of us.

"Ma, why aren't you answering?"

Still nothing. I began to wonder if she'd had some kind of attack, a stroke or something.

Nick took another step closer. "You want me to call the doctor in here? Why aren't you talking?"

Finally she shook her head, but it was only one small shake. Her eyes didn't seem to be blinking.

"Maybe you should call someone, Nick," Dilly said softly. "A nurse, at least."

Sharon shook her head again and leaned forward as if to rise but instead drooped back against the chair. "No. I just need a little more time to rest, that's all."

"That's why I should take you home—so you can sleep. Not in a chair."

"I can't leave Sierra, Nick. You know that."

Dilly left Sierra's side to kneel in front of Sharon. "Sharon, I know you're worried about Sierra. And I know you don't trust me. But we have a bond, you and me. It's Sierra. We both want her to be well more than anything else in this whole world. But we can all see how tired you are—it's all over your body. You need to go home and sleep. I'm going to stay here, and I'll see that Sierra gets the care she needs. You don't have to worry about her or about me doing anything to her. The nurses are constantly here; the doctors are checking in on her. They're making all the decisions, not me."

I couldn't tell if Sharon had been listening, at least up until those final words when she looked at Dilly at last.

Here was a woman who—this very day—had all but called my sister capable of murder. Again. If I hadn't heard it myself, I never would have guessed such a thing. It was hard not to believe in miracles as I stared at my sister, or at least in the power of God's love and the way it could work through someone like Dilly.

Dilly stayed where she was, waiting until she received some kind of response. "Nick can call Cyd and have him come to the hospital, if he's willing. You can have him watch my every move. I'm telling you the truth, Sharon. I only want what's best for Sierra. She's my life."

Sharon didn't offer anything, but Nick did. He went to his mother's side, putting one of his hands on one of hers, another around her shoulders, and pried her slowly to her feet. And Sharon went, without a struggle, without a word.

She left Dilly with Sierra. Alone.

I knew I hardly counted.

# 35

"DOES SHE feel warm to you, Hannah? Feel her forehead."

Dilly had done nothing except obsess about that for the last couple of hours, but each time I followed her lead and checked, Sierra felt cool. A little clammy, but cool.

This time I was fully prepared to repeat what I'd said earlier. *She's fine; no fever.* But when I pressed my hand to Sierra's skin, the words died before I could say them. She did feel warm. In fact, very warm.

"Maybe you should call the nurse again to check."

Dilly nodded, even though the last time the nurse had looked as though she'd been pulled from something more important. Dilly pressed the button, and a voice came over the intercom.

"Is there something you need?"

"Yes, we were wondering if you could check Sierra's temp again? She feels warm. Really warm this time. Please?"

Sierra had slept off and on and seemed to be sleeping now, but the intercom noise had made her eyes open. They'd removed the mask, which I thought indicated things were getting better, but that didn't explain why Sierra was weakening by the moment.

The nurse came with an ear thermometer, barely looking at either one of us. She pulled it out, simultaneously looking prepared to turn and leave. But then, reading the little pad, she stopped. She checked the other ear.

"She does have a fever. I'll be right back."

But it took nearly fifteen minutes for her to return, and along with her came another doctor, not Dr. Faulding but someone new. He introduced himself as Dr. Warren, another hospitalist.

After listening to Sierra's chest and checking her nose and ears, he said, "I'm going to have her taken down to X-ray again. I know her lungs were clear earlier, but I can hear why the ER doctor first diagnosed pneumonia. She's pretty crackly in there, and now with the fever, I think she may be headed that way. As a precaution, we'll step up the nebulizer treatments, add an antibiotic to the IV, and intubate if absolutely necessary."

"Intubate?" I asked.

"Help her breathe."

"Like a . . . ventilator?"

"Not so drastic. This is just a tube that'll be inserted down the throat to force air into the lungs. But we're not there yet; it's just a possibility. Has her pulmonary doctor been notified?"

Dilly nodded. "I don't think he'll be here until tomorrow." It was already past seven in the evening.

For the next hour, I was fully prepared to pick up the pieces as Dilly fell into the anguish of worry. Instead, I watched her pray. I saw tears that never spilled onto her face. I saw desperation in her eyes softened by folded hands. And when she asked me to pray too, I did.

Nurses came and went, preparing, then wheeling Sierra to X-ray, returning her far quicker than our last visit to the radiology department. It had been only a matter of hours since the last check, so I wondered what it could possibly show, but I didn't question anything. I didn't know enough.

With another influx of nurses came our parents. Their entry was sharply reminiscent of a few weeks ago, when Dilly had been in this very hospital with her broken ribs.

Neither of our parents had ever been especially demonstrative in their affection, but when Dilly saw them, she fell into our mother's open arms. Dad came up beside them, a hand on Dilly's back.

"She'll be all right," he said. "Everything will be fine."

Seeing the comfort Dilly received from them, I longed for Mac to be here and tell me the same thing. *Everything will be all right.* But I told myself running to Mac was the last thing I should do. I needed to get through this for Dilly—*without* depending on Mac.

"How long have you been here?" Mom asked at last as all three moved as one unit closer to Sierra's bed.

"Since around noon."

Mom shook her head. "Nick just called us. We didn't know."

"We'd have been here sooner if we did," Dad said. "We called over to your house, but there was no answer."

"We thought maybe the two of you had come to Springfield for the day," Mom said. She wiped a tissue beneath her nose, then tried to smile. "Shopping or something fun." Her forehead wrinkled and she looked at Sierra, the oxygen mask once again in place, the IV hooked to her hand. "Not this."

"They think she has pneumonia, Mom," Dilly whispered.

Mom had kept an arm around Dilly, and she pulled her even closer. "You been praying, honey?"

Dilly nodded.

"That, and all that the doctors are doing around here, is all we can do."

"You got to hope in the Lord, Dilly," Dad said. "The Good Book says no one who hopes in God will ever be put to shame. Count on that now."

As much as I hesitated to admit it, having my parents there made me feel better too. Before that day, I couldn't have named a single incident when having my parents around had improved things for me, but all of a sudden I had one memory after another. Of when I was sick and my mother tended me with her chicken soup. Of my father buying me new shoes for my eighth-grade graduation. Of them driving all the way to California to see me graduate from college.

I was glad they were here.

Before long Sierra's fever went to 103, then 104. It came down again only to soar anew, frustrating everyone.

Sierra had been moved to the pediatric ICU and placed under the care of a peds intensivist, Dr. Nolan. We couldn't all be in with her at one time, so most of the time I sat in the waiting room with my parents. And Nick had come back—perhaps he realized papers would need to be signed, insurance or otherwise, permission granted, official custodian needed. He provided all of that—without Sharon and only after Dilly looked everything over.

Shortly after his consultation with a pulmonologist and a neurologist, Dr. Nolan ordered Sierra to be intubated. The procedure was done right there in ICU, and Nick came out to the waiting room with a sheen of perspiration covering his suddenly cottony-white face. All he said was he couldn't be there any longer, although Dilly didn't rejoin us for some time.

When she did, she sat beside me. "It's over—the procedure, I mean." She looked wrung out, incapable of anything but breathing. "I'll go back in a minute, but I just had to sit down for a bit."

"I'll go," I said, and Dilly nodded.

Sierra lay on a bed, tubes sticking out in all directions. IVs, oxygen, the tube that must have been traumatic to insert based on how Nick and then Dilly had reacted. I felt a little woozy myself, seeing my niece so weak.

I spoke to Sierra as best I could, telling her we were all here, just in the other room, praying and waiting for her to get better. I told her to rest, to sleep and dream about her mom singing to her, and said that I looked forward to the day we could sing along. I promised to read her more books—I didn't have one with me but would see about getting some.

I kept talking because I knew if I stopped I would sit down and cry. Sierra couldn't possibly be strong enough to withstand all of the machinery she was hooked up to. No one could. And if she could barely survive the equipment helping her, how would she ever survive without it?

We took turns going in and out of the ICU. Past midnight, when my parents dozed on the seats nearby, I watched Dilly and Nick make the exchange. I expected them to pass by one another as they'd been doing all night, but this time Nick touched Dilly's arm on his way into ICU.

"I'm signing papers to put you back on the list for medical information. It has to be done through Sierra's pediatrician."

"Thanks, Nick." Dilly looked like she would have kept walking but stopped. "What about Sharon? Will she be okay with this? You know, after the emergency is over and Sierra is okay? The fever's down. I think she'll be better in the morning."

Nick rubbed his face, then folded his arms on his chest. "You know why my mother almost lost it earlier, Dil?"

She shook her head.

"She wasn't trying to blame you about the meds."

I wanted to smirk but didn't want to give away that I was so blatantly listening. I looked at Dilly; she didn't let on that we already knew what Sharon's real fear had been.

"Okay, so she did try to make it seem that way. But she hasn't slept for a couple months, and for three nights straight it's been really bad. Ma's been doing it alone, the way you used to, but she didn't tell anybody. She's so tired she thought *she* messed up the dosage. Not you."

Dilly shook her head. "But the dosage was written down, and the mix looked the same color it always does. It didn't look any different from usual. Sierra's here because of her lungs, the thing we feared all these years."

"You feared," Nick said. He rubbed the back of his neck. "I didn't even know what to worry about. I'm not much of a dad, am I?"

"You're here now," Dilly said. "And God gave her to both of us, Nick. I haven't figured out why yet, but all we can do is our best for her. Always."

Nick didn't reply. He left the little waiting room we shared only with our sleeping parents and headed toward Sierra's ICU station.

Dilly came to sit beside me. "Did you hear all that?"

I nodded.

"It's hard to believe Sharon admitted she was afraid she'd done something wrong."

"Maybe lately she has a better appreciation for what you went through."

Dilly leaned back on the couch, her head resting on the faux leather cushion. I could see she was tired. I'd dozed a little earlier but was now wide-awake.

"You should try and get some sleep."

"I can't," she said. "The fever's down, but I'm not sure it's under control. She's so weak." Though she'd denied any ability to sleep, my sister's eyes closed. "You're praying, right?" she asked.

"Yes. Right along."

"Does this mean you're not mad at God anymore?"

"Who said I was mad at God?"

Dilly looked at me. "Your whole life has said it. From when we were kids."

I glanced at my parents, listening to make sure their breathing remained the even kind that went with sleep. "I wanted to forget God existed; I wasn't mad at Him."

"That's worse. At least with anger you'd have some kind of relationship."

"I'm just tired enough that it makes sense," I said.

"Did you want to forget about Him because of the way Mom and Dad raised us? That family altar in the corner, kneeling when all we wanted to do was go to bed or read a book—or have a television. All the rules?"

This was a conversation I didn't want to have at all, much less when either one of my parents might hear it. I said nothing.

"Here's the thing, Hannah. Mom and Dad are happy with their faith. They chose the church they go to, same as I did, because it matches the way they are."

I let my gaze fall on the two we were talking about. I couldn't picture them any other way. Maybe Dilly was right; it wasn't the church that made Mom and Dad so rule-crazy. They just . . . were.

Dilly was looking at them too. "Their faith never hurt me. Maybe I was embarrassed a few times because of them, I'll admit that. Embarrassed because we didn't have a television and never went to movies or ball games, so we couldn't talk to other kids about the things they all knew so well. But with Mom and Dad we didn't have to wonder what was expected of us. Believe in God, live clean, work hard. What's wrong with that? You're like that now, whether you see it or not. I think we had a good home and a good church where everybody knew your business, but if you asked for help they were there for you."

Her words reminded me of what Mac had said, about reality and perception sometimes being two different things, at least in my mind. But there was one area I knew I hadn't misjudged.

"The way they were there for you years ago?"

Dilly sat up and faced me, only inches away. "How many times do I have to tell you? I never asked for help." Her brows drew together and she broke her angry stare. She rubbed one arm in a nervous, jerky way, and I could tell she had more to say but was trying to figure out a way to say it. "I kept myself from everybody back then, even from them. You know I stopped going to church the day I married Nick; Mom and Dad hated that. How was I going to ask for help from them, or from anybody in the church? I'd turned my back on all of them before Sierra was ever born."

"Mom and Dad should have known. They should have seen you needed help whether or not you went to church." The same way I should have known.

"I was as good at acting happy as you are, Hannah. When someone offered, I refused. I had it all under control. No one could take care of Sierra the way I could." She met my gaze again so that I had no choice but to look her in the eye. "It seems to me that you have a tougher time with forgiveness than I do, when I'm the one who had so much more forgiven."

All of her words mixed together in my tired, confused mind. She thought I was *acting* happy? Wasn't I happy . . . enough? And forgiveness. She'd reminded me many times how God had forgiven her. She sure didn't need my forgiveness, no matter what she thought.

"You've gone around forgiving everybody just as freely as you say God forgives you, Dilly. Starting with me."

"Who ever said *you* needed to be forgiven? I never once thought you did anything wrong." She smirked. "Well, except for one thing. Wasting six years of your life and topping it off by coming back here to live. Talk about guilt. It's okay for you to feel guilty about not being here for me, but according to you it's not okay for me to feel the same way about the choices you've made—because of *me*."

Her voice had risen somewhat and I stood. "Let's go out in the hall." I wasn't entirely sure she would follow. But before she could, my mother stirred.

"Don't leave on my account. Or your father's, for that matter. He can sleep through anything."

I turned to my mother. "How long have you been awake?"

"Long enough to learn a thing or two. For one, Dilly thinking she couldn't ask for our help because she didn't go to church anymore. It's not true, you know. We were disappointed because we always wanted the best for you. Walking with God is part of that—at least it is for your Dad and me."

Dilly nodded. "It is for me, too. Now."

Mom patted Dilly's knee. "We know that, honey, and couldn't be happier for you." Then Mom looked at me and I wanted to slink from the room. Somehow I didn't think whatever she'd just learned about me was so easily cleared up. "And what you girls talked about made me think I was right all along, about the real reason you came back to Sugar Creek, Hannah."

I returned to my seat, irritated. "Neither one of you understand. I'm glad I came back."

Dilly and my mother exchanged glances and I saw they didn't believe me.

My mother stood, joining me on the couch I'd chosen, the one closer to the door. "We're glad you came back, honey. You've been a good sister to Dilly. But it seems to me you don't really want to be here except for her, the way you'd rather sit in front of that computer and work than spend time with us or neighbors. Seems to me the only time you really smile is when you're talking about California or if that Mac fella is in town."

I stood again, giving them both my back. If leaving the room was one way to end this conversation, I was ready to do it.

Dilly came up behind me. "Hannah—" her voice was barely above a whisper, and I doubted Mom could hear her—"you've been taking care of me since you returned. And it's not your job. Or Mom and Dad's anymore. It's mine. You'd see that if you could get past all the guilt you built up around yourself."

I didn't reply, didn't have one. Yes, I felt guilty. I'd been carrying it around too long to deny its existence. I just wanted the conversation to end.

But Dilly didn't let go. I could see there was more coming from the look on her face. "You know how people are always saying you have to forgive yourself? I guess if that's something you can understand, it's a good thing. But that's not how I look at it."

As much as I was tempted to walk away, I was curious enough to prompt her when she was quiet through a long pause. "Okay, so how do you see it?"

"I think forgiveness is only important inside a relationship."

"I suppose. But you can feel guilty about something all by yourself."

"That's what I'm getting at. There's no reason to if the relationships you have are put right. If you wronged somebody, and they say they forgive you but you don't feel it, then either their actions don't agree with what they said or maybe it's something else. Not so much forgiving yourself but accepting God's forgiveness. God and other people you have a relationship with are the only ones that matter as far as forgiveness goes." Dilly leaned closer. "Hannah, have I ever once made you feel like I blamed you for what happened all those years ago? like I thought things might be different if you'd stayed in Sugar Creek?"

I shook my head.

"Then it's not me you're having trouble accepting forgiveness from. It's God." She smiled. "And, Hannah, He's the easiest one of all to get that from, after all He did for us, making sure we knew about it because it's written down in the Bible."

My mother was looking at me, as if ready to keep the conversation going. I knew I'd have to ponder what Dilly had said, which was something new for me. I wasn't quite ready for my baby sister to be teaching me about life. But right now I wished I were somewhere else. I wished I were by the ocean so I could see my mood reflected there no matter what it looked like to others and be comforted by the empathy it offered. I missed the ocean. I missed Mac. I wanted . . . something I couldn't quite name.

I wanted Mac, but I'd seen him with one too many women to think he'd ever be happy with just me, forever, no matter what he said about me being the first choice. I'd seen what a cheating husband could do to a woman; Dilly's trial had brought that out in more detail than I ever wanted to hear.

I went back to my seat on the couch again, closing my eyes. The only way to end this conversation was to withdraw.

But no matter how good I was at pretending to fall asleep, my thoughts kept me wide-awake inside. God had been a lot easier to ignore before He started invading all my conversations and relationships.

By midmorning the church that I'd so confidently attacked for not having been there for Dilly had sent three messengers. One with flowers and a card, another with food to eat in the waiting room, and a third who'd come to pray and assured us the rest of the church was praying too. All messages had come with a clear urge to let them know if they could help in any other way. My parents played the hosts in the waiting room while Dilly, Nick, and I continued to take turns at Sierra's side.

Against Sharon's wishes Nick had called the physician who'd tended half the town since before I was born. He diagnosed Sharon with complete exhaustion and a touch of the flu and she was under no circumstance to come near Sierra until her bug was gone. I couldn't help being relieved.

Throughout the next twenty-four hours Sierra's fever continued to fluctuate even as antibiotics were given and the intubator did her breathing. The following afternoon I went home once for a quick shower and to bring a change of clothes for Dilly. I retrieved my cell phone and checked my e-mail while I'd been there. No messages from California. Not one.

Maybe it really was over.

If he'd called, just once, or sent me the most casual of e-mails, I'd have called him in an instant, brought him up-to-date about all that was happening. Asked him to pray, told him I'd found myself praying alongside Dilly. That I was finally beginning to believe God was after me, the way Mac had laughed about so long ago.

Most of all, I'd have told him how amazing Dilly had been throughout this ordeal. How strong she was, watching her daughter struggle for her life and yet not falling to pieces. Her faith, I was convinced, held her together. Not me.

But he hadn't called, so I didn't.

# Dilly

I remember one time I stole five dollars from my dad's wallet. I was thirteen, and there was a movie I just *had* to see. *City Slickers* released in June, and before summer even started, everybody was talking about it. I had to see it.

But of course movies were something my parents never approved of, even if it did have a PG-13 rating and I'd turned thirteen.

Convincing Hannah to drive me to the theater was no big deal. That was her last summer home, before going off to California for college. She never asked where I got the money; both Dad and Uncle Steve used to pay me for the work I did. But I never saw a cent. It went straight to my bank account. At the time I thought it really unfair, but it came in handy when I planned my wedding. Mom and Dad didn't want me to marry Nick, but they'd always told me I could spend the money I'd earned when I was eighteen. They didn't appreciate my spending it on a wedding to a guy they didn't approve of, but they didn't go back on their word.

But when I was thirteen, I couldn't touch a dime of it. That's why I resorted to swiping money. Turned out there was such a heavy hand of guilt on my shoulders I couldn't enjoy the movie anyway. These days I'm so grateful to be forgiven for the really big stuff in my life that I *should* find it silly when this little sin still comes back to haunt me.

That was the only time in my life I ever stole anything. I don't count taking the receipts from Nick's wallet for things he bought for his girlfriends. I kept track of how much money he was spending on other women. It started after I'd found a hotel receipt in the glove compartment of his truck, and after that I was always looking for evidence. Not that I needed such a thing after a while. He flat out told me he was seeing other people and if I didn't like it I could just leave. But where was I supposed to go? Home, where marrying Nick might have been thought of as a mistake, but divorce was one of those sins that could never be forgiven? At least that's what I thought my parents believed in those days. When everything came out at the trial about Nick cheating on me, they said I had "biblical grounds" for the divorce. Would've been nice if I'd known that sooner.

Anyway, here I am stealing something for the second time in my life. Hannah is in with Sierra, even though I know I have to get back in there as quick as I can. Hannah's being a real trooper about all this, but I can tell it's scaring her to death.

Here it is, in her jacket pocket. Hannah's cell. I don't have a cell of my own, although Dad has one and he told me he's going to get one for me, too, so he can reach me no matter where I am on the farm. I'm in no hurry to be that accessible, so I haven't reminded him about it.

I slip the phone into the pocket of my own jacket, then head downstairs and out the door, where I can use the phone freely. It's not as if I'm really stealing it. I'm just borrowing it to make a phone call I don't want her to know about.

I have no idea how to use it, so I slide it open and start pushing buttons. Thankfully my search brings up a list of names. My parents, Aunt Elsie, other names I don't recognize. And there it is: Mac.

I press the green phone icon, hoping it's going to connect to his number. There's a delay, almost long enough to make me think I might have done something wrong, but then it rings.

"I'm glad you called."

It's Mac, all right, and he sounds so happy he must think Hannah is on this end.

"It's me. Dilly."

"Oh, hi, Dilly. You're calling on Hannah's phone?"

"Yeah. We're at the hospital in Springfield."

"Is she okay?"

The worry is so quick to come through his voice that I know a moment of envy. Must be nice to have someone instantly worry about you.

"Yeah, she's fine. It's Sierra."

"What's going on?"

"She's pretty sick, Mac. We've been here for a couple of days. Hannah's been here with me this whole time. I guess since you didn't know about Sierra being here that Hannah hasn't called you."

"No, she hasn't."

Mac really ought to do something about hiding his emotions. His disappointment is so clear in those few words that I'm feeling sorry for him, even while I'm eager to get my message to him so I can get back upstairs to Sierra.

"How's Sierra doing?" His tone is better now, concerned instead of sad. "Is she going to be all right?

"We're working on that." I don't say more, because I can feel my throat tighten with worry. "But that's not why I called. I was talking to Hannah last night—about lots of things. I guess being in a hospital makes people open up a little more. I don't know where you guys stand, but I think you need to come here. If you come right now, while she's needing a friend, then she won't be able to send you away again."

"Think so? She's made it pretty clear she doesn't want to depend on me."

"We're all worried about Sierra. Hannah hasn't gotten any more sleep than I have in the past couple of days. I know she needs a friend right now because I've needed my friends. The thing with Hannah, though, is she doesn't have any around here. She needs you."

There's a silence like he's considering what I'm saying. I wonder if I'm doing the right thing, interfering this way. But part of me isn't one bit insecure. How many times has Hannah interfered in my life?

"I'll be there as soon as I can."

Then, without even a good-bye—*don't they exchange hellos or good-byes on these phones?*—the line goes silent.

# 36

IN THE morning, I tried getting Dilly to eat breakfast, but she refused. I had trouble eating too, but I did manage a bagel and some juice. Nick and my parents were still in the waiting room, but despite everyone trying to coax Dilly, she didn't eat a thing.

She went back to Sierra's side, and not long afterward she came back to the waiting room with the first smile of the day.

"They're extubating Sierra—taking the tube out!"

I jumped from my seat, the first to reach Dilly. We celebrated the news, listening as Dilly told us how they thought Sierra was strong enough to breathe on her own, how this meant she wouldn't be in danger of becoming dependent upon equipment to do the breathing for her.

"She *must* be getting better!" Dilly said.

Nick took the good news as permission to go home. He said he would be back, and this time even I believed him. Throughout the afternoon, my parents, Dilly, and I took turns sitting with Sierra. Although she was hooked up to one fewer machine, she still looked far too sick to me, but because I knew Dilly would be able to tell if I didn't, I forced hope into my thoughts even as Sierra's fever continued to fluctuate.

Eventually our parents went home but told us they would be back the next morning. They'd been depending on Beacon to do the hog chores—his wrist now healed and fully functional—but I knew they didn't want to impose on him for long after having given him such short notice to begin with. After they left, the waiting room crowd usually consisted only of Dilly and me, despite the comings and goings of two other families.

Near six, Tom Boyle arrived with quiet concern and hamburgers. As I watched Dilly politely eating the food Tom had brought, I couldn't help thinking this wasn't exactly the way I'd hoped they'd share a meal. And while I was glad Tom had come, gladder still that Dilly was eating something, this whole scenario in no way matched my original plan.

Especially when, after eating only half of the hamburger, Dilly set it down. "I can't eat any more."

Both Tom and I had already finished ours, Dilly had fussed with hers so long. "You've hardly eaten for over two days," I said. "Don't give up yet."

Dilly sent me a half smile, shaking her head just the same.

"I don't care if you give up on the hamburger," Tom said, "just so long as you're not giving up on everything else. She's going to be all right. Everything's in God's hands."

"And they took out that awful tube," I reminded her. "That means she's getting stronger."

Dilly's eyes filled with tears as she looked between Tom and me. "I'm not giving up. That's just it. It's the not knowing. If she's on the mend, why can't they keep the fever down? I can handle either way this goes. I just don't like not knowing."

"Either way?" I asked.

She brushed away a lone tear. "Don't read anything into that. But shouldn't I long for heaven for Sierra? I'd be lost without her, not having her here. So is it me I'm worrying about? my life? I know it'll be all right in the end, whenever that may be. Eternity is a long time compared to a lifetime or two."

I heard the certainty behind those words and once again I was struck by Dilly's strength. Here she was, facing every parent's worst nightmare: a child in ICU. And yet she still functioned, still prayed, still hoped. She was assured that whatever happened, she could still trust God.

I wanted that assurance, that belief that God loved me so much that even if I spent the rest of this life alone, I could find enough good in it to keep trusting He had something worthwhile for me to do. I thought I was supposed to take care of Dilly; that was worthwhile. Or share my life with Mac. That was a life I once thought I wanted.

But if I couldn't have that and Dilly didn't need me, then why had God brought me home? Even my mother didn't think I belonged here anymore.

I thought of my parents and of Sugar Creek. I couldn't help believing coming home had been the right thing. I knew my sister better now than I ever had, and we'd survived more than a couple of rough spots. I could also see my parents through the eyes of an adult, see all of Sugar Creek with a new attitude. Seeing it through Mac's eyes had taught me it wasn't the boring, strict place of my memories. It had its share of problems, like anywhere else. But it was full of people who cared about one another. Was it a place I could live?

According to my mother, that meant I'd have to spend less time by myself, mix in with the community. I used to do that because of my job, back in California. Could I do it here?

I was barely listening to Tom and Dilly. Instead of talking about Sierra's care, which was all Dilly had been talking about for the past two days, they spoke of the town. It was all so normal, and judging by Dilly's face I guessed the conversation was exactly what she needed.

Dilly's friend Sandee had been there twice, along with Aunt Elsie and Uncle Steve. I'd seen more people in these last two days than I'd normally see in a week at home. Dilly had been quiet through the visits, as usual, but each visitor left her a little stronger, I thought, instead of drained, the way I was feeling. They'd brought their love and concern. The way Tom did now.

I knew if I'd let him, Mac would be here for me the way the town was here for Dilly. I could call him and he would drop everything if I told him I needed him. California might not have provided me the same quantity of community, but in Mac I had the same quality.

Only I'd tossed it away.

"Mrs. Carlson?"

A young nurse stood at the waiting room door. I hadn't seen her before, but then who could keep track of all the personnel we'd dealt with?

"You'll want to come with me."

Dilly lost whatever peace had settled on her face while Tom had spoken so calmly, so normally as he sat on the nearby chair. She popped from the chair and followed. I went along. There weren't supposed to be more than two of us in the room at the same time, and Tom went only as far as the ICU door.

"Sierra's breathing has become labored again," the nurse was saying as we walked. "The doctor wants to talk to you about it."

A physician met us at Sierra's ICU station, not Dr. Nolan but another intensivist.

"Sierra's throat hasn't responded well since we took out the tube, Mrs. Carlson," he said. "She was getting along well enough for a time, but breathing is becoming hard for her again. We might have to reintubate her."

Dilly shook her head. "No . . . no. If she's reintubated, she might—she might *never* breathe on her own. She could depend on that, and then—"

The doctor nodded but at the same time held up a hand to still Dilly's protest. "I understand your concerns, Mrs. Carlson. There is the possibility of her body depending on equipment to breathe, and chances are a second intubation will be harder to get over than a first. It also leaves the last resort—a tracheotomy procedure, if necessary."

"A trach!" One of her hands went to the side of her face, and I grabbed the other; it was as cold as ice.

"You still have two choices, Mrs. Carlson," he told her. "Reintubate or we can try a BiPAP, a tube that'll be inserted through the nose. The difficult thing with that is it has to stay in place. I know

Sierra doesn't have much control over her limbs, but if she thrashes or pushes at the tube it won't be as effective as she'll need."

"If it'll keep her from having to go through the intubation again . . ." Dilly was near tears now, I could tell, but she didn't give in to them. She shook her head. "I don't want her intubated again, if there's any way not to."

He nodded. "But my point is we may be resorting to that anyway, if necessary."

"But the BiPAP—that doesn't take any anesthesia? It's through the nose, you said. And it's easier to take out?"

He nodded.

She took a step closer. "I can be right by her side, make sure it stays in place."

"And I can help," I said. The words were out before I knew what I was saying. Could I really help? Sitting beside Sierra and talking to her, occasionally holding her hand, was far different from this. Could I really hold something in place that—if I held it wrong and couldn't tell if I was helping or hindering her breathing—could *kill* her?

"All right, then. You might have to live up to that promise. We don't have the staff to do it for her, which is why reintubation might be necessary anyway."

New equipment appeared in the room almost immediately, the nurses and doctor hovering over Sierra to hook yet another machine to her frail little body. I didn't want to stay, I didn't want to watch, but there was no moving Dilly, and so I stayed with her, still clutching her hand.

The doctor motioned for Dilly to come closer and gave her quiet instructions on the machine, the pressure needed, the consequences of letting the tube slip out of place. I listened, and now that I wasn't holding Dilly's cold hand, sweat started to seep out of mine.

Dilly held the BiPAP in place. It was a narrow tube that forcefully delivered oxygen to Sierra's lungs, through her nose and with a mask that fit over her forehead. Dilly told me Sierra always hated having something in her nose. She squirmed and moved her head back and forth as if to shake the tube away and might have succeeded if Dilly didn't firmly hold Sierra in place.

For the next hour, Dilly sang to her daughter again, never letting up her gentle, steady hold. I sat nearby, wanting to help, dreading my turn. I knew in that moment who were the strongest in the room: Sierra for surviving; Dilly for doing all she could to see her daughter through the next second, the next minute, the next hour.

Admiration filled me, seeing Dilly so strong and steady, even though underneath she was the most worried of all. I felt a tinge of my old anger at God, knowing how much they'd both sustained. It never ended, not even now. How could I have ever doubted Dilly's strength? Who else could withstand all she'd faced?

"Aren't you angry, Dil? I mean . . . at God?" Fear and fatigue must have compromised control of my tongue. I knew Dilly had enough on her mind without me challenging her faith right now.

Instead of answering, my sister looked at me for what seemed an oddly long period of time. Then something entered her eye I didn't expect. The light that was always followed by laughter. A laugh came, not long, not loud, but a laugh just the same.

"Why should I be angry with the one person who helps me make sense of anything? I'm not the only one in the world to see somebody I love suffer." She looked at Sierra and my gaze followed. Sierra was sleeping, as soundly as she could with so many machines hooked up to her. "Look at her. I remember when she was born, the moment I first saw her. I thought she was perfect. This little person who's part of me but her own, too. Separate and beautiful. She's still perfect, Hannah. Only nobody sees that except me. And God. Someday, when we're in heaven, everyone will know how perfect she really is."

I might have doubted Dilly's sanity just then, with such extraordinary words on the heels of that strangely timed laughter. But as she gently stroked Sierra's hair, I saw the truth. No wonder Dilly never complained about tending to Sierra's needs, never looked at her as though she were misshapen or different. Dilly had accepted her daughter exactly as she was. The way she'd been created. Love, familiarity, acceptance . . . all made Sierra perfect.

Then, instead of talking, Dilly bent over Sierra and started singing again. This time she sang "Amazing Grace," and after a while I joined her. When she came to the last verse, words I could barely recall from singing the hymn as a child, I saw Dilly's eyes moisten and her hands tremble. "'When we've been there ten thousand years . . .'" Her voice quivered until the final line, when I joined in and her voice was strong again.

"Back when I did what I did . . . before then," Dilly whispered, "I used to live with an ache inside of me. All the time, day and night, day after day. I never even thought about heaven. But now I do. I know we'll be there together, me and Sierra." She gave me a half smile. "You'd think I'd do anything to get us there, wouldn't you? But the thing is, every time I think of that ache, I know I have hope now. And I'm grateful for the life God gave us. There's nothing I wouldn't do to give both of us, me and Sierra, the best of life now. His gift. Here and now. Life is God's greatest gift, Hannah."

I nodded, feeling myself relax with her words, knowing what they meant, having witnessed the actions that went with her beliefs. And I knew I had nothing to worry about, either, at least about Dilly and Sierra.

I also knew what I had to do now. Pray for the strength I'd need. Help Dilly. I couldn't avoid the clock forever. Dilly had been holding the BiPAP for almost two hours.

"Are you tired, Dil?" I asked, even though every part of me still didn't want to ask. But I'd waited too long already, and after that prayer the question had come out of my mouth before I could stop it. I saw Dilly was tired by the bend of her shoulders. She couldn't last much longer, and Sierra must still need the machine or the doctor would have returned.

Dilly nodded, as I uneasily expected. Stepping closer, I placed my hand on Dilly's, letting her slip away.

"Am I doing this right?"

"Of course you are," she said gently, "so long as the tube stays in place. She's resting easier now. Maybe she won't fight it anymore."

The muscles in my arms were tense with fear; in my back they were pulled taut. I wasn't sure if I was applying too much pressure or not enough, but I was grateful that Sierra seemed to still be asleep. Then she moved, and I nearly lost my tentative hold.

"It's all right," I said, and perhaps Dilly thought I was trying to soothe Sierra. To my relief, the tube was still in place.

And there I sat. Dilly stayed for fifteen minutes, and all of the time Sierra barely moved. When my sister said she was going to the bathroom and would stop and talk to the doctor, I only nodded. Despite the wish to hide my unease from her, I didn't want her to leave. What if I needed her help? Sierra could move at any moment. But I let her go without a word, allowing only a quick glance to the nearby nurse's station to make sure someone was still nearby.

Despite my resolve to match Dilly's strength, my hands began to tremble, and my eyes were stinging from tears held back too long. My back and shoulders ached from leaning at such an odd angle, keeping the tube in place, holding her head steady. By now Dilly had been gone over a half hour and all I wanted to do was lie down beside Sierra and fall into sleep. But I knew I couldn't.

And so I prayed . . . again. Did I believe what I'd seen these past two days? that the strength of no less than a Creator God was shoring up Dilly? Why couldn't He do the same for me? Why had I only thought of Mac, wishing him to be here, keeping me sane, keeping me strong, so I could be that way for Dilly?

Dilly had faith; maybe I didn't, after all. Maybe that was why I didn't have the strength I'd seen in my sister, the very sister I'd come here to help. To save. What a puny thing that was, my offer to help. Dilly was so much stronger than I'd ever been, and she'd proven that a thousand times. I only realized it in these past two days.

"Oh, God," I whispered. "Oh, God . . . help me to believe. Let me be stronger, like You've made Dilly."

Sierra wiggled just then and I nearly lost my grip on the BiPAP, but it held after all. I watched my niece, her eyes opening above the mask, and she looked right at me.

"You're so strong to stand all of this, Sierra," I said gently. From somewhere, I felt a smile on my lips; having her look at me must have made it possible, given me the strength I needed to fight curling up and falling asleep right next to her. "I guess I can depend on God to help me to be what I need to be . . . maybe even as strong as you and your mom."

I don't know if she heard me. She closed her eyes again, and I heard the oxygen going into her lungs through the tube beneath my hands.

Just as I considered calling for a nurse, Dilly came to the other side of the bed with the doctor at her side. He told me to step back so he could examine her, and I moved stiffly away, my arms initially uncooperative, like they weren't attuned to my brain messages anymore.

The doctor had barely listened to Sierra's breathing before he turned to Dilly with a smile. "Would you care to say good evening to your daughter? She's wide-awake."

Dilly went closer and I saw Sierra's gaze land on her. Dilly grabbed her hand. "Oh, sweetie, I've been waiting to say hi to you all day, do you know that? You're going to be just fine."

"Let's see how she's doing without this, shall we?" the doctor said, reaching for the BiPAP.

I stepped closer, and though Sierra's gaze began to wander as it usually did, it didn't settle on me again. But that was okay. God had awakened her just early enough to get me through those last few minutes.

"Go out to the waiting room, will you, Hannah?" Dilly said over her shoulder.

I wasn't sure I wanted to go; I wanted to tell Dilly, somehow, that just a moment ago, right here at her daughter's side, I felt a miracle happen. But I didn't know how to put it into words.

So I obeyed and left the unit.

I was so tired I watched my feet take each step to the waiting room, thinking of how good it would feel to sit. In the past two and a half days I'd gotten no more than a few hours' sleep. How in the world had Dilly survived so many sleepless nights for so many years on her own and Sharon so many years since? I wouldn't last a week.

"Hannah."

I stopped, convinced for a moment that I'd lost my mind. During the last hour in ICU I'd gone from exhaustion to euphoria and just now back to exhaustion. Now I was hearing voices?

I sensed a shadow in front of me and I was almost afraid to lift my gaze. So many things went through my mind. Was this God's way of telling me I wasn't strong on my own, that I should just go ahead and admit I needed Mac, and so I'd dreamed him up? I knew I wasn't coherent enough to figure out any of my emotions. I only knew one thing: when I lifted my eyes, if I didn't see Mac in front of me, I'd just fall to the floor in a heap of disappointed exhaustion.

But there he was. Not exactly smiling—his face was too somber, even though the look in his eye was one of pure love. He closed the last step between us and I fell into his arms instead of to the floor.

"You're—you're here?" I leaned into him, everything about him instantly and intimately familiar. The feel of his chest, of his arms around me, of his hand stroking my hair. I wanted to melt into him, to become part of him, so I'd never be without him again.

But then I pulled sharply away. I pounded his chest once, as if he'd accosted rather than embraced me. I felt him stiffen, but other than that he didn't react, didn't even remove his hands from my arms.

"You're here!" I shouted. "Just when I was trying to convince myself I could get through this on my own—okay, with prayer, but without resorting to you for support, the way I always have." Tears streamed from my eyes, but I did nothing to clean them away.

"Hannah, what's wrong?"

I wanted to pull him close and strike at him again all at the same time. Pulling him close won out.

"I'm sorry. I—I don't know what I was thinking. How did you know?"

"Dilly called me from your phone. I got here as soon as I could."

I looked behind me but couldn't see her through the closed ICU doors. "She didn't tell me." I became aware of the tears still on my face, of nurses passing behind us, but I knew in this unit they'd seen emotions run a wider gamut than mine. I wiped tear remnants from my cheeks.

Mac was studying me so closely I wished I knew what he saw. But I couldn't make out a thing just then. How was I ever, ever going to get on without him when having him here rejuvenated me more than anything else had so far? For a moment I'd believed I possessed an ounce of my own strength, but here he was, his presence disproving that short-lived theory.

"I don't understand. Why wouldn't Dilly want me to know she'd called?" I eyed him. "Did you tell her you weren't coming?"

He tilted his head. "Why would I say that? I couldn't get off the phone fast enough to see how soon I could get a flight."

I leaned into him again. "Let's go sit down."

"You look beat," he said. "Dilly told me Sierra was in bad shape, but just now when I saw her, she said things were looking up. It sounds like you've all had a tough time, especially Sierra."

"She looked at me for the first time since we got here, just a little while ago." I led the way back to the waiting room. "Like she's back to herself after all she's been through."

The waiting room was empty except for the image of the newscaster on a cable news channel. Tom was gone. I took a seat, but Mac only joined me after turning off the television.

"What's going on? Why didn't *you* call me?"

I wanted to take his hand, tell him I loved him, tell him I'd purposely not called because I needed to prove to myself I could be all Dilly needed. But I'd proven something else instead. Dilly didn't need me. All she needed was her faith in God. Maybe that was something I needed too.

"I'm a complete failure." I should have said something else, but those were the only coherent words that made it past my lips.

He put his arms around me. "What? All Dilly said when I showed up was how grateful she was for you, how you were just now taking turns holding some kind of machine in place, that she couldn't have done it alone. Nick wouldn't do it, Sharon couldn't, your parents have been great but had to get back to the hogs. Only you."

I'd heard all of the words, and they even registered at some level because a wash of relief went through me, as if I'd needed to hear exactly what he said. As usual. "But I hardly helped at all. Dilly did it most of the time." I sighed, then tried to smile. "When I left, the doctor was taking it away."

Mac put a gentle hand beneath my chin, tilting my face his way. "How are you, Hannah?"

More tears pricked my eyes. "I don't know how to do this, Mac. I don't know how Dilly did it. For that matter I don't know how Sharon has done it either. It's been nothing but bad news, more bad news, a little good news, more bad news, a trace of hope. I'm so exhausted I can't sort my thoughts anymore."

He leaned toward me and pulled my head to his shoulder. "Then just rest. I'm not going anywhere, and if Dilly needs someone to take turns in there again, I'll do it."

I had every intention of arguing. Only one thing stood in my way. I put off my objections just long enough to fall asleep, right there in the ICU waiting room. In Mac's arms.

# 37

I WOKE to the sound of voices talking from the other side of the room. Unfamiliar people, familiar tone. Somber, worried over a loved one in ICU.

I sat up, aware of the same sweater I'd worn for a day and a half now, needing a shower. I looked around. Had I dreamed Mac's arrival? I must have, because he was nowhere to be seen.

The ICU nurse's station was just inside the double doors. I approached, at the same time spotting the clock that hung above. One o'clock. In the morning or afternoon? I didn't even know.

I saw the unit where Sierra lay, but the curtain was drawn.

"Your sister is with Sierra now," a nurse told me before I could inquire. She smiled. "They're both asleep, the last time I checked. Sierra's been breathing on her own for several hours now. And no fever."

Taking a breath of relief, I carefully walked closer to the unit Sierra occupied. She was there, the oxygen still tented above her, IVs still hooked to her little hands. And there was Dilly, in a padded chair right beside her. Sound asleep.

I went back to the waiting room, and my heart twirled. So Mac hadn't been a dream, after all.

"I wondered where you went," he greeted me. "I was only gone a minute to the bathroom, and when I came back, you'd disappeared."

I didn't join him. Instead, I lingered by the doorway. My mind was still muddled, and I wondered if any parts of my dream were true, if I'd really been angry when I saw him, if I'd cried.

Just then I needed the bathroom, and I told him so.

Alone at the sink, I splashed warm water on my face, not wanting to see how awful I looked but unable to resist. Old mascara shadowed my puffy lower lids, deepening the circles left from exhaustion. My hair, no doubt from sleeping on the couch, was a disaster, sticking up on one side, matted on the other. Mac and I had once been stranded overnight at LaGuardia because of a snowstorm, and I thought I'd been a mess then, but I'd been a beauty queen compared to now.

I ran my fingers through my hair, smoothing it. Then I washed my face, rinsed out my mouth, and even as I made such efforts, I realized what I looked like didn't really matter. Not now, not when we still didn't know if Sierra would be all right.

When I got back, Mac was watching a news story on the television someone had turned on again. It somehow still amazed me that the news was on twenty-four hours a day, even now in the middle of the night. That there was always news to report.

"How long did I sleep?" I asked as I sat nearby. Not too close—I was too much a mess for that—but this was clearly our corner, while the other family occupied another. A man snored while his wife watched the television.

"About four hours," he said.

I raised my brows. That was longer than I thought, although I knew it must have been some length or I wouldn't have felt so rested.

"And Dilly?"

"She was here a few minutes after you fell asleep, then went back in by Sierra."

"She's sleeping now."

There was a long pause; each of us glanced at the television screen, but not a word registered in my mind. I wanted to talk, just not here. Not when we couldn't be alone.

"Thank you for coming all this way," I said, low. The television wasn't loud enough to drown out our conversation, but it did help to give us a little privacy.

He grinned at me. "You didn't seem all that pleased when I got here."

I looked away, my face heated. "I'm sorry. I was just so tired—"

He reached to grab my hand; I let him. "I know. And four hours still isn't enough. Why don't you try to go back to sleep?"

We sat there, constrained by the other worrying family, mindful that a doctor or nurse could come in at any time and tell us Sierra needed something else, some new machine or medication. Or Dilly might wake and join us. But eventually I did fall back asleep, just after I heard Mac's even breathing beside me.

My parents returned in the morning, surprised and glad to see Mac. Shortly after them Nick returned too. I introduced Mac. Nick told us Sharon was on the mend and hoped to be at the hospital tomorrow. I wanted to ask if he'd told her about putting Dilly back on the list to share medical information, that he'd deferred to Dilly on almost every decision that had been made since Sierra was admitted. But I didn't; he would have to deal with Sharon himself.

When Dilly joined us, all I saw was her smile. She looked as fresh as if she'd slept at home in her own bed instead of on a chair beside her frail daughter.

"The doctor said he thinks Sierra will be all right." Then she threw herself at my parents, who hugged her as if they were used to such a thing.

"They're going to keep her in ICU for a while, though, just in case anything changes. But everyone who's seen her in the past hour has said it's a miracle. She's breathing on her own; she even smiled at me. And no fever."

Dilly looked at me over my mother's shoulder, mouthing "Thank you." I didn't know what she meant. I hadn't done a thing.

I caught Mac's eye then, who looked more somber than the occasion warranted.

That afternoon while my parents stayed with Dilly, Mac took me home, where I enjoyed my much-anticipated shower. There, with warm water pouring over my head, the worries of the last few days seemed to slide down the drain. I hadn't prayed so often since I was a very little girl and wanted to please my parents.

Only now I saw it all differently. That moment in ICU when Sierra had opened her eyes to look at me, it was as if God had instantly answered my prayer. I knew things here on earth didn't often work that way, and as I'd reminded Dilly not long ago, God wasn't a genie, there to grant our wishes.

But this had been different. Peace had accompanied that moment, a glimpse of the kind Dilly had. From God.

I was sure Sierra had opened her eyes as a direct answer to my prayer. It had been just what I needed, a sign that everything was going to be all right and everything we'd done would be worth it.

Had that been any different from Mac showing up? Why had I thought, even for a moment, that Mac's arrival had been anything other than God showing me it was all right to depend on those He placed in my life? Hadn't that been exactly what I'd been telling Dilly to do all along? Why was it all right for her to need me (when she really didn't) but I shouldn't need Mac?

I'd been an idiot.

When I emerged, the smell of food led me to the kitchen. Mac had cooked a full meal—tender chicken with crisp zucchini stirred into lemon-flavored rice.

He ate too but not nearly as much as I did. I savored each bite, thinking food never tasted so good as after worries were left behind.

His gaze settled on the glass ball he'd given me, the little piece of the ocean intended to bribe me back to California. I kept it in the center of the kitchen table, not because it was big enough to be a centerpiece or because that was the most aesthetic place for it to be, but because I liked starting every day by looking at it.

"Has that been sitting there since I gave it to you?" he asked.

"Here, there, and everywhere." I was too embarrassed to admit I'd taken it to bed with me more than a few times. "I take it where I can see it."

"I thought you'd use it as a paperweight or something. On your desk."

"It's been there, too."

He smiled but not for long. Pushing away the plate in front of him, he reached across the table. I put both of my hands in the one he offered.

"Mac. We need to talk."

He nodded. "Yes, we do. I was sitting here thinking that very same thing."

I smiled. "You were?" He looked far too grim to have been thinking anything along the lines of my own thoughts.

"Yes. I was planning to come back one last time, to try convincing you to come home with me. I was going to bring you a plane ticket, thinking if I could get you back to California, even for a weekend, I might have a chance. Then Dilly called. For one wild minute I thought this might be it, the excuse I needed to come and get you when I knew you wouldn't want me to."

He looked at me, pulling away and leaning back in his chair. I saw the sadness in his eyes. "When I got here, she told me how bad it was, that doctors have told her from the time Sierra was little that when she dies—whenever that may be—it'll be because of pneumonia. I wondered what she would be doing if you weren't right here, facing whatever's ahead alongside of her."

"But Sierra's going to be okay. She's made it through the worst of it; she's on the mend."

"Maybe. I understand better now, though, about why you want to stay."

I shifted in my seat, leaning closer still. Since he'd leaned back, he seemed too far away. "I'm glad I was here for her, Mac. But here's the thing: In these past few days, it wasn't me giving Dilly enough comfort to get her through. It was God."

He smiled again, but the serious look in his eye didn't disappear. "Glad to hear you're crediting God with something for once."

"All I could do was pray, ever since Sierra was admitted. It occurred to me nothing makes any sense unless there's a God who created all of us, someone who made us for a reason. We wouldn't all care so much if we were just some chemicals all mixed together by chance, would we?"

"So you did read that book I sent you," he said.

I nodded. "But it didn't sink in until these past few days."

At last he leaned forward again, reaching over to stroke my cheek, and I wanted to turn my face and kiss his hand, but something held me back. That look in his eye, that reserve. I couldn't figure out why it was still there.

"I learned something else in these past few days, Mac. Did you hear what I said a moment ago? It wasn't me getting Dilly through this; it was God."

"But God used you," he said. "He helped Dilly through you. That's why I know now that it's right for you to stay. I'm a slow learner in some things, Hannah, but one of the things I'm realizing is that God's plans aren't always mine, and I have to go with what makes the most sense. Not selfishly, not because of what I want. But what's best."

"So now you're convinced I should stay?" I was astounded. What horrible timing.

"Dilly needs you."

I paused, considering what to say. "Remember when you told me to look at Dilly in a new way? to see the strength she has? I saw it, Mac. She's so much stronger than me, and it's because her faith has been stronger than mine. Until now. We talked about a lot of things while we were in the waiting room. One thing that I remember was her saying all this guilt I'm feeling about letting her down had to be because of some kind of relationship. Either the one with her or the one I had with God. And you know what? My little sister was right."

"What did she say, exactly?"

"That I wasn't feeling guilty about things because of her—she never blamed me, and I knew that. I was feeling guilty because I've been so mad at God all this time. Forgiveness counts most inside a relationship—either with somebody else or with God. Once I figured out the forgiveness was there, both from her and from God, there wasn't any reason for my guilt anymore."

His brows drew together. "I saw her tell you thank you, there in the waiting room. Maybe she realizes she couldn't have gotten through this without you."

A little laugh bubbled up inside me. "Let's ask her."

He shook his head. "No, because you know what she'll say, no matter what the truth is. She wants you to believe she can get through anything on her own, no matter what the reality is."

"And I'm telling you that of the two of us these past few days, Dilly was the stronger. I saw it; I can admit it. If I can admit it, you can believe her when she tells you the same thing."

Mac leaned closer to me, his face barely inches from mine. Something new was forming in his eye, taking the place of the bleakness that had been there before. Hope. "So . . . what are you saying, Hannah? That you think—that you finally believe she can manage on her own? Here? Without you?"

I nodded. "I'm ready to come home, Mac. That is, if you want me to."

He laughed, but I had one last thing on my mind. "You told me I didn't have to worry about measuring up, but I have to admit it's been scary watching you go through so many dates over the years."

He put his hands on my face, one on each side. "Who could live up to you? I've been looking for a woman I could trust, Hannah. Someone with the kind of loyalty I've never seen—until you. These last years have proven there's nobody else out there for me except you.

"Then I guess you're stuck with me, Mac. Forever."

# Dilly

"This little girl is lucky to have a mom like you," the doctor says from the other side of the bed.

I want to bask in the words, but I have to glance at Sharon because I think she'll take the moment away from me. To my surprise she doesn't even look at me; she's still looking at Sierra. I wonder if Sharon heard the doctor's words, because if she did I can't believe she let the comment pass without a contradiction. Maybe she's just too tired to talk. She looks about as wrung out as Sierra was looking until last night's peaceful hours of sleep.

The doctor pats Sierra's arm, tells her she's doing a good job at getting herself well, then before leaving the room reminds us she'll need to sleep again, so we can leave her alone for a while.

He's just given us the best report I could have prayed for: Sierra is on the mend. Nothing's guaranteed, of course, but she's been breathing on her own so many hours now that he thinks she's past any danger. Still, I don't think it's a good idea to leave her alone. I know the nurses will check on her, but I've barely left her side since she got here and I want to stay. If Sharon will let me. At least to take turns with her.

Sierra is still wearing an oxygen mask and still needs her regular secretions pulled out, but her eyes have been open and alert for some time now. Not only is she no longer coughing, she's calm and peaceful. She even smiles on occasion, although I think the doctor's right about her getting tired again.

"That doctor said it just right," I say. "You're so strong, Sierra. You did it; you got better. I'm proud of you."

I glance up at Sharon, who still says nothing. Nick probably filled her in on all of the procedures Sierra has been through in the past couple of days, because she didn't ask any questions when the doctor was here.

"Sharon," I say softly, "I want to thank you for bringing Sierra in when you did. You did the right thing in getting her here."

She sighs and grips the metal bar on the side of Sierra's bed. "I thought . . . I might have waited too long. But I've brought her in before when it turned out to be nothing. I didn't want her to be poked and prodded like a pin cushion."

I shake my head, even though I'm secretly surprised she's admitting any doubts to me. "The pneumonia was only just building," I remind her. "They didn't even catch it at first."

I look down and see Sierra is starting to fall back asleep. Sharon must see it too, because we look at each other and then without a word walk from the room. Maybe Sharon is still exhausted from her own lack of sleep, but this is the most civil conversation I can recall having with her. Best to keep it short, I suppose.

We come to the waiting room and the first voice I hear is Tom's. I notice my insides do a little dance, something that hasn't happened since . . . I can't even remember. I guess it could be that I'm just happy about Sierra getting better.

But no. Tom is here again, and I'm starting to believe Hannah's opinion. He's acting like more than just a nice guy.

I feel a smile already on my face as I get ready to greet him.

# 38

MAC AND I had just arrived back at the hospital, where we found not only my parents and Nick, but Tom Boyle as well.

Tom greeted us with a smile. "Doctors say Sierra is a miracle. Dilly's in there with her. With Sharon."

I shot a glance Nick's way. "Sharon . . . and Dilly together? With Sierra?"

Nick nodded just as Tom stepped around us to the door, stuck his head out, then faced us with a smile. "And no fireworks coming from that direction," he said, "so I guess they're getting along."

"I have a whole new respect for Sharon," I admitted. "After only a few nights without sleep, worrying over Sierra, I don't know how either one of them have done this for any length of time."

My mother nodded. "God has given them both the strength they need. I think Sharon's ready to trust Dilly again after this."

I exchanged a glance with Mac; if it was true, that would be more than I'd hoped for.

Just then the ICU doors opened and Dilly emerged with Sharon at her side.

"They'll be moving her to a regular room in the morning," Dilly said. "And maybe we'll get to take her home in a couple of days."

"Tom told us even the doctors think she's a miracle," Mac said.

Dilly nodded. "She is. She really is."

Nick retrieved a covered paper cup and straw from one of the end tables. "Here, Ma. Doc said you're supposed to keep up your liquids."

She accepted the drink and for the moment we were all quiet, although Nick seemed fidgety, as if he had something to say but wasn't quite sure how.

"How are you feeling, Sharon?" I asked.

"Better, thank you." She hadn't met my eye, but her face was placid. Or was she still just too tired to send me and the rest of my family the normal icicle daggers from her eyes?

"That's not really true, Ma," Nick said. "You're worn-out. When Sierra gets home, you're gonna need help. Dilly's help."

"She knows she's welcome. She's been welcome most of the summer."

"I mean more than just a couple hours a day. I mean nights, too. You willing to do that?"

I was vaguely surprised by Nick's tactic, making the inquiry with all of us around—the family she blamed for so much. Maybe he thought she'd have to curb her reaction if she had an audience. Especially this one.

"I'm willing to do what's best for Sierra. Same as always."

"You need help. Overnight help."

Sharon's gaze, which so far had been straight ahead and aimed at the opposite wall, now bounced from her son to Dilly and then back to Nick. "I'm back on the list for a respite worker. That'll help."

"Ma, you're as stubborn as they come. If you can't find some-body in town to help, you're sure not gonna find somebody to make a long drive. You don't have to look, though; you've got help right here, in Dilly."

"You know I'll do anything for her, Sharon," Dilly said. "I know how hard the nights can be."

Sharon didn't look at anyone for a moment, but it was different from the last time she'd stared straight ahead. I could tell she was still with us, thinking hard. At last she looked at Dilly. "You're welcome to help with Sierra. Day or night."

My sister's eyes sparkled at the words, and she smiled first at me, then at our parents.

"Sierra's sleeping, and I'm planning to stay a while longer," Sharon said. "Some of you've been here right along. No need for all of us to stay."

She was trying to get rid of us, I could see that, and yet there wasn't a hint of any effort to banish us. Perhaps just a touch of discomfort because we all knew she'd finally, fully caved in on her resistance to Dilly.

"You need a break, Dil." My statement was followed by affirmation from all directions. I was about to offer her a ride back home with Mac and me, but Tom Boyle put a hand on Dilly's arm.

"I was planning to take her home for a while and grab something to eat on the way. If that's okay with the rest of you?"

He looked at my parents, as if he actually needed their permission. I smiled. I wasn't sure how many people were a natural fit in this family, but surely Tom Boyle was one of them.

"Maybe your parents would like to take a break too?" Mac asked. "Hannah and I have eaten, but how about we go somewhere for you to get something?"

As he went on about letting them eat and then the four of us sharing dessert, I couldn't help but think he was a natural fit for this family too. A Californian, just as I'd become, but one who'd want to return with me to visit back home. Often.

We walked from the waiting room, leaving Sharon and Nick with Sierra for the time being. But Dilly would be back as soon as she could; I knew that without a doubt. I watched her walk away with Tom, convinced she was in good hands. Between him and God, she certainly didn't need me.

I stepped next to Mac and followed him out with my parents at our side. He held open the door for my parents to get into the backseat. When he opened the door for me to slide in front beside him, I detained him just long enough to kiss him before letting him go around to get behind the wheel. If my parents guessed at the delay, they didn't protest.

## AUTHOR'S NOTE

*My Sister Dilly* was inspired by a combination of true stories: By mothers who've been to the darkest place a mother could go, survived, and found their love survived with them. By other mothers who face each day not knowing how long their children will live and yet make it through with incredible strength. By women who feel they've let others down, not from lack of caring but rather from lack of confidence. It's been said to me on more than one occasion that God allows into our lives only what we can handle, but the truth is we can't handle anything well without Him. My prayer is that the characters in this book would be companions for those of us who've overcome hardships or made mistakes and who realize forgiveness is most relevant within the context of relationship.

## ABOUT THE AUTHOR

Maureen Lang has always had a passion for writing. She wrote her first novel longhand around the age of ten, put the pages into a notebook she had covered with soft deerskin (nothing but the best!), then passed it around the neighborhood to rave reviews. It was so much fun she's been writing ever since.

Eventually Maureen became the recipient of a Golden Heart Award from Romance Writers of America, followed by the publication of three secular romance novels. Life took some turns after that, and she gave up writing for fifteen years, until the Lord claimed her to write for Him. Soon she won a Noble Theme Award from American Christian Fiction Writers and has since published several novels, including *Pieces of Silver* (a 2007 Christy Award finalist), *Remember Me*, *The Oak Leaves*, and *On Sparrow Hill*.

Maureen lives in the Midwest with her husband, her two sons, and their much-loved dog, Susie. Visit her Web site at www.maureenlang.com.

*have you visited*
# tyndalefiction.com
*lately?*

Only there can you find:

- ✢ books hot off the press
- ✢ first chapter excerpts
- ✢ inside scoops on your favorite authors
- ✢ author interviews
- ✢ contests
- ✢ fun facts
- ✢ and much more!

Sign up for your **free** newsletter!

Visit us today at: **tyndalefiction.com**

---

Tyndale fiction does more than entertain.

- ✢ *It touches the heart.*
- ✢ *It stirs the soul.*
- ✢ *It changes lives.*

That's why Tyndale is so committed to being first in fiction!

**TYNDALE FICTION**